Jeremy and Corbyn

A Post-Truth Novel

SIMON L BAXTER

www.jeremyandcorbyn.com

Copyright © 2016 Simon L Baxter

All rights reserved.

ISBN: 1542454409
ISBN-13: 978-1542454407

To the uprooted,
And to Amalia.
For Ever More I Love You.

CONTENTS

1	REASON'S PRECIPICE	1
2	THE ALLOTMENT	24
3	INNER STEEL	47
4	THE DISCUSSION	69
5	THE DEBATE	88
6	THE DEMONSTRATION	108
7	OXI	129
8	TO THE MINERS' GALA	145
9	WELFARE REFORM	168
10	JEREMY IN LIVERPOOL	186
11	INNER PANIC	208
12	CORBYN IN CAMDEN	229
13	AMALIA'S EXPULSION	246
14	VICTORY	265

CHAPTER 1
REASON'S PRECIPICE

All facts, in the course of their unfolding, become fiction.
Victory became defeat, labour became new,
and the union became traded.
Iraq invaded Blair and the credit burst into debt.
And those who had once managed, found they no longer could.

1

He had begged him to stay away, but his brother would not listen. He had tried to show him how the party favoured his offering, but his brother would not see. When in defeat he packed his bags, he pleaded with him not to leave. But his brother left, passing over water and into exile. And for many years, he heard from his brother not.

2

Year's end was fast approaching. Edward was alone in the bathroom cleaning up. As he washed his hands the soap stung beneath his pink nails. They were bitten to the wick.

He splashed his face and looked in the mirror, wiping the puckered grooves beneath his eyes. He was in his forty-fourth year, no longer a sapling, but now risen to the full stature of the mature English male. Half a decade's preening was drawing to a close.

Inspecting his nostrils, he listened to *The Red Flag* on his wife's MP3, wincing as he pulled at an enclave of hair. The anthem of British labour poured into his ears:

> *The people's flag is deepest red,*
> *It shrouded oft our martyred dead*
> *And ere their limbs grew stiff and cold*
> *Their hearts' blood dyed its ev'ry fold*

His pocket trembled. It was big brother:

"Happy New Year from New York! Love from David and family."

Since Ed won the party leadership contact had been a rare thing. That was five years ago. Their contest had been brutal, and the party blood-soaked by its conclusion.

He often wondered if it had been worth the price: to win a party, and lose a brother. It was something he had never fully come to terms with, the terrors of an ancient cannibal past seizing him whenever he recalled the brutal days of struggle for the party leadership.

He stroked over the message, scrolling it up and down, and the sting of his bitten wick was momentarily dispersed. Oh, how he longed for his brother's return...

> *Look 'round, the Frenchman loves its blaze,*
> *The sturdy German chants its praise,*
> *In Moscow's vaults its hymns are sung*
> *Chicago swells the surging throng.*

He returned to the mirror. His face had crumpled somewhat since his ascendancy; a consequence, no doubt, of the guilt he still carried.

It was either that or the diet forced upon him: nothing but cottage cheese and saltless nuts and mean milligrammes of fruit. He was allowed the occasional piece of protein, but no red meat. As a consequence his waking moments were forever dogged by hunger. *How does one manage a party when forever famished?* His friend Eddy said it was the only way to manage, though he was one to talk. Ed could not remember the last time he had a steak.

One of his consultants even suggested smoking, discreetly of course, the better to mark a little experience upon his baby-cursed face. Burn away the 'puppy fat', they said. But he declined. His face was as battle-ready as it would ever be, and people would just have to jolly well get used to it. Next year this fuss would stop. Next year he would be his own man and sink his teeth into as much meat as he liked.

> *It waved above our infant might,*
> *When all ahead seemed dark as night;*
> *It witnessed many a deed and vow,*
> *We must not change its colour now.*

He was about to reply to his brother when from out of the dark edges of his vision a man migrated into view. Ed jumped. He thought he had been alone among the plastic plants and patchouli that masked the smell of urine.

The attendant was a small man with big, kind eyes, dressed in a grey-striped waistcoat and white bow-tie. Ed thought of his nostrils. *These chaps must see all kinds of things...* The man offered Ed a set of white teeth and a towel.

'Oh, yes, of course,' he said nervously, acclimatising to the man's presence.

As he dried himself he peeked at the man from behind his towel. To Ed's eyes there was something... uncertifiable, about him. What kind of establishment would employ someone to work in a toilet in this day and age? And on New Year's Eve? It did not add up. Could it be that he had been taken to one of those places that was still exploitative of labour? He looked at his watch. It was later than he thought.

The evening had suddenly become uncertain. He thought of the great British public that his team were forever explaining to him in bold, colourful graphics. He knew what Eddy would say. *Why take the risk?*

Then again, why should he not converse with whomever he liked? He was the leader, after all. It did no harm to make conversation with the general public from time to time. The attendant eyed him curiously. On the other hand, was it wise to risk becoming the recipient of 'difficult information'? This man might disclose the details of his arduous journey to this fair and green land. He might disclose the conditions his masters kept him in, once his shift had ended. Did his shift come to an end? Or did he live here, in the laundry baskets, under the stairs?

What if, after being bludgeoned by such a revelation, this fellow took matters further? What if he ended up in a court of law and he, the leader of the British Labour Party, was forced to give evidence? The towel hung from his chin as he looked toward the exit... Could he scurry off without so much as a wet-flannelled thanks?

> *It well recalls the triumphs past,*
> *It gives the hope of peace at last;*
> *The banner bright, the symbol plain,*
> *Of human right and human gain.*

No, it would not do. His only option was to engage his attendant in a pre-emptive prattle. It was a technique he acquired when but a lowly Doncaster MP, and had worked quite well when the little people had become overexcited. He lowered the volume on his earphones and prepared to engage the man on the subject of his 'living' - a conventional opening move.

'You know, it's really quite funny, I was just pre-preparing a focus in this... arena,' said Ed, with a gestured smile and sweep of the bathroom. 'This arena, that you're... transitioning. It was about the robots coming out of Japan. Are you briefed, at all, on Japan?' The attendant offered him some cologne, but said nothing.

'They're engaging in some cutting-edge initiatives, don't you know? Very cash-neutral. Even in secondary quintile arenas - such as journalism, for instance.' He was momentarily transported to a world of automatically generated headlines. *The machines will be our friends.*

'Once the Tory cycle goes offline, we can re-contextualize growth-orientated efficiency savings, and move on from their failed economic paradigm.

> *It suits today the weak and base,*
> *Whose minds are fixed on pelf and place*
> *To cringe before the rich man's frown,*
> *And haul the sacred emblem down.*

The attendant furrowed his brow and rearranged the golden platter of condoms and aspirin, gum and cologne, chap-stick and lubricant, all sat beside him in cellophane wrappings on the bathroom shelf. It dawned on Ed that his friend might not speak English, but he resolved to roll up his sleeves and persevere:

'Envision, if you will: fully automated re-distribution of all these… quality deliverables.' He flopped an arm at the attendant's carefully arranged effects. 'A Labour government would empower its core base by upstreaming such initiatives and diversifying front-line ownership models.' The man maintained his smile. A toilet flushed.

'It's the future, don't you see? Machine journalists, digital teachers, virtual nurses, robotic… bathroom strivers. It's absolutely shifting the dial!' But the man said nothing. It seemed Ed's message was not getting through. A hairline of exasperation thread its way into his voice:

'You do understand my meaning? Clearly we're not pitching "personalised repurposement" - that you become, in any way… "automated". Wouldn't dovetail.' He pondered on the thought. The attendant again said nothing. The poor fellow clearly did not speak English. *Fancy coming all this way, only to find you were in need of a severe upgrade.*

> *With heads uncovered swear we all*
> *To bear it onward till we fall;*
> *Come dungeons dark or gallows grim,*
> *This song shall be our parting hymn.*

He may have not been in a position to help the man, but he had staved off an outpouring. The least he could do was tip him for his trouble. Pushing his fingers down into his silken linen pocket he found only a bank card and a twenty-pound note. The exchange had been trifling, but was it worth a twenty? He rubbed the note against the raised plastic impressions. His fingers sung out.

'Awfully sorry, are you... contactless?'

'How can a robot order cologne?' declared the man.

He spoke English after all! He knew they had been speaking the same language. *If one was only prepared to be patient with them.* He was forever telling Eddy to speak with Femi, the large Nigerian lady he often met vacuuming party HQ late at night, when everyone else had gone home. She was jolly good fun. But her schedule seldom seemed to overlap with Eddy's. *Labour should be tough on immigrants, yes, but that doesn't mean foregoing civilized conversation.* Ed ceased his feigned fumble and pulled out an earphone.

'Well, you make an absolutely valid point. Labour-saving technology: it's such a fraught issue, isn't it?' Then he lowered his voice and drew closer to the attendant, as if to enter upon a conspiracy: 'Zero-hours - is that the bottom line? Final Quintile Precarian?' The attendant went dumb again. Ed hoped he had not caused offence.

'Don't worry - we're on the same team, you and I. Clearly, we all need to make savings in these difficult times. It's in the national interest. Your gov'nor would say the same. He needs to cut costs, of course, but we'd insist he had insurance, software updates, maintenance checks, health and safety – you know? Rebalanced, but in our direction.' The attendant nodded unconvincingly.

Were there cameras in this bathroom? Perhaps his friend felt unsafe. He looked up at the ceiling, but saw nothing. It was his understanding that some of the wealth-creators could be rather forthright when it came to their upward strivers.

> *Then raise the scarlet standard high.*
> *Within its shade we'll live and die,*
> *Though cowards flinch and traitors sneer,*
> *We'll keep the red flag flying here.*

'Let me be clear – we're moving the goalposts, not downsizing them. At the end of the day, they need labour like us.' He straightened up and broke the conspiracy. *You need Labour like us... Britain needs Labour, like us... Britain likes to Labour, with us?* He stuck a pin in it.

'I mean, theoretically, robot attendants might be remotely prioritised. Automatic re-stock triggers. And don't even get me started on 3-D printing! But in that case, I'm afraid there wouldn't be any real need for robotic stock coordinators. But you might become a warehouse mobility facilitator. Or a vehicular goods enabler? You know, some of these Robots even sprayed perfume out of their finger?' Ed's eyes bulged with terrible, swollen possibility. 'Incredibly amusing,' he said, no longer seeing his new friend, but looking through him. He was transported to a distant world that was just around the corner.

Then he turned back to the mirror, pleased with himself, and checked his hair and revisited those marks beneath his eyes. *The lights in this place are awfully bright.* He placed one sore, bitten finger on the thin skin below his eye, exposing the pink flesh beneath. He had quite failed to notice that *The Red Flag* had come to an end. Silent hissing played out the final seconds.

Then the track shuffled, and a familiar song began to unwrap in his ear. It was the melodious plink-plonks and toddling soft steps of a turn-cranked music box. It sang:

Never smile at a crocodile
No, you can't get friendly with a crocodile
Don't be taken in by his welcome grin
He's imagining how well you'd fit within his skin!

Comfort wrapped him, and he was removed from the hard lights and the masked urine on the bathroom floor. He was amid the bold, xylophonic colours of his children's playroom; he was wrestling with the after-school bundles of energy that clung to him around his knees as he walked through the front door. He was with his wife, and the hot little souls of his boys, fast asleep on his chest...

A sense of unease crept upon him and the moment did not last. The work-life balance was upsetting. Fishing the device from his pocket, he mashed the buttons and his thumb seared. His childrens' song was no more.

Ed smiled his embarrassment at the attendant, reading for signs of betrayal. But the attendant seemed blissfully unaware of any misdemeanour, merely offering a smile in return.

He relaxed, but even as he did, he sensed that the bathroom had closed in on him. He brought his face to the mirror again. Narrowing his eyes, he caught sight of something floating over his shoulder. It was a human head.

'Peter!' He jumped. 'I didn't hear you come in.'

Nobody ever heard Peter come in, for he was the Lord of Silence. He slipped in and out of Party HQ as an apparition, leaving one unsure as to whether he was in the building or not. And so in this way he was always present; the wise among them working under that presumption. Often the first one knew was his words unfurling in your ear; or the dumb frost that had fallen upon a room and choked the air dry.

'Conversing with the help, my boy?' Ed stood aside and yielded Peter his basin, though two beside were free enough. Peter rolled his sleeves and daubed his fingertips in soap and water and stroked them over his old, elegant hands. His skin was translucent, and Ed thought he discerned the faint outline of a liver spot beneath the surface.

Lord Peter was a 'senior' gentleman, in the language of the party, and carried himself immaculately. Viewed straight, his face appeared borrowed from a younger man, and traced only a few lines. Around him he carried a cultivated air of accomplishment, and a grey badger's undercoat dignified his kempt side-parting. It was only the pink skin around his neck, beginning to slacken into a jowl, that betrayed his years.

'Is this man bothering you, Kenneth?' asked the Lord, taking a towel.

'No, boss,' said the attendant, laughing. Ed cocked him a suspicious eye.

'And how are you, young Edward? Looking forward to the great campaign, I should not wonder.' Lord Peter towelled his hands drily. His manner of speaking was mild, but not weak. Rather, it was the speech of one so self-assured that he could not but filter through the world as he received it, while others, impatient in their haste, were forced to adjust themselves to his presence.

'Yes, yes, all systems go,' said Ed, his smile rooted to the spot, fighting the urge to address his Lord as 'Sir'. He had never been Ed's boss directly, but that was of little consequence. Lord Peter was grand among the grandees, and someone not to be trifled with. He was looking straight into Ed's eyes through the reflection in the mirror.

'You remind me of an old friend, my boy. He was much like you: young, enterprising, the world at his feet and a twinkle in his eye.' He saw Ed's smile falter. 'But also, not without the occasional butterfly in his stomach.' He was paternally seductive and eased upon Ed rows of sympathetic teeth.

'Obviously, the polls have not been… despite our best triangulations,' said Ed, his voice shrunken.

'Pay no heed to the polls, my boy. You must look to yourself; that is all one can ever truly do. Believe in yourself and the rest will follow. The polls will fall in line and the whole world will dance to your tune… if you wish it.' Ed was impressed.

'If I might be so bold, I think you have been through a rough time of it these past few years, ever since the leadership contest. Perhaps more than you like to let on?'

'I… suppose you could say that.' Ed felt something was reaching inside of him, holding him calm.

'And it is not the gossip, dear boy, nor the party members; they are all right behind you, that you must understand. But what I believe you have a hard time with is that unfortunate business with your brother. Am I being fair?' The Lord seemed to know something of his anxiety. He was probably one of the few people with the experience to understand his position, thought Ed.

'The path to Downing Street is not easy, my boy. It is lonely and perilous. One hundred hours of weekly service, a mean-spirited media, and a party staffed by creatures who, shall we say, are not known for their approachability? Rather, you are kept awake half the night by their phone calls and second guesses. And by a boy that wets the bed.'

'How did you…?'

'All little boys wet the bed, Edward. This job can get the best of you, if you are not careful. If that were not the case, we would not be human.' His eyes flickered.

'But remember, your brother is a big boy. We talk often, and he often asks after you, did you know that? He bears you no ill-will. He is across the pond now, building bright causes of his own.'

'He just sent me a New Year's message.'

'Well, there we are then. We all go through crises, my boy. And Lord knows, you've been through tougher times than most of us should have to. But crises are part of life. Birth is a crisis; so too is adolescence; and, as I am sadly discovering, old age is a crisis also,' he said, offering Ed a confidentiality. Ed drank down the medicine Peter spooned him. It felt like a vote of confidence, an intimate sort of comradeship - something in short supply at party HQ. He wanted to share something in return, although he was not sure what.

'What can one do?' said Ed, a punt for all occasions

'All one can ever do: You must weather the storm, my boy. A weak man will allow a crisis to consume him, but a strong man weathers his crisis and emerges stronger for it. I can see an inner strength in you, my boy, an inner... formidability. You will come out of this, and tempered, you need not worry.'

'I have some concerns, Peter, about our message. Our 'big idea', so to speak. How does one exactly... square the circle, if you get my meaning?' The Lord bade him continue.

'Well, the Prime Minister is bottom-lining the debt. More with less - I understand that. But how does one proactively facilitate our obligations whilst dovetailing it within our own ecosystem? How do we unite the nation under our guiding principles? Especially after Scotland. It's such a fraught issue.'

'Trivialities do not concern you,' said Peter. 'Polls, message, ideas; the polls do not rule us, they have never done. Whatever position you wish to set out, you really have very little choice. You can only say one thing, and that is what comes from within.' He adjusted his tie and checked his cufflinks.

'You still opinion-irrigate at the leader's office? Self-represent? War-game?' It appeared from Ed's puzzled look that they no longer carried on any of the old practices. *Not altogether unexpected.*

'So you think we should long-grass the issue, going forward? Until after the election?'

Peter peered into Ed's eyes, as if trying to read something in them of which he could not be certain.

'Because... well, I think it would be far more productive if we could stick a pin in it until the election's been and gone. But Eddy, he wants to nail our colours to the mast. "Manage expectations", he says. Yes, the ratings are rather dim, but won't they be even dimmer if we do something like that? Damn these polls! Everything's so blasted presidential these days. What your face looks like, how you speak, how you eat…'

'Poppycock and balderdash,' said Peter, with a new firmness. 'You are the leader, are you not?' Ed confirmed that he was.

'It is you who will have to rule this country, not some brown-nosed lickspittle. The direction of travel is the way the leader sees fit. Otherwise, you are not leading, you are being led. Your troops selected you, and now they must be right behind you, my boy. You are about to go over the top - there's no turning back. Only conviction begets leadership, young Edward. You must make your own path - it is the only path you know.'

Ed looked into the eyes of the Lord and realised that he was right.

'You know,' Peter continued, softening once more. 'I do not think you realise how much you have done for our little party. One cannot very well begin to lead, if one does not first understand what one has already accomplished.' He placed a hand lightly between Ed's shoulder blades and looked up toward the bathroom ceiling.

'The responsibility we must presume, is something of… an art, my dear boy - quite beyond the comprehension of most party members; even beyond the likes of the Prime Minister and those foolish Tories.'

Ed did so hate the Tories. Even in his Oxford Union days he could never quite bring himself to eat and drink and sleep with them after the debating had finished, like the other Labour boys and girls.

'We really must talk more often,' said Peter, pressing his hand into Ed's vertebrae and steering him toward the exit.

They were half-way out when Ed remembered his friend. He turned back and made the scribbling gesture people make in restaurants, mouthing that he would leave a tip at the bar. Then the door swung open, and they were gone.

The attendant was left alone. He shook his head and dropped the towels into the laundry basket.

3

On the other side of the club sat the brothers, Chuka and Tristram. Not brothers in body, but nonetheless of a spiritual fraternity; a fine meeting of minds and the great hope for the future. Brothers, but from different mothers, they confided intimately to each other when taken by the bubbles, and each other.

They lounged in the VIP area beyond the velvet rope, either side of a divan, cupping their crystal brandy glasses and taking good care not to crease their crisp suits. But the thin velvet line had no special significance that evening as there was no one present to man it. The party was a free event for all with an invitation:

"When everyone is a VIP, no-one is a VIP"

it read, in a navy blue font. But the raised platform was their usual spot, and upon arrival they quickly sought to claim their rights, putting distance between themselves and all before them.

At their feet gathered herds of Labour MPs, and MEPs, and grandees, all with their staff of courtiers and other special friends of Labour. It was the modern, moderate, majority wing of the Parliamentary Labour Party - the PLP - and they shook the disco floor.

A disc jockey had been hired, but he was under strict instructions not to turn the tables. His sole responsibility was to facilitate the disco lights that swung their beams emptily over the corners and crooks of the room that had filled with the sound of MPs bellowing thir resistance to the theme of the evening. Others had not understood the rules:

'Bring our own music? Next they'll make us bring our own drinks! Honestly, this party...'

Others heaved at the sides, breathless, overtaken by the great novelty of it all, regardless of whether they had understood or not. The entire basement converged into a raucous cattle drone that rose like trapped methane beneath the streets of London, serving to drown out the other sounds that sweeten the air when hundreds of politicians and their hangers-on toss their flabby bits in close quarters.

The brothers bore witness to this indignant spectacle. It disrupted their ability to converse far more than the banging of tunes that usually played out their evenings. They watched on, hypnotised by the herd, until they were distracted by an unusual sight. They spied the leader emerging from the bathroom, and right behind him, PM. The two men were nodding away, holding each other's shoulders in deep conversation.

'Looks like PM has snared himself a *wabbit*,' said Tristram. Chuka looked on, sipping his soda stream.

They were still observing the wildlife when a woman approached the velvet rope from off the dance floor, perching herself on Chuka's side of the divan. She was of little consequence, not even an intern, merely a treasurer of one of the local London parties.

'Are you two ever going to get off your bums and come dance? Or are you just going to mope in the corner and drink your expensive brandy?' Chuka ignored her, too interested in the movements of the leader, who had now parted company with PM and was doing a sort of walking dance across the floor toward the bar.

'It's Italian Irn Bru,' said Tristram, leaning forward. 'Bespoke. I acquired a taste for it on our campaign this summer. It's crafted by an Italian soda grandmaster, far greater depth than the stuff they sell in the shops.' He swirled the fizzy rust before his eyes.

'Soda? You do realise you are at a New Year's party, don't you?'

'It's not that type of party.'

Looking around the disco the young woman saw everywhere her fellow party members drawing from bottles of mineral water, or glasses of colourful bubbles that she had taken for shorts. She looked down at her gin and tonic and felt ashamed. *Why didn't they tell me?*

'But, what about John?' she asked, flicking her head in the direction of the former Deputy Prime Minister, stood holding a pint of bitter and sharing a set of earphones with his wife and looking lost.

'That's John, he's old fashioned,' said Tristram. 'You'll see a lot of the younger crowd wear sobriety bracelets these days - helps them stay the course. It's important for us to stay clean in our game. Of course, there is a bar. No-one's forcing you not to drink.'

She did not like that one bit and marched away to order a mineral water.

'The leader's just knocked Margaret's drink over!' shrieked Chuka with a singular joy, startling his brother. 'The little worm - right down her dress!' He studied the scene intensely and chuckled to himself, and his brother joined in.

Then his interest in the unfortunate scene extinguished as suddenly as it had begun. His eyes deadened. He turned to Tristram:

'That reminds me: You need to get her to clean her walls and bleach her feed if you're going to progress any further.' Chuka slumped against the arm of the divan. His joy had died.

'You wanna go down MDen's? This place is depressing.'

4

Ed barricaded himself at the shoulders, not wanting to catch an eye at the bar. His comrades conversed in huddles, none of whom had failed to notice the cherryade that had just gone flying over Margaret's striped shirt-dress. One of the waitresses had taken her away to the kitchen. He fixed his eyes on the fridge behind the bar and waited for his soda and wished they would all just go away.

He recalled his brief encounter. Was this the same man who so many had warned him against? Who had been so unspeakably encouraging? Who had at least listened to him and did not smirk at his misgivings, but had advised him to be himself and speak his truth? Hardly the Machiavellian master of shadows his detractors made him out to be. He sighed. *It's all just politics.*

What's more, his advice seemed so honest in its simplicity that he could not help but wonder whether he had not been barking up the wrong tree all these years. He really should have made the effort to meet Peter earlier and not allow himself to be guided by *lickspittles*.

The barmaid brought his soda. It was his fifth of the evening, and he could feel the bubbles had gone to his head. He loved to belch, especially a suppressed burp in good company that burned through his nose like horseradish sauce.

He thought back to his time in government. He used to suppress all his burps around Gordon in those heady days in late 2008 when he was forever running Downing Street's corridors with hods of paper at his shoulder, hods he and nobody else would ever read. He thought back to Gordon in his office, the *"S"* of his favourite t-shirt showing through his white cotton shirt:

'How could this happen!?' thundered his former leader, bringing his clenched fist upon the table and his rosy jaw shuddering.

As he reminisced, a silent belch burned between his eyes. Ed imagined himself standing on the podium outside Downing Street in 2008 as the Prime Minister would have done, talking to the nation's assembled press.

> *'The invisible hand has decided! From now on this Labour government will outlaw banking in all its forms. Bank chiefs have twenty-four hours to turn themselves in, or be declared enemies of the state! The government will compose an official register, freely available to the public, which will allow people to know if a former member of Britain's banking system is living in their neighbourhood.'*

Ed thought again of Peter. He thought of his brother, separated by the vastness of the sea. He had not replied to his message. He thought of his father; he could just imagine what he would say. His voice spoke to him:

> *'Thatcher and her class were victorious in their struggle against the workers. They destroyed their livelihoods, and a large section of the capitalists dedicated themselves to the ever-growing market of lending lost wages. To the victor go the spoils and to the vanquished went the debt. Into the cracks of this problem seeped the bankers. In defeat our movement stopped flowing and started haemorrhaging, and when the bleeding stopped the wound congealed into a scabrous crust.*
>
> *'Out of the frying pan, into the fire. The banks collapsed because workers' debts became unpayable. Jobless workers can't buy, so bosses couldn't sell. How to sell moneyless workers, money? What do you sell it for? They trade it for the future. Absurd, isn't it? A future repayment - with interest. They bought and sold debt and, for some, it became the sole source of their income – trading shackles. The bankers turned a loss of livelihood into a business opportunity.*
>
> *'But debts must be repaid. Some took out a second loan to pay the first. Some took a seventh to pay the fifth and sixth. Others self-medicated and swallowed austerity long before it was forced upon them. But the bosses didn't like that because those workers would buy less. Once they were debt free, they were uninteresting. A worker in the red, who served and paid tribute, was worth ten in the black.'*

These things he knew to be true, but he feared to shine a light upon them, consigning them to a dark recess where their ugliness went undisturbed. His father continued:

'Like drug pushers, they shoved little plastic cards down the workers' throats and letterboxes, year after year, until one day they vomited it all up. They could no longer eat any more debt.

'First one set of workers got sick - no longer workers of interest. Their houses were taken and on the scrap heap they went. The bosses and bankers had to make good their threats, lest others become emboldened and dishonour their agreements, too.

But dishonourable they became. More and more defaulted, and more and more the banks lost the money they had loaned. They lost interest as things became more interesting. A worker without debt is a worker without a house; a bank without debt is a house with no bricks.

'The disease jumped from worker to bank and spread like fever. Mad Pecuniary Disease. Bank would not go near bank, for fear of the pustules that burst around their swollen pits. They didn't know who had touched whom, and suspected all. Because a ten-pound note is a ten-pound note, no matter the serial number. In the rapid blur of exchange it all became the same: average, homogeneous, and riddled with disease.

His father's voice faded, and as he returned to himself he realised he was staring at the barmaid's bottom, which through no fault of his own had moved into his field of vision. Swiftly he averted his gaze, darting eyes from side to side, checking to see whether he had been found guilty. That was the last thing he needed. The bar was wet around his elbows.

The barmaid passed him a towel. Wiping his sleeves, Ed turned to face the dance floor where he saw Shadow Ministers wiggling beside party aides. He saw long-standing MPs delivering gentle bops, abandoning their dented shields of irony, the elastic of their party hats cutting like a butchers' string at their quaggy maws.

Ed screwed one eye and looked into his glass and saw that his fizz was drained. He ordered another, this time with a cordial lime twist.

Why can't we just acknowledge it? We bankrupted the country by handing over billions to people who, in any other industry, would be allowed to sink to the bottom to have their carcass picked over by the nematodes. We shouldn't have handed them free money -

we should have taken them over. A hostile take-over:
"Gentlemen, these things are far too important to be left in your hands: you are relieved. Compensation? You might be out in three-to-five."
We should have gone much further than RBS. We should have taken the bloody lot!

5

Eddy and Yvette were the dream dance floor pairing. He barrelled forth, carving out a circle and stomping around her like a sweaty cockerel, scraping dirt with his heels, and rolling forth his mashed potatoes. She held her nose and wiggled down for the swim. They were a dreamy Westminster success story; such humility evident in their sardonic swings, such good-natured British humour, such graceful condescension.

They had not lost the common touch, and the young staff members held tight their bracelets and fawned at this beautiful example of matrimonial labour. This beautiful example of politics and life gracefully balanced as one.

He drew her close and prepared to mock the Tango, bending her over one arm. She could feel his heart working hard through his soaked dinner jacket. He was a purple sponge with eyes grinning inanely into hers. Leaning back, droplets of sweat caused her to screw her eyes as she prepared to be taken.

Then, out of the night, she saw the leader in the distance, waving at them from among the crowd on the edge of the dance floor. *The Message.* She indicated to Eddy, who looked up and then rolled his eyes to her apologetically. The dance was at an end, and her shoulders dropped without protest.

'Adieu, fair lady,' he said, and bowed to her, but she was already on her way to the bar. He fastened his smile and turned to face his leader.

'Mr Ed, I presume! Are you enjoying your evening?' He put a sweaty arm around his leader and pulled him close. *Please, please, please don't mention the message.* They took a seat at a nearby table.

'Not a bad night this lot throw, eh? Not such a bad crowd, after all.' He pulled his calf over his knee and re-tied his laces.

'I think we need to touch base about the message.' Eddy sagged.

The Message, The Message, The Message. Every day for five long years. Oh, how he hated *The Message*. And he also hated *The Big Idea*, which, as far as he could tell, was just another name for *The Message*. *The Message* had become inseparable from the face of the man that sat before him. *The Message* was something to be fought. *The Message* was something to be jumped upon and wrestled to the ground. The ringing in of the New Year was all the sweeter because it brought down another year on *The Message*.

A moment ago he had been Prime Minister of the dance floor. Now all Eddy wanted to do was wring his leader's scrawny neck. He waited a moment for his rage to deposit in his arteries, and looked Ed up and down. An intelligent, complex man, Eddy considered. To be treated as something of a puzzle - a political Rubik's Cube - each day bringing a new challenge.

'Oh... it's the same old thing. I really think we just need to bite the bullet, suck it up, be like the Greens - go anti-austerity and reject the debt.' He seemed more belligerent than usual, Eddy thought. How much soda had he had?

'I don't like this cost-of-living triangulation,' said Ed, slumping in his chair and loosening his tie. 'We say it's bad, but on the other hand we're going to say we have to keep to Tory spending and reduce the deficit. But isn't the cost-of-living crisis a consequence of reducing the deficit? Honestly, I thought I'd have more to work with when I became Prime Minister.' His face stretched with anguish and his eyes pouted into their fierce puckered bulges.

'Well,' said Eddy, 'I think we know where this ends, don't we?' He leant back in his chair and freed his chins from his hot damp collar. Ed detected a haughtiness of manner of which he disapproved, but resolved to let it go - this time.

'We all agree that our economy is in a mess, and that the world economy is in a crisis. It was the banking system that caused it all, not bloody Labour! I mean, how could we cause the biggest economic crisis of our lifetime?' Eddy laughed, and Ed consented.

'On the other hand, whoever... done the stink... we'd all agree, it's in everyone's best interest if it's cleaned up as soon as possible.'

'Well, yes,' said Ed, 'to a point. But it isn't dirty laundry, is it? Its people's lives we're talking about. And they didn't make this mess, did they? So why should they clean it up?'

'Didn't they? I mean, alright, we all know that some bankers were irresponsible. You always get a few rotten apples, a few... unscrupulous purveyors of insurance policies, shall we say... Oh, hello Tom!' Eddy waved at an MP shifting past their table. 'But can you say that every banker is universally a bad egg? Come off it, you know that's not credible. And are we saying that we don't need bankers? We don't need banks? Of course not. And are you saying that working class people didn't have any say in the matter? That they couldn't have abstained from taking on more debt?'

'They didn't have any choice!'

'Not everyone one went out and got credit cards, you know. Many lived within their means.' He platted his fingers. 'My nana lived off her pension book and nothing more. Are you saying that ordinary, hard-working families didn't have a choice? Of course they did! You know what you're doing there, don't you, by championing this... narrative? You are robbing people. Robbing them of ... agency.' Ed looked alarmed. He certainly didn't want to do that. *Check.*

'Our game-plan must be to relate to the public as grown-ups. Let me be clear: the Tories go too far. Yes, we have to deal with the deficit, and say it plainly. Why? Because it's in the national interest. From the immigrant family on the corner, to the stock market guys in the sky - and all the other wealth creators - we have to say that Labour will be accountable. Labour will reduce the debt. Labour will match Tory spending. You know these loony Greens and SNP-ers; no one takes them seriously because they don't live in the real world. People don't buy into their anti-austerity fantasies, save a few miserable students.'

'OK, really, well what about Scotland then?' advanced Ed. 'The SNP got forty-five per cent! How do you explain that?'

'Wasn't all SNP, Ed. But yes, it's true; there was a "noisy minority" in the referendum. But that was a one-off; a protest, not the General Election. We can't base our strategy on a one-off, never-to-be-repeated set of circumstances. People bang on about the Scottish referendum like we lost it! It was mid-term blues, that's all; people wanting to give the Tories a kicking - can't blame them for that. But at the same time, we've got to fight that kind of irresponsible politics. Imagine if the Scots had got a majority? What then? An anti-austerity Scotland? Fifty Labour seats down the toilet? The end of the United Kingdom? Good heavens above!'

'Well, at least they wouldn't have any debt,' said Ed. 'They'd be a new country.' None of the Scottish MPs appeared to have shown up, but then again New Year's celebrations were reported to be jolly good fun up at the Scottish office.

'They'd soon take it on like a sinking ship, once the oil runs dry and the big firms pull out. And you know that we'd have to pull the plug; close lines of credit, call in our debts. Otherwise, you'll have Wales and Northern Ireland and Cornwall and the bleeding Isle of Wight clambering for it next!'

'Well, yes,' said Ed, 'and that's what I think is, well, rather unfair. What you're saying is that you'd sabotage their decision! Money doesn't have wings. It doesn't just start flying out of countries of its own accord. Someone pulls it out, devalues the currency, creates inflation. It'd be those horrid bankers again, who you say we should let off the hook! In your example, if the Scottish people had another referendum, the banks would mobilise a massive bloc-vote against them in the form of pounds, shillings and pence. You know how I fought against bloc-votes.'

'Exactly,' said Eddy, 'and that's why we can't let matters get that far in the first place. And besides, the referendum's over and done with; it's not going to happen again.'

The countdown began. *'Ten! Nine! Eight!'*

'That bloc-vote business was Foot's fault,' said Eddy.

'Seven! Six! Five!'

'And we've been paying the bill for thirty years. Thank god we've cleared it up at last. Or rather, you cleared it up, Ed. You showed real leadership there.' He offered his leader a pressed set of lips and leant over and slapped him on the knee as a token of his appreciation.

'Four! Three! Two! One!'

'Happy New Year!'

Party horns unrolled and confetti fell from the ceiling as the two men continued their discussion. On the dance floor everyone who wore earphones pulled them out and were reunited with the ill-equipped who had been forced to do laps of the field in their underwear. The disc jockey was given the nod and *'Auld Lang Syne'* was played and they all linked arms. Ed and Eddy watched for a moment.

Ed noticed that not many of his trade union friends were among those ringing in the year. It was not as if he did not appreciate them anymore. He hoped they weren't too upset. Whatever one said about the unions, you would have to agree that the new party rules were an improvement: One Member, One Vote. Peter had certainly thought so.

'Consider it another way,' said Eddy, his sweaty tufts now layered with colored bits of paper. 'If Scotland had left, debt or no debt, the wealth creators would have withdrawn their money from Britain. Too much uncertainty – only sensible.' Ed did not know where he was going with this, but he accepted his logic for the time being. An intern came up and placed a red and yellow paper chain around his neck, and then ran off giggling.

'But if they start withdrawing money it will mean less business, and therefore less revenue. So you've got to start cutting back, unless...'

'Unless what?'

'Unless you nail down everything that moves. But you can only do that by nationalising: you can't control what you don't own. But you know the logic in that. It's a globalised world. No matter how much the Greens whinge about tax-havens, there's no escaping it. If you start nationalising then the next day they'll all be trying to take out their money, like ships pulling out of port. Then what can you do, but take them all over? Before you know it – bam! You've nationalised the entire economy. And what's that called? Socialism. Congratulations, you're the new Castro.' Ed wilted in the face of Eddy's merciless logic.

'And we all know where that gets you,' he said. *Checkmate. Shove that up your big idea.*

Ed was crestfallen, and Eddy knew that his leader was beaten. It had not taken long. He was glad to be there for him. *The bubbles go to all our heads, every so often. And when that happens, you need a friend to pull you off the ceiling.* He had become decidedly agitated as the General Election drew nearer, Eddy reflected. *Thank God I'm here.* He looked into his leader's eyes and decided to offer an orderly retreat.

'Look, we all saw what our friends in the unions were up to in Scotland,' he said. 'Playing silly buggers.'

'Well, absolutely,' said Ed.

'Good job we nipped Falkirk in the bud. That was a Clause Four moment. I tell you, Ed: It's those types of fellows who want to whip up this "anti-austerity" nonsense. Yes, we say no to those extremist Tories, but we must say yes to managing the deficit, no? That's why we're a party of government, unlike the loony lefts and trade unions. We must position ourselves to the left and the right so we can appeal to as many people in the centre as possible. It means being tough on the deficit, but also tough on the causes of the deficit. That's what the unions never understood, and in my opinion we couldn't have dealt with them soon enough. Their undemocratic bloc-vote was an accident waiting to happen.'

'Yes, I suppose you're right,' Ed conceded, feeling somewhat calmed by Eddy's terrific power of reasoning.

'Now any worker can participate on an even footing in our great party; One Member, One Vote, and primaries of supporters. And it's all thanks to you, Ed. Mark my words: bring the public in and you'll find them a darn sight more reasonable than these anti-austerity labour movement types. That road leads in the direction of chaos.'

'Well, nobody wants that,' said Ed.

6

Many months later, Ed stood at the edge of a cliff. Behind him, an eight-foot plaque was being unloaded out of a white van. He could not bear to turn around. He fancied he would rather skid down the rocks and dive into the sea and swim away from it, and everyone, than continue with this blasted election. He heard the slab *thunk* against the car park floor.

Ed looked out to sea where dull-grey mounds reared and drained, and washed into the miserable clouds and the blue-grey asphalt that crumbled beneath his polished shoes. In the wind his police-blue trousers rattled against his legs, and his streaming tie made him look as if he were straining on god's leash.

The fold of activists, dragged up from the nearby town, huddled together and beheld the Stele as it was raised before them by a system of pulleys and levers. The elections were less than a week away. Everywhere he travelled he seemed to end up in the same tea-stained, dog-bitten, out-of-town motorway rest area, speaking to a feeble-minded cross-section of the party faithful.

One of his team crossed the asphalt and sidled up to him.

'Just got off the phone with London,' said the advisor. He had a soft American accent.

'Sturgeon's left another message saying for you to please return her calls. Eddy's secretary says no need to hurry back, he and Yvette are having family time tonight.'

'Again?' Eddy had been spending an awful lot of time with his family recently. From under the cliff the wind swept, drowning their exchange.

'Look, are you quite sure about this?' cried Ed.

'I'm positive - says he needs to spend time with the family and kids.'

'No, I mean the stone. Is it really such a good idea? Isn't this a bit of a... gimmick? A bit, well, cheap?'

'Not for seven thousand,' said the advisor.

Ed turned and saw the sorry little crowd gathered with hope around the semi-erect monument. He rubbed his thumb along the screw-top of the jar in his pocket and his thumb sung out in pain. He felt reduced, thinned. He was in deep now.

Walking gravely over to the propped monolith he donned a castor oil smile. He greeted the camera operator and his congealed colleagues and the workmen who stood apart from the proceedings, and rattled off his speech.

***

In the first four months of 2015 more than fifty-five thousand humans crossed over the borders of Southern Europe.

CHAPTER 2
THE ALLOTMENT

1

The afternoon was bright in early May. Corbyn dozed in his deck chair at the top of his allotment, his bucket hat pulled over his eyes. The radio buzzed, and he half listened, drifting between sleep and the spring air.

> *'The Labour Party has won Britain's General Election of 2015, becoming the biggest party in parliament; not quite with an outright majority, but is expected to form a government with the twelve seats won by the Green party, who recorded their best ever result in a General Election.*
>
> *'We now cross over to the Rose Garden in Downing Street where Ed Miliband is about to make his first announcement to the media following his party's victory.'*

The radio crackled over its frequency, and one could hear the hollow *tub-tub* of a microphone. Then the unmistakably earnest, nasal voice of the leader pleaded across the airwaves:

> *'The people of Britain have elected me as their leader, and the Labour Party as their party, for a fairer Britain, rejecting austerity, that puts the young first and is no longer prepared to accept the cost-of-living crisis.'*

He went on to make the usual tributes to his wife and children, his parents, the people of Doncaster and of Britain. A joke about a new cat was made, and he paid tribute to the plucky political cub scout activists who made Labour's victory possible, and who asked not for reward, nor influence, nor respect, but who lived only to do a good turn.

But then he said something Corbyn did not expect:

'I would also like to pay tribute to our fallen soldiers, those who were unable to win their seat this time round. I would like to mention in particular a very special MP who the Parliamentary Labour Party of 2015 will be poorer for having lost. One of our longest-serving parliamentarians, a man close to my father and who was, until last night, the representative in my own London residence. A man who epitomises the grassroots activism at the heart of our movement. That man, as you know, is Jeremy Corbyn.'

Corbyn turned in his deck chair as respectful clapping followed. The new Prime Minister continued:

'Jeremy did not make the journey with us last night, his Islington seat being lost to our new partners, the Green Party. For years a stalwart of the Left, one of the first MPs to speak out against Blair's shameful oil wars, and a campaigner for the oppressed everywhere; from the communities of Islington, to the Miners, to the Print workers, to his courageous stand against the Poll Tax, the Chagos Islanders, the disappeared student teachers of Ayotzinapa, and many, many more. It is for these reasons that the loss of Jeremy Corbyn is a loss to Parliament, to the labour movement, and to the national interest.

'Although I am certain that Jeremy would not accept a place in the House of Lords, I hope to speak to him soon to see how he can continue to work alongside the new government in an advisory capacity. I look forward to working with our new partners in repairing the damage done by five years of brutal austerity.'

Corbyn rolled from side to side and woke abruptly with a snort.

The newsreader murmured the afternoon news, reciting the names of various party leaders caught en route to the polling booths that morning, partners outfitted in hand. He had done no such thing. His rag-tag bunch of local party members had traipsed the streets of Islington late into the previous evening, trawling estates and balancing door steps, requesting and suggesting and counting on votes. Afterwards, they had all gone for fish and chips, and that morning had risen early to do it all again. Now he was decamped in his allotment for some time alone.

The usual roll of clouds had come in off the sea and carried away the morning-blue sky. Finally off his feet, his back ached and ankles throbbed and into his bucket hat he had slowly slipped, until his dreams had stirred him.

He reached for his flask and poured green tea into his Labour Party mug with its locally sourced slogan:

"Controls on Immigration"

A dozen of the horrid things gathered dust in his shed, a gift from party HQ. He had potted them with cacti.

Before him his little strip of garden sloped down to a stream running along the back of the allotments and consisted of a set of perfectly arranged oblongs, marked within a greater rectangle. Nearest him stood the cane around which his red currants grew. Behind them, the potato patch, sprouting green shoots from beneath the earth, and recovering well after last year's plague of aphids. Then came the rhubarb in its robust ranks, rowdy leaves densely packed and always overstepping the mark. He was quite taken with their unruly vigour and found pleasure in their curtailment. Next grew fledgling blocks of Indian Summer sweetcorn; little golden cobs speckled red and purple and grey-green. In the autumn he and Laura would make corn bread out of them. After that was the neatly heaped compost, well contained within thick wooden planks. Each of the garden's cells ran at right-angles to the strip of turf that allowed Corbyn to walk from the tool shed at the top, to the greenhouse beside the bank of the stream. Inside the greenhouse was a stone floor he and his sons had laid together many years ago, and in which grew his tomatoes and begonias and various potted plants. Leaning against the glass house, a single sturdy apple tree branched not far from the ground.

It was his little Versailles, perfectly perpendicular to a blade, and to tend it was his satisfied distraction. Into his kingdom came birds to sing, and an Englishman's peace prevailed among the vegetables that gradually transformed the earth and sun into the foundations of human culture. From his seat he marvelled at his speckled sweetcorn and the gradual, steady march of evolution.

As he surveyed his land, his attention became slowly drawn to something moving in the far corner of his eye. Beside the greenhouse on the bank of the stream, a bundle of clothes was flapping in the breeze.

Rising from his deck chair, he took a few steps down the strip of lawn and saw that the bundle was a man squatted on the flats of his heels, the back of his head rising and falling and arms flaying from side to side. Corbyn moved closer. He wrenched the pitchfork, stuck at an angle in the compost heap, and his back wrenched with it. He really had overdone the doorsteps that morning.

He halted at the greenhouse and straightened himself as best he could. The afternoon breeze moved through the leaves, flapping his untucked shirt. He pulled back his bucket hat and called out:

'Hello, there. Do I know you?' said Corbyn, standing tall. The bundled man said nothing and continued to throw his sticks. Corbyn stepped closer and, on inspection, saw that the man was old, perhaps of a similar age; and that he was not raving, but throwing twigs and stones into the river.

'Hello. Who are you?' He poised his pitchfork, but with no intention of using it. The man stopped what he was doing and Corbyn went tense. Then, he rolled off his haunches and stretched out on the grassy bank.

'Hello old friend,' he said. 'Don't you know me?' He wore a relaxed smile and was remarkably similar to Corbyn in appearance; the same rough-spun white beard; slighter of build and seemingly younger, which perhaps accounted for the easiness of his face.

'Jeremy!' said Corbyn, relieved, pushing the pitchfork back into the compost heap. 'What are you doing here?'

'Where else would I find you on a fine day like this?' said Jeremy.

Corbyn squinted. 'Well, I'm afraid I don't get up here very often,' he said, somewhat defensively. 'You know how work always gets in the way.'

'Is that so? I rather got the impression you get up here as often as you liked.'

'I haven't seen you for quite a while.'

'Well, today I thought you might be in need of me.'

Did you indeed. Corbyn held his tongue. Jeremy continued to flick stones in the stream. *Plunk!*

'Say, do you remember when we were boys and we used to go butterfly hunting?'

'I remember when I used to go butterfly hunting,' said Corbyn.

'Well, I think I just saw an Adonis Blue, fluttering above the stream.'

'Oh, yes?' said Corbyn, with apparent disinterest. 'That species is in decline, owing to the destruction of its natural habitat.' He took a furtive peek at the stream below.

'You'd have been impressed. It was a brilliant bright blue with white trim ... But then you called out, and it disappeared.'

His childhood with Jeremy had been made up of great butterfly hunts, across the fields in the light of the morning that rose gently behind the family home. For Jeremy it had just been an excuse to go down to the river and play stepping-stones. Corbyn had always wanted a butterfly collection, but Jeremy just wanted to splash his feet in the cold flow of the stream. That was what it had been like between them as children: Jeremy plunging headfirst into the flow, but not always with the most productive of outcomes; Corbyn some way behind, treading water. Although, now that he recalled it, his childhood dreams of desiccated insects were no longer as appealing as the thought of placing his poor trodden feet in the icy cold stream.

'Did you know they drink crocodile tears?'

'What?'

'Butterflies. They drink crocodile tears. Something about the salt, I seem to recall.'

'Staying long this time?' said Corbyn. He had no time for one of Jeremy's tangents. 'It's always a pleasure, as you know, but I do have work to be getting on with. You can make yourself useful if you like.'

He turned back to his rectangles and meandered among them, feigning concern for his potatoes. His only plan that afternoon had been to snooze amid the polling station treacle that smeared over the hourly bulletin. He pottered over to the big plastic barrel that collected rain water from the shed gutter. On tiptoes he peered over the oily surface where the dead leaves floated.

Squatting, Corbyn poured his watering can and swept the potato-invading aphids away. He held a glistening leaf between his fingers. Jeremy stood over him.

'You can wash away the mites, but they'll be in your rhubarb by morning.'

'Maybe so,' said Corbyn, straining at a weed. 'But gardens need to be maintained. Hedgerows need to be cut back, vines need to be pruned. Otherwise, you'll end up in a mess.'

'Quite right, old boy,' said Jeremy. Ignoring his tone, Corbyn dug down to the root.

'Do you know what a brush fire is?' asked Jeremy.

'Yes, I know what a brush fire is, thank you very much.' He could feel Jeremy's tangent about to launch. He pulled the root free.

'In places like Canada and Australia they've always favoured preventing brush fires by discouraging people from smoking in the woods, and lighting campfires outside designated areas, that sort of thing. And the fire services are really on the case.'

'Right,' said Corbyn, scanning the dirt with the tips of his fingers.

'Well, it turns out, precisely because of the success they've had over the years, the forest floor has collected so much fallen dead wood - so much combustible material - that they are inadvertently creating the conditions for what is termed a "forest super fire".'

Corbyn looked up at him. 'Then they need more firefighters, more resources, better regulations.'

'Before man intervened, the fires fertilised the forest with the ash they left behind, and pinecones opened in the heat, releasing their seeds into the soil.'

'So you're saying, what, exactly? That the rangers should start forest fires to clear away the dead wood?'

'No, I'm not saying that, although that is what the article I was reading proposed: *"Occasional forest fires prevent cataclysms further down the road."* Not sure it would work, though. Controlling nature allows you to potter around on this allotment - but then it ups the stakes.'

'So, that's your solution is it, to do nothing? You've certainly changed your tune,' said Corbyn.

'Well, there isn't a solution, is there? I mean, in the complete sense of the word. No final conclusion where we all get up and go home; only growing understanding. The forest will light up whether we like it or not, be it by a discarded cigarette or bolt of lightning. Far better to understand nature, in order to intervene in it, not let it take us by surprise. That's what I understood by it, anyway.'

'But we're part of nature,' said Corbyn. 'And it's perfectly natural to put out a fire when it leaps up and singes your whiskers.'

'Nature isn't conscious. It doesn't plan in advance, only we do that. We're part of nature, yes, but we're also apart from it.'

'You're either part of it or you aren't,' said Corbyn. He looked down toward the stream and his feet ached more than ever. Then he wiped his brow and looked at Jeremy. He wondered how his tomatoes were getting on.

'We can see things that don't yet exist,' said Jeremy. 'We can imagine things in our heads and then plan them on paper and set about to make that plan real.'

'Just as the spider spins his web.'

'But the spider always spins the same web.'

'And the great tear it up,' said Corbyn. They exchanged a smile and Corbyn felt genuine warmth for him for the first time that afternoon. *He may talk a lot of nonsense, but it isn't so bad. Not after such a long time.*

'Well,' said Jeremy, 'I don't suppose we're under any threat of super-fires on this little patch. Not any time soon. Our English rain would soon dampen your combustible material.'

Standing, he was slightly taller than Jeremy. It was typical of him to appear today, of all days, he thought. He would have put good money on it.

'Talking of which, this election isn't looking half as tidy as your allotment,' said Jeremy. Corbyn sauntered to the greenhouse. 'Particularly in Scotland, wouldn't you say? The party looks a bit, well… ragged?'

'No - I wouldn't say so. The Nationalists lost, and now that's over and done with. Now they need a party of government. The British people are known for their common sense, Scots included. We might take a few hits, here and there, but we'll hang on to the lion's share. Scotland has always been Labour.'

'Well, I'm not sure that's entirely accurate. But I think you'd be wrong to underestimate what's taken place. The independence referendum had the highest turnout this country has ever seen. Doesn't that tell you something?'

'Yes, that it was a freak.'

'I'm not so sure. Look, what's been solved? Scotland is still in

Jeremy and Corbyn

Britain, meaning it's still ruled at present by a bunch of shrill Etonians hell-bent on austerity. It might as well be a foreign occupation!'

'Don't exaggerate. You think the Scots don't feel part of Britain? That they would be better off under the nationalists? I must say, Jeremy, you sound more and more desperate each time I see you.'

'That's not the point. All I'm saying is that people responded to a call for change – "anything but Westminster", and the austerity that goes with it. And all the while, where were we? With the Tories, waving the Union Jack.'

'So it's "We", is it?' teased Corbyn. He fed his begonias a little water. 'You have a point, tactically speaking. Jumping into bed with those hooligan Tories was not in our best interests. We should have had our own campaign, on a class basis, against dividing the British workers. Not all this *"Better Together"* nonsense.'

'What's a little flag-waving between the sheets, when we've been "better together" with them on the councils carrying out the cuts for the last five years?'

'Well, yes, but come on,' said Corbyn. 'I think you need to be realistic. We all know that we couldn't just oppose the cuts on every single council. We'd have been lynched by the press. And the Tories would have just overruled us from central government anyway. Then we would have looked foolish! And they would have taken it out on ordinary, decent, hard-working people with severer cuts - ground-zero kind of stuff. Which makes sense, from their point of view: make an example of any council that gets out of line. Believe me, the Tories are vicious. Far better to throw up the Labour shield, to soften the blow - kinder cuts. Yes, we've worked with the Tories, but only to hold them back. It demonstrates the benefits, in practice, of voting Labour.'

'I always thought you'd be an outstanding hostage negotiator, did I ever tell you?'

'Scotland was a blip,' said Corbyn, beginning to feel a little cross.

'A blip on the seismometer! The British working class was very nearly split in two. And it would have been all Labour's fault,' said Jeremy.

'Not "We" anymore?'

'If *we* had spent our time fighting the cuts, and not carrying them out with the Tories, then the Scottish workers wouldn't have a reason to look elsewhere for a solution.'

'It's a nice idea, Jeremy, but Labour isn't in that line of work anymore, don't you know? Defending workers! Where have you been for the last twenty-five years?'

'That can change. It has to. What about the SNP? It was never a working-class party, but now I'm not so sure... Its trade union section is bigger than the entire Scottish Labour Party. All Labour had to do was dock ship and ask those workers aboard, but it didn't. And now they're on board with the SNP instead. What happened in Scotland can happen in the rest of the country. Did you know it's the biggest party in the world now, as a proportion of the population?' He admitted he did not.

Corbyn reflected on his prior allotted peace with renewed appreciation. He bore Jeremy no particular ill-will - he was a part of him in many ways - but he did possess a profound propensity for transforming perfectly sensible topics of conversation into the most arrant nonsense.

He would talk about the masses, and the inevitability of their struggle, and even interpret things in quite an original way - you had to give him that - but it was always symptomatic of some great impending change. And if there was one thing Corbyn knew, it was that things did not change. Not really, not fundamentally. One might make a small difference here, win a little victory there, and, who knows? Eventually, in the passage of time, those incremental adjustments might just add up to something. Of course, everything did change, just not as impatiently as Jeremy demanded. Change was something that took place gradually, imperceptibly, under tremendous geothermal pressures and over vast geological expanses.

'You know, the French have a saying: *"The more things change, the more they stay the same."* It's something that's held me in good stead over the years. You'd do well to remember it.' Jeremy rolled his eyes.

'You are right, of course,' Corbyn continued, 'we all want change. But how? That's the question. What exactly is it that you propose? What you say might be fine talk among learned professors in their seminars, but people are afraid, you know? The change you talk of means a leap into the dark. People want change they can see, they can touch, they can feel. I'm not sure it's something you've ever truly understood.' He looked at Jeremy for a reaction, but he offered none.

'To serve the community and to represent their interests; small changes, little kindnesses; it all adds up you know. You'd find it very rewarding. News soon spreads of the chap who has done this, who fixed that, who took a stand against the other. You might offer bright ideas, but they're always dependent on one thing: *The Movement*. *The Movement, The Movement*, and once again, *The Movement,*' said Corbyn, moving his hands like a conductor waving a baton.

'And if I have learned one positive, irrefutable truth these past five years, something I should have learned long ago is that - as if to carve it upon my nose - in the very moment when it should have become an absolute blinding necessity: your movement of the masses - where is it? It's nowhere to be seen. Why? Because it belongs to a bygone era. Where are the strikes? Where are the mass demonstrations?' Jeremy tried to interject, but Corbyn was in full flow.

'While my poorest constituents have been turfed out of their homes because they use an extra room to store equipment for a disability; while the hospitals are cut to the bone; while a number of my constituents have actually died after being declared fit to go on a wild goose chase down the job centre; while even people with jobs now need to go to food banks: where is this so-called movement, beyond a few spindly protests? General strike kicked into the long grass. Unions surrendering their bloc-vote. Where's the pressure from below? There isn't any. People don't care. We've become a society of individuals who walk by, on the other side, when they see someone begging in the street. I'm sorry, but Thatcher burned away any revolutionary spirit this country had when she beat the miners. And Blair poured white-wash over their charred embers.'

'You know your problem?' said Jeremy. 'You think the world would be a better place if only we would all just sit down togather at the table with a nice cup of tea. You think the lion and the crocodile can sit on the riverbank and discuss their differences. It's so... shallow.' He felt mean for saying it, but there it was.

Corbyn had heard it all before. It was Jeremy's understanding of reality that had little depth, and faith in the masses was a religious idea. Yes, he knew they moved, but to say when and in what manner was an article of faith.

The lower layers from time to time seemed to flare up; that much was apparent. But who could have predicted the London riots? More besides, what good were they? The masses simply could not be divined, and even if they could, what would be the use?

Perhaps in other countries there was a genuine working-class movement, even in Scotland one could seemingly argue, and he might concede the point. But fifty million Englishers? They were too many, they were too heterogeneous, and they lacked the Celtic flame of the Scots. The English workers of today were warmed in sturdy, three-walled partitions, answering telephones between comfort breaks and team-building exercises. A miner would have given his right arm for that kind of life.

He was not seeking a confrontation with Jeremy. That never got them anywhere. He attempted to steer the conversation back onto polite terrain.

'You know, before you arrived, I dozed off for a moment and had a funny dream. It was tomorrow and we'd won. Ed was giving a speech to the press in Downing Street. He was announcing a coalition with the Greens. Can you imagine...?' He turned to Jeremy with a smile, but it went unrequited.

'The funny thing was that in the middle of it all, Ed declared that despite the victory, Jeremy Corbyn had lost his seat in Islington, and what a tragedy it was for the party! I rather think they'd be popping the champagne corks if they got that into the bargain! '

Jeremy smiled, regarding his friend curiously. 'And what would you think of that?' he said, leaning against the greenhouse door.

Funnily enough I felt quite comfortable with the whole idea. It's been a hell of a stint, though it hardly feels like thirty years. And I've done it in my own way, not cowered to the buggers, stood my ground. It's been a lot easier since John came on the scene, as you know.'

He pressed his hand against the small of his back and the ache eased a little.

'I can see myself retiring, after this next parliament, perhaps. Come up to the allotment more, begin making red currant jam.'

'A charming idea, old boy, I reckon I've heard you say it before. But who would champion the people of Islington North?'

Corbyn fiddled his trowel around the tomato stalks. 'Oh, I'm sure some young left could be found to take up the mantle, perhaps even a local. I could still participate in my CLP as a local activist. I used to be quite good at the sort of thing, if you remember?'

'Yes, you've always been the organised one... But why not just pack it all in then? It's not as if you've much to look forward to, other than being ignored by the leadership for another five years.'

'Bit late now. Ask me again in five years' time,' he said, exiting the greenhouse and making his way back to the tool shed. Jeremy followed.

'Or, announce you're going tonight! You'll make an interesting little footnote in the all-night coverage.'

'Very amusing. And what if it came down to one seat?'

'Imagine their faces,' Jeremy laughed. 'Well, whatever you decide, I'll be there for you, as always.'

The radio still buzzed as Corbyn sat back in his deck chair. He looked over his land and poured another green tea into his locally sourced mug. Jeremy sat down on the grass beside him. They were silent for a moment. Corbyn sometimes found that if he was quiet long enough, Jeremy would tend to go off and find other things to amuse himself with.

But he was not so bad, Corbyn considered. A friend has to challenge you. Keep you on your toes. *He's always done that. Even when he's away, he never really goes away. He's always asking those questions.*

'Well, here's to my defeat,' said Corbyn, raising his mug.

'Victory in defeat,' smiled Jeremy, holding an invisible cup in return.

2

Later on, Corbyn made his way to the polling station. It was on the cusp of evening by the time he met Geraldine, the local party treasurer, at the gates of the community centre.

A mole-ish librarian in her mid-thirties, Geraldine came from that thinned ring of party members who had survived their weaning during the primacy of Blair. A BBC-checked inoffensiveness dominated her, and she rarely wagered a point of view. Invariably her contributions at meetings were prefaced by: 'I thought a woman should speak, so…' and were always administrative in nature.

From the gate, Corbyn had already spotted three Greens; an earthy gentleman in sandals and a grey ponytail, and alongside him, two fresh-faced students. Enviously he admired them straddling his path. He had always found the Greens to be thoroughly decent people, and their local candidate was ever such an agreeable young lady.

He improvised a non-toxic joke with Geraldine to put himself at ease. A few members of the public were filtering in after work. Far better to vote now, and be seen by them and the local party, than early in the morning when the place was deserted.

As they approached the entrance he was relieved to spot some party members, beyond the bright Green youth. He was about to greet them when he was accosted:

'When are you going to join us then, Jeremy?' said a young woman, handing him a leaflet. The other Greens lingered nearby. Geraldine grasped her wrist and scowled at the younger woman.

'Oh! Not quite just yet, thanks,' said Jeremy, a broken laugh catching in his throat.

'You'd be much more at home in our party than Labour, Jeremy. We're against nuclear weapons, against privatisation and against austerity.' He loathed getting caught up in conversations like this.

'Well, I have a lot of respect for Caroline. I'm always trying to convince her to join Labour,' he said, and hurried on as politely as he could.

'But Jeremy, how can you be in the same party as Blair? The party that invaded Iraq?' He stopped mid-step.

'You're absolutely right; I don't know how I do it either.' Geraldine looked at her feet. 'But the point I always make to Caroline is, Labour is a broad church, and we need to bring in more progressive types like her - and you guys. It's all very well protesting from the side-lines, but we need a party that can form a government in order to have things like a proper environmental policy. It's as simple as that, really. You should join us!' Then he smiled and walked off as briskly as he could.

'We're the future,' she called after him. 'Biggest youth group in the country!' Her words unsettled him. *He who has the youth has the future*, Jeremy always said.

He had become damp around the neck and happily fell into the arms of the nearest member along the path; a local Labour rank-and-file activist named Bob, an old revolutionary socialist, or something like that. Nevertheless, he was someone who could be relied upon to support the party, come rain or shine.

'Bob! Hello, Bob,' cried Corbyn, and Geraldine chafed at the enthusiasm given to the irksome old-timer. He was even more worn than Corbyn.

A former athlete, Bob went everywhere by bike, which had the effect of naturally moulding his white hair into an aerodynamic wisp. He wore aviator sunglasses over his pink face and a bright yellow hi-visibility jacket all year round, and his hands were splashed with sovereign rings. No one, not least Corbyn, could forget Bob. Nor did Corbyn forget to avoid eye contact with the *Revolutionary Newspaper* Bob held against his chest.

'Fruit and veg giving you bother, Jeremy?'

'Oh, only trying to recruit me,' said Corbyn, shaking a sparkling hand.

'Cheeky buggers. I'll go over there and give them a salad dressing, if you like.' Corbyn appreciated the solidarity, but hoped no one overheard. 'Got some good policies, mind. Could do with some of that in Labour,' said Bob.

'That's what we were just discuss... by the way, Jeremy, have you met our new comrade, Amalia?' He gestured to the young woman beside him helping to hand out Labour leaflets and sell the *Revolutionary Newspaper*.

'One of our bright young members in Islington North. From Greece...' he made sure to add.

Corbyn had heard mention of the young Greek girl from the local university who had shown up at the CLP. For an enthusiastic youth to join and attend a party meeting was quite an event. To come back a second time, and then actually to become involved; this alone made her exotic.

She was quite beautiful, as Mediterranean women often are to dilated English eyes. He reached to shake her hand. Tangles of baked clay kelp fell swinging as she made an awkward half-curtsy.

He glimpsed the freckles that swept over her Hellenic nose, tracing the plumose hair beneath her ears, past her neck, fading as they approached the sternum. Corbyn swallowed. He felt stripped of decency around beautiful young women, and tried to maintain eye contact.

Further along, he and Geraldine passed a dejected looking Liberal Democrat handing out his party's leaflet, but they saw no Tories or UKIPers.

Inside, the little queue stirred on his arrival. He greeted politely all those he knew, and a little old lady squeezed his hand and blessed him. A man he believed was a long-standing member half-joked, half-argued with him as to why he should not vote UKIP. The conversation finished with Corbyn unsure as to whether the man was joking at all.

After five minutes he was shown to a booth. His hand hovered rebelliously over the Green box for a heartbeat. He had half expected Jeremy to turn up. Then he marked Labour and made his way out of the centre, and home.

3

It was well past midnight, and the results were soon to be announced. The hall roared, masking the tense, mundane, giddy observations that had entwined and became poisoned. The brick walls absorbed them all, drowning each in the raucous anonymity of a public pool.

Corbyn ached from his neck to the small of his back to his knees.

Alone under the bright lights, eyeing the stage and twiddling his watch strap, a parliament of little old ladies had swooped down and surrounded him. They blinked through thick glasses, and the ringleader demanded he taste her cake.

'Mmm… yes, I must say Mrs Barnett,' said Corbyn in mouthfuls, eyes scouring the hall for his wife.

'I really don't know what Islington Labour Party meetings would be like without…'

A shaky arm guided another spoonful toward his face, layering crumbs upon his white whiskers.

'Mmm… I just don't know what we'd do without your sponge cake.'

'It's Lemon Drizzle,' said an unamused Mrs Barnett, and the old ladies broke into a back-fence twitter. *The lemon must be homeopathic.*

As they cooed, he slipped free of the knitted scrimmage. Sneaking to the far end of the hall, he disappeared behind the stage.

Once alone, he surrendered to his weary shoulders and mopped the back of his neck with his handkerchief. He propped himself against the scaffolding under the shade of the stage and pressed the cold metal piping across the wet patch that had spread from shirt to jacket.

At his feet plastic sacks were strewn across the floor. Earlier they had been carried to the hall and emptied of their content. Now the secret will of Islington North was being sifted by a tiding of volunteers, who broadly speaking divided into two social types: There were the rare young people, so taken with politics that they hoped to make a living by it. More common were the doughty guardians of democracy who, between elections, could be found raging against the yellow lines, or the fouling of the dog.

Piled beside the sacks was an untidy heap of blue crash-mats, weighed down with dust. Corbyn imagined himself falling backwards into them with a cavernous thud…

He screwed his eyes and refocused. Fishing out his glasses and a little brown note book, he thumbed the pages of his speech. He had prepared a few simple notes on the expectation that he would win, and Labour would win the country. But at Ten o'clock he and Laura sat astonished in the living room as Dimbleby threw their expectations overboard:

> *'Here it is. Ten o'clock. And we are saying the Conservatives are the largest party.'*

Big Ben groaned in despair.

> *'And here are the figures… quite remarkable this exit poll. The conservatives on three-hundred and sixteen, that's up nine since the last election in 2010.*
>
> *'Ed Miliband for Labour - seventy-seven behind on two-hundred and thirty-nine, down nineteen on the last election.'*

Elections filled him with dread even when they were a sure thing. Now he had to re-write his whole speech at a moment's notice. He picked his white beard and scratched his throat and struck out his ode to Ed with his little IKEA pencil. Laura brought them back in handfuls after each outing. Officially Corbyn disapproved, but it did not stop her, and he had not pushed the matter as they were rather convenient.

He had never been pleased with his dedication to the leader, yet resented far more its redaction. It had taken many hours to arrive at the perfectly balanced weak-lemon tribute.

Ed had been far kinder to him than the other lot. Nevertheless, one could hardly say that his stewardship had been inspiring. Bewildering was nearer the mark.

The tabloids had picked up on the cruel physicality of that fact; the gormless awkwardness and vulnerability of the kid who tries to run with the big boys in the school playground. Corbyn pitied him.

Something positive. Thank you, etc., etc., thanks to Laura my wife, thanks to the local party, the public... He had done it a thousand times, unknowingly resenting the routine of it all.

It was at this point that he heard the light tapping of Jeremy's voice at the threshold of his thoughts. He wondered what he would say about all this. Then Corbyn turned to find that he was beside himself.

'Say what's on your mind,' said Jeremy, his elbow resting on the scaffolding, one hand splayed in his hair.

'And what's that?'

'Oh, I don't know,' said Jeremy. 'Something like: "If Miliband loses it'll be because he was too much of a pathetic little jellyfish to stand up against the cuts." How's that?'

'Shall I make that the opener...? Don't be so preposterous,' said Corbyn. He turned his back on Jeremy and mined the speeches of his memory for suitable combinations.

'The Labour Party. The Labour Party is... the people's party.'

'The party of the working class,' said Jeremy.

'The party of the poor, the party of the oppressed, the party of - the community.'

Corbyn scribbled it in his little brown notebook.

Jeremy winced.

'Write this: "Without organisation, we are nothing but raw material for exploitation."'

'Too risqué - you do realise there are little old ladies out there, don't you? How about:

'"Without community, we are helpless individuals in the face of Tory austerity?"'

'Yes, but it's not just the Tories - they're just the errand boys. You give them too much credit. Call them what they are:

'"…in the face of austerity, carried out by the hired thugs of the bosses."'

'That's far too complicated,' said Corbyn, thinking of the little old ladies.

'"In the face of austerity, carried out by the bankers and their… hired representatives".'

Corbyn scribbled it down. 'Nobody likes the bankers.' They continued to wrestle over the script:

"For many years, *some might argue*, our party ~~has been hijacked by big business~~ *lost its way*. Many *might have* said we had ~~come to resemble the enemy we were built to defeat~~ *stopped representing those in need*. ~~Certainly among the leadership. Who can deny it?~~ And they *might have* had a point. But the Labour Party has deep, deep roots in society. *In our community*. New Labour *may have* left a bitter taste in *some* people's mouths. ~~Mine included~~. ~~'Understandably, many~~ *Some* looked elsewhere, to other parties, ~~which say they are more Labour than the Labour Party.~~ *But I say to them: stop complaining; stop fiddling on the fringes, stop moaning from the side-lines. If you don't like the Blairites then join us in Labour to take the party back!*"

This time it was Jeremy who thought the tone too much, but he agreed with the sentiment. He proposed an alternative:

"But I say to them: We must unite! All the anti-austerity forces, whatever tomorrow's outcome, let's come together in a united, working-class front to fight to overthrow what's at the bottom of austerity: Capitalism.

That means fighting for a socialist society!"

'Steady on, old boy,' said Corbyn, lifting his head from his notebook.

'You're always asking people to join Labour, and it's always to fight austerity, to fight the Tories,' said Jeremy.

'Reasonable enough… but if you don't offer a raised horizon or two it doesn't mean anything. Why don't you talk about what we're fighting for?

'That young Green put you on the spot earlier, didn't she? Well, the Greens and the SNP can say they're the anti-austerity parties, but they don't say anything about socialism. That's our tradition, and you should tap into it. God knows no one else does.'

'Yes, because it's entirely abstract,' said Corbyn. He struck a line through the passage. But he so desperately wanted to appeal to the Greens and their bright young people, although few of them were present in the hall at that late hour.

'Let's just say: "And may I just congratulate…" what was her name again?

> '"May I just congratulate what's-her-face and the Greens for conducting a very moral, very decent campaign that raised many important issues.
>
> '"I think we both agree that there is much that unites our two parties, not least the question of protecting our environment."

'There, how's that for reaching out?'

'Congratulating the Greens? That'll piss off Geraldine…'

'What, and your way wouldn't?' Corbyn kept it. 'Differentiate Labour and the Greens from the rest, appeal to the Green youth on the basis of unity. They had twice the youngsters we had knocking on doors. Can't praise them too much though, most of their ideas are ours.'

'They were,' said Jeremy.

'Where was I?' said Corbyn. 'Something about the Tories…'

> "The Tories are the servants of the capitalist system. They handed over our money to the banks."

'Wait - Labour did that,' said Jeremy.

'People know what I mean.'

> "~~These Tories in Labour's clothing~~ *They* bailed out ~~capitalism~~ *the banks*. Any ~~worker~~ *hard-working family* understands that when one of us gets into debt, we have to pay for it. But when the Tories' rich friends in the city get into the same trouble - it's us again who have to pay for it. Double standards. Taxpayers' money went to bail out the ~~capitalist~~ system, but ~~it cannot be repaired. Y~~you only have to look at history; the merry-go-round always ends in tears. And as night follows day, the rich make the poor pay.

Don't forget the Liberal Democrats,' said Jeremy.
 "These people are the reason why hospitals are closing.
 Why our schools are being run into the ground."
'This is very good stuff,' said Jeremy, barely concealing his pleasure. When it came to his friend, he knew when to take his winnings and leave the table.

'You don't think it's… too much?' said Corbyn. He had been so rushed, and he was so tired by this late hour, that he no longer trusted his judgement.

'Not at all! I must say, I'm a little impressed - even with the edits. You have my full backing. Best thing you've produced in years. '

Corbyn hesitated at the thought of going back out, preferring the shade of the stage to the throng and the members and Mrs Barnett's bland drizzle.

The ranks were far more daunting than the careerists he side-stepped in Westminster; always talking about how 'courageous' he was. It was not false modesty that made him cringe, but the debt with which these sincere souls saddled him. It was a debt he had no confidence in paying back. In his lowest moments he wondered if he was not merely a repository for their grievances, for their poverty-stricken fantasies. Was he just someone to be whined at? Someone to delegate responsibility for their life to? It was not his strength, but their weakness, that maintained him in office.

'Who wins if Labour wins?' he asked the plastic sacks. If they knew, they kept it to themselves. The workers had been deserting since the 1980s, while he and a bloody-minded few had hung on by their fingernails. Many had tried to trim them, leaders had come and gone, but they were not clipped.

'Yeremy!' The voice of his wife broke his thoughts. Laura was at the side of the stage, her loud Mexican whisper more insistent than usual.

'Dees is where you have been? Dare announcing deh results!' She swung on her little black heels and threw her handbag over her shoulder. 'Come on!' she said, tilting her head toward the hall.

Corbyn returned his glasses to their green leather case and placed them in his shirt. Unhurried, he patted his pockets and started after his wife.

The hall no longer roared, but had settled into a serious murmur.

Eyes were falling on him, causing him to become self-conscious in his walk.

He kept his eyes on Laura. She looked back at him and stopped. His beautiful companion: petite, coal black hair and eyes. He drifted to her like a dog and smiled and waited for the blessing of her kiss, before the ceremonial tribulations took him.

But she did not bless him, and instead her big dark eyes grew wide in alarm.

'What is that on your mouth? Cake?' With a licked thumb she wiped his white beard clean of Mrs Barnett's drizzle. 'And where is your rosette?' she said, jutting her chin in the direction of his chest and tugging at a bare lapel. Jeremy looked down and then twisted back toward the stage.

'Maybe it came off backstay...'

Laura re-entered his field of vision from behind, heels clacking on the wooden floor, shoulders small hills of irritation.

He untwisted and, inches from his face, found himself confronted by Simi, the local party Chair.

Simi was another graduate of Geraldine's thin dry ring, only a few years younger. Corbyn disliked her, considering her rather juvenile.

'So it looks like five mins yeah, Jeh-Ray-Me...' she said, drawing out his name, which he found it most irritating. 'I think we're doing fine, no murmurs from the counting table; Mrs Barnett's girls are circling. Everyone's gathered over there,' she pointed to a stackable table close to the stage, where a small troop of hardened members had collected. 'Perhaps a few final words before you go up?' she said. He did not feel as if he was being asked.

'Speak to the young ones Yeremy, day look up to you,' said Laura, returned and re-fastening his rosette.

All Corbyn saw were a few old ladies and Bob and Geraldine. They were all sending him burdensome smiles. His shoulders pinched.

'Do we really have the time?' he said, a little bit of himself sinking into his blood stream.

Then he saw, beside Bob and his brood, the young Greek comrade he had been introduced to earlier - and she was speaking with Jeremy!

'Alright, let's go,' he said. But just as he had begun to walk over, he was cut short. A stout bingo-caller took the stage and the microphone thudded.

'Could candidates make their way, please?'

'Oh, well, here we go...' he said, with regretful relief. He looked over at his knot of supporters and saw Jeremy and the Greek comrade waving at him with open smiles. Laura brushed him for crumbs one last time and straightened his rosette and gave him his kiss.

The last to ascend the stage, Corbyn perused his rivals. It had certainly been an extraordinary campaign - the most unusual in his memory. The usual two-way tug-of-war had become a sight more tricky. When you included the SNP, it resembled a six-way game of musical chairs.

At the opposite end from Corbyn stood the UKIP candidate.

Local. Young for UKIP. Eyes don't swivel. He suspected a used-car salesman. *He must be a pretty twisted creature to have survived in Islington among all the blacks and Asians and bleeding-heart lefties. Unreformed Thatcherite. Hopefully chipped away at the Tory support, though.*

A trickle of sweat beaded past the Liberal Democrat's ear. His Adam's apple protruded, and his face matched the colour of his rosette. He seemed a nice fellow, Corbyn thought, but the Liberals appeared to have far lower expectations of themselves than the Tories, all things considered.

He reminded himself to make a point of being friendly to the Green candidate before the night was out.

The Tory next to him was young and handsome, with a rugby smile and hands folded in front of him. He pretended to pay no notice to Corbyn. *British Psycho.*

The winner was announced. Corbyn's mind went blank. Down at the table his members moved like a fizzy watercolour. He heard their whistles and cheers in the distance. What had he meant to say?

He glimpsed the pages of his notebook, but it was just a jumble of crossed scribbles. The cheers of the local party lifted his arm automatically, and his smile defaulted, and then he was shaking his Tory's hand.

He steadied the microphone between gloves of sweat. Looking over the hall, the concentrated knot of delight set their attention at his feet, as the fragments of the other parties went peeling into the night.

He had forgotten what he wanted to say.

CHAPTER 3
INNER STEEL

1

As always, they began with global forecasts.

'Of course, my boys, it all comes down to the question of the debt, which bears down on everything as a low pressure tearing through the world economy. That is the starting point for an understanding of the situation. It makes conditions ever more volatile on the high seas of the world market.'

Peter twisted his reading glasses between his thumb and forefinger, hands hanging loosely off his crossed knees, the occasional strand of hair creeping out from beneath his cuffs.

'How much is the debt, PM?' asked Tristram.

Asinine question…

'Worldwide? One cannot precisely say.' Peter did not let his disappointment show through. As always, he was quite prepared to persevere with his student. 'But the best estimates are around two-hundred trillion dollars - a figure even our Clientele cannot entirely comprehend.' The brothers turned in their seats.

'Think of it this way: It is three times what the entire economy of the planet produces in a year. That is to say, the debt could be repaid in only three years' time… if we could get the little people to work without pay.' Tristram looked perplexed.

'I don't think that would go down very well, PM.'

'Quite right my boy, quite right.' He had long ceased expecting fireworks from his young apprentice, but he admired his trying little squibs, brought to him like a faithful golden retriever. *The mediocre student who endeavours can climb high,* say the Chinese, *a brilliant student who does not will fall low.* His other student would be brilliant, if only he would apply himself.

'This is why it is important that we continue to pursue our projected aims. Our Holdings here, and in the media, are dedicated to talking up the economy – very important for morale. Do you recall what Napoleon had to say about morale?'

Tristram's face became constipated. It was on the tip of his tongue; his Lord said it so often.

Much to Peter's irritation, Chuka merely peered out of the high grated windows. It was a sunny morning. He saw oarsmen skimming over the waves that rippled along the Thames, before escaping under Westminster Bridge.

'*The moral is to the physical as three to one,*' said Chuka, putting Tristram out of his misery. 'Something which our former leader never understood,' he added, slouching disinterestedly in his leather arm chair.

'Do sit up and pay attention, my boy,' said Peter, a mother's despair pregnant in his plea. Chuka complied.

'Of course, we must understand that this… necessary fiction, is contradicted by the facts. In America the figures show it is the weakest recovery in history, and elsewhere matters are worse. What that means, regrettably, is that predictions for economic growth are revised down on a routine basis. Ultimately, that erodes confidence; like chasing a pot of gold at the end of the rainbow.'

Tristram nodded in solemn comprehension. He learned long ago that there was little point in chasing rainbows.

'Now, you are both keeping up with the *Financial Times*, are you not? It is paramount you do, and that you bring your findings here to discuss. The *FT* is the only completely open channel we have. I have shown you which writers to read, and if you do read them,' he tilted his head toward Chuka, 'then, of course, these meetings will become a little less one-way, and we will save ourselves a great deal of time if I don't have to…'

That Lord Peter declined to finish his sentence was all the sign the boys needed, and they both promised to keep up with their homework. Tristram jotted down a reminder in his notebook to take out a subscription to the *Financial Times*, underlining it several times.

'Pay attention to the interest on the debt... thank you my dear,' his secretary brought Peter his tea in a delicate china cup. 'It denotes the health of an economy, like the charts the doctor keeps at the bottom of a patient's bed. And after that: investment levels - they indicate the flow of oxygen through the system. In America, capital investment as a whole is at an historic low, and state investment has been falling for the past five years. This shows the prevailing mood, not just of our Clientele, but of the entire bourgeois. Their reasoning is simple: demand is so weak that it is near impossible for them to know whether to sow fields they may never harvest.' Tristram turned to Chuka with a plea for help written across his face.

'What's the point in buying new machinery and building new factories,' explained Chuka, 'when they can't make a decent profit from the ones they already have?'

'Precisely,' said Peter.

Tristram did revere his brother. He simply could not put things like he did.

'And in Britain,' Peter continued, 'of all the money that is undoubtedly sloshing around, less than a fifth is in new production. Most is being spent by companies on their own shares in order to keep the price high, which is quite understandable. If one cannot invest, better to keep the shareholder happy than let good money sit idle.'

Peter's mouth curled ever so slightly. 'One of our Clients is apt to say: "You can buy a throne with money, but you cannot sit on it."'

The boys made polite noises like laughter.

'Yes, most droll,' said Peter. 'Therefore, and as we have said before, the problem is not for lack of money. Vast sums have been injected - even conjured - since the crisis, but to no avail. To be perfectly honest, all that printing did was increase the public debt, with at best negligible results. Despite the best wishes of our aforementioned Client, around one-and-a-half trillion dollars are little more than thrones piled high in the bank vaults of Europe and London. Plenty of sore bottoms, I think you will agree.'

'All that would go a long way toward paying off the debt,' said Tristram. 'In that case why have we printed our money, PM? Seems rather silly to me.'

'Well, the Clientele are not very well going to pay the debt themselves, good heavens!' said Peter. 'They would not be Clients very long if they did so.'

Chuka bit his bottom lip.

'Oh, it was desperation, in the main - the need to be seen to be doing something. We had our reservations, naturally, but even our influence has its limits. After all, if we were omnipotent, what would be the point in being organised?'

The boys again made noises like polite laughter. It was a favourite maxim Peter's, and as he believed repetition to be the mother of all learning, the boys knew the sound of it well.

'What the world needs is a severe detox, not printing more debt,' asserted Chuka, fondling his wrist. 'Go cold turkey. That's the only way to do it.'

Peter admired his student's ruthless streak; if only it could be harnessed. Combined with the boy's 'ethnic good looks' he could be Blair re-born. Or, dare he dream, the British Obama? But did he possess Tony's instincts?

'Well, you are quite right, my boy,' said Peter, offered his palms and exposing more dark, wiry filaments.

'Only, of course, this only goes to show why global forecasts are so important.' He suspected the boys did not appreciate this most fundamental of questions. They always seemed to brighten up when the discussion moved on to organisational matters.

'We are not academic eunuchs. We discuss economic forecasts for one reason, and one reason only; insofar as it informs our understanding of the class struggle.'

'In the interests of the Clientele,' said Chuka, nodding enthusiastically. Once Peter guided his man to the battlefield, he could usually understand the terrain. But Tristram shifted uncomfortably in his seat.

He had only been attending these meetings for the past year; Chuka much longer. The three men usually met on the first of the month, every month, in Peter's office, but on this occasion it had been held back, owing to the General Election.

At first Tristram had joined them only occasionally, and the discussion had been quite informal. He was flattered to be invited into the confidence of his Lord, but for an occasional doubt that smouldered, like indigestion, in the hollows of his rib-cage.

PM often talked about the 'class struggle', and used terms like 'capital' and 'proletariat' and 'bourgeois' quite freely. Tristram felt awfully embarrassed when this happened, struggling to know where to look.

'We discuss developments in America;' said Peter, 'China's slowdown, and the consequential drop in the price of oil; the effect that has on our oil Clientele; how that in turn plays out in the arena of international relations; the Euro Crisis and its effects on morale; all for one reason: the class struggle.'

'The fall-out from 2008 has not gone away. It persists, like background radiation. But it is no mere Three Mile Island. We cannot evacuate. We have no choice but to live among it; to keep taking the Iodide and persevere, in the national interest, as you so rightly said, my boy.'

Peter talked for some time about the class struggle in China and the growing pessimism of the East Asian Clientele. China represented one of their greatest triumphs, and far better managed than what had transpired in Russia.

But he offered a word of warning: The Clientele was now questioning whether they had not been too successful in their Oriental endeavours; whether their success was not in fact provoking instability between the classes.

Tristram did his best to grasp the essence of what was being said, trying to look past the exotic language Peter and Chuka employed. He was learning that questions of stability were real concerns for Peter's friends. It was an alarming picture, as far as he could understand. The Chinese simply did not have the infrastructure in place to deal adequately with the brewing discontent. 'Safety valves', Peter called them. The British had perfected theirs over many centuries, whereas the valves made in China were cheap and plastic in comparison, and poorly installed. He reported that increasing numbers of Chinese clients were travelling to visit Peter personally to discuss how they might manufacture to British standards. It was one of the few growth industries.

'Yet, rule by the sword remains the most common practice,' continued Peter.

'It is all rather uncivilised. But a necessary evil, one must concede, when you have not laid down the many centuries of sediment, as our forebears did.'

They went on to discuss the precarious balance of the classes internationally, and the key battle fronts in South Africa, in Venezuela, in Mexico. They discussed the troubling developments in Europe and the worrying signs in Spain and the appalling situation in Greece, which they all agreed was the greatest danger in the present situation. Finally, they arrived in Britain.

'What characterises the situation here, of course, is the advanced understanding of the national interest that the little people have.' Chuka and Tristram nodded wholeheartedly.

'Not that we have not had our occasional difficulties,' continued Peter, with a serpentine smile. 'The Prime Minister had an uncomfortable start when the students threw out their toys. Our Liberal Democratic friends played an admirable role in all that...' His voice trailed off into a sigh, and for a moment he stared, glassy-eyed, through the high grated window.

'There draws to an end one of our finest projects.' A moment's silence descended upon the little gathering.

Presently Tristram ventured:

'How do you mean, PM?'

'He means the SDP,' whispered Chuka. 'It was one of the first directives that helped build the Tendency. Don't you remember? We discussed it a few months' ago - about how the Clientele was forced to split the party in eighty-one? And how it then brought some back later, and fused the rest with the old Liberal Party to form the Lib Dems?' Of course he remembered.

'...but this is business,' said Peter, regaining his composure, 'and last week's result has knocked them out of the equation. However one might feel personally.'

'And the so-called General Strike remains in the long grass,' said Chuka.

'Quite right,' said Peter. *Go to the top of the class.* 'Our people at the TUC made short work of that. Of course, some of the union leaders continue to be tiresome, but we maintain stout Holdings and wide Secondary Holdings among them.'

'And we also have "Holdings",' said Tristram, wielding the word unsteadily, 'in the left groups and campaigns?'

'We do,' said Peter, 'one or two gritty fellows who do not mind that sort of thing. In small groups it is often as simple as sniffing out the demoralised elements - and our men can smell demoralisation a mile off. Their mandate is quite straightforward: to keep these groups safely partitioned from the Party.'

Tristram found this the most gratifying revelation he had stumbled upon in their year-long meetings, and was by far his favourite topic of discussion. He loathed the Left with such a hideous pleasure that he took care to keep its true depths hidden from all sight, even from Peter and Chuka. It was secreted behind a palatal flap at the back of his throat, and it lactated each time they discussed the question.

'But what the General Election proves, in laboratory fashion,' said Peter, 'is what we have always said. The British are the most advanced people on earth, and therefore the most sensible. I suspect it comes from getting our bourgeois revolution out of the way so early. A king's head was not a bad price to pay, in the long run. Once the fires petered out, the path was cleared for hundreds of years of slow, gradual progress and peaceful cooperation.

'Naturally, one cannot discount the influence of foreign ideas that excite the blood; particularly in this era of instant communication. But if the last period has shown anything, it is the superior good sense of the English.'

'You mean the British?' said Tristram.

'Yes... and who would have thought it? After five years of quite brutal cuts to their treasured "welfare state", they hardly made so much as a peep.

'The occasional protest was bound to flare up, naturally, but we keep such developments so far away from the party that they dissipate into thin air, thank the Lord. If only one could keep them out of the unions...

'And so the little people voted back the same pro-austerity government. Only the German can boast the same success. How can one argue with that?' The boys nodded in furious agreement.

'I have to say, even I underestimated the little people,' said Peter, with a broad, rascally smile.

'At least, that is what I have concluded. I never had much faith in Ed, as you know.' The boys raised their eyebrows in concurrence.

'But of course, he will always have our eternal gratitude for raining down that mighty blow upon the unions - surprised us all.'

Peter took a sip from his bone china cup. The tea had gone cold. It happened every time they met. *If only they had a little more to say.*

He had let the discussion veer, and they agreed to move on to business. On the agenda were just two items: the leadership contest, and reports from Holdings. They spent the lion's share of their remaining time on the contest, talking late into the afternoon. Their strategy and tactics flowed seamlessly from their political conclusions. They were all agreed: It was time to reclaim the Labour Party.

2

The next evening Chuka and Tristram dined together in Soho. Inspired by their new joint venture, Tristram was full of questions. They were much the same as Chuka had asked many years ago when he had joined, and as he spooned his Sugar Puffs he did his best to answer the questions as they were fielded. Tristram ate up every answer, so much so that he was hardly able to finish his big bowl of Frosties with chocolate milk.

Their organisation was called the 'Inner Steel', explained Chuka, the chivalric title a consequence of their earnest student origins. More often, however, they referred to themselves informally as 'The Tendency', and fellow members as 'Intimates'.

It would be enough to be told that someone was 'Intimate with the Tendency' to understand they were a member, although he explained that one had to earn many years of trust before you were deemed ready to be introduced to the wider organisation. They were a disciplined force, clandestine, and were nothing without the ideas around which they organised.

'After all,' he said, 'before we can fight together, we have to understand what it is that we are fighting for.' That sounded reasonable enough, thought Tristram.

'So what exactly are the... core beliefs?'

'We work under the direction of the Clientele and at their

discretion. The core beliefs can be summarised in three words: "Modernism", "Moderation" and the "National Interest".'

'I've noticed PM often refers to "The National Interest".'

'It might sound like a euphemism,' said Chuka. 'I assure you, it is not. We're vigilant against that kind of thing slipping into our internal communications. Of course, every craft has its own specialist language, but if you unpack it you'll find the term is quite logically… flawless.'

Chuka explained how the Tendency strove for total internal clarity. Managerial circumambage was a tactical necessity, of course. Evasion, misdirection, ambiguity; these were all tools of their trade. But to wield them internally would be fatal.

'When we talk about "The National Interest", we are describing the preservation of the status quo; the Clientele's established order of things,' he explained. 'Of course, we all accept that the free market is the only possible system.'

'You mean capitalism?'

'Exactly. If you don't get that clear in your head, and keep it at the forefront of your thoughts at all times, you're lost.

'Simple enough,' said Tristram.

'For us, perhaps, but you'd be shocked at how many people in the Labour Party have a hard time hearing it. I mean, it's not like there is an alternative. But that's the essential difference between ourselves and the rest of the party - they haven't thought it through.

'The Labour Party ranks live in a sort of collective denial. They reject logical thinking outright, for fear of where such clarity would lead them. It's a defence mechanism. There are few non-Intimates in the party who come close to the understanding and foresight we possess.'

'Non-Intimates?' said Tristram, grinding his flakes between his molars.

'Everyone outside The Tendency.'

'I see. And I suppose once you are clear that there is no alternative to capitalism, certain things flow from that?'

'Exactly- you're a logical thinker. But we're not so naïve as to worship capitalism. We understand it has some serious defects; o-eight showed us that quite clearly.' Tristram slurped his lime soda, captivated.

'We don't believe in an "Invisible Hand" that will just correct the market if left to its own devices. The same way you wouldn't expect your garden to tend itself– it would soon grow wild.'

'You'd need to hire a gardener,' said Tristram. His mind drifted to his local constituency.

'Precisely. We're very much like gardeners. We check for rain, we test the soil, we prune the vines; we plant, we channel, we unearth.'

'And I suppose you sow, too?'

'We do indeed, brother,' he said, leaning across his bowl of Sugar Puffs and raising his cream soda in a toast. 'And in a few months' time we'll reap the harvest.'

'Long may he reign,' said Tristram.

'Long may we reign, my friend.'

Chuka continued his explanation. The problem with the free-market dogmatists was that they believed the state should not interfere. If they had had their way they would have allowed the entire capitalist system to collapse. If the banks had not been bailed out by the state, their so-called invisible hand would have been bleeding cash machines dry across the planet. It would have led to anarchy, war, revolution - *instability*.

Such people were all well and good for propaganda purposes. One could provide them with a professorship and a healthy disbursement. But they should be kept safely confined to whatever backwater department one finds them in. It was dangerous when propaganda rose above its station - tactics should not dictate strategy.

The bottom line was that there was no such thing as perpetual motion. The system needed maintenance. It needed managers. In the past, you might have relied on tradition and mother Church to lend an inert hand - but they were no longer reliable.

That said, Inner Steel had no time for sentimental traditionalism. If anything it nurtured a low-key contempt for the decrepit bishops and lords and ladies that had managed to cling on to their hereditary titles. Nothing like PM of course, who had earned his peerage.

'My father too,' said Tristram, proudly.

For the most, the old nobility were time consuming profligates. However, just because something was old, it did not necessarily make it less modern. The British state was extremely modern, Chuka explained, because it was the model of managerial obliqueness.

'The British system is not a set of rigid and inflexible rules,' explained Chuka, 'but of precedents and ancient traditions. Some can be brought to the surface at one moment, and pushed into the background at the next. We can rearrange them as we see fit; bury them one minute, revive them the next. It's a beautiful labyrinth, an intricate pantomime, and it can absorb any shocks because of its rubbery demarcations.

'For instance: Who is the Queen? What can she really do? Does she have a say in running the country? Or is she just window-dressing? Most little people wouldn't be able to answer such questions with any degree of accuracy. They'd soon end up contradicting each other and cancelling each other out.

'That's what makes the British state so thoroughly modern. In disturbed times, it's an important moderating force in the hands of the Clientele. And for that, Britain commands a great deal of respect among the nations.

'Did you know that the British state is the basic model for all call-center queuing systems?' Tristram did not.

'That's why we're the envy of the world. PM says even our American Clientele would like nothing more than to adopt the British model and re-write their naked and self-contained constitution, all there to see in black and white. But of course, when they wrote the thing they never imagined that one day the little people would be able to read.'

'Yes – very short-sighted,' said Tristram. He found this all wonderfully refreshing. It was not as if he had not suspected such things. A little understanding he had gleamed from his discussions with Peter and Chuka. But it was so liberating to hear such correct ideas articulated, not only perfectly sensibly, but by people who were serious, and who put their money where their mouth was, and were well organised. That lent their words weight.

'The crisis in o-eight shows why defending the national interest is synonymous with the preservation of the capitalist system,' said Chuka. 'Only the state was able to come to the Clientele's rescue.'

'The half-trillion pounds of taxpayers' money?'

'Yes. You see the Clientele *are the national interest*. And the nation-state is our tool for preserving them.'

'But why say "The National Interest"?' asked Tristram. 'Capitalism is a worldwide phenomenon. You can't say the two things are completely identical.'

'But there isn't a world state, is there?' said Chuka. 'There are international relations, of course; international treaties, blocs, and the like. And our Tendency naturally operates internationally. But everywhere we work, we do so through the ready-made machinery. That means the nation-state.

'Theoretically, I suppose one might imagine a single international capitalist super-state. But the Clientele prefer to have a number of local departments to work through. Why put all your eggs in one basket?'

'So how does the Tendency view the EU?'

'We'll work anywhere. We're not purists. NATO, NAFTA, the IMF. Hell, we'd work in Islamic State if there was an angle to it. But these things come and go. What remains is the national interest. That is what the system is based upon. Yes, capitalism is global, but it rests on individual nation-states which the bourgeoisie have built up over centuries, and which the Clientele are in no hurry to dispose of.'

'How many people are involved? It all sounds so wonderful, but I've only met you and PM.'

'You've met more than you think. But look, we're careful. There's no membership list. We're small in the name of discretion. But truthfully, I don't know how many members there are. It exists, and it must exist, that's as far as I know.

'I'm held in intimacy by PM, and I had Holdings in you - before we became intimate. And there are others, higher up, that PM has intimate relations with.'

Higher than PM? Goodness, they must be ten feet tall.

'Besides, we don't need a big set-up. The Clientele sees to it that we are well financed. And with a decent flow of Holdings, our Intimates can have an impact far beyond their number. I have a portfolio of Holdings and Secondary Holdings, but it's not my place to talk to you about them. The little people that keep you informed in your constituency; you should consider them Holdings. It bodes well to maintain a limited portfolio outside of Westminster.'

'By Holdings, you mean apprentices, am I right in saying?'

'Not exactly. PM is responsible for both of us, and reports to

Intimates higher up, even Clientele.

'Eventually I might take you out of PM's hands. Then we can be intimate with one another on our own projects, and have intimate discussions by ourselves.

'Holdings and Secondaries are more like influence. They are either someone you meet with on a regular basis and bring round to our way of thinking - before a crucial vote at the NEC, say - or someone you know we have influence over, but choose to deal with them indirectly, through a Holding. It can often be better that way. For a long time, you were a Secondary Holding of PM's. Then for the last year he has held you directly, and now we're all intimate together.'

Tristram felt slightly objectified to be discussed in such a way. Bur he did not dislike it.

'Have you ever thought what it might be like to join the Conservative party?'

The sinful question that had niggled at Tristram over the years suddenly let fly. It felt good to get it off his chest.

Chuka did not flinch. It was a question that often came up during an Intimate's induction, and showed he was developing well. But it was not an option. The Conservatives were a very important element in the equation, and Inner Steel was very active inside of it, but members of the Tendency inside the Labour Party had a crucial role to play.

'We are valuable members of Inner Steel, much more than your equivalent Tory. The Tendency tries to put people where they work best: in parliament, in the unions, in the local parties - anywhere they are needed.'

The crucial role played by Labour Intimates, Chuka continued, was their stewardship of a deep and dangerous fault line which the trade unions created over a hundred years ago when they created the Labour Party. The original idea was harmless enough - that the little people should have their own voice in parliament. But of course that did not necessarily mean they knew how everything worked.

While there was an open question as to its long-term usefulness, the Labour Party remained an extremely important lever that the Clientele wished to keep their hands on. Sometimes an industrial lubricant was needed to keep the party from careering out of control:

peerages, honours, roles in the state; not exactly suitcases of cash one should understand. That was too crude, and liable to leave fingerprints. Nevertheless, the positions and the combinations to those suitcases were 'made available' if and when necessary.

'You know that most union leaders never take a worker's wage? Well, that was us. At one point there was a counter-current against it: "Workers' representatives on workers' wages" - even for Labour MPs!'

'Gosh! That would cost me half my salary,' said Tristram. 'Not very worker-friendly.'

'Indeed. Thankfully, these days union jobs - MP's jobs, even local councillor positions - are well-lubricated. And everything runs smoother as a result. What was really magnificent about that particular accomplishment was how we tapped into the historic Labour demand for waged MPs.'

'How do you mean?'

'Parliament used to be a gentleman's sport, attended by those rich enough not to have to earn a living. The Tendency took Labour's historic demand and turned it to the Clientele's advantage, you see? Today they all defend the wages system.

'It speaks no words, it leaves no trace, but it has a lot to say all the same. That's when we work best.'

'Of course, there are still troublemakers, like the Firefighters. They pay their General Secretary a high wage, but he donates a large slice of it to political causes and in reality only takes what the average firefighter does. It's a problem, but relatively isolated. At least they're no longer affiliated.

'But you get the picture. It's important that all levels of the Labour movement are "priced in", so to speak. Without a price things can become unknowable, and even unmanageable.' Tristram understood.

'Once we've broken them in, ninety-nine per cent of the labour movement leaders become the most accommodating chaps to work with. Often, they were so rigid before that, once they snap, they lose all resistance... Did you know that trade union organisation is one of the most upwardly mobile professions? Our Intimates at the top accomplish a great deal because they often come from actual working-class backgrounds, you see. They rarely start out as place-seekers or bargain-hunters, and some can be too wild to be put to good use, but you'd be surprised how many former proletarians we're intimate with. It's like the armed forces - important to bring a few up from the ranks. They talk the proles' language, and that's all round better for morale.'

'Which is three to one,' said Tristram.

'Very good,' said Chuka, chewing his puffs, 'you're learning. What makes our work such an art is the balance we must keep between two opposing forces. The little people are always wanting more: more money, more wages, more health care, pensions; things like that appear to interest them.

'Our Clientele, on the other hand, always wants to claw those wages back so they can be better invested. The workforce is quite an expense, you know?' Tristram had heard as much.

'The difficulty I suppose,' said Tristram 'is that we can't categorically make them go away. I mean, we can't have a country without… workers. Although, I suppose we could have a country without the Clientele?'

It was something that Tristram would never be able to say in public, but it gave him a sense of freedom to speak it plainly, knowing he would not be mistaken for some rotten socialist.

'None of us wants that, of course.'

'Exactly,' said Chuka. 'Can you imagine a world without the Clientele? But that's why it's important that Labour is priced in. If you don't, it might spin out of control.' Tristram could see the logic in that.

'Which is why it's paramount we don't foster illusions.'

'I thought that was the name of the game?'

'I mean internally, inside the Tendency - between Intimates.'

'Oh yes, of course.'

'Inner Steel is a realistic force for moderation. The only logical alternative is Russia and gulags and war.

'Unfortunately, the world is made up of different people, all occupying different positions and with different outlooks. You can't persuade all of them, all of the time. So we accept that there is no perfect system, only one of temporary stability within a greater chaos. The weeds never stop growing.'

They moved on to some of the finer points of membership.

'Directives come from the top down - no democratic nonsense. Clarity doesn't mix well with democracy. Our directives are determined by logic, not votes. Every so often forecasts are reviewed, refined, re-approximated; sometimes spawning entirely new directives and projects, all flowing from our overall global forecast.'

'I know I shouldn't ask, but... is Blair an Intimate?'

The question caught Chuka with his spoon between bowl and mouth. 'No. And no, you shouldn't ask. Don't do it again.'

'Really!' he exclaimed, so loudly that he disturbed his fellow diners. Munching ceased in the Soho restaurant.

'I'm sorry, I know I shouldn't have. I was just... so certain.'

'Shocked me too, first time I heard it. Technically he's only ever been a Holding of ours. PM says he was too unalloyed to be brought into the Inner Steel. Talks about him like he's the Messiah; says he didn't need to be held - that he was too pure.

'Every directive the Clientele passed down Blair already anticipated. I don't know how much of an exaggeration that is. Don't know the guy. Anyway, that's why he was never organised - there was no call for it. He was only ever intimate with himself, says Peter. The way he tells it, half the time Blair was directing us.' Tristram was disappointed and impressed.

'Payments are made offshore every quarter. But you won't need for money anymore. The Tendency takes care of you now.'

'Right, OK.'

'And Tristram, you must understand, we never lose anyone. Once you become intimate with the Tendency... I'd like to say that it's based purely on loyalty, but you know we require a deposit.'

'Yes, I... understand.'

'PM says it used to involve a Polaroid and an Alsatian in the old days - that's students for you. Before the internet. Now it's more straightforward. Of course, in your case, the Tendency is more than satisfied with their security.' Tristram went bright pink.

'Don't worry about it. We're all human.'

'Yes, quite,' said Tristram. His Frosties had gone soggy.

3

A few days later Lord Peter summoned the boys, insisting they meet in the parliamentary tea rooms on urgent business, the details of which he would not disclose over the phone. Neither suspected anything out of the ordinary; last-minute mid-morning conferences happened all the time.

They sat by themselves in the middle of the democratic din. Only a few weeks had passed since the General Election, and Westminster Palace had not yet settled into its usual rhythm. Amid the mash of noise, occasional gasps escaped, all relating to the coming Labour leadership contest:

'It's going to last three months.'
'You can vote for just three quid.'
'Who is Mary?'

As planned, Chuka had lost no time in announcing his candidacy. At that moment he felt all eyes were on him, and he bathed in it.

Crowding the entrance of the tea rooms was a tiding of new MPs on their induction tour. Tristram noticed there was a substantial Scottish contingent among them.

'Bit out in the open this meeting,' he said, cutting into his cake.

'There's Liz's camp,' said Chuka, nodding discretely at a thicket of MPs stood around one table. 'They're talking about us.'

'They're scared,' said Tristram. 'I've spoken to one or two members who are considering transferring their support now that your hat's in the ring. Although I have to say, I'm surprised how many have already plumped for her. But a worthy opponent - better than the other weaklings.'

He chewed guardedly, glancing sideways at the thicket.

'They're saying Andy is the favourite and apparently the trade unions are backing him. Can't believe how quickly they've organised. We should be able to get out the support in Stoke.'

Chuka was inspecting his brogues and not really listening. He was familiar with the general structure of the conversation.

'Well I'm not surprised; you've always been a staunch local MP.' He folded one leg over his knee and thumbed the polished leather of his shoe.

'That's right,' said Tristram, washing down his cake with a gulp of tea. 'One of the little fellows said the same when I was up there last. You know I put in two straight weeks in Stoke in the run-up to the election. I don't think I've ever worked as hard in my life!'

'Is that so?'

'Bit of an ugly bunch, I must say. Very pasty - could do with some sun. Funny sort of place, faces seem to change every time I visit.'

'The unions can't do too much for Andy,' said Chuka 'they're a spent force. They've been threatening to take their ball away for years. Maybe this time they'll honour us.' Tristram did admire Chuka's devilish streak.

The morning sun passed behind a cloud, and the room dimmed slightly. At that moment the mash of noise faltered. Lord Peter had entered.

As he neared, he did not slow or meet their eyes, but walked straight past them without so much as a smile and continued toward an isolated corner of the tea rooms, near to the gap in the service counter through which the waitresses passed. Two large Tory gentlemen sat there enjoying bacon and eggs, minding their own business.

Tristram and Chuka watched silently, and so did the rest of the tea room. The tubby Tories, seeing Peter approach, rose from their seats, and one almost unbalanced in his chair.

Soon they both developed watery smiles and began nodding pensively. Then they gathered their eggs, their mugs, papers and briefcases in clumsy bundles and vacated the table with good will.

Peter took his seat, extracted a handkerchief and lightly dusted the table. The boys approached, and he did not stir, but merely sat cross-legged, staring into nothing and indifferent to the world around him. Presently the Lord looked up at them with the inner peace of a grandfather wakened from a dream.

'Hello, my boys. Please, be seated.'

Soon the tea room returned to the usual bludgeon, although one or two eyes continued to twitch toward the wholesome little threesome nested in the corner.

A waitress immediately brought Peter a pot of tea. The briefest of small talk was had, and then Peter asked them:

'And how do you feel about the present predicament?' Tristram suspected his meaning.

'I was only just saying to Chuka, a lot of chaps have already promised themselves to Liz's camp. I mean, early days yet, but they really have moved ever so quickly. All in rather bad taste, I thought.'

'It is not the contest, my dear boy… and yet again, it is. Have you not read the papers?'

Tristram understood that Peter enjoyed testing them, but this was far too cryptic. The boys looked at each other, neither knowing Peter's meaning. The Lord leant back in his chair for a moment and pressed the tips of his fingers together.

'There's no easy way to say this, my boys, so I'm afraid I'm going to have to just come straight out and say it: We are pulling out of the race.'

'What!' blurted Tristram, indignant for his friend. Chuka looked down at his shoes.

'What's developed, PM?' asked Chuka.

'I do wish you boys would keep up with your reading. What has happened is this,' he said, producing a bundle of photocopied sheets from inside his jacket and landing them on the table. They were of a national newspaper and underlined heavily in biro.

'New directives?' asked Chuka.

Tristram looked about him.

'Isn't this a bit out in the open, PM?'

'It is in the newspapers, my boy - hardly top secret. Not that anyone here is giving it the attention it deserves, what with this blasted leadership contest. But the Clientele certainly is.'

'What does it say, PM?' asked Tristram.

'Oh, it says many things, my boy, many things I'm sure a clever lad like you might have guessed.' He sipped his tea.

'It contains the most advanced analysis of the General Election to date, and tells us that our previous conclusions were, well, quite unfounded. For us, the most important headline is the Labour vote. According to the data, it was the most middle-class in the party's history.'

'Surely that can't be right,' said Tristram. 'If we had captured the middle ground, how could we have possibly lost the election?'

'Because,' whispered Peter grudgingly, leaning forward in his chair, 'the proletarian core did something we failed to price in… They deserted the party in their droves!' He banged the flat of his hand on the table, causing his tea to upset. Eyes blinked from the corners of the room. Tristram was confused. It did not seem to him something to be all that upset about.

'But doesn't that show that we're winning? Isn't it proof that union influence is on the wane?'

'My dear boy,' said Peter. 'There is no point advancing on a position if you leave your rear exposed. The proles are our base - money in the bank. '

'So where have they gone, PM?' asked Chuka with dead eyes, reconciled already to the new situation.

'Scotland, of course, but we were aware of that. But also to UKIP. And the Greens took the youth, also an important base.' Tristram could feel Peter's weariness radiating.

'The Clientele are up in arms about this and are calling in a revision of the entire forecast. It will be the third revision in a year,' he sighed, longing for more innocent times.

'We knew that UKIP was undermining the Tory base with this immigration nonsense. But to give Ed his due, he seemed to have positioned himself well enough to check that on our flank. The mug even said we needed to be tough on immigrants. I really did not see this coming.'

He finished his sentence in his tea, taking a prolonged gulp. The boys waited in silence, concern dawning upon their faces.

'It is true we were initially surprised that we had not provoked a rebellion,' said Peter, his cup drained. 'Some local difficulties at the beginning of the Prime Minister's term, yes, but nothing monumental. These figures, however, provide us with a comprehensive snapshot. The Clientele says it shows the situation is D.U.D.'

'D.U.D?' asked Tristram.

'Deep Underlying Discontent,' said Chuka. 'They've mentioned it before, in regard to China and Southern Europe. But it couldn't happen here, surely? Our union Intimates would have picked up on it, wouldn't they, PM?'

'I don't know, my boy, that is what worries me. The unions no longer seem the sensitive instruments they once were. Zero-hour contracts have been good for the national interest, of course, but the unions do not seem to know what to do with them.'

'Useless,' said Chuka. 'You should have a word with them, PM. Tell them to get organised.'

'Perhaps,' said Peter. 'But in the meantime what the Clientele is demanding is a radical repositioning of Labour. They have already had to let go of the Lib Dems - and I can tell you what a sorry fuss was made over that! We picked up a lot of liberal support, but little else, and of course the middle class is not what it once was. The core losses to the SNP and UKIP the Clientele consider intolerable.

'Apathy is fine, but this kind of political re-distribution threatens stability,' continued Peter. 'They want normal working relations to resume as soon as possible. The Prime Minister needs to govern in peace.'

'Apathy means contentment - one only has to look at my constituency to see that,' said Tristram. 'Only, I thought the Clientele would be pleased with the outcome. After all, the Prime Minister doesn't have to work with that awful Clegg anymore.'

'The Prime Minister had to promise a referendum on Europe to stop half his party defecting to UKIP,' said Peter. 'Having the Lib Dems as a shield actually worked out surprisingly well for him.'

'Yes, but now the election is over with, surely he can renege on one little referendum?'

'And risk splitting the Conservative Party? The Clientele would be appalled. Do you know that half the Tory backbenchers voted UKIP at the election? The Prime Minister is having a hard enough time trying to bury that English Parliament nonsense he cooked up - he only has a majority of twelve. If he reneges on Europe he will lose his majority. That will provoke instability. No, no; the Tories must be held together. We made it through Scotland... I am afraid we will just have to weather another plebeian supervision.' Peter tapped his fingers on his lips. Chuka had never seen him so agitated.

'So I am afraid what this blasted contest now needs is not another moderniser, but a bone to throw to the proles. It has become the Clientele's number one priority - stop Labour's bleed. That means pulling the whole thing to the left. Can you believe it? Unfortunately, my boys, that is the price of stability.'

'And what about Liz - is she going to be stepping down as well?' asked Chuka.

'Too suspicious. Besides, we need someone to carry the standard, my boy, but that is not going to be you. If you ran, you might win, and the Clientele considers that too much for the Prime Minister.

'But look, she is not going to win. She is there to keep our lot on the map. We have big ideas for you, but they will have to wait. Your time will come.'

'Anything to serve the national interest,' said Chuka.

'That is the spirit, my boy. Take it as a compliment.'

'As for now, we need to start working on a whole raft of new directives that have just come down. They are even talking about creating a genuine labour youth group, good heavens above!

'I need you boys to start scouting for a candidate of the Left; someone with a bit more about them than the last one. Work through your Holdings and report back to me. And be thorough - I fear there is not much to choose from.'

***

In the month of May forty-thousand men, women and children, fleeing war, entered Europe.

CHAPTER 4
THE DISCUSSION

1

Tristram and Chuka worked together intimately throughout the rest of May, reporting back to Peter regularly. He had been right - there was very little to work with, and it occurred to both men that Inner Steel had quite neglected to invest in the left of the party.

Peter did his best to supplement their efforts with the benefit of his experience. However, amid every ruinous dwelling of the left-wing that they uncovered, they found little in the way of Intimates or Holdings - not even Secondary Holdings through which they might operate. And Tristram, being new to the Tendency, was limited by his underdeveloped portfolio.

Toward the end of May a break-through was finally made. The Queen had invited all her loyal MPs to join her (once her Lords and Ladies had taken all the good seats) for the state opening of Parliament.

Keeping warm on her paltry state pension was no easy task for Mrs Windsor, particularly after her application to the Community Energy Fund had been rejected, so she wore a short-tailed weasel around her shoulders to fight off the cold as her subjects gathered at her feet. Beneath her stoat she wore a wedding dress to lift her spirits - the opening of parliament was always such a dreary affair. As this left her with no pockets, her speech was brought to her by the Lord Chancellor, bowing and scraping on his knees, as any grown man might.

Mrs Windsor had never lost an election in her life and was therefore well positioned to advise parliament that the law enshrining a trade union's right to strike was not half as democratic as it might be. She announced that her new government, elected by fewer than a quarter of her subjects, would make the withdrawal of one's labour illegal unless forty percent of a workforce voted for it - whether they were in a union or not.

Chuka was late. He wormed his way through the MPs crammed in dignity at the back of their Lords' house. He had been working around the clock on their directive.

Their nearest point of contact had proved to be at least three times removed from them, and Holdings and Secondaries still yielded no direct connection with the left, particularly the little Socialist Campaign Group which they had established as their primary target. Tristram had even discovered when and where the group met, but neither could go near the meetings, nor approach the members of the group directly, for fear of raising suspicion.

The brothers' ability to wield influence had also come up against other limitations. Holdings often could not fathom what the brothers were proposing, and, once the penny did drop, half of them dismissed it as preposterous.

Under such circumstances, circulating the message among Secondaries proved near impossible. And even if a Holding was on board, by the time the message reached the socialists it could be transformed into something quite different. This had even caused some damage. A message urging one witless member not to endorse Andy had been transformed into a nomination for him, much to their despair.

'What have I missed?' whispered Chuka in his brother's ear.

'Queenie's just announced all the benefit freezes: income, child… pretty standard fare. Dave looks pleased.' Both were tall enough to stretch on tiptoes and see the Prime Minister and Harriet, Labour's interim leader, standing side-by-side.

From the edge of her enormous golden throne the Queen declared her endorsement of the plan to stop scroungers below the age of twenty-one from claiming housing benefits.

'Jolly good ma'am - levelling the playing field,' said Tristram. 'We're all meant to be in this together, but these youngsters sell their labour so cheaply that my older constituents find it awfully difficult to compete - about time the youth gave something back.'

The Queen's eldest, tired after his trip to meet with the leader of Sinn Fein, yawned as he slouched in his seat between mother and wife.

'I think I've found a solution to our problem,' whispered Chuka.

The Queen's crown slipped. Her osteopath had told her that morning not to wear the one with 2,901 encrusted diamonds. But she soldiered on, describing how her government would continue to assist the poor by taking no more than three thousand pounds a year from their benefits.

'Best idea I've heard all year,' whispered Chuka. 'That'll get those shirkers off the couch and back to work. Did you know the majority of those households are single-parent, or have a child under five?'

'No, I didn't.'

'Some people can be so irresponsible.'

2

After the ceremony was over and the brothers had trawled the froth of exiting members for Holdings, they ventured outside of the Palace of Westminster, meeting at a bar on Windmill Street in Piccadilly. Tristram had heard they did a superb line in retro Panda Pops.

Chuka laid out a piece of paper on the bar and began explaining his solution:

'Imagine this line represents the Labour Party,' he said, drawing an arc from one end of the page to the other. He doodled two stick-men in the right-hand corner. 'We're here.'

'Don't forget PM,' said Tristram, drawing a third man beside them. *The three amigos, together always.*

'Our target audience, however, is located in this tiny bubble here,' said Chuka. He drew a circle at the opposite end of the arc.

'Right.'

'To get from one end to the other, we have to move along the line, passing all these different points,' he said, placing notches along the arc at intervals.

'This isn't one of those Greek riddles, is it?' said Tristram.

'No. The problem we have is every time we send out a message it gets neutralised by the time it reaches the first or second point along the trajectory. Or sent off on a tangent. Or it returns to us without having reached its target.'

'I suppose the question is: Does the message travel at all?'

'The question, my friend, is how do we get our message to travel from one end of the Labour spectrum to the other without it hitting one of these obstacles and careering off into deep space?'

'Gosh,' said Tristram. 'You'd have to somehow overcome the left-right continuum through some kind of… wormhole.'

'Exactly,' said Chuka. 'And I think I've found one.' He folded his paper in half, bringing the two ends of the arc together.

3

June arrived, and Corbyn's shoes slapped the ancient flagstone. He strolled without a care, veering in rebellious zigzags through Westminster's winding passages. The late spring sun poured through the palace windows, and the ancient dust danced in its waterfall. He was in a fine mood. That weekend Arsenal had beaten Villa to win the FA Cup.

As he hopped up the stairs of glory he dropped his shoulder in a pivot, emulating his favourite player. At the same time he reserved pity for the poor Villa fans; not for the hammering they had received, but for the Prime Minister who had contrived to elect himself among their number.

He had given no serious mind to the meeting he was about to join. It was a mere formality. The scrappy little socialist campaign group had met twice already since the General Election, both times ending indecisively. The third he expected to be no more fruitful. It seemed that the task of agreeing a candidate for the leadership contest might well prove beyond them.

The group had been left in a sorry state by Labour's defeat. The Scottish members were no more, although an injection of young MPs from among the new intake had partially replaced them. Yet they had been taken by surprise by the sudden announcement of the contest.

Before they knew it the nominations process was sown up and the party doors closed to them. It was a sad and familiar experience for the veterans of the group.

The mood among the members was easy enough to divine. Almost all participated as if they were doing community service in lieu of a custodial sentence, merely going through the motions, with no belief in the task they had set themselves.

That was no less the case for Corbyn. He considered his duty done after volunteering early in their first meeting. It had been an offer glazed in irony, and the confusion of those first weeks of May quickly swept the discussion along before his comrades could give it due consideration. Some deliberately 'forgot'. Even among the socialists, Corbyn was considered something of an indecent proposal.

He was late entering the tiny committee room. Even though the previous meetings had both been near full, no one had thought to arrange a larger room.

As usual, Diane placed herself square in the centre of the little horseshoe table. Dennis assumed his favoured position next to the exit, beside the ex-miner MPs Ronnie and Ian. Next along from them was his old friend, John, who smiled as Corbyn entered, before turning his attention back to Diane:

'I just can't believe how quickly those rats have turned on Ed,' said Diane. 'All four of them sat in his cabinet, and now they're taking turns to stab him in the back. He must be feeling awful. Like it or not, the party produced its best ideas for years under Ed.' She shook her head beneath her fringe and closed her eyes in disapproval. Corbyn wondered what Jeremy would have thought of that.

On the other side of the horseshoe sat a small contingent of new MPs: Cat, Clive and Richard. They were a refreshing sight thought Corbyn, and contrasted agreeably with the veterans near the exit. He supposed that he too was now a veteran in the eyes of the new generation.

Despite their losses, he could not think of a time when the group had benefitted so much from the new intake. One General Election after another Labour seemed to assemble ever longer lines of the lawyers, or law graduates, who now packed the house with their immaculately-waxed white bites. Few, if any found, their way to the meetings of the little socialist campaign group.

At the beginning of the new parliament one or two might turn up, fidgeting apologetically in their seats as if they should not be there. Whether they had come to the wrong room or, as Jeremy suspected, were put off by the interminable reports and arguments over minutes that swallowed half the meetings, the result was they were rarely seen again. Not even by chance in the tea rooms.

But these new chaps appeared not to mind. They too were quiet, but seemed to rest on one another, and had been at each of the group's meetings so far. They were polite, contributed not a word to the procedural wranglings, and always voted to move the meeting on to the politics.

In the meantime, their phones kept them busy. Corbyn did not understand much about that, and some among them (those who only used their mobiles as an excuse to take a break from a meeting) thought their constant scrolling rude.

But for Corbyn life had at last found its way into the group, coming to resemble something to which he was more accustomed. Not the masses that Jeremy placed all his hope in; yet it was a meeting of ancient mariners which now had a following of youth to whom they could pass on their wisdom. It meant that, in some dim and distant future, their ideas would once again take to the high seas.

Corbyn was side-stepping his way toward the far end of the horseshoe when he spied the only remaining free seat being taken by none other than Jeremy, greeting the youngsters as he did so. He sat down and took out his notebook.

What is he doing here?

'Would you expect anything less,' spoke the soft and ever reasonable John. He held on to the ankle of his crossed leg, shaking his white head into his chest in disapproval. 'Of course those creatures have abandoned him, Diane. He put Blairites in his cabinet in the belief that he could hold the party together. And he spent the next five years exposed to their poison.'

'Oh, they're all Blairites, to one degree or another,' said Diane.

'What on earth are you doing here?' Corbyn whispered to Jeremy, barely suppressing his anger. He had not seen him since before the General Election.

'Oh, hello old boy. You here too?' He handed Corbyn a smile, before turning his attention back to John and Diane's exchange.

Corbyn fumed, feeling the members' eyes on him.

Corbyn detested personal matters interfering in politics, and he considered Jeremy a very personal matter. He looked to John for help. *Sorry about this.*

John returned a sympathetic nod, as if to reassure him.

'You know, there are spare seats at the back, old chap. But I suppose you want to sit here, don't you?' Jeremy yielded his seat to Corbyn and removed to the back of the room, taking a folded chair from the stack. He nearly scalped the young crop of MPs as he carried it over their heads, setting it down behind Corbyn.

'Happy now?' Jeremy teased in his ear light-heartedly. 'I simply didn't think I could miss another campaign group meeting; things have become so lively, haven't they?' Corbyn ignored him and took out his notebook.

'I think worst of all is what Andy has come out with,' said Diane, peering over her spectacles. 'And he's supposed to have the unions backing!'

Corbyn raised his hand, and she brought him in. 'Hello everyone, so sorry I'm late. Haven't the unions shown any interest in one of us standing?'

'None whatsoever,' said John.

'I mean, did you hear what he said?' continued Diane. 'He called Ed's policies the "politics of envy". Of envy! It's that type of... narrative, that is such a betrayal of our movement. It's recycling the old idea that socialists are just grumpy, middle-class types who want to make everyone equally poor.'

'And you could hardly call his policies socialist!' called out Jeremy from the back of the room. Corbyn turned and threw his friend an icy stare, but Jeremy just smiled warmly back, not noticing his irritation.

'Well, quite,' said Diane. 'As if relying on the welfare state was motivated by some kind of character flaw and not because people are suffering and fear for their children. You know where he said that?'

'Speech to city,' said Dennis, slouching in his chair, hands in his pockets.

'At the headquarters of Ernst and Young... a stockbroker!' said Diane. 'I mean, do you want to be any more symbolic? It's very clear who he was making his pitch to.'

The room went momentarily silent. The young MPs stared at the floor.

'Well, I wouldn't resent any working-class parent bitten with a little envy,' said Jeremy. 'Or perhaps just a plain sense of injustice when they see the Prime Minister and Chancellor feasting at the Lord Mayor's banquet in penguin suits, sat on thrones of gold, lecturing people about tightening their belts.' Corbyn's ears began to warm as if Jeremy was breathing directly onto the back of them.

'I'd say envy of that kind is pretty justified,' continued Jeremy, 'when they see the Queen reading a speech telling them they are having three grand taken out of their pockets.' The back of Corbyn's neck went damp. *Why does he have to say such things?* A murmur spread along the horseshoe. *No one cares; he's only prolonging the meeting. Doesn't he realise these things can run on all night?*

'Well, I think Jeremy's quite right,' said Diane, doodling her biro and glancing sideways at him below her fringe. 'This is precisely why we need to change the... narrative. If we could just get in the race, we'd have all the way until September to make the anti-austerity voice heard. I would say it is incumbent upon us. If only someone were willing to stand.'

'But is that so necessary?' said Ian. 'Wouldn't we best spend our time supporting Andy, to keep Liz out? Back the lesser evil? Andy may have said a few things off- colour, but the unions are behind him. Remember how close we were in 2010? We could have ended up with the other brother. If we support Andy, wouldn't that be the best way to change the, what Diane says... narrative?'

'Hear, hear!' said Dennis, arms folded defiantly. 'Even if we got nominations - and we won't – no one's listening... Look at Scotland, leadership went to that right-winger. Scottish membership's collapsed - what's Left going to do without Scots? Look how rest of country voted. Not exactly inspiring, is it?'

'Well, sounds like Dennis has thrown in the towel,' said Diane. She was not a chair with a light touch, often thrusting her thoughts without hesitation into any passing exchange. 'I think we should remember that the Tories only managed twenty-four percent of the electorate, and we go twenty-three. It was a lot closer than people think.'

'You just can't say that people voted for the Tories,' said John, anguished by Dennis' sentiments. 'I was as bowled over as you,

Dennis, when I saw the votes coming in. But the beastly truth is as Diane says - they didn't get a quarter of the country. You know, I think that if we get on that ticket we should say that it's high time we had a proper system of proportional representation.'

'And compulsory voting,' added Diane.

'With PR, the Tories wouldn't have been able to form a government,' said John. 'We could have been talking about a coalition with the SNP, the Greens and Plaid Cymru. Many of the trade unionists I've spoken to are saying something similar. Greece has a system of PR, and look how well they've done recently – elected an anti-austerity government.

'And did you see how many people are now represented by that one UKIP MP? I don't cry myself to sleep for them, but… four million? It's ridiculously out of proportion. If every MP represented that many people, Westminster would stand for almost half the planet!'

Corbyn was uncomfortable with the way the discussion was going. He had been sat with his hand raised for some time. It was his silent protest, disliking the way some colleagues just butted in. A moment passed in silence until John brought Corbyn to Diane's attention.

'Thanks. Look, it's not the first time we've heard this question of electoral reform.' Dennis and the veterans were already nodding their heads in anticipation.

He hoped John did not find him rude in opposing him. He tried addressing his remarks to the youngsters, rather than appear too confrontational.

'I think we've always got to remember that these PR systems on the continent, clever and clean as they might seem, fundamentally don't allow for local representation. The connection with the MP and the constituency is severed, and then it's the party that sends MPs to Parliament, and the leadership draws up the list. And you know who they would put at the very bottom of such a list! I'm sorry John, but I've heard the argument again and again over the years. I can understand the frustration, but if we manage to mount a candidate, I don't think we should muddy the water with that sort of thing.'

'Is that necessarily true? About the local link?' asked Diane, not wanting to discourage Corbyn. She had always had a soft spot for him.

'Scottish Labour did just that, Diane,' said Corbyn. 'Probably accounts for half the mess they're in today.'

'I think we're missing the main point,' said Jeremy. Droplets of sweat ran down Corbyn's spine. 'No matter how you arrange the deck chairs, it's the policies that matter. Syriza hasn't come to power in Greece because of the voting system. PR isn't an 'anti-austerity' system.

'Of course, smaller parties have more of a chance. But it cuts both ways: coalition government… not a good thing. Blair cynically established a PR parliament in Scotland so the SNP would have to share power. A fat lot of good it did. And were the Tories any better in coalition with the Liberals in the last government? Not a bit. Europe is riddled with coalition governments. If they can manage it, they consider it far better to have the socialists prop up the Tories, like in Germany. Is Germany any more left-wing? I don't think so. The reason Labour lost is not because how the deck chairs were arranged, but because we completely failed to inspire, because we offered nothing fundamentally different from Tory austerity. That's the question we need to address.'

The veterans applauded, and everyone joined in, even Corbyn reluctantly. His friend had fought his corner, but he was not sure he approved of how he had gone about it.

'Well, this is not Scotland, and it's certainly not Greece,' said Ian. 'You can't say the British people are like the Greeks. And the voting system isn't the point, as Jeremy says. If there were genuine feelin' out there, we'd know about it, but we haven't seen anything like that. So let's not kid ourselves. The time's not right.'

'I don't know,' said Cat, 'I have a feeling things are changing more than some people think. What about the protests in Bristol and London? Thousands of people just spontaneously came out after the elections. And wasn't the one in Bristol called by a group of schoolgirls on Facebook?' The rest of the new contingent nodded in confirmation.

'A few thousand kids on't twitter is not masses,' said Dennis. 'Where are workers? Where are unions? Ian's right - I regret to say it - but there's no mood for that kind of thing here. Not in this country.'

'Well, perhaps not from the unions,' said Diane. 'Pathetic bunch. Did you hear McCluskey after the Queen's speech? Pleading with the government to reconsider! I mean come on, give me a break, grow some balls.' Dennis cackled, and the others round the horseshoe smirked.

'What happened to the General Strike? That's what I'd like to know,' said John. 'I've been asking Len about that for years, and he still says it's on the agenda for the next TUC meeting. It was proposed in 2013, for pity's sake.'

'Dennis, you say only a few thousand,' said Richard 'OK, but these are kids organising at a week's notice.... I agree with Diane; I think it indicates something.'

From the back of the room Jeremy could be heard: *Hear, hear!* The hot damp spread across Corbyn's lower back.

'And don't forget,' said Ronnie, 'the tube workers are on strike this week. They've not got their heads down. This new Tory government might be the signal for a fight back from the unions.'

'The tube workers are always on strike,' said Ian. 'If their tea is cold in the morning they go on strike. If there's no loo roll, they down their tools.'

'Yes, and that's why they have decent wages,' said John. 'They're prepared to take action. But going back to what was being said: I remember my secretary telling me that there are plenty of people going to this big anti-austerity march on June 20th.'

'More than a hundred thousand now,' said Richard.

'You see. I don't think we should confuse what the union leaders are doing with the mood on the street,' said John. 'Particularly because so many young people are casual workers who are not in unions.'

'There's a woman in my constituency,' said Jeremy, 'good activist - therapist in the NHS. She told me that almost all of her colleagues are on zero-hour contracts, not employed by the NHS, but by between three or four different agencies. 'When she contacted the union to ask them what she could do about it, the answer she got was that there was nothing that could be done. Can you believe it? If they get clobbered by this next government, it'll be their own rotten fault. Hopefully it'll knock some sense into their heads.' Corbyn worried his sweating had become visible, causing him to sweat further.

'Some of our union sponsors wouldn't like to hear you speaking like that,' said Ian.

'Now, come on, said Diane, 'I think Jeremy has a point. We should be raising this in our meetings with the unions.' Diane was enjoying Jeremy's spark this evening. He often just seemed to hide in the corner, causing her to sometimes wonder whether he was not a little depressed.

'I'll give you another example,' said Jeremy. 'Every year since I can remember I've been going to Brighton to attend the civil servants' conference, PCS. And every year I see the same tired, ashen faces. They're the same ones that have been there since the 1980s.

'And it's the same throughout the unions: tired, well-meaning old warhorses who, to be perfectly honest, are often in Brighton, Bournemouth or Blackpool for an annual jaunt, as much as they are for union business.' The veterans' end of the horseshoe rearranged themselves in their seats. It's part of the routine: fish and chips and yes, pass the mustard please, catch up with old friends and reminisce. There's no youth breathing new life into the unions. And a lot of the leaders rest on that fact - I tell you.'

The backs of Corbyn's knees dripped like a tap. The room was silent again, but this time for far longer. The young MPs scrolled their thumbs vigorously. Dennis remained slouched with his arms crossed, a great grin grown across his face. Diane's eyes roamed the room, searching desperately for a raised hand.

'Anyone wish to add to Jeremy's very... candid thoughts?'

'Jeremy undoubtedly has a point,' said John, transmitting to Jeremy and Corbyn an amused smile across the horseshoe. 'Although I think those kinds of remarks are probably best kept within this room.' Suppressed smirks disfigured the young MP's faces.

'But to get back on track. Richard says that there are more than one hundred thousand signed up for this June 20th protest. That says something, doesn't it? That so many people are attending a demonstration against austerity...? And I think there's one in Glasgow, too.

'We need to be clear on this: coming only a month after the General Election, this event can send a clear message of opposition to the Tory government. We should all be on that march.' Again the veterans re-sat in their seats.

'If we stand a candidate, I'm sure we could get them on that platform. They wouldn't give it to any of the other lot. For that reason alone we should stand a candidate.'

'You're getting ahead of yourself, John,' said Dennis. 'First we have to get on bleedin' ballot. But if you're so convinced of need to make fools of ourselves, why not stand yourself?'

'You know, I don't think it would be completely out of the question for us to get the nomination,' said Diane. 'I was speaking with some black caucus colleagues and - as you know, some of them are real Blairites – but... and this is confidential, you understand...'

'Oh aye, Diane's got a bit of gossip!' interrupted Dennis, sitting up in his chair.

'No, not gossip, Dennis.' She closed her eyes in disapproval at the old curmudgeon. 'But they seem to think we really stand a chance. Quite a few MPs are talking about supporting us, apparently. Like when I ran.'

A little collective gasp escaped across the horseshoe.

'You know, I got the impression that they're pretty aghast at the... narrative, some of the candidates are spinning. You can say what you like about Ed, but a lot of MPs served under him for five years, and I really think the sentiment is... well, a little bit of revulsion at the way some are talking about him. I have to say, I think I was being given, shall we say, an unspoken nudge?'

'Well, I think there's a mood for it,' said John. 'But twice bitten, thrice shy, Dennis. 'If there is genuinely no one else, I'll do it. But you'll have a harder time convincing my wife than me. I really think one of you work-shy buggers should step up.'

They laughed, but Jeremy did not. However nice Diane might be, he thought it was quite shameful how she had elbowed his friend out of the way in the last contest in 2010, taking nominations that should have been John's. And then to go begging further nominations off the Blairites. It left a bad taste in his mouth.

'If you want to be the sacrificial lamb,' said Ian, 'then I won't stand in your way.'

'Yes, and you won't be helping him either, will you?' snapped Diane like a mother scolding a child for hurting his brother. 'Honestly, throwing your nomination away to Andy like that...'

'I did that because I thought none of us was getting their act together. Besides, it's what the unions – for who you seem to have so little respect - are asking for.'

'And you didn't think to consult us first, Ian?'

'Now, now!' said Corbyn. 'Let's not fight among ourselves. More light, less heat.'

'Sometimes it seems that *certain people* behave like our group doesn't exist,' said Diane.

'I think "sacrificial lamb" is a bit much,' said Clive. 'I mean, have you seen this online campaign...?' They had not. 'A lot of MPs I've been speaking to say they're being flooded with requests to back a left candidate. And they don't mean Andy.'

'You see - there's a mood there!' said Diane, glancing Ian a sideways raspberry with her eyes. 'We have to go for it - it would be irresponsible if we did not. Especially at a time when there are so many signs for change taking place. I mean look at Scotland...'

'Scotland's no example, Diane!' said Dennis. 'If we had kept Scotland, we might be in government right now and not sat here in blinkin' mess.'

'Don't like Scotland?' said Diane. 'Ok, well what about Ireland?'

'What about Ireland?' said Dennis.

'Didn't you see the referendum on gay marriage last week? If that's not a sign that things are changing, then I don't know what is.'

'Sixty-two per cent in favour,' said Richard. 'People were travelling back home from around the world to vote. That's part of how Ireland has dealt with the crisis - exporting its young workers overseas to lower the cost of unemployment.'

'That's how they've always done it,' lectured Dennis. 'Since potato famine onwards...'

'Well, I think it's incredible,' said Richard. 'Only twenty-two years since homosexuality was decriminalised. Nineteen years since they legalised divorce... and now they've leap-frogged Britain!'

'It's a huge blow to the dictatorship of the church,' interrupted John, 'which has been a pestilence on the Irish people. They talk about Islamic fundamentalism - Ireland was the Saudi Arabia of the Catholic Church. It's not just change – it's an earthquake!'

'They'll be legalising a woman's right to choose next,' said Diane.

'Aye,' said Ronnie. 'That'll be the next one.'

'Attendance at Sunday mass was ninety per cent in Ireland in the

1980s,' said Jeremy, 'now it's less than twenty. A monumental pillar of the establishment has collapsed. When these pillars come down, people can see the empty space where they once stood. Remember the News of the World…?'

Diane smiled in admiration. It was good to see her old friend in such fine spirit.

'After the Ryan Report came out in 2009,' said John, 'about the thousands of children raped, and the way they transferred priests between dioceses to keep them out of the public eye. And then the hundreds of children's skeletons uncovered in that mass grave in Bon Secours - it was only a matter of time before people moved against the church.

'As Jeremy says, when people realise the status quo is not invincible, not eternal, but rotten, they start looking to themselves to make up the difference. It demands a new sort of courage from the oppressed.'

He exchanged understanding looks with Jeremy and Corbyn.

'Well, we need to get to the point,' said Diane. 'Selecting a candidate… I propose we adjourn all other business to another meeting. Is that acceptable?'

The new intake immediately raised their hands. Diane paused, as if a thought had entered her head.

'Did you see what happened in Spain last week? That new party: Podemos? Means "Yes we can". They won in Barcelona, Madrid, Zaragoza, Cadiz, lots of big places, in an alliance with other left parties. They only formed in January last year, but within six months they were in the European parliament. Now there's an example of change.'

'Yes, and do you know what one of their main planks was…?' asked Jeremy. 'They said no to a Euro MP's salary and promised to take the average workers wage. Not only did they say it, but they did it! Made them hugely popular. Their leader, Iglesias, says we need to "democratise the economy". And the new mayor of Barcelona, Ada Colau, has said she'll take a workers' wage, too. Jolly good, I say.'

'Things are different here, Jeremy,' said Dennis. 'As Ian said… Britain isn't Greece. Britain isn't Spain. It isn't Ireland, neither. And it aint Scotland!' Dennis pointed a crooked finger Jeremy's way. 'Things don't change here. British people aren't like Europeans.

They're far more reserved - Engels said that.'

'What about what's going on in America, then?' said Jeremy.

'What's going on in America?'

'Oh, you mean the Black Lives Matter movement?' asked Diane. 'That was really incredible, after those racist shootings by the police. Did you see all those black youth occupying Westfield's in Shepherds Bush the other week? What do they call it, a... "Die-in"? Talk about solidarity, that's really changing the... narrative.'

'Well, yes, that's another incredible example,' said Jeremy. 'Although, I was actually thinking about the Democratic Party nominations... Have you seen this Senator, Bernie Sanders? Have you seen the slogans he's using? *"Against the one percent"*, *"Against Wall Street"*, *"For a Political Revolution against the Billionaire class"*? You can talk about continental Europe being spontaneous and revolutionary, and having different traditions from the British and all that, but this is America - the belly of the beast! Aren't they supposed to be politically backwards Anglo-Saxons, like us?'

'You can't just say that just because some loony Senator in't US has lost plot,' said Dennis, 'and is running for Whitehouse - something that will not happen in a million years, by the way – don't mean owt has changed. But yes, Yanks are more like Brits, which is why nowt will change here neither.'

'Well, I say the Americans have a revolutionary tradition,' said Jeremy, 'as do we. Have you seen that man, Cromwell, standing outside this building...? Kings and Queens were bumping each other off for thousands of years, but it was here that the people took a King's head. We all know this whole place is decorated as a shamefaced apology for that fact. You call Sanders a "loony left". Well, maybe so - don't know much about the man. But the fact that he is gaining support, small donations from workers here and there, is a symptom of the times. He might get beat, will probably get beat, but I wouldn't be surprised if he causes some fireworks along the way. You have to understand this Dennis: things are changing!'

'Ok comrades,' said Diane. 'We've gone slightly off track. If we want to get home at a reasonable hour we really do need to make a decision. Let's recap: There may, or may not, be the possibility that a campaign from the left could get an echo among the public, who most of us can agree are looking for a real alternative to the Tories. And that's something the candidates so far are not offering. I would go so far to say that actually, for the very soul of the party itself, one of us needs to stand. Otherwise, the… narrative, will be dominated by the kind of patronising aspirational rubbish we've heard already. It's dull, it's uninspiring, what they have to say could be automatically written by a computer.

'We have a moral duty to stand,' she continued. 'The young comrades have informed us about the online response. We know that a number of MPs have approached us, and in my opinion some seemed quite favourably inclined. If we can make even the slightest impact on the Blairite automatons and swing some of what they say leftwards, then that would be an achievement in itself. Of course, you know I've ruled myself out, I'm already running for the London Mayor's position.'

Ian had been quiet for some time. For him the discussion could go to the devil, for all the good it would do. 'I propose Jeremy run - something's got into him this meeting.'

Suddenly all eyes fell on them. Corbyn hesitated, caught by surprise and unable to fully digest what had just been proposed. Then it dawned on him. His heart stopped pumping.

'I assure you, I don't…'

'Hear, hear! A fine suggestion,' said John. 'Diane and I have already done it, and this lot are too depressed and past it,' he said, thumbing in the direction of the veterans. 'It's your turn now comrade.'

'Oh Jeremy, I think it's ever such a good idea,' said Diane. 'I can help you, after all the things I learned from when I ran. Not to mention my broadcasting experience.'

The youngsters leant forward and nodded and clapped with big, hopeful smiles written on their faces.

Corbyn felt everyone's eyes on him, and he began to shrink in his chair. He saw John, and his heart resumed its pumping as he looked into his old friend's watery eyes. Sweat filled his shoes, soaking his socks. The floor had begun to sway, as if he were on the deck of a ship. He felt a hand on his shoulder. Jeremy was standing over him.

'All right, I'll do it!'

4

Twelve days later the candidates were crossing the finishing line. Corbyn was not present. He and Jeremy had had a blazing row after the socialist campaign group's meeting, sending Corbyn into a long sulk. His rage had eventually cooled and congealed, coating his arteries.

Jeremy attempted to make the peace by showing him the online petition in circulation, urging MPs to support Jeremy Corbyn's candidacy. It already had a few thousand signatures.

'That'll be John's doing,' said Corbyn, noticeably cheered. Jeremy tried to explain to him that it was a rank-and-file initiative, but Corbyn insisted.

If Corbyn was in a sulk, Jeremy had become energised. A week later, at the hustings of the parliamentary party, he had been an exotic offering to the moderate mainstream majority, contrasting brightly with the other candidates' two tones. The PLP departed entertained, if nothing else.

John spent the week begging nominations and calling in old favours. He had little choice but to approach right-wingers, so determined was he to get his friend on the ballot. But it was an uphill struggle.

In that two week book-end of time, a short but distinct historical period in their later recollections, Jeremy and John happened upon Chuka and Tristram more than once along the same slippery corridors through which they ran.

But they passed by on each others' side, smiling politely, too occupied by their respective missions to pause and reflect on the mirror alien movements of their fellow comrades.

Days before the deadline, Tristram finally managed to crack Mary, scooping out as many of her nominations as he could carry away. At the same time Chuka organised their fellow Intimates and mobilised what Holdings they had been able to convince of their cause.

On the day itself, and with only half an hour before the deadline, the little socialist campaign group were still four nominations short.

Chuka slouched against the corridor wall near the voting table, chewing gum, hands in his pockets, an apparently disinterested spectator. Jeremy stood holding a mug of tea, a mellow, nonplussed smile upon his face. They watched as John harangued each passer-by, imploring their aid, but with little result.

With fifteen minutes to go, Chuka let two fingers drop by his side. At the end of the corridor Tristram took the signal. He sent Sadiq and Jonathon marching down to nominate the candidate of the left.

Their appearance caused fits of delighted confusion from John, who kissed them both. The MPs mumbled something, leaving as quickly as they could.

With five minutes to go Chuka signalled for another. Frank was dispatched.

With only a minute remaining John was on his knees, pulling at an MP's leg, begging their reconsideration. If only he had known that, just around the corner Alan, Angela, Ben, Caroline, Stella, and Margaret were all queued and ready to deliver them their vote.

Chuka held back on the off-chance that John and Jeremy might secure the nomination without further assistance. He was keen to ensure they went through with as few of his fingerprints on the process as possible. He hesitated to the very end, fighting his natural instinct to hinder, not help, the Left. With ten seconds remaining Chuka finally signalled again to Tristram. Margaret was sent running.

CHAPTER 5
THE DEBATE

1

Liz talked long about what kind of person she was, and little else. Attitude was all, and she was determined to be the best head girl.

Into Jeremy and Corbyn's vision she jarred, the stage lighting bouncing an aura off her polished black coif. Beyond her, Nuneaton's parishioners heard the sound of her accomplishments ringing off the church walls.

It was now evening. From upon the stage, built over the church altar, the bright television lights were a pollutant on the candidates' vision, concealing all but the first few rows before the darkness crowded in. Further back, cameras craned quietly above the pews and dipped like the thirsty silhouettes of dinosaurs.

As Liz talked, Corbyn looked through her. He was not there. He was back in London, in Islington, standing at his front gate. A little garden sat beside the path that ran to his front door, and a rose bush twisted up its frame. Through his ankles El Gato tiptoed with his tail in the air, purring a welcome home to his faithful tenant.

Corbyn pushed at the gate, but it was jammed. He looked up and saw, towering above him: Blair. Only, it was not Blair. It was a tall man that leaned against his gate in one of those grinning Blair masks, grim and rubber. El Gato crouched and flattened his ears, asking

Corbyn what he proposed to do.

With a single shove, Corbyn pushed against the gate and entered upon his path. The rubber-masked man went flying and El Gato leapt aside, cursing mankind for its brutishness. As the man fell to the ground Corbyn grabbed the mask and pulled it from his face. What landed amid the untidy tangle of bushes was Margaret Thatcher, stranded on her backside.

As she rose to her feet Thatcher stared at Corbyn through hollow, black eyes. Her lips were receded, revealing a set of purple gums stuck with soiled teeth. Single white strands fell from her otherwise hairless head, and below her eye sockets bruises spread like polished conkers. Then she hissed and leaped the fence, and was gone.

For too long, we have been infiltrated by Tories in Labour's clothing.

He had been too tired to argue with Jeremy over the opening remarks on the train coming up to Nuneaton. Now he was alert and unhappy. He could hear the blinking of hundreds of eyes in the darkness, and the giant salivating eye of the BBC watching over him.

Why had he agreed to this?

He turned the key and stepped inside. It was a humble home. The staircase immediately confronted him, the downstairs corridor running away to the right to the front room and the kitchen. He took off his shoes and placed his jacket on the hook and crept up the carpeted stairs.

Mid-way up he came across an enormous water-wheel turning against the adjoining wall of the terraced house. *What on earth was Jeremy thinking?*

Inside the wheel stepped two donkeys. On their backs rode Rupert Murdoch, the media tycoon, and Lord Sugar, the reality TV capitalist, a torn Labour brooch hanging from his jacket.

Cigar smoke fogged the air, and they clinked brandy glasses as they rolled on their asses. The donkeys' fur was soaked in sweat and their hind legs bled from the stabbing of the men's heels. The pain brayed out of them and Corbyn's insides shrivelled.

Yet the beasts walked the wheel. They did not buck, and their eyes did not stray from the piece of string dangling before their eyes.

Our leaders became tools of the press, tools of big business. They stopped fighting for the working class. We need to make Labour a

> *socialist party once more. That means fighting against austerity, fighting against the cuts, fighting for a complete transformation of society. It means kicking big business out of Labour if we want to fight for a world run, not for the private profit of the one percent, but by the needs and aspirations of the ninety-nine. It means overcoming this antiquated capitalist system, in order to live in peace and harmony, rather than poverty, uncertainty and constant wars of plunder.*

It really would not do. It would not do at all.

He reached the landing at the top of the stairs. The bathroom was directly in front, from which one could look out onto the back garden. He needn't walk around the entire house - it was only a forty-five second speech. The landing followed round to the bedroom, and then to a spare room facing the street, which was used as an office.

In the bathroom tub sailed a little boat, water lapping against its sides. Across its hull in bold white was painted *"Labour"*, and upon its deck sat a very fat, white Persian cat. It was larger than El Gato, and far smarter dressed (To be clear, El Gato is no scruff. He keeps an immaculate black evening coat which, along with his Mexican accent, proves irresistible to the alley queens of Islington North. He was only born over the river in Plumstead, but he keeps that to himself). This giant fluff-ball was wrapped in a fine waistcoat, and wore a monocle and top hat. El Gato could hardly compete with that.

The cat was surrounded by a hoard of mice in pirate hats. There were young mice, unemployed mice, working mice, immigrant mice, mice on crutches. They wielded tiny swords and high-pitched jeers and prodded the cat toward the end of the plank until it went *splash!* The mice cheered and set course for the rim of the tub, and all gathered on deck around a giant cat-bowl that cast shadows beyond the ring of rodents as they basked triumphantly in its golden glow.

> *Ultimately, we need to draw a line under Blairism and re-found the Labour Party. We need to re-find our party's socialist principles and put at its heart, as a fundamental human right: everyone is entitled to a job and a home, if they so wish. Only in this way can Labour stand up for the young, the unemployed, the workers, in Britain and around the world; stand up for those who are sick of this system that puts power and money first and people*

last. It means turning Labour around. It means fighting for revolutionary socialism inside the Labour Party, in order to fight for socialism everywhere. Thank you.

Applause, sit down.

How had he arrived here? Only a few weeks ago he was living the life of a humble constituency MP. He had never asked for more. Now he was being cooked under the studio lights.

Why had he prepared so little? Flanking him were the legitimate and bastard scions of New Labour's political machine; anaemic striplings, plucked and plaster-set radio-friendly smiles and focus-filtered word-combinations at the ready.

Why had he dreamt it all up on the train to this god-forsaken town? These people had whole teams of advisors. He and Jeremy had talked with John at length in recent days, but John was still in the process of assembling a team. For now he had only Jeremy.

Why had he prepared nothing to say about himself? The others seemed to pack so much into their forty-five seconds. Would it seem arrogant? As if he assumed people should know him already? Panic stampeded his thoughts as Liz drew her remarks to a close.

Politely-paced English clapping escorted her back to her seat, as it had for Andy and Yvette before her. She looked so pleased with herself, thought Corbyn, that she must have spoken well.

Jeremy was poised to stand. Corbyn wavered. They had agreed on the train that Jeremy would speak, having been the one who had written the opening remarks, but surely he could change his mind? Tears of sweat gathered behind his ears. Would it look strange? Would Jeremy mind? What if he caused a fuss on live television?

Then the weight of his piling concerns collapsed into a singular point, crushing any hesitation. Springing from his seat, he landed square on the stage's night, and without a moment for his friend to raise complaint, he began:

'I… was elected to parliament thirty-two years ago,' he
said, tiptoeing before the audience.

Jeremy was left standing. He smiled into the darkness and lowered himself back into his seat.

'And I spent my time in parliament,' continued Corbyn, 'representing my constituency and standing up for rights in Britain and all around the world.'

Why is he talking about himself? He hates personality politics.

But Corbyn was gone. He was at his front gate, a rubber-faced Tony Blair towering over him, mocking him with his black grin.

'I believe that is the function of the Labour Party.'

He pushed at the threshold, but his gate would not open. Blair was growing. He looked down and saw an inflating foot wedging shut the gate. He was almost eight feet and rising.

'But I also think that over the years we've lost our way. We've become cowed by powerful commercial interests.'

He heard a hissing sound. Blair was deflating.

'We've become frightened of the press.' Blair deflated some more, panicking as he saw the ground approaching.

'We've become frightened to stand up for what we absolutely believe in.'

He pushed open the gate and Blair crumpled in the wind. The mask went flying and so did the decrepit Thatcher that nestled inside, landing in a thicket of briar Corbyn had never seen before. He marched on.

On stage his eyes had begun to adjust. He flitted from face to face, fearful of resting on any one person. They were not faces, exactly, rather recognisable fragments of people, overlaid with the passage of his home. On the stairs the donkeys brayed, and their masters' heels dug in.

But among the fragments he began to detect something, something Jeremy had already noticed quite clearly. Now Corbyn began to notice it too. It was the people – they were not booing. He saw no frowns, no shaking of heads. In fact, they appeared receptive, and the front row had become streaked with an open smile. As he spoke, he felt the audience grow reassured, and that reassured him. It was as if they wanted him to do well, and he forgot the six beady eyes pointing at his back.

He climbed the stairs and hovered at the bathroom door and saw that a storm was raging, localised directly over the bathtub.

The little Labour boat was being tossed on the high seas. The waves pummelled against it and the sides of the tub, drenching mice and cat alike.

'I want a more equal society, I want a fairer society; I want a society at peace, not at war. I want the Labour Party to be the heart of the community that is demanding those things and demanding jobs, homes and hopes for everybody, so that they can live in a society that is more equal. We're moving in the wrong direction at the present time, let's turn it round and move the other way. Thank you.'

A rush blew from the stage and squeezed him in a bear hug. Gasping for breath, he was hauled back to his seat, heels screeching rubber across the stage. As he took his seat the clapping did not halt, and when his lungs once more inflated he felt the adrenaline thump out of his heart and carry on his veins to every extremity. It felt good - like stumbling across a manhole he had only seen in pictures.

In the minute that had passed, Jeremy's disappointment had become replaced with something else, something unfamiliar.

It was the movement of the crowd that had caught his attention. He was not sure what it was, but it seemed to move in a way that reminded him of something he had once read in a book. The applause was strange. There was an embarrassment of inequality between the response his friend had received and the other candidates.

'How was that?' asked Corbyn, looking pleased.

'Not bad... hell of a response, I think you even got a "hear, hear!" on your way back,' said Jeremy. *'Only, I thought I was going to speak? It seems we got away with it - but you really should let me know next time you do that.'* Corbyn sipped his water and looked out into the crowd. He was pleased.

Laura, the moderator of the debate, had to wait for the applause to settle down. It did not go unnoticed by the other candidates.

'Our first question tonight,' she said 'comes from Paul, a retired teacher who's sixty-two...'

The cameras emerged like insects, lowering over the teacher. A voice radioed in Laura's ear:

'A little too much for Corbyn there, don't bring him back in for a while.'

'As an old Labour supporter,' said the teacher, 'my question is: How do we get away from the legacy of Tony Blair and rebuild a left-wing party?'

Jeremy and Corbyn exchanged looks. *'Good question.'*

Like an infectious yawn, the other candidates turned simultaneously in their seats, their manikin mouldings running like candle wax in the teeth of the hot question. Static shattered in Laura's ear.

'Thefuck?' barked the voice.

Laura unguardedly brought her finger to her earpiece, before turning it into a neck scratch.

'What did you bring him in for?'

She checked her notes, certain he was the man she had spoken with before they went on air. All the questions had been submitted and vetted in advance. Did she have a rogue element in the room? Corbyn tried to get her attention

'Don't let him back in,' the voice ordered.

'Andy,' said Laura, somewhat panicked.

Andy inwardly frowned. Was the moderator out to get him too? Everyone seemed to be having a go at him these days.

'Well, I don't think we want to do that...' said Andy.

'*He certainly doesn't,*' whispered Jeremy.

'...because Tony was the Prime Minister that won three elections for Labour.'

Andy saw that the teacher was unmoved.

'But he didn't get everything... right. So we have to learn from the mistakes of that Labour government. But he did a lot of things right, and he spoke to peoples' wishes to get on in life... we want to be the party that wants to help everyone get on in life...'

'We want to be the party that asks the lamb to lie down with the Crocodile.'

Corbyn shuffled away from Jeremy, trying to catch Andy's remarks.

'...we'd build on our past and make Labour stronger going forward,' finished Andy.

The audience queued no applause.

'Liz, people see you as the Blairite,' said Laura.

'Yeh, look, I'm not Blairite, Brownite, old Labour, new Labour. I want to be today's and tomorrow's Labour.'

Meaningless

'But the lesson I learned from our victories in 1945, 1964 and 1997,' she said, 'was that we had leaders who understood how the world had changed... Like Andy, I'm very proud of things that Labour achieved, but the world has moved on, and the party has got to move on... jobs change and close in what seems like the blink of an eye...'

'That's true - if you don't fight for them.'

'We're all living longer, we're getting much older, so our public services need to change to improve support for older people. The same policies we had in 2010 won't be right for 2020. We keep our values, we move on to the future.'

'Good grief.'

'Will you be quiet,' said Corbyn, turning to Jeremy. *'I need to hear what they're saying; otherwise I won't be able to respond.'*

Respond to what? But he kept that to himself.

'Right, let's get away from that,' buzzed the voice. *'Throw them a bone to scrap over - deploy the tension point on "baggage". But let's just keep it between the real candidates.'*

'Liz...' said Laura. 'Do you think Andy and Yvette have got too much baggage, having been ministers under Gordon Brown and worked under Tony Blair, to be the next leader?'

'I think that we do need a fresh start, and I don't have the baggage of the past, but that's not why I'm putting myself forward to be leader...'

Laura interrupted:

'But the other two do, you said you don't have the baggage...'

Liz carried on, but the moderator was no longer listening.

'Well, Yvette,' said Laura, 'I mean, Liz is saying very clearly then: It can't be you because you've got baggage from before.'

'Well, I don't think that's quite what Liz was saying...'

Yvette sat forward in her floral summer skirt, clasping her hands against her stiffened knees. She suppressed a deposit of hate into her bloodstream; hate for the host, and hate for the skipping rope she was being made to jump.

'But... sounded quite like it, I don't know if the audience would agree,' said Laura, appealing for rotten fruit. But she won only a saccharine sneeze.

'I think there is an advantage to having experience, and I certainly make no apologies for running a hundred billion pound department, and also perhaps more importantly being the minister who rolled out Sure Start which I'm really proud of, or being someone who voted for the minimum wage which again I think is so important for our country and I think to go back to your question,' she said, addressing the teacher, 'in the end this can't be about taking a narrow party and moving it to the left or moving it to the right...'

Laura's ear vibrated.

'Alright, let's bring it back to the teacher very briefly to close this down. Don't give it to Corbyn, whatever you do.'

Laura interrupted Yvette, causing her to suppress another deposit:

'Paul... You're clear we've got to move away from the legacy of Tony Blair. What do you think of what you've heard there?'

'I don't think the idea that we can stick to policies that are totally centre-ground...,' said the teacher, 'we seem to be on the same ground as the Conservatives doing that - and they've won. I don't think we're making ourselves distinctive enough and I think we're leaving behind some of the underprivileged, some of the people without jobs and people like that.'

Such a comment could not very well be left hanging in the air, but Laura did not trust any of the real candidates to deal with it. She brought in a man nearby, hoping he would clear the discussion's palate:

'It's not so much the Tony Blair era, the Gordon Brown era, etcetera,' he said. 'It's just that the electorate during the last General Election, the General Election before, were saying: "We cannot see the division between line between Labour and the Conservatives." The line has blurred.'

Paul the teacher nodded in agreement.

'Not good,' buzzed Laura's ear. Then Andy butted in:

'I think that's a fair point...I think where we got things wrong... I believe we let the market too far into the

National Health Service…'

Jeremy leant over to Corbyn:

'Wasn't he minister for health?'

'Yes,' said Corbyn.

'Well, Andy, if you will insert your private sector, you've only yourself to blame.'

Corbyn was not amused. He shuffled further in his seat, putting space between himself and Jeremy.

'You should get in there; you know what to say on this:

"Tony Blair and Gordon Brown were Tory infiltrators who let their business friends get their hands on the NHS and bent the knee to the highest bidder. We need to kick the money-lenders out of the hospitals and hand them back to the doctors and nurses, publicly and democratically controlled."'

'Yes, yes,' said Corbyn. 'She'll let me come in soon enough.'

Andy continued:

'…what I say is, let's take the best of New Labour, but the best of Old Labour, and create a distinctive Labour offer - that deals with the problems of here and now. This government isn't doing that, it is destroying the health service, and it is leaving so many people behind.'

Laura's ear whispered to her:

'You'd better let in Corbyn; we don't want the BBC to look unbalanced. Give him some rope, enough to hang himself with.'

She moved automatically.

'Jeremy, Jeremy Corbyn. The question there was pretty clear,' said Laura. But she rephrased it anyway: 'He says all these three kind of sound the same and sound a bit like the Tories to him. Maybe you, sir, might sound a bit different?'

Corbyn's patience had been rewarded.

'Well, I've never considered myself very much part of New Labour,' said Corbyn, 'so let's put that to one side.'

The audience liked that.

'There were some serious problems with the way that Tony Blair and New Labour approached things. One was to restrict democracy in the Labour Party and the Labour movement by centralising decision making.

'Secondly, was the promotion of markets rather than a

planned economy...'

'Hear, hear! Well said, more of that please!'

Corbyn was put off. Then he bit the air, realising why Jeremy was cheering him. His mouth ran dry.

'Or... any level of planning in an economy... so we ended up with more deregulation than we should have had.'

'Than we should have had?'

'But thirdly, and this is the elephant in this room and everywhere else. Why, oh why, oh why, did Blair have to get so close to Bush that we ended up in an illegal war in Iraq?'

A deep murmur of approval rolled its way toward the four seated candidates, and a few of the audience openly shouted their agreement.

'And we're still paying the price for that...'

Before he could finish what he was saying, they broke spontaneously into open applause.

'Where did we get this crowd?' The interference in Laura's ear spiked painfully.

'I thought they were meant to be handpicked. I thought this was a typical constituency, not a nest of bleeding reds. Not good!'

The applause was long and loud, and it offended Laura. Who did this scruffy little tramp, with whom she had cultivated no professional relationship, think he was? She attempted to shut down the applause.

'But, but, but, but Jeremy Corbyn.'

They paid her no heed, carrying on their long applause defiantly.

'But, but Jeremy Corbyn...'

Satisfied, they withdrew, and allowed her to place her 'but'.

'The gentleman's point, and Paul's original question, was: "How do you move away from the legacy of Tony Blair?" Perhaps some people might think there's no point rehashing what happened in 2003?'

'The party has an opportunity now,' said Corbyn, 'to rediscover its principal roots, rediscover the issues of... equality.'

Jeremy sighed. At least his friend seemed to have found some spirit, even if he still fudged his words.

'...rediscover the issues of public service and, err...

promotion of council housing in order to solve the housing crisis which Andy mentioned earlier. I think we've got the opportunity to do that now.

'But if we're just going to say: "Well, this policy needs changing a little bit, the Tories did this, so we'll do this, and it's sort of endless triangulation to get yourself to some slightly better position - doesn't work. People are looking for some fundamental change in our society that gives them real security,' he said.

'So say what it is!' said Jeremy, poking Corbyn in the ribs.

'Real security,' said Corbyn, visibly annoyed, 'comes from work, comes from decent public services.'

The crowd again broke into a spontaneous applause, causing Jeremy to become quiet. It was evident that however hedged his friend's words were, he could do no wrong in the eyes of the audience.

The response was embarrassing the other candidates. Yvette and Liz squirmed, and Andy nodded in wonder like a weathercock.

How is this senior citizen so cost-effectively dovetailing his marginals?

'Right, deploy the UKIPers,' sounded the command. Laura moved automatically:

'For many previous Labour party voters, that meant turning to UKIP in the last election.

'Now, Glen was a Labour Party voter for many years, and turned to UKIP to vote in the last election. Perhaps we can hear what he wants to say to the candidates here:'

The alien mic moved swiftly over the audience and craned over a tidy looking man in his forties.

'Um, I'm, actually... I'm actually a fireman,' he said, retarding Laura's woven fabric.

'Fuck!'

'I've been a fireman for twenty years, and we're faced with cuts, savage - quite savage cuts.

'Um, as I seen it, before the election, Conservatives were gonna continue with these cuts, and subsequently the cuts are gonna run deeper and deeper. How are Labour going to address this issue, particularly in the public service?'

'Whothefuckarethesepeople?'

A whining feedback perforated Laura's ear drum.

'I thought we had a guaranteed bunch of racists at the ready?'

Then she heard an even angrier voice in the background. Her static interference was pleading with it:

'We checked the local party... we had promises: all the live wires weeded out - I swear!'

Then, everything crashed into white noise, and she could no longer hear her director's voice.

'But, just to be clear, Glen,' said Laura, composing herself, 'you chose UKIP, rather than place your faith in Labour?'

'I chose UKIP because I didn't hear any sign of support from the Labour Party. I certainly wasn't going to vote Conservatives for what they've done to our profession. And I seen UKIP as just another, err, option vote - a protest vote, if you like.'

Laura quickly handed the floor to Liz while the voices continued arguing in her ear. Liz skilfully arranged *'equality'* and *'public finances'* with an *'in order to deliver'* and an *'under control'*.

Laura's ear finally settled, and an instruction came through:

'Move on to the immigrants.'

Yvette was waving her hand amiably in the air, but Laura ignored her and declared it was time to move on to the second question, although in truth it was the fourth in fifteen minutes. She was not enjoying herself.

At last the audience showed signs of behaving. Her man in the sweater asked what Labour was going to do about immigration control. She relaxed and brought in poor Yvette, who was fit to burst.

Yvette had no intention of answering such a silly question, but she needed the air time, and so proceeded to explain the need for sensible debate with sensible answers, doing her level best not to offend the sensibilities of all the sensible voters gathered in the aisles.

'Let's deal with immigration,' she said.

'Fair', *'enforcement'*, *'rules'*, *'sensible'*, *'reform'*, *'fair'*, *'not unfair'*. Yvette placed the sharp edges of the question in the stream of her imagined three-pound public and pulled out a perfectly spherical pebble that faced all ways at once.

Jeremy and Corbyn

Liz kicked Yvette's pebble into the English Channel, where migrants jumped on lorries from Calais, and who really should start putting more into the community than they take out. And respect our culture.

That said, it was also important to learn from other cultures. The excellent Australian points-based system, for example, based squarely on the national interest and a commitment to Pacific paradise island housing for immigrants of all creeds and colours - whether they liked it or not.

A shiver went down Jeremy's spine. *'The only skill a migrant needs is to be worked and not heard.'*

A woman with braces asked whether the points-based system was not a UKIP policy, and a bearded man said that immigrants had made this country what it is.

Then the other candidates all weathered their cocks, but the bearded man declared with Corbyn, and their wax wilted.

> 'If we weren't going around starting illegal wars in these countries,' said the bearded man, 'then perhaps they wouldn't be fleeing to come and live here.'

'Good point.' Corbyn agreed.

What a night, thought Laura.

Andy said he agreed with the gentleman, and that as an ex-health minister he was perfectly positioned to understand that if it was not for immigrants we would not have such low NHS waiting lists... Only, the waiting lists were high, because of the Tories, of course.

His father had worked overseas, which meant he was a sort of immigrant himself, and he had migrated out of the Westminster bubble to somewhere near his constituency where the only English speaker in a workplace had spoken to him in English, telling him how horrible it was to work there.

We all needed to remember not to forget to stop foreign labour being used by some – possibly - to undercut the wages of others. We must not forget, nay, we must remember, and we must understand.

> 'I think you live in a different world from me,' said a man in a checked shirt.
>
> 'You honestly do, I'm not being disrespectful. But I see it; it's on our door step. If you're gonna put plans for your future - forget the past, 'cos you're not gonna change that

- you've gotta tell me, convince me, how you're gonna put this country right and so far I've heard nothing - I know its early doors, but... you must have an infrastructure to absorb these three or four-hundred thousand people a year you're bringing in and allowing in – and that's only what you know about... there's other people coming through the back door - you've said it yourself...' Liz nodded. 'You acknowledge it - it's a massive, massive problem, and it's an ongoing problem.

'Now the problem is, when you drop your borders, you get rid of your police - the police in this country is gone down...

'He's right there,' said Corbyn. 'Even Thatcher didn't hurt the police because she was sending them against all the rest. She knew which side her bread was buttered.'

'Yes, which just goes to show how desperate they are,' said Jeremy. 'That's why it's meaningless to call the cuts "ideological". If it was just a mere Tory whim, the last thing they would be doing is going for the police.'

'The 'ealth is rock bottom,' continued the checked man.

'The fire brigade is rock bottom, all these services are at rock bottom, and you keep leading and letting people into this country - I'm not racist, I'm being sensible.

'Sounds like a racist to me,' muttered Corbyn.

'What do you expect if all he hears are these geniuses' beside you not explaining the crisis? If Labour offers no real explanation then of course some people are going to look elsewhere for an understanding. He's not going to say: "Oh well, I don't know why that's happened" and sit on his hands. He's going to try and work it out himself. And when his job goes the media aren't going to show him fat mountains of uninvested cash with a capitalist on top piled next to his closed-down factory. No, he's going to be shown in the direction of the foreign brown man who has a better job than him. And he's going to be invited to draw conclusions. All those immigrant mugs you keep in your allotment may give you a vague superior satisfaction, you may look down your nose at this man, but his point of view is understandable given that Labour has completely failed to explain the crisis. If Labour was to offer a real explanation we could unite our class against the bosses and cut across all this racism. He clings to St. George's flag, because the red flag is palest pink.'

'And I fear for England, I fear that we're going down a

slippery slope that we won't recover from, because we're not...'

Laura had all she needed from him and cut him down. But he was determined to stagger on:

'...manufacturing enough...' he said, but she shot again, and he stumbled against the bullets of his learned submission.

But he was a big fellow, and before the arrows of deferred reverence laid him low, he uttered a redeeming last word:

'One thing: Don't try and run the services as a business. It's a different thing.'

And he was silenced.

'Thank you, sir, let's try and deal with your point on immigration,' said Laura. 'You're clearly very worried for the future of this country, you say you're not racist, but you're really worried.

'Jeremy Corbyn, what do you say to him? What would you do as Labour leader?'

'Nicely done,' buzzed the voice in Laura's ear. *'Keep on that message: subtle suggestions that the public are racist. They clearly need work on their morale.'*

'First of all', said Corbyn, 'if there hadn't been immigration into this country, what kind of health system would we have? What kind of transport system would we have? What kind of education system would we have? We would be in a much more difficult place than we are at the present time.'

Spontaneous applause broke out.

It's the same point Andy made, but he got a far better response. Why?

Andy looked cheated. However, Corbyn's uttering of his incantation appeared to breathe life into the man in the checked shirt:

'But why have all the doctors and nurses left the industry then?' he cried out from beyond the grave. 'Why have they left? Because they had them in the first place. When you got rid of the matrons and you got the accountants in to run the business.'

'Can't you see the essence of the man's point?' said Jeremy. *'He's asking: What made the health service starved of workers in the first place? He*

says it was the accountants, the pencil pushers; in other words, the privateers in the service of her majesty's government who boarded public services, plundered desirable jobs, and contracted them out on the cheap. If there had actually been a labour shortage in the NHS, what made it so unattractive? It's a fair question. Isn't it equally racist to say migrants should be praised for doing jobs British workers allegedly "won't do"?'

'Oh come on,' said Corbyn, 'look at him; he's clearly a bigoted man.'

'The health service is a major employer,' said Corbyn to the checked shirt man, 'and is very effective at running a good health service, and I think Jamaican nurses and others that came here in the 1960s did a fantastic job, and we should recognise that.'

He would not criticise the NHS, even in order to explain its privatisation. That was the move the other candidates wanted him to make.

Laura tried to shut him up, but the audience came to his rescue and shut her up instead with another big round of applause. They asked him to finish:

'If I may finish,' Corbyn said to Laura, feeling the audience at his back, 'we should also recognise that migrants that come here actually contribute net to the economy, claim less, pay more in tax and work.'

Yvette and Andy tried to assail him, and Laura was apt to assist, but Corbyn's voice filled with a rare passion that pushed them all back. He spoke directly at the man in the checked shirt:

'If there is a shortage of housing, that is our failure... and we must plan for need in the future,' he said, reeling back and finishing.

Then he immediately hoped he hadn't been too harsh on the man.

The others circled around the question, smelling blood, waiting for their turn to pick at the carcass.

Jeremy leaned over to him and whispered: *That was what I was saying - a planned economy!*

The debate continued, and when the applause bled heavy Laura gradually learned to stymie the flow. But she could not stem it entirely.

2

After the debate they returned to London and met with John at the Lyceum Tavern on the Strand. It was late, and they were famished. Jeremy ordered the Steak and Kidney pudding and a pint of ale, and Corbyn had the vegetarian curry with a glass of lemonade.

John had watched the debate on the television, declaring Corbyn the winner hands down. Corbyn said he would say that, although privately he felt it had gone far better than expected. Jeremy agreed, although he was still annoyed by his friend usurping his place in the debate.

A report was given by John on his attempts to assemble a campaign team. They were a bit thin on the ground when it came to old hands. But he did report many youngsters wishing to volunteer. They came largely from the Labour Representation Committee, and were not without experience, some having been around the group since the short-lived 'Socialist Youth Network' ten years ago.

'I think that's a splendid idea,' said Jeremy. *'He who has the youth has the future!'*

'Yes,' said Corbyn, 'but aren't there any people with a bit more experience? Who can handle the media? It's going to be a tough few months and I don't think we can afford to have someone learning on the job.'

'We're overflowing with "experience",' said John with an exasperated sort of smile. 'Haven't you ever been to an LRC conference? I agree with Jeremy, it's the young ones who have the energy, and they're on top of all this social media that seems so important these days.'

'Here, look at this,' said Jeremy. He showed Corbyn his mobile phone and scrolled through the comments they had received since the end of the debate that evening. Corbyn put on his reading glasses and peered at the screen.

Badger him as he might, Jeremy had yet to convince Corbyn of the advantages of the technology. His friend skimmed the many messages of support.

'I see... and people just write what they feel on there, do they?'
'Rather useful, isn't it?' said John.
'Yes, well that's all very well and good. Perhaps we could have

one of these youngsters take care of that side of things - moderate the discussion, and so forth. But what I'm talking about is mass reach. There are almost two-hundred thousand members out there. Few have the knowledge to load up a computer and find their way to this... chat room.'

'Well, John and I were discussing earlier that what we need to do is...'

'Really?' said Corbyn, interrupting Jeremy abruptly. '"Discussing", were you? And when was this?' He appeared visibly annoyed.

'After the PLP hustings...' said John. 'Jeremy asked me how he spoke. I told him that he spoke very well, but that he may as well have been talking to the wall.'

'What we thought was needed,' added Jeremy, 'was a decent tour of campaign meetings, up and down the country – we certainly can't rely on the PLP for much support.'

Corbyn looked shocked. The two of them seemed to have developed quite the conspiracy.

'I don't know. That would take an awful lot of work,' said Corbyn. 'Which is why I'm so keen for us to get a press officer. You reach more people through the media. That is... if you know how to use it correctly.'

Corbyn gave Jeremy the slightest of guilty glances, but Jeremy caught him in the act.

'Oh! Is that why you jumped into my place this evening?'

Corbyn stared into his lemonade. 'Look, Jeremy, if we want to keep the media onside, we've got to be sensible. They'll crucify us if we carry on the way you do.' Jeremy stared at Corbyn resentfully.

'Did you see,' said John, attempting to defuse the situation, 'that bit between Liz and Andy? When he said the party comes first, and she interrupted him and said, what was it, something about the national interest... oh yes: *"The country comes first"* - you should have seen his face. I almost wet myself!'

'We shouldn't have anything to do with the mainstream media,' said Jeremy. 'They're a mafia. Intimidating here, bribing there, terminating careers when it suits them and rewarding their most loyal toadies. We don't need them.'

'How many meetings are we talking about?'

'Jeremy and I were thinking twenty, maybe thirty,' said John.

'Good grief. We'll be exhausted.'

'And we need to raise funds,' said Jeremy. 'In America Bernie Sanders raised one-point-five-million dollars in twenty-four hours after he announced his presidential campaign.'

'Goodness. Who backed him? Wal-Mart?' said Corbyn. 'I thought he was the socialist candidate?'

'He is. It's all come through small donations. He hasn't got any big business backers; he says he doesn't want them. The average donation to the Sanders' campaign is something like thirty dollars. We should do something similar. It's a political question. He doesn't want to be ruled by any corporate interests, and at the same time it engages people – asks them to put their money where their mouth is. We shouldn't underestimate that.'

'I think it all sounds rather eccentric. And we need to be realistic... at least for the time being. Perhaps we could arrange a meeting with someone like Lord Sainsbury? I like his new slogan: *"Live Well for Less"*. What do you think of something like that for a campaign slogan?'

'You're joking, aren't you?'

'Well, not exactly that, obviously.'

'I think we should say: *"Bring back Clause Four",*' said Jeremy.

'Far too backward-looking. We need something that speaks about the future, something about all the changes that are taking place around the world, like the things we discussed at the campaign group meeting. I really think that hits the mark. After the debate tonight more than one person from the audience approached me to say how refreshing it was to hear some straight-talking, honest politics for a change.'

'Did you ask them if they were being ironic?' asked Jeremy.

'I think a slogan is a good idea,' said John, 'but perhaps we should give it some more thought.'

They continued talking into the night. Corbyn got his way on the position of a press officer, and John promised to investigate potential candidates. Jeremy and John managed to get Corbyn to agree to a Bernie Sanders-style financial appeal, and a modest plan for a tour of the country was agreed.

CHAPTER 6
THE DEMONSTRATION

1

'I think what has happened to the Greek people has been absolutely appalling, and the very poorest people are seeing their schools closed, their hospitals underfunded, sleeping in the streets.'

Jeremy sipped his morning coffee and yawned into the microphone. He had stayed up to an unreasonable hour the night before, glued to the coverage of the stand-off between Greece and the notorious *"Troika"* – the alliance of the International Monetary Fund, the European Central Bank and the leaders of the European Union. Corbyn had told Jeremy that he should get some rest; they had a long day in front of them. But Jeremy had not listened.

Seeing that his friend was falling asleep, Corbyn offered to take over the rest of the interview. Jeremy handed him the headphones with sleepy gratitude.

'They're not the ones that caused the crisis in Greece,' said Corbyn, 'and I've got a great deal of sympathy for the Syriza government and what it is trying to do.

'I know Alexis Tsipras, I've been to Greece and talked to them and talked to many other people there. I think the ECB's treatment of Greece is patronising and unfair, and I think they should recognise that what the Greek government is trying to do is improve the economic situation of everybody, remove the worst levels of poverty in Greece and actually invest in public services. Is that not the way forward?'

'Well, if the Greek government is going to do that,' said the host, 'surely it's got to be able to run an economy which produces the resources to allow that to happen. We're not talking about the desirability of social ends, but the resources that are required to make it happen. And if it simply says we'll run an economy that hasn't delivered in the past and has produced a great deal of poverty in that country, and will just depend on German tax payers to fund it, then it's not a very credible position to take.'

'Well, what the Greek government is trying to do is improve tax collection, and it's doing that. What it's trying to do is invest in infrastructure; it's trying to do that. What it's trying to do is... invest and rebalance its economy. But if instead it's forced into paying what is frankly an immediately unpayable debt in quick-march time, then how can you possibly achieve any of those social ends?

'The Greek people, the founders of democracy, have spoken very strongly about what they're trying to do. They want to work hard, they want to improve the economy, they want to improve their agriculture and all those kind of things. But if they're forced into this position, what happens? Are they going to be forced out of the Eurozone? Are they going to be forced into the kind of disaster that seems to be down the road if the central bank carries on this way?'

After the radio show Jeremy and Corbyn jumped on a train bound for Stevenage to participate in a leadership hustings.

They bickered most of the way there. Jeremy was thankful to Corbyn for stepping in, but he thought his friend might have taken a little more care with his choice of words.

'I may have been half-asleep, but I heard what you said. Making the economy better for "everybody". Who exactly is this "everybody"? It's always the same with you – you're always muddying the class question. Can't you say "the working class" for once?'

'Well, if things improve for the Greek working class, then surely everyone benefits?' said Corbyn.

'And how is that going to happen? By "collecting taxes" and "working harder"? You sounded like one of the EU's inspectors.'

'That is what Tsipras is trying to do; it's only a statement of fact, not your... propaganda.'

'You're not an advocate for Tsipras. You should be giving him critical support; not providing an uncritical description of the workings of the Greek government.'

'It's not for me to criticise the Greek peoples' choice of government.'

'You know, that presenter had a point when he said that the Greek economy cannot deliver if it just carries on as before. That should have been your cue to say: "Yes, you're right, that's why Tsipras needs to rip up the debt and declare the Greek economy socialised!"'

'That's just what they want you to say. And within hours the headlines would have been: *"Corbyn attacks Syriza government."* Our comrades in Greece would be over the moon with that, wouldn't they?'

'So instead you say that the Greek people want to "work hard" and "pay their taxes". Do you even know what you're saying? The Greeks are among the hardest workers in Europe. They work far longer hours than the Germans. If working hard was the answer then they would be masters of Europe and it would be the Germans who were in Greece's thrall. They're outcompeted because the German bosses have invested and the Greek bosses haven't. That doesn't make the Greek workers "lazy"!'

'I wasn't saying that. In fact, I was attempting to refute all this nonsense about them being lazy. I was just saying they need to be given a chance, that's all.'

'I know you mean well, which is why I'm saying be careful how you choose your words. The Syriza government is trying to collect more tax, but you might have mentioned that they're also trying to get more of it from the rich. I have my reservations about Tsipras and Syriza, but you might have mentioned that. The British people need to hear that these kinds of things are being fought for in other parts of

Jeremy and Corbyn

the world. The great weakness of our labour movement is its ignorance of the working class struggle internationally.'

'I did say that. I said the government is trying to rebalance the economy.'

'And you need to stop with these euphemisms,' said Jeremy. 'Tell me, what exactly is it that you mean when you say "rebalance the economy"? More industry over services? More exports over imports? I hadn't even considered you meant taxing the rich more and the poor less! If you mean progressive taxation, say so. Because it's not the same as the economy. You must say what you mean. Otherwise, you'll never mean what you say.'

Corbyn fiddled his watch strap. 'Well, it can mean all those things – I'm in favour of all those things. That's why it's such a good, all-round phrase. It's not a "euphemism".'

'It's such a good phrase that the Tories and the Blairites say the exact same thing… Just explain yourself, won't you? Society needs trade and industry, but if you start saying that we need to revive industry in order to "attain greater exports" and "close the trade deficit", well, you're straying into the field of nationalism.'

Corbyn looked up. He did not like the sound of that.

'Germany has a very healthy trade surplus precisely at the expense of southern Europe,' continued Jeremy. 'Because it exports cheap, efficiently-made goods produced by the technology the German capitalists have invested in, and can therefore out-compete its rivals and run their industry into the ground. We should be talking about socialist cooperation with the people of Greece and Europe - with the people of the world, in fact – not beggar-thy-neighbour policies and more Greek tragedies.'

'You can't say such things on the radio, not with the time you're given. Even if I did, they wouldn't accept it,' said Corbyn. 'You've got to speak their language; the language of responsibility. We can't just say things like "take over the banks" and "plan industry democratically", valid proposals though they might be.'

'You know,' said Jeremy, 'sometimes you sound like you're trying to win this contest. I thought it was meant to be about getting the message across?'

'The group agreed on an anti-austerity message and that's what we're delivering.'

'Do you honestly think we can fight austerity without proposing anything to replace it?'

Their bickering continued for a while, until they eventually settled into silence. Corbyn worked on his notes, Jeremy caught up on his sleep.

2

The morning was still young when Amalia arrived at the old London Wall. The June sun blazed, but in the shadow of the giant stone corridors that led to the Bank of England her Attic sensibilities suffered a decided chill.

Along the deserted road she walked, coffee in hand and a rucksack full of *Revolutionary Newspapers* rubbing against her shoulders. Little life could be seen. Four hard-hatted workers discussed beneath a scaffold, and a police van already lay in wait at the juncture, its officers visible within, pressed and detached against the tinted glass windows. Further along, a pasting table was unfolded, manned by one of the many socialist groups that wanted nothing to do with the Labour Party. But she could not see her friends. She did not even think to look for any other members of the Labour party. At the last branch meeting the flyers she had passed around had received scant attention, only the occasional English smile amid the hand-wringing over Labour's electoral defeat.

She considered it equally unlikely that she would come across anyone from Syriza. They were a small group in London, mainly university students, and Amalia considered most rather superior and sour-faced. She had not told them she was in the Labour Party; they would have sneered at that. But, living in London, what was the point of being only in a Greek party? Labour was no coalition of radicals, but she could see no other party that was, and at least Labour was the traditional workers' party in Britain. That's what Bob said, and it seemed sensible enough. Although, apart from him, when it came to actual party members, the only real difference she saw with the Syriza crowd was age, not attitude. She could quite easily imagine the Greek students settling down in London in the future, becoming old Labour members. At least the actual Labour members seemed to have a bit of life in them - in the cantankerous way that the elderly often do.

Nevertheless, the parties unwittingly agreed: *'Britain isn't Greece'*, and *'Greece isn't Britain'*, both said with a forlorn expression of regret in the face of life's invincible inevitability.

Amalia arrived at the agreed corner, releasing her shoulders and lighting a cigarette. As she leant against the traffic lights, the sun bit the back of her neck. Home seemed not far away. Pulling her sunglasses from atop her Aegean tussle, she breathed smoke into the bright blue sky. Helmets turned under scaffolding, heads pressed against tinted windows, and a young man at the socialist table considered giving her his leaflet.

She did not need to look: it was either there, or it was not. Male regard did not upset her as it seemed to upset so many in this land. It was something natural. If Geraldine or Simi had been present she would have felt uncomfortable. But for now she was free from the unsolicited indignity her Northern European comrades presumed of her.

The Greeks are not known for their punctuality. So when the others finally arrived she made sure to boast to them, one by one, about how empty The City was early on a Saturday morning. They dithered over the positioning of the trestle table for some time. Someone forgot to bring sign-up sheets, and so Amalia had to improvise one with a page torn from her notebook. They spread their banner and pinned their posters to the table legs, and arranged and rearranged their books and pamphlets and *Revolutionary Newspapers*. Two of them went off to scout for the arrival of the coaches that were carrying protesters into London that morning from all around the country.

They waited. The street was deserted. Occasionally a pedestrian passed by without stopping, glancing bemusedly at the contents of the stall and the young people who flanked it. Another group established a table. They stood by their posts, watching each other on the tumbleweed frontier.

A while later, and with traffic only a passing trickle, Amalia took some posters advertising the *Revolutionary Newspaper* to place along the route. Ross, a Scottish student in London for the weekend, accompanied her.

Ross was shy and short; shorter even than Amalia, and not the most presentable young man. His hair was an unplanned tuft; his jeans were too long and frayed at the hem, and his face - always somewhat smudged. Yet he was grave and sweet and blushed in Amalia's company. Men able to converse about the struggle of her country, beyond the usual platitudes, she was willing to extend due respect. Which was all to the good for Ross, who had not yet mastered the art of conversation beyond politics; indeed, did not know of its existence. They progressed along the Moorgate Road, fastening their posters to the feet of the granite giants.

'Did you see three billion euros was taken out of Greece this week? They say it will be five billion by Monday,' said Ross.

'Yes, well they missed the third payment this week,' said Amalia.

'Why is Tsipras still discussing with the Troika? They act for the banks, don't they? Do you think he realises that?'

'I don't know... They're demanding pension cuts,' said Amalia, 'because pensions have risen to sixteen percent of the GDP. But that's inevitable if you make the economy collapse by a quarter!'

'So the pensions haven't increased a penny?' asked Ross. 'Like fish in a shrinking pond.'

'Not only have they not increased, they've been halved! It's like a shrinking fish in a pond that's shrinking even faster... The Troika are as bad as these feminists, no? Who complain about men sitting with their legs open when the bus service has been cut?' She let out a brassy laugh, causing Ross to blush.

'No, it's really disgusting what they're doing,' she said, becoming serious once more. 'I Skyped my mum the other day and she told me that my cousin was sacked by the supermarket on his birthday. Can you believe it? Because the minimum goes up when you're twenty-four.' They arrived at a bus shelter and stuck up a poster.

'So they fired him and got someone cheaper?' said Ross. 'Joins the fifty percent of youth without a job?'

'More like sixty. Now he and my auntie rely solely on my grandma's pension – and the Troika are trying to cut that again!'

'Ach - they're just the banks' puppets,' said Ross.

'True, but they have their own interests. The money they lend goes straight out again to pay the banks. So Greece stays in debt, but to other European countries - central banks, instead of private ones. You can see that why all the governments have a common interest in making us pay.'

She tapped a cigarette out of its box and offered one to Ross.
'You don't smoke?'
He did not, to his infinite regret.
'So is that why they're so determined to make Greece pay?'
'Yes. It's the banks, like you say.'
She crooked her neck and flicked her lighter, but the flint faltered. Looking around, she saw that the street was empty of shops.
'But it's also the example they need to set. They have to think about Spain and Portugal and Italy, and all the other countries with massive debts. If the Troika gives in to us, even a tiny bit, it'll be a big morale boost to all the other anti-austerity parties, like Podemos in Spain. They need to humiliate us, in order to send the others a clear message: "There is no alternative."'

'Aye, so why is Tsipras negotiating with them? Does he think he can get them to back down? Hasn't the Greek parliament declared the debt illegal? If that's the case, surely he has to reject the whole thing?'

'I don't know... Many say Tsipras will betray, and that he already did so when he nominated Pavlopoulous for the President in February.'

'Who's he?'

'He's a politician for the New Democracy. They're like the Tories. It's as if Tsipras was trying to show the establishment how reasonable he was. It seems so... naïve,' she said, but even as she did so, she did not entirely betray her feelings on the matter. A secret part of her still smouldered with hope.

'So what do you thinks gonna happen?' They arrived at a lamp post.

'Maybe Tsipras will give in... And then, who knows? Maybe the government will fall? Maybe Syriza will split and become another PASOK?'

'They're the Labour Party of Greece, right?'

'Yes, the same basic ideas. They have a working class tradition. They accepted the debt and carried out the cuts, and because of that were almost wiped out in the elections in January.' She fumbled the tape and it went rolling into the road. Dutifully, Ross went to fetch it and, as he did, spied a man, some way in the distance, reading one of their posters. He was about to call out to Amalia that their efforts were gaining an audience, when the man ripped their poster off the wall.

'You see that?' said Ross. 'What a prick!'

Amalia screwed her eyes. She could see that the man was deliberately walking up to each and every poster and tearing them down.

'Is that legal?' asked Ross, impotently. She could hear in his voice that he did not want a confrontation. Without saying a word she marched up the street.

The man was tall and bald and wore a dark grey square suit and thick glasses. An official badge was pinned to his pocket.

'Excuse me,' she said, as he tore at another poster. He ignored her. 'Excuse me,' she said again, 'but could you not do that?'

'You responsible for this?' he said, turning to her. She was responsible enough not to answer that.

'It's not hurting anyone. Why can't you leave them be?' Ross caught up to them.

'You know this is City of London property? Look at the marks your tape has made – it's criminal damage. You could be fined up to a hundred pounds a poster.' Amalia's heart jumped as she calculated the cost of the ten or fifteen posters they had stuck up. She could hardly believe it. In Athens such a demand would be inconceivable - it was the posters that stopped the buildings from falling down.

'Are you serious?' demanded Amalia.

'That's ridiculous,' piped up Ross.

'I don't make the rules,' he revealed, 'but if these are yours, miss, I would think seriously about taking the rest down.'

'But what harm is it doing? It's just a few posters. They're for the demonstration.'

But she saw he was paid to be impervious to reason. He said he did not know anything about a demonstration, all he knew was that "rules were rules". She pleaded with him freedom of expression; she pleaded democracy; she pleaded good will and natural justice and gave a solemn promise to return and take them down once the protest was over. But he was overruled, whatever his private opinion on the matter. The truth was that long ago his private opinion had conformed to his wage. How else could he carry out his job?

Embarrassed for Ross and his limp solidarity, she conceded defeat. It appeared that free speech relied on a human consensus, and some unseen individual had wielded a veto.

'They'd better not be up in fifteen minutes,' said the grey square man, taking his leave. They returned to the stall, but left the posters up. The man did not return.

3

Both Jeremy and Corbyn were shocked by the booing the other candidates had received upon refusing to criticise the benefit cuts. Corbyn disagreed with them, of course, but he could not condone such treatment. After all, they were only stating what they absolutely believed in.

Even their insane support for weapons of mass destruction, Britain's 'Trident' nuclear submarine system, did not warrant the hisses and calls of 'Shame!' according to Corbyn. There was no need for unkindness in politics, and all the unnecessary fall-out it caused.

Returning by train from Stevenage, Corbyn revealed to Jeremy his anxiety that the media would use the behaviour of his supporters against them. Jeremy offered no sympathy. He had found the whole affair most refreshing.

'It's not as if you planted them there, old boy. It was the honest reaction of the audience.'

'It was unhelpful. If our supporters behave like that, how can we reach out to Andy and Yvette - even Liz - and hope to change their... narrative?'

'So you'll support their right to say whatever they want, but you won't do the same for your own supporters?'

Jeremy recalled with glee the look on their faces when the booing had begun. He tactfully omitted to mention the same look he had seen written across his friend's face.

'Every time something like that happens,' said Corbyn, 'it just pushes them further from us. If we want to get through to them, we need to demonstrate a new politics - a kinder politics. Perhaps in that way we can help make them understand that the Left isn't so bad; that it isn't so childish and unreasonable as some... would lead them to believe.'

Jeremy laughed about it all the way back to London, mistaking Corbyn's earnest misgivings for irony. But Corbyn only sulked.

Toward the journey's end, Jeremy straightened up. He told his friend that he mustn't be so sensitive. With genuine concern, he said he would be mad to go through the next three months worrying about what the media thought:

'We've thirty years of transgression on our permanent record,' he said. 'They're hardly going to make us head boy! You say we need a new, kinder politics, and that we need to shift the "moral narrative", all that nonsense you pick up off Diane no doubt.' Corbyn wrinkled his nose. 'Well, that's the first time I've been to a Labour hustings and heard booing... no – I'm serious this time. Those people who booed today did so because of you – and it's not a bad thing! Forget the "new", "kinder" politics. That was a new kind of politics. It was angry and frustrated; demanding real answers – and you were the reference point. You were like the rod around which the solution crystallises.'

Corbyn did not answer. He was not sure he wanted to be a rod. Neither was he sure he that he wanted a solution crystallising around him.

In any case, they were agreed on one point: the nuclear question. Corbyn admitted that the other candidates' position was quite insane, and Jeremy conceded that, nonetheless, it was still a point of view

Outside King's Cross they hopped on their tandem and rode down Bloomsbury Street, passing the British Museum and Leicester Square, and came out beside the National Gallery. There they alighted, walking their bike the rest of the way.

The noise could be heard before it was seen: A vast flotilla, rolling out of the Strand and down Whitehall toward the river. They walked across Trafalgar Square and merged with it. The giant trade union balloons pulled at the chains of their Lilliputian escorts, towering high above the banners and placards:

"Education is not a commodity", "Defy Tory Rule", "Is this the queue for the food bank?"

The hairs on Jeremy's forearms prickled. He could see the banner of the Green Party; Save Legal Aid; Goths against Austerity; Disabled People against Cuts. He saw the banner of the National Gallery workers, who were at that moment in a prolonged struggle, and the firefighters' banner with their slogan:

"We save people, not banks."

There were socialist groups, environmental groups, and local union banners from every corner of England and Wales (the Scots were holding a separate demonstration in Glasgow). Even the purple flag of Spain's Podemos was on display. Greek flags, rainbow flags, red and black, and red flags; all flew in the afternoon sun, and the roar echoed for miles.

Marching were those who had not succumbed to the centuries-old inertia, despite the derisory quarter of the vote their rulers had tried to saddle on them. Corbyn could not help feeling a little satisfied, and wondered whether they could be heard in Buckingham Palace. The organisers had expected eighty thousand, but it felt far larger.

Many banners, many grievances. Yet throughout the demonstration they hardly saw sign of the Labour Party. One or two youngsters in tweed and leather elbow-patches were leafleting for the campaign; stalwart young members of John's following. But no one for the other candidates appeared to have bothered. It made Corbyn nervous.

The whistles and kettle drums made it difficult for Corbyn to be heard among the old friends that he met, and the new ones he made along the way. Many came over to shake hands and have their photo taken with them. Some said they had listened to them on the radio that morning, and often they were cheered for managing to get onto the ballot sheet and 'making a go of it'.

The noise-making novelties irritated Jeremy. He said they drowned out the political songs and slogans. But he conceded that the salesmen that fed the edges of the movement were part of its development. One day, when the millions of voices became a voice of millions, they would put away the rattle.

4

Parliament Square heaved. So many people stopped to speak to Jeremy and Corbyn that they found it impossible to fight their way toward the front. They decided to abandon their Tandem, locking it to the railing outside the Red Lion pub.

The sun was high, and beat down among the ever more tightly pressed bodies, causing Corbyn to feel quite faint. Jeremy found him some water, after which he improved a little.

Most of those who shared the stage gave very 'democratic' speeches, in the sense that they sounded much the same. They were the victims of austerity, re-telling the familiar crimes of the Tories, crimes of which the gathered assembly was well acquainted.

'It has its place,' said Jeremy, 'but where are the proposals? Where are the raised horizons? That's where we'll have to come in.' Corbyn merely smiled and sipped his water.

The highlight for Jeremy was when a soap actress gave a very rousing speech, mentioning socialism for the first time that afternoon.

'At last!' said Jeremy, clapping vigorously. 'You see old boy, if she can say it, then...' He turned to Corbyn, but his friend was not there.

Moments earlier Corbyn had wriggled out to the side and was now walking the long way round, tracing the perimeter of Parliament Square, where the crowd was less dense. In the context of the crowd few recognised him. Some approached, but this time he did not stop. Aggravated by the heat from above, and the ground-heat below, he could only apologise and fiddle his watch strap and explain that he was needed on stage.

Jeremy searched with growing concern for his friend's welfare, worrying that the heat might have overcome him. He tried hopping above the ranks of shoulders that held him tightly in place. He paddled in circles.

'Corbyn! Corbyn!' he called out, concerned the current might have dragged his friend under. He dived beneath the surface, but saw nothing.

Now out of the thick of it, Corbyn was feeling greatly improved, making progress on the other side of the square. He found the back of the stage, ascended the clanking metal steps, and loitered at the top until a small, concentrated lady with a Geordie accent caught sight of him. They had been worried sick, she said. Taking his damp hand, she guided him toward the front and did not let go until it was time for him to speak. He found most this most distracting, and all the while could not concentrate on his opening remarks, only on his oily palm pressed against hers.

Two-hundred and fifty thousand were in attendance, she told him. *Surely it couldn't be as much as all that?* Corbyn looked down and saw that the Geordie lady was smiling with every muscle in her body.

He felt confused, and somewhat pitied her. It was not as if it would amount to anything. One could concede it was the right time, but it was in the wrong place. It was outside the party, like the movement against the Iraq war had been all those years ago. Then, before he knew it, the sound system was blaring out his name to the cheers of the crowd.

Jeremy was submerged beneath the waves at that moment, and did not hear Corbyn being introduced. Stumbling through an opening, he came across a small stall. It had been set up hours before, judging by its position, before the rising tide had rendered it inoperably swamped by the crowd. A girl he recognised stood beside it, a spiral galaxy burned across her cheeks; long strands of seaweed shining on the surface of the water.

Corbyn searched the horizon. The armada was still pouring down Whitehall, twenty heads wide. The square seemed to have grown ten times larger, and the Palace of Westminster, to his right, diminished as a result.

He walked to the microphone. All at once, two-hundred thousand apprehensions fell upon the little grey man, stood on the edge of his precipice. He began:

> 'Friends... Friends, first of all, demonstrations are very important; they are part of our political process. And I say thank you to each and every one of us who has come here today to say: It is possible to have a different world.'

The sound system doubled throughout the square, and the crowd cheered. Jeremy, having become engaged in conversation with Amalia, had quite forgotten his search for his friend when his voice suddenly amplified across the square.

'There he is!' Amalia laughed at the old man's enthusiasm.

> 'We are giving the message that the austerity we've had for the past five years is not necessary.' Then he raised his voice: 'Hands up anyone here who created the banking crisis in 2008.' His eyes scanned the crowd for the inevitable joker. 'There's one hand over there' he said, pointing. *Is that Jeremy?* 'There must be a merchant banker over there somewhere.'

Jeremy appeared to be shouting something, but Corbyn could not make it out. He continued:

'No... Was the banking crisis created by nurses, by teachers, by school workers, by street cleaners, by the unemployed, by the disabled, by the homeless?'

Jeremy and Amalia joined in the singular cries flying off the surface of the water. Then the mass behind them boiled over into a singular, unadulterated:

"No!"

'Of course it was not. You know it was not. It was created by an unregulated banking system that sucked up billions of pounds of our money in order to... survive in this system.' More applause.

'What he means is that we should socialise the banks. If you want to regulate them, you have to separate them from capitalism and take them over, because you can't control what you don't own.' Amalia quite agreed.

'Initially, the nationalisation of the banks was good and the right thing to do.'

'Initially?'

'There is now no case whatsoever for now selling off RBS shares - at a loss - that somebody can make a greater profit out of our money in the first place.' Applause rang round.

'When was there a case? There's no case for selling them off at a profit, either!' Jeremy turned to Amalia, apologetically. *'He's not the best communicator.'* She understood.

'But as soon as the coalition government was elected in 2010 it took an axe to the welfare budget; it took an axe to the local government budget; it took an axe to all the other areas of social spending. It privatised, it cut. As a result, what has happened? One million people in Britain use food banks regularly, and we are the fourth richest country in the world. Is that necessary? Is it right?'

"No!" roared the crowd.

'Absolutely not. Not even if we were the fourth poorest. Not here; nor in Tasmania; nor in Timbuktu!'

'Of course it's not necessary, and of course it is not right. Inequality has got worse and worse...'

To his surprise, Corbyn was finding the crowd quite worked up. It was infectious - and distracting. *Glasses. Notes. Ah, yes.*

'The hundred richest people in this country now own the

equivalent of the wealth of thirty percent of the entire population. That is ghastly inequality on an industrial scale! And if these next rounds of cuts go through - and I'm sure the government intends to put them through - then the situation is going to get worse and worse.

'I travel around the country a great deal, at all these debates and hustings and so on. And everywhere, you meet people that are begging on the street; you meet people who are sleeping on the street; you meet people working zero-hours contracts unable to make ends meet, getting in to benefit problems because they don't know what their income's going to be.'

Corbyn stepped back for a moment and the square called out to him. It was as if the thousands and thousands at his feet were feeding him his speech like an auto-queue. Taken by their enthusiasm, he shook his head violently:

'Is it really morally right, or just, that anyone should be forced to sleep on the streets of this country at any time?!'

"*No!*"

'Instead of extolling the virtues of the ever-rising prices in the property market, particularly in London, I've got a different idea!'

His voice had changed and become commanding. He no longer felt himself - he was not himself. He was the yawning mouth of an awakening giant, through which a terrible voice was approaching like the trains arriving at the platforms beneath Westminster. Jeremy was impressed. Corbyn was impressed.

'One: Build. Council. Housing. For. Those. People. In. Need!' The crowd yelled, their cheers carving definition upon him. 'Two: Regulate the private rented sector.'

Then, ever so politely, the momentum shifted to clapping.

'*Regulate?*'

'We're spending eleven billion pounds a year on in-work benefits subsidising low wages. We're spending at least twenty-five billion pounds a year subsidising landlords charging extortionate rents in some parts of the country. We need a different narrative... and a different story...'

He felt their enthusiasm dampen.

'What tale would you tell them?' Jeremy bit the air, as if something had caught in his throat.

> 'So I say this: The people who marched in this square in the 1850s were the People's Charter; didn't achieve very much that day. They were dismissed as out of date, out of time and irrelevant. Within fifty years, we had a national insurance system.'

'Oh no - he's lost his place. He always rambles on about the past when he loses his place.' Amalia grimaced.

> 'Within twenty years, we had a national education system. Within seventy years, we had council housing. Within a hundred years we had a universal health service.'

'A hundred years?' said Jeremy, and not quietly.

'Talk about growing your way out of the crisis - he wants us to evolve out of it!'

'I think he's just trying to say that things can change, no?' said Amalia, giving her MP the benefit of the doubt. But Jeremy was not so sure. *'He never mentions 1926. He never talks about 1917 or May '68.'*

> 'Those people were real visionaries. And so when people tell me that the only thing that's practical and what matters in politics is being fiscally responsible, paying off the debt, and paying off the debt in record quick time, I say this:'

'Give us a hundred years?'

> 'The objectives for any society should be: eliminating homelessness, eliminating poverty.' Long cheers let out.
> 'Reducing the levels of inequality, investing in productive work and productive jobs.'

Jeremy yawned and looked about him. His friend may well have been advocating tax-and-spend capitalism, but he had to admit, they were hanging on his every word. He supposed that was only to be expected after so many years of drought.

> 'But we are short-changed when the media tell us that all that matters is finding somebody to blame. So, UKIP comes along and says: "A plague on all your houses, blame every migrant that's come here." No! I stand with those people that have come to this country, worked, contributed as part of our society.'

'And the ones who can't find work, and the students - he means them,

too.' Amalia smiled politely. She did not work, but her parents certainly made a contribution, if that's what the grey man on stage meant.

> 'That would be the humanitarian and decent response to those poor people who are victims of war that are dying in the Mediterranean trying to reach a place of safety.
>
> 'I am not prepared to join in a campaign of Benefits Street and attacking the so-called benefit scroungers. I want us to stand up, as brave people did in the 1920s and 1930s, and said: "We want a state that takes responsibility; a community that takes responsibility for everybody that ensures...'

His eyes went wild and his face pink, and then he said with real muster:

> '...that nobody is destitute!" We each care for all, everybody caring for everybody else. I think it's called socialism!'

The crowd roared with what was by far the biggest cheer of the day. *'Now that got a response!'* Amalia smiled in agreement. *'Well done, old boy, well done.'*

> 'And the last point I want to make is this. We've all been in this square many times, to oppose wars, to oppose nuclear weapons, and to oppose so many other things.'

He saw arrayed in front of him many friends and family members exchanging secret glances. As he spoke the words, it occurred to him how young their faces were. He struggled to spy a grey hair.

> 'The world is not an easy place, the levels of injustice are appalling, the levels of greed are almost overwhelming. Are we going to solve any of those problems by spending a hundred billion pounds on new nuclear weapons? Are we going to solve any problems by global reach of our defence capability to start wars everywhere in the world? No. Let's try to rebalance ...'

'Good grief!'

> '...rethink our society, a world at peace and human rights, social justice for all at home...'

'And abroad. He means abroad, too.' Jeremy glanced at Amalia, who maintained a polite smile.

'...but above all, remember those who came before us; we stand on their shoulders those people that achieved so much for all of us, for education, for health, for housing. Let's go forward with confidence... and optimism.

'This anti-austerity movement *is a movement*. It's not - absolutely not - about individuals, and absolutely not about ambitious individuals. This is about a social movement of all of us that can re-change our society into something good rather than something that is cruel and divided. You all know the way forward. Thank you!'

Applause blew in from farthest reaches of the square and carried him off the stage.

"Jeremy! Jeremy!" cried swathes of the crowd.

As he walked down off the podium Corbyn's follicles burst at the base of his skull and spread across his scalp, nestling in his inner ear. Endorphins streamed across his brain, and he shook many hands he did not remember.

5

Corbyn was still riding high as they cycled home. He asked Jeremy what he thought of it all.

'All very good. The mood was clear to see.'

'It was jolly good, wasn't it?' said Corbyn, somewhat dreamily.

'But you need to think through this housing position.'

'Why do you say that?'

'Well, yes, a crash plan of council housing – can't disagree with you there, old boy. They're much needed, especially among young families.'

'And building them to meet that need would create thousands of skilled jobs and offer thousands of young people high quality apprenticeships. What's not to like?'

'You don't say anything about the hundreds of thousands of empty homes. You'd have to build fewer houses if we seized the ones that are already built and just lying empty.'

'But what about all the apprenticeships?'

'We shouldn't just employ people to dig holes and fill them in. We should have an economy geared to what society needs. There are one-and-a-half million people waiting for council housing, and you'll reduce it to near nothing if you do it that way. And it would create jobs, too. Think of all the renovation work a project like that would require.'

'You do realise those houses are owned by other people, don't you?'

'Yes, by rich people, more and more, and corporations who have nowhere to park their capital. Safety deposit boxes for the wealthy; items of speculation for the Conservative Artists.'

'They'll go potty if we start raising ideas like that. It would be… an infringement of property rights.'

'Yes, that's right. But so what? In their eyes your rental regulations amount to the same thing. Telling them what they can and can't charge on their properties – they'd say it's an offence to their liberties. And they'd be right; it would be a trespass against capitalist law. But if you attempt to police the landlords against "misdemeanours", you'll need a bureau of inspectors so large it'll have to have its own post code. And even then, you'd fail.'

'So you think we shouldn't regulate them?'

'You know what I'm saying - if you try to muzzle a crocodile, you'll end up between its teeth. We should say we'll abolish landlordism from day one.'

'Don't you think that would make some people rather unhappy?'

'Undoubtedly. But I think there'd be many more who'd be over the moon. London tenants pay seventy percent of their income on rent. In the rest of the country it's almost half. It's a monstrous fact, considering the pile of bricks you live in costs less than five percent of wages to maintain. Can you imagine? These parasites complain about a lack of demand in the economy, while they are sucking that kind of purchasing power out of it through rent. Evictions in London are the highest they've been for five years - and there are already twenty thousand homeless in the capital. And for prospective home owners the cost is ten times the annual wage – for a house that has already been built!'

'Ah, well, now that is a serious question,' said Corbyn. 'Surely the laws of supply and demand determine that if we build more houses, the price will go down?'

'Yes, and with the same argument you could justify giving council tenants the right to buy. That also widens the supply for the market.'

'Well, I know Thatcher didn't have the best intentions, but it certainly proved very popular... Look, we're not out to promise the moon. We're campaigning for a kinder, more equal society. Don't you think it would be kinder and more equal if, as well as allowing council tenants the right to buy, we allow private tenants that right, too? Then we deal with your landlords, but in a way that's more... digestible - for public opinion.'

Jeremy paused, glancing back at his friend for a moment with suspicious eyes as they bumped along an empty cobble-stone lane.

'I take my hat off to you. You're quite devious when you put your mind to it. You want to take a well-known Tory policy, despised by the labour movement, and turn it against the small landlords?'

'Yes, I suppose, only more reasonably put. What do you think?'

'I think it's awful. Few tenants will have the cash to take it up. Landlords will push up rents to recoup as much as their mortgage as possible, for fear of being forced to sell. You'll mobilise the entire landlord class against you, while leaving them a free hand to keep milking their tenants to fund their war chest. And to boot, you'll foster the provincial Englishman's fantasy about his home being his castle. Yet it is devious, in a completely reckless sort of way.'

By the time they returned home, several miles of fresh evening air had passed through Corbyn's lungs, cooling him considerably.

'I mean, I suppose it was just the Left we saw today, wasn't it? Doesn't necessarily fit the wider mood, really... but at least you can see, undoubtedly, some people are willing to protest.'

'You think the 'Left' is two-hundred thousand strong?' said Jeremy. 'I don't think so. Ten thousand, at most. And did you see how young the crowd was? There were more than the usual activists out there. It was a wider layer. And it's just the tip of the iceberg. Each one of them will know four or five people who feel the same - and there are more besides that.'

'Yes, but is it enough?'

'One step at a time, eh? You're not running for Prime Minister - yet.'

***

Throughout the course of June, fifty-five thousand travelled across the sea to seek refuge in Europe.

CHAPTER 7
OXI

1

In the days following the June 20th demonstration angry protests filled Syntagma Square outside the Greek parliament. The Syriza government promised the Troika that it would tax the poor; that it would tax the islands; that it would keep the programme of privatisations; that it would increase pension contributions and raise retirement to sixty-seven. However, they also proposed to raise corporation tax, as well as a one-off tax on companies. All told, it amounted to eight billion euros of austerity - three-quarters of which Syriza said the poor would pay. Yet the Troika was unmoved.

The Communists demonstrated. So did the pensioners. Even supporters of the government demonstrated, speaking out openly against their Prime Minister.

Amalia's father told her that support for the government was falling rapidly; that the negotiations were confusing people and that they should never have begun. But her mother kept the faith. Each evening she lit a candle for Tsipras and a room in Belgium where the light did not enter. Tsipras will deliver, she said.

Amalia could do little else but follow events as they unfolded. She had to agree with her father: What kind of negotiations were these, when one side gives all, and the other, nothing? Yet, and despite everything, she found that she worried for Tsipras, and Varoufakis his finance minister who accompanied him on his trip to Belgium. Strung with tension, she also hoped for them. More often she was haunted by the shame of national capitulation. But then she reasoned: Why spend five months negotiating an 'odious, illegitimate and illegal debt' (as parliament had determined it) if you were just going to give in? It had to mean that they would not give up. They had no choice but to stand their ground. The Troika were fools for thinking otherwise.

Within days of the demonstrations the Troika rejected the Greek government's proposal, returning the offer struck through with the desperate red lines of a teacher at the end of his tether. *Must do better.* The comments in the margin demanded that the workers and pensioners pay more and pay faster, and that taxes on the 'business community' were to be dropped.

Then Tsipras did something Amalia did not expect. He declared the talks at an end. The Troika's terms would be put to the Greek people. A referendum was announced.

The next day the stock market closed and an indefinite bank holiday was declared by the government. The day after that the Greek parliament approved Tsipras' referendum.

Fresh hope overtook Amalia. The interminable sapping inertia was broken, and all seemed flooded with expectation. Tsipras had saved the day, and he was wonderful. He had understood that the people must be the measure of all things. Now they would give their answer in the language of Greek democracy, and it would be historical. Her mother had been right all along.

Studying became impossible, and Amalia was forever leaving the library for cigarettes and coffee in order to check the news on her phone, to the point where her throat became quite sore. Her British friends took an interest, but as they did a partition was placed between them, and she longed to return home. Amalia's country was about to be washed clean and only once would she be able to place her feet in the flood.

Once, before the beginning of a study group, she overheard a fellow Greek student confess to her professor her shame about what was happening, and then Amalia felt an angry shame for her. On Facebook, Greeks would tell her she had no idea what was going on, and that her opinions meant nothing because she was not there. It was an argument she could not answer. They were Greeks living in Britain more often than not, and their concern over her worthless opinion should have been all the answer she needed. Yet she felt she must go home.

2

Following the announcement of the referendum, Corbyn added his name to an open letter asking the Prime Minister to call a European-wide conference tasked to *'agree debt cancellation for Greece and other countries that need it.'*

He signed the document without consulting Jeremy, annoying his friend, and when Jeremy saw it published in *The Guardian*, it led to a falling out.

The letter was signed by, among others, John and Diane, the general secretary of the TUC, and the general secretaries of both the Unite and GMB trade unions. It explained that debt reductions were to be *'funded by the banks and financial speculators who were the real beneficiaries of the bail-outs'*, that austerity was causing *'injustice and poverty in Europe and across the world'*, and urged the United Nations to create fair rules for dealing with the debt crisis in order to send a signal to *'the banks and financiers that we won't keep bailing them out for reckless lending.'*

Jeremy told Corbyn he thought it was foolish. To appeal to the Prime Minister - Britain's champion of austerity - to call for an end to austerity in Greece! It was like calling a conference of crocodiles to discuss the merits of vegetarianism.

What's more, such a debt conference had already existed for many years and was fully backed by the Prime Minister. It was called the Troika.

Corbyn did not understand why Jeremy was so offended. It was an entirely reasonable demand, and with historical precedent. The London debt conference of 1952 agreed to write-off half of Germany's war debts, including some still left over from the Treaty of Versailles - and on very favourable terms too.

It was a misleading comparison said Jeremy, and was nothing more than a recycled version of the same old argument he made about the British debt. After World War Two Britain had a far greater debt than today - twice what the entire economy could produce in a year - yet it was paid off without the austerity currently in place. In fact, the Labour government had created the NHS at the same time.

It was a misleading comparison, said Jeremy, and was nothing more than a recycled version of the same old argument he made about the British debt. After World War Two Britain had a far greater debt than today - twice what the entire economy could produce in a year - yet it was paid off without the austerity currently in place. In fact, the Labour government had created the NHS at the same time. But he said that what Corbyn always omitted to mention, was that the USA profited so much out of the Second World War that it was able to accumulate half the world's gold reserves in Fort Knox, and was therefore quite prepared to bankroll Britain and Western Europe against the Soviet Union. It bore no resemblance to today; the Americans were just as much in hock. And what about the little detail of the post-war boom? Twenty-five years of historically unprecedented growth and full-employment? World War provided the 'creative destruction', as today's economists so delicately put it, of factories and people demanded by 1930s capitalism. For them the war's most important role wasn't the defeat of Fascism, but the destruction it caused, and the profitable fields for investment that were created as a consequence, leading to the long and virtuous post-war upswing.

Jeremy conceded that if Britain was making money hand over fist, and so was the whole world, then capitalism could probably burn away the present debt without the need for austerity. But that was not the case, and Corbyn would just have to face facts. Besides, it was not his job to provide solutions for capitalism. It was his job to overturn it.

Corbyn countered: If the Greek people vote against the austerity in the coming referendum, then the EU would be forced to convene such a debt conference.

But the EU did not respect democracy, said Jeremy; one only had to consider the Treaty of Lisbon to understand that.

In any case, what most annoyed Jeremy was that by signing up to this useless letter he was reinforcing the illusion that if Cameron,

Merkel, Schauble and all the rest of them were really willing to offer debt relief then it could be done. As if it were a matter of personalities, or even policies, when the truth was that all they could do was represent the system's will.

If they were to act to the contrary, Jeremy explained, it would provoke a stampede among the poor that would completely undermine their allies' efforts in southern Europe who had just spent the last five years shoving austerity down their people's throats. It was Utopian, just like all his talk about the cuts being 'ideological' - as if the crisis was just the product of the Tories' vindictiveness, and not a worldwide consequence of the contradictions of capitalism. And if he had wanted to write an effective letter he might have posted it to the right address. Not Downing Street or those eunuchs at the UN, but the Maximus Mansion in Athens, pointing out to Tsipras that he did not need a referendum; that he already had a mandate; and which he should have acted on months ago.

'He needs to take over all the monopolies,' said Jeremy, 'and big companies, and put them into the hands of the people, in the name of democracy - real democracy, that does not loiter at the threshold of the economy, but crosses over it and brings it under its control.'

But the letter was written, Corbyn was not going to write another. That would only cause confusion. The conversation finished abruptly. Soon after, Corbyn took to his bed. The same off-colour sense of sickness that had taken hold of him during the June 20th demo seemed to have returned. In the days following Tsipras' announcement of the referendum it developed into a fever.

Laura made him a bed on the living room sofa so that he could keep up with the news. He found it all most frustrating. There were so many hustings and trade union conference to attend, as well as the many Greek solidarity demonstrations that were now being called. But whenever he felt like he might be on the mend, he quickly fell back upon himself, and Jeremy had to attend to his duties without him.

3

There are six million Greeks of working age, three hundred thousand of which are scattered far and wide by the fair winds of free trade. In those days in late June many looked long toward Athens, considering whether they might return. The referendum offered no postal vote, reducing most to watchful and helpless observers.

Amalia was among the fortunate. Her family had lived comfortably in the years before the crisis, and once it arrived the economy had furnished them with enough fat to cushion its worst excesses.

Her father was a kindly old man who doted on his three daughters. Even though he ran a small business, his roots were to be found in the Communist side of that historical divide that runs through Greek society, and even Greek families - a divide arising from the partisan resistance movement against the Nazis, watered by the military dictatorship of the sixties and seventies. As June became July, and with her father's assistance, Amalia secured a flight to Athens.

It was a flight was unlike any she had experienced, apparent from the moment she arrived at the departure gate. Absent were the British, Germans and French that occupied her country each summer. The flight was completely Greek.

All talked, not that that was unusual, Greek people happen to enjoy each other's company. What was different was the way they talked. The only subject on offer was politics, and not the haughty, cringe-worthy politics of the campus. They spoke of politics with abandon; with improvisation; with meaning. It was desperate talk, unbridled by the qualified caveats of politically educated speech.

The inward-bound flight appeared uniformly opposed to the Troika. Amalia noticed some remained quiet; the predominantly middle-aged and middle-class. But they were few, and sat quietly on the edge of the flight and passed unnoticed while the young talked about everything under the Greek sun. Among them the biggest divide was to be found not between the No of OXI and the Yes of NAI, but within the OXI itself.

Many sympathised with the Prime Minister's point of view. *"He's trying his best; one should not expect miracles overnight..." "Varoufakis has a plan — he will sort the Germans out..."* "Germans" had become synonymous with "Troika". *"How could they not allow concessions? There must be some give and take - surely we've more than paid these past five years - Greece is bled white, can they not see? You cannot get blood from a stone..."*

Others doubted the government: *"Why did Tsipras make a coalition with those nationalists, Anel?" "They want to kick us out of Europe!" "At home they say Syriza is nowhere to be seen -why do they not organise assemblies in the Squares, as in 2011?" "The baker spends five days sifting the flour!" "Greece has always been weak because it was dominated by the Ottomans and the British..." "We should go back to the Drachma..."* Amalia was not sure about that. What difference could a new currency make?

"With our own currency we can devalue and compete against the German and the French. Now we have no independence. It's dishonourable..." How can you make money 'cheap'? asked Amalia. It seemed absurd. By printing more, came the answer. It sounded like peasant magic to her.

'Greeks prefer to swat flies than compete with the Germans,' said one young man. That raised the temperature in the crowded aisle. Eyeballs rolled, and it was suggested that he had bought into the hatred that the foreign media was actively cultivating against the Greek people.

'Malacas,' said a young woman, 'the Germans work seven hundred hours a year less than Greek workers.'

As Amalia kneeled on her seat and gripped the back, she occasionally saw quiet eyes following the mid-air debate, only to look away when her eyes met theirs.

'What I mean,' the young man qualified, 'is that Greece is corrupt. Of course the people want to work.' But everyone knew that.

'You think Britain is any different? What about the MPs and their expenses?' said Amalia. They all agreed she had a point. But no one did corruption like the Greeks, with the possible exception of the Italians.

'There are worse off countries. The problem is the people expect too much. They can't accept that Greece is a third-world country now,' said the young man, attempting to assail the debate once again. 'You see the people lived beyond their means. Now they are too ashamed to show that they are poor. It is the classic peasant mentality; born with trousers and ashamed to be undressed!'

Amalia had heard the same argument made about the Brits and their Eastern European tomato pickers. She supposed it existed in every country in one form or another, as long as assholes like this had tongues to speak. *The exile, superior, singing songs outside the circle of the dance.*

She thought back to her high school days, pleased to find she could hold her own amid the in-flight assembly. She could not have imagined such boldness on her part then. Many were impressed with her among the critics of Syriza, while others were confused and asked how she could be a member of a party that she criticized.

4

Days had passed and Amalia was back in Athens, or rather, its outskirts. Her parents lived in the foothill suburbs and were isolated enough for her mother to insist on driving her to the metro station.

Alone on the platform she waited. Her younger sisters had already gone to town to join the protest. She had arranged to meet them later. It was evening and it was quiet, far quieter than Athens proper, and all that could be heard were the grasshoppers. A few OXI posters were visible here and there. There were hardly any NAIs - few were willing to risk open association with the Troika. But they existed, indoors, out of the sun - her mother assured her.

All the family had been actively campaigning for the OXI. Her mother even had OXI t-shirts printed for them, and had handed Amalia hers proudly upon greeting her at the airport. It was proof to her daughter that even though she lived far away, she was not forgotten, and that her family were always with her in spirit.

'It has been easy!' her mother had protested as they had driven home. They had leafleted the neighbourhood that week as part of a group organised through the free clinic where she volunteered and, aside from a man who pulled over to shout at them from his BMW, the responses had been encouraging. People approached them upon seeing their t-shirts, embracing them and asking questions and saying silly things that betrayed their excitement. It was true that her mother's brother had been beaten up by the Golden Dawn in Thessaloniki, but not seriously, and that was hardly typical. In truth the Fascists were a small sect despised by the workers, despite the disproportionate attention gifted them by the media.

Amalia politely declined to wear her t-shirt, but as she waited on the platform it certainly felt liberating to have discarded the denim and socks and slipped back into clothes that made her feel a woman. The greatest wonder of summer was when the sun lowered in the sky, and she could pass through the evening in nothing but a flowing dress and sandals.

The English anaemia had been quickly lifted following immediate and dedicated time on the garden sun lounger. Now she was dark syrup, for the most part. She wore a full-length skirt that was light and shadowed her form, and a sleeveless black top into which her freckled embers naped. She wore beads around her neck, and a small leather purse hung off one shoulder. In their sandals her feet-fingers stung against the ground heat, having not fully come to terms with the new terrain.

When the train arrived it was near-empty. As it trundled toward the centre she watched the people enter the refrigerated carriage with relief. *Some will vote NAI even though they hate the Troika, out of fear.*

Her mother talked with disdain of the middle-class hens that surrounded her in the foothills, but she too was a victim of the TV channels that gripped suburbia, and so set her on edge that she dared not desert the box even on this most hopeful of nights. It was apparent she was smoking far more than the usual forty-a-day.

As the train pulled in, Monastiraki station swelled. Her plan was to see Athens a little before heading to Syntagma. As the escalators funnelled her onto ground level, a chant broke out among the evening commuters:

"Ock-ee! Ock-ee!"

In Monastiraki square battalions of youth and Greek flags swayed. They did not loiter long, but quickly marched out into the street's night. Around the perimeter of the square old people sat and talked in the open as always, and the restaurants continued to serve up Souvlaki to the few tourists who had not abandoned Athens to its fate. Here the OXI posters piled high and, while there were some queues at the cash machines, they were not as long as Amalia had been led to believe.

Outside Monastiraki Square the streets were well-kept for the foreigners who climbed the Parthenon at any time of day. But soon Athens closed in on her as she followed the flow, re-absorbing that which she could not retain: the decline of her home city, shockingly expeditious in the short time she had been away. Her mind's eye tended only to a fairer Athens. Yes, a Labyrinthine white sprawl, but a sprawl unbowed, a sprawl unstressed. A sprawl that had dignity. Each time she returned she re-learned the truth from the crumbled houses and shuttered shops and formerly prosperous ladies and gentlemen picking their way through the garbage. Each time she returned the streets had slipped and the paint had peeled some more; and the odour of burnt wood, resident everywhere, had climbed higher above the dry-cracked walls stitched together by posters; and the black burn marks shone like creeping bruises along the unlit side streets.

She weaved her way through the dim for some time. Then, hearing the chattering of a stream someway off, she followed it to the flow of Ermou Street, where the window-dressing reappeared.

She stepped into the stream. She was carried along, past the ancient Byzantine church of Panaghia Kapnikarea, flood-lit against the night sky.

As she drifted the street began to pack and its white water echo against the rapids of Athens' discounted central ravine. The noise grew rapidly and terribly, as if it was the Apostolos Nikolaidis on the day of the derby of the eternal enemies. A howling wind blew overhead. Black banshees of the night wailed and multiplied, horrifying and wondrous against the darkness. Alone among the densely packed shoulders Amalia could see little. She was being pulled by the sounds and even the smells of the torrent, and had lost all sense of direction. Then a critical point was reached. A word dropped, and among them and for a moment the night was expelled. Around her all was exposed in a soundless flash. The procession, charged and polarised in the night air, split the street:

"*Ock-ee! Ock-ee! Ock-ee!*"

She was no longer in a crowd, but in Hermes' crucible, forging into the night-river, wading with her brothers and sisters. Unforeseen, she was overtaken. Her eyes filled, but there was no one to turn to. A moment's desire to flee and smother herself in her mother's breast seized her, but then it loosened its grip.

She was returned. She was with her people who, seeing her, only smiled for her tears and burst upon her skin, and grasped her thighs and spine and shoulders, and the fine soft hairs on her cheeks, and did not stop shouting at the night. But all the same, they saw her. *This is what it is like.*

Hermes poured into Syntagma Square, which had become a vast ocean and into which humanity flowed upwards from the commuter drain-pipes below. Greek flags and OXI banners rocked like masts in the moonlight, and the floodlights on stage bathed all in a blue light.

"OXI, Nein, No"

read one enormous banner floating its way over the crowd, submerging hundreds beneath its wings. *"Forget it Schauble"* read another. The German finance minister was more hated than Chancellor Merkel at that moment.

Few party flags could Amalia see, and not one for Syriza. There were no Communist Party flags, of course - they were boycotting the whole thing.

As she spread into Ermou's delta, Amalia could see the space in front of the parliament where the barricades had recently been. The new government had removed them, as they promised they would.

Entering the square, Amalia pulled herself out of the rush and onto the right bank, stopping to light a cigarette. Then she walked along the shore of the mass. A little girl on the shoulders of her father smiled and cried 'OXI' at her, waving a little plastic Greek flag as they passed. She meandered up the sloping street to the monorail platform where she had agreed to meet her sisters. They were not there, and so while she waited she studied the society of the square. All along the shoreline gathered knots of people. Wily old ladies sat on the low walls in their best dresses. Young men with beards and pony tails and thick arms gathered under the citrus trees, clacking Komboloi between their fingers.

She phoned her sisters, but they did not answer. Amid the din and the rush she forgave them by text message and strolled back down the slope to the square.

To her right, a young bearded man in round spectacles stood on stage, floodlit and grasping his notes, crying at the sea. She could not make out what he was saying, but the crowd roared approval, while a giant beach ball danced before him, mocking his words. Amalia drew near a group of young people who had received word that the demonstration was a hundred-and-fifty thousand strong, and still more were marching down Ermou Street. It was without doubt the biggest show of force she had seen in her small country - at least since the occupation of the squares.

The rumours of a low showing for the NAI demonstration across town came as a surprise. The TV stations had strained so hard to associate NAI with the people's desire to stay in 'Europe'.

That they desired not to be cut adrift from the continent they had helped form was without doubt true; though if asked Amalia would have been hard-pressed to place the Europe the TV stations spoke of on a map. From the slope above the square she saw no gaps, no spaces, not even along the edge. Just a single black mass. At her back the monorail rumbled. Out they poured, pushing her onto the pavement. Then they subsided and she walked on, forgetting her sisters, drawn toward the conversations that burned all around her.

'The bourgeois want to overthrow the Syriza government!' shouted a leathery man, moustache and cigarette hanging from his mouth. 'They openly say "regime change". They think they can tell the Greek people how to vote!'

From his fury one would assume he was engaged in bitter argument, but for the uniform nodding that surrounded him.

'They say it is a choice between staying in Europe or not,' said another. 'The Europeans, the Americans, they want to demoralise us. They are mobilising all their puppets. Did you see them wheel out all the old prime ministers? Just to tell us how to vote. It makes me want to say "Fuck You" even more!'

'The Mayor tried to get our protest cancelled. We should go to city hall and surround it until he resigns!'

A young woman in a soft, clipped voice, remonstrated with her friends. She said she had given up on television months ago; now she got all her information online. She said the Greek media outlets were colluding with each other in a conspiracy of lies and sabotage against the Greek people:

'They show old ladies queuing outside cash points in South Africa and say it is here. They try to threaten us and say we will have to leave the EU if we vote OXI. They show Turks in fur coats boarding buses last winter and say they are immigrants preparing to "overrun Greece" if we leave the protection of Brussels.' A young man besides her agreed:

'There have been solidarity demonstrations,' he said. 'In London, in Frankfurt, in Brussels, in Barcelona, in Paris, but you would not hear that from the TV. It makes me so angry I just turn it off.' Athens had indeed become a wireless city, overflowing its channels.

Others mentioned the demonstrations throughout Greece and the great solidarity that existed among the OXI, something which the NAI simply did not possess. More still warned not to underestimate the NAI; that just because you could not see them, it did not mean they were not there. The opinion polls were narrowing - NAI was catching up.

A skulk of old ladies in summer dresses squatted on the low wall overlooking the square. They were discussing the health of the Prime Minister and the state of his nerves. He was a good boy, they concluded, but he needed to eat more.

'I signed the petition to bring him and the other boy back from the negotiations,' said one proudly. All good Greek boys listen to their mothers.

'He should not have negotiated in the first place,' said another. 'We elected him in January, what more does he want?' If she were Tsipras' mother she would have clipped him round the ear.

A rotund, moustachioed man turned from his ice-cream and butted in:

'And what if he loses? Then everything will go back, and it will have all been for nothing.'

'Not for nothing,' said the second old lady. 'The Troika and the NAIs might overthrow him. But then all of Greece will know that the Europeans sing the song of democracy too high.'

'If OXI wins they say the banks will take thirty percent from anyone who has more than eight thousand euros,' replied the ice-cream, melting in the evening heat.

'What do you care? You haven't got that kind of money!' said the second old lady, stretching out her spotted arms. The skulk cackled. She must have been his mother. *Tough old foxes*, thought Amalia.

Below, the square was drunk and even brutal with motion. But Amalia was assured by it. If she had been on the other side of town she could only imagine her discomfort. Here, everyone's rough thoughts and sentences were clad by their nakedness.

The bespectacled beard had finished. The solid centre broke into a roar:

"Ock-ee! Ock-ee! Ock-ee!"

We know what we don't want. That is the first step.

Further down the slope she saw an old man nodding alone at the edge of the mass. At his waist he held a newspaper. She recognised it. It was the paper her sister had often brought home. The headline read:

*"Massive No: An order to break with the Troika
and the oligarchy!"*

He was a small man, shorter than her, and so distracted by the enormity of all around him that he had quite forgotten his task. She asked for a copy, giving him a ten euro donation and a cigarette.

It turned out he did not know her sister, but all the young comrades had gone 'in there' he said, exhaling cigarette smoke and pointing to the edge of the deep.

'It's incredible. I haven't seen anything like this in forty-years. The young generation have become militants tonight.' He did not smile. His eyes were fixed, dilated by the mass, as if it were lava. She bade him farewell with the courtesy she always afforded her elders, wading into the hot human lake.

All around her people muttered in the dark. Not to each other, but as they do to their television sets. Between the speeches Greek partisan songs played, and old men cried for a past that seemed returned. They had lived under a new Junta, they said. Now there was a new revolution.

Then the protest hushed and all focused on the blinding lights of the stage. A famous actor emerged and said that the Greek people wanted Tsipras as Prime Minister, but the Troika wanted him to fall. The waves of shoulders murmured around her in agreement. She waded further from the shore, and sometimes the shoulders rose so high that for periods she could only see the actors reflected in the uttered séances of those around her.

'They are trying to remove Tsipras and Syriza from power,' said the actor, 'so other left-wing parties don't succeed in Europe - like Podemos in Spain.' Amalia added her murmur to the many.

Then Tsipras appeared, and there was the biggest murmur of all. The overlapping shoulders interlocked, focused on a single point. Tsipras distributed his words among them. They passed them from front to back, feeling each between their fingers.

He spoke of bringing democracy back to Greece and they

cheered. But when he said: *'No matter the outcome, it is a victory for democracy,'* the response was mixed. It left Amalia cold.

'No matter the outcome' sounded so defeatist - almost as if it was spoken in defiance of them. *We want a lot more than a moral victory.*

But into the cracks of his ambiguity they poured themselves, and when they did they recognised their Prime Minister easily enough. Then they embraced him as their own. Not for his soft abstracts, but for his solid stand. The ancient walls of Athens stood with him.

The square had retained the heat late into the evening, and Amalia thought she saw the light catch on a tear of sweat trickling past Tsipras' temple.

When he finished the ground moved so violently that he reached out to steady himself on the actor's shoulder. Anyone might sway after days spent beneath Brussels' fluorescent tubes, Amalia reasoned. The crowd receded, and music played, and the Prime Minister was gone.

She went with the drift and saw that her sisters had tried to call her, leaving several messages. But she felt like floating back by herself, anonymous among the receding people. Sunday was written. Like a child her excitement exploded her thoughts and re-made them, over and again, and in all directions.

The next day Amalia slept long and late. Once risen, her and her sisters talked of nothing else but the previous night, until the evening when their thoughts turned to the referendum. It was a strange day, not quite whole, and the sun went down on an Athens that hummed differently in the distance.

Into the night her mother sucked her cigarettes and shouted reports from the television screen as the girls lounged, but the news never really changed.

She did not oversleep - the old woman made sure of it - she and her three daughters arrived before the polling station opened. Many old ladies were already gathered outside.

Her sisters went home after voting, but Amalia and her mother stayed and were given blue shirts as official representatives of Syriza, to monitor the elections and count the votes at the end of the day. They carried out their duties with pride.

Later that morning various representatives of parties came, including a member of the Communist Party, who handed out a

leaflet:
> *"Against the deal of the EU and the deal of the government."*

The man looked uncomfortable and did not stay long. Despite the leaflet, it was clear that many Communist Party members and sympathisers came to vote during the day. It was also clear that there was only one way they were voting. The NAI representative showed up even later, looking even more sheepish. Often Amalia felt she could tell which way people were voting just by looking at them. OXI voters loudly proclaimed it on their way in and out, often punching the air with dignity and determination as they exited.

Others entered and left without a word, eyes darting to the sides. She suspected NAIs, but could not be sure. The OXIs, answering in the negative, acted as if they were constructing something positive - as if adding their brick to the foundations of a grand new house. And they did so in parties, with friends, with workmates and with family members. Most of all, they did so with enthusiasm, and departed the polling station with the grubby cleanliness of faces licked with hope.

Later, as Amalia and her mother counted the vote in the closed hall, remarks among the tellers soon escaped, making it clear the OXI was in front. Then their phones began to say the same thing. Across the evening Greece was lighting up.

They became emotional and doubled their counting, possessed by a single thought: that throughout the salt olive groves and snake-dry brush of their withered land, people just like them, crouched over with sore backs in echoed halls, were registering the same proud strike, ballot after ballot: OXI.

CHAPTER 8
TO THE MINERS' GALA

1

Corbyn's condition deteriorated throughout the weekend. By Sunday he was suffering cold sweats as the exit polls became known.

It was later than he had thought. Laura had left them some nibbles to snack on with the rolling reports and gone to bed. Prostrate on the couch, a pillow under his neck and a blanket to cover him, Jeremy had found Corbyn in a wretched state. Green tea and biscuits squatted beside the patient on the coffee table, but he was too far gone to swallow anything solid. It had become difficult for Corbyn to speak, so much so that he had acquired a slow blink in order to signal the affirmative. Jeremy found this altogether irritating. Occasionally Corbyn would beckon for his cup, which Jeremy suspected he could easily reach himself, but all the same he passed it to his friend as he lay there, eyes half open and mouth agape, attention periodically drawn to the sound of the coverage, yet far from able to absorb anything.

It was not as if Jeremy had no sympathy for his friend; he had suggested they both turn in and get some rest. But Corbyn insisted on rolling out the white noise, bathing within the tension points of the coverage.

Periodically, Jeremy would ask after his friend's comfort. Yet deep down a private fist of resentment was building for the man who would fall ill at such an auspicious moment - when the drama taking place on the other side of Europe had captured the nose of the world and balanced it between its fingers. Whether or not he was fully conscious of his sore feelings, Jeremy kept them to himself.

The OXI movement had won and the Troika's austerity measures had been rejected. Over sixty percent voted against their terms. Among the workers and unemployed it was over seventy percent, and eighty-five among the youth. That was not surprising - three-fifths of Greek youth were unemployed. Nine out of ten Communist Party supporters voted OXI, despite their party's abstentionism, and all of Greece's constituencies also said OXI, and most by wide margins.

Corbyn drifted in and out of himself while Jeremy eulogised the heroic Greek people. They were far greater than the individual heroes of the ancients, he said. This was a revolt of the whole people. He turned to Corbyn, but he appeared not to be listening. Undeterred, Jeremy continued: It was beyond a rejection of the technical terms of the austerity, especially considering the terror campaign they had suffered. Closed banks, unpaid workers, unpaid pensioners; all the black threats of impending doom spoken from every corner of the Troika's infinitely-cornered 'international community'. Such sentiments had been recycled ad nauseam by the Greek media.

Perhaps it was the sheer volume of what had washed from the slack mouth of the establishment, the blind brunt of its twentieth-century atomic muster stampeded of all subtlety - perhaps it was that that had caused it to fail? The professional commentators, now forming an orderly queue below the shadow of the Parthenon, said the result confounded all logic.

'It's all so frighteningly hopeful, don't you think?' said Jeremy. 'But why has Varoufakis resigned? He said he'd go if there was a NAI, but they voted OXI - he won!' Corbyn strained his stiff neck toward the television.

'I bet they're panicked in Brussels,' continued Jeremy, looking over at his friend. 'Want some more tea?' Corbyn lowered his eyelids in confirmation.

'It'll be a huge morale boost to the workers,' said Jeremy, taking Corbyn's cup on his way to the kitchen. 'It's what they all already know, but affirmed as a class: "Greece rejects austerity". Some might debate the meaning of Syriza's election in January, said it wasn't clear enough and all that, but this is as clear as day, and from the land that invented democracy. That puts the seal on it!'

'Slave-owning...' Corbyn gasped.

'What's that, old boy?' said Jeremy, poking his head back into the front room.

'It was a slave-owning democracy.'

'Maybe so, my sick friend, but that was long ago. Time has moved on since then. The slaves have the vote now. Naturally, the masters try to keep them divided. They let them roam free, but with a guard posted inside their head. But you can't guard all of the people, all of the time. Especially when you can no longer pay the guards! All this austerity has united the slaves against them. Soon they'll be the masters!' He placed Corbyn's fresh cup beside him.

'But it's as I said before,' said Jeremy, falling back into his armchair. He was far too excited to let his friend rest. 'Now the money will begin to fly away if they don't act fast. Tsipras should nationalise the banking system immediately, without compensation, and declare all small deposits guaranteed. Otherwise the old masters will bide their time and use the banks to engineer economic sabotage. Learn from the Paris Commune. In fact, learn from Venezuela Mr Tsipras. You can't make half a revolution; you've got to see it through to the end! Call on the people to form local assemblies to defend the OXI in every town and village, and to keep the economy running in these critical times. The natural leaders will rise to the top.'

Carried away on his thoughts, Jeremy shouted at the television triumphantly:

'It will be the basis of a new state, a state for the workers! Put your faith in the people Mr Tsipras, they will provide the answer!'

Laura stamped her foot on the bedroom floor.

Quietly bringing their eyes down from the ceiling, they lowered the volume and resumed the coverage. The news showed thousands pouring into Syntagma Square in celebration, their great achievement dawning in the summer light. Stranger embraced stranger. Brother and sister, separated at birth, became reacquainted. When the news came through of the resignation of Samaras, the leader of New

Democracy, a fresh round of cheers spread among the victors.

'It's the beginning of a revolution,' said Jeremy, careful not to let his excitement spill upstairs.

'Not as many as there were Friday,' whispered Corbyn, coiled under his blanket. Jeremy peered at the pictures of the decidedly smaller crowd. Corbyn was right. But their spirits were just as high.

'Well... you can't expect people to be out on the streets indefinitely,' said Jeremy. 'I imagine some have stayed at home out of caution - worried about recriminations. I'm sure the elite will be re-doubling their old efforts: complaining that the poor are uneducated and should not be allowed to vote; that those who haven't voted before should not be allowed to vote now; that the elderly should be given more votes for their experience; all the elitist dirty tricks they try to make a dumb rattle of when the workers assert themselves with confidence.'

'Forty percent... that's more than just the elite,' said Corbyn, hissing at Jeremy through his blanket. 'There'll be worried workers among the NAI.'

'Yes, worked up by the media. But there will also be a lot of NAI voters who were split in their hearts and voted better the devil they knew, but will be happy for the outcome.'

'What was the turn-out?'

'Sixty-five percent.'

'So a forty percent minority... and another thirty-five percent who did not vote.'

'Come on old man,' said Jeremy, beginning to feel a little cross. He was not going to allow Corbyn to rob him of their victory. 'You know abstention is a vote for the majority - whatever that majority might be.' But he felt his argument was not entirely water-tight.

'That's the same type of argument the Tories are using against the unions. Besides, if there was less than complete support for Tsipras, it was because he cost himself so much goodwill dithering for so long over the negotiations.'

On screen a young man appeared whom the reporter introduced as a 'financial expert', who said that Greece had just signed its own suicide note. Then the German vice-chancellor, a Social-Democrat, was walked out to declare solemnly that: *'Tsipras has burned the last bridges.'*

The reporter beneath the Parthenon said Greece was due to pay three-and-a-half billion to the European Central Bank by July 20th, and if the Greek government put money into their banks, or issued a new currency, it would mean ejection from the Euro.

'Pfft!' said Jeremy, rolling his eyes. 'If the Right were still in power they'd find the cash. Greece represents a piddling two-and-a-half percent of the EU economy. They could save it if they wanted to. That's where the cuts do get "ideological", I'll give you that.' Corbyn's eyes were closed.

'But even then such ideology, which might seem unnecessary when one looks at Greece in isolation, becomes - from their point of view - an economic necessity when you think about the political effects it would have internationally. If they could bail out Greek capitalism secretly, in isolation, with no further consequences – which we know is pie in the sky, of course - they'd take the hit. They'd pay up. But surely now, even if he isn't exactly a revolutionary, Mr Tsipras has to take over the banks? It's the least he can do in order to stop the money racing out? If he did that, and made an appeal to the workers in Europe to rise up, he'd get a huge response - especially in Italy and Spain and Portugal.' Then Tsipras appeared on the TV, as if invited to field Jeremy's question:

> *'I understand that voters have not given me a mandate against Europe, but a mandate for a sustainable future,'* Tsipras declared into the cameras.

'Well, that doesn't answer my question.'

The anchor reported that Tsipras had called a meeting of Greece's party political leaders to discuss the way forward.

'But they were allies of the Troika!' said Jeremy, indignant.

'Why on earth is he wasting his time with them - unless he's giving them twenty-four hours to get out? What possible agreement could one arrive at with those who supported austerity and opposed the referendum from the very beginning?'

> *'Now, as we know,'* said the anchor, *'the controversial finance minister, Varoufakis, handed his resignation to the Prime Minister shortly after the referendum result. This evening he was replaced with Euclid Tsakalotos.'*

'You-could sack-a-lot-us?' Jeremy repeated, with widening eyes.

> *'He is regarded,'* continued the reporter, *'as one of the most*

sensible figures in the ruling Syriza party, and increases the outcomes of a solution to the impasse in Greece. Mr Tsakalotos insisted that the Syriza government was "fundamentally pro-Europe" and that it wanted "a viable economic programme inside the euro." His appointment is said to be critical to bridge the gap between the difficult reforms the government will be forced to implement and the objections raised within Syriza as a deal gets closer.'

'What deal?' said Jeremy, loudly, asking too much of the television, so that once again Laura's brought down her foot upon the ceiling. He continued in a whisper:

'They talk as if the referendum never happened.'

Corbyn coughed and turned under his blanket. He was asleep.

2

Chuka and Tristram were in Peter's office for their usual beginning-of-the-month meeting. It was one of the hottest days of the year. The air conditioning system, squeezed between the cracks of the sinking palace, wheezed hard as it strained to cool the high ceilings of the rooms of Westminster.

As always, they began with Global Projections. The discussion started with a review of the economy. Peter was keen to impress upon his students the grave nature of the present situation, transmitting the mood of pessimism that had trickled down from the Clientele.

To Chuka the clientele were forever seized between a state of mania and depression these days. Now it seemed they were once again fretting over a global recession. The Euro was apparently the most likely epicentre, said PM, and the collapsing Chinese stock market bubble was an ominous symptom of the current fragility of the system. The Clientele reported that the coming slump would be one that very few would be able to withstand.

'We are all sitting ducks', said Peter, with the eloquence he assumed in all matters high, and not so high, unmoved by the weight of his words as he unfurled them. 'One clever chap in our employ has been so colourful as to state that the world economy is like the Titanic: 'going down'. Only that this time, we are rather short of lifeboats.'

'Why's that, PM?' asked Tristram.

'Well, despite interest rates being at rock bottom for years, our risk-takers have not recovered the animal spirits necessary to borrow and spark a recovery. And the state debt – our life-boat in the analogy - can hardly take on any more water.' Tristram concentrated as hard as he could, but the heat was wilting. All the air conditioner appeared to do was produce noise without ventilation, and Peter's office was flooded by the distraction of the summers' day.

'China, once again, is a problem,' said Peter, moving his face out of the reflection of the Thames and into the shadows.

That came as no surprise to the boys. The blessed Chinese were forever being troublesome.

'And while China was responsible for four-fifths of the world's growth only a few years ago, this year it is expected to account for only a quarter.'

'Isn't that because America and the rest of us are doing so much better and picking up the slack?' asked Chuka.

'I am afraid not, my dear boy. One only has to look at shipping figures to see that world trade as a whole is in decline. And the raw material producers that feed China: Argentina, Australia, Brazil, Russia - all suffering as a result.'

'Couldn't we just print some more money, PM?' said Tristram. Chuka shifted in his seat, rubbing the bridge of his nose between his fingers.

'What we have regrettably learned,' said Peter 'is that much of this printed money failed to work in the national interest. Individual Clients do not refuse it - naturally enough – however, they do often complain of the clutter it causes when used by others. It tends to make bubbles, our Chinese friends being a case in point. Much of their print-run has ended in shadowy banking practices, or spiralling property prices.'

'Like in London,' said Chuka. 'I know some people who've done quite well from their town houses.'

'But now all that is fast disappearing,' said Peter. 'What is happening in China appears to be a classic example of the "law of diminishing returns". As with an opium addict, the more they take, the less effective it becomes. I dare say a few sorry chaps will be left holding the bag. The state will most likely pick up the bill, one way or another. If not from more bank bail-outs, then from increased unemployment benefits.' Peter sighed.

'And less tax revenue,' said Chuka.

'Quite right, my boy, quite right,' said Peter. 'And the silly thing of it all is that taxation is the only real way the government has any money.'

Bubbles and pyramids, sitting ducks, benefits and bail-outs: it all sounded quite bad to Tristram. 'I suppose the Chinese could always lower their benefits bill? Worked well here.'

'Not good for the internal pressure, I'm afraid,' said Peter. 'You do recall our discussion about the poor quality of Chinese safety valves? No, no. The real problem, as everywhere, is demand - as I am sure you have come to understand.' The boys exchanged empty looks.

'Put simply, there is not any,' said Peter, suspecting the penny had not dropped.

'One of the documents currently circulating among the Clientele is about the possibility of printing it instead.'

'Print... demand?' asked Tristram. He understood one could print money, but how could one print demand?

'Yes, in a manner of speaking. *"Helicopter money"*, they're calling it. Put simply, we drop a few thousand pounds into Jim and Jemina's sticky little paws - rather generous, I think you will agree - and in that way the Clientele believe it will act as an "economic defibrillator", so to speak, jump-starting the economy.'

'*De-fibril-lator*,' muttered Tristram, scribbling in his notepad.

'The problem up until now,' said Peter 'has been that all the money we borrowed, or printed, was merely dropped into the vaults of our banking friends. But as has been shown, the banks do not necessarily spend their money as little Jim or Jemina do... The thinking runs as follows: If we place money directly into the proles' pockets, then they will not proceed to buy shares in themselves as the banks and companies have done. Most are not even publicly listed. Rather, they will buy television sets and washing machines and... fridge-freezers... and all the other effects that their little hearts desperately desire. Under those conditions, so our Clientele say, they would be quite prepared to recommence production - as I am certain would most reasonable capitalists. But until that happens, as much as they would like to, they say they are simply unable to invest without the corresponding demand.'

It was so simple, thought Tristram. Why had it not been thought of before? For every malady, there is a remedy. The only thing was to determine how to deliver the medicine. *Thank goodness for us.*

'Whether such an approach is adopted, I am afraid is another matter,' said Peter, and Tristram was once again deflated. Who could not see the merits of PM's case?

'I'm afraid, my boys, inertia plagues us at every turn - even among the Clientele, it must be said. Nevertheless, such dilemmas highlight why our tendency must endure. Today is not all that matters. We must not lose time. We must prepare, and ensure that our people – the best people, those most qualified, those who have Inner Steel - are in place at the right time for when such seemingly novel ideas become the new normality. Now, more than ever, our Tendency is so necessary.'

The boys responded approvingly.

'Most regrettable, really. I do so wish I could retire to a yacht on the Mediterranean.' The boys watched as Peter's lips curled, provoking from them noises like laughter as they turned in their leather seats. 'But we remain optimistic,' said Peter, sighing once again. 'We maintain an unerring faith in the innate reasonableness of the little people. Once they are given the freedom to act rationally, of course.'

Quite right, thought Tristram. Chuka shifted again in his seat. The leather rasped.

'And of course, matters are not helped by these difficulties in Greece,' said Peter.

'It seems like only yesterday they were hosting the Olympics,' said Tristram.

'Quite so,' said Peter. 'Amid all the euphoria of the juggling and the flame-throwing, it seems our counter-parts made a number of over-sights... Of course, they have not had the historical good fortune of the British, one must be admit. I imagined it would be complicated enough managing two workers' parties, let alone having these Syriza fellows thrown into the mix.'

'This Tsipras chap seems quite mad,' said Tristram, tonguing his palatal flap. 'I understand his party is a coalition of all those awful socialist sectarian grouplets. Imagine allowing them into Westminster. One shudders!'

'The majority of Syriza actually come from the Communist movement,' said Chuka. 'Something we had failed to invest in until recently.

'Yes, and we have been playing catch-up ever since,' said Peter. 'Fortunately for these types, events themselves can play a sobering role. You recall our discussion about Mr Scanlon? He didn't like the view very much either.'

'Abysmal fellow,' said Tristram with a shiver, recalling a previous discussion they had had on the struggles of the 1970s. 'So we're priced in then?'

'So it would seem...' said Peter, deep in thought. 'But the worst of it all is, if this had happened in the past - say in the thirties, or even the sixties - broken safety valves would prove no major upset. There were always a few plucky chaps available to plumb the situation. Not ideal, I grant you, but they were only ever a stop-gap until matters improved. Nowadays, however, the proletariat in Greece seem so very... belligerent. Not least because there are so many of them. That's one thing about the proles - they will insist on breeding. And I must say, I am not altogether certain our people have complete control.'

'Well, I saw that our people on the Greek TUC, the GSEE, managed to come out for the NAI,' said Chuka.

'Yes, but to what end?' said Peter. 'Six years, five General Elections, and now our chief vehicle is destroyed.'

'PASOK?' said Tristram.

'Very good my boy. Yes, PASOK.'

'And the amount of General Strikes they've had is atrocious,' said Chuka. 'You should have a word with them, PM.'

'Ah, yes, but you must understand my boy,' said Peter, 'we are not dealing with the same circumstances as in Britain.' The Lords lips parted, revealing a row of successional teeth. 'You are quite right, of course; we must hold the line against any General Strike. But once that line is crossed - and it was crossed long ago in Greece - it is important we re-evaluate tactics accordingly. I do not know how many times it has been, but our people in the Greek unions have been staging General Strikes for years now. It keeps the little people running around for a day or two, up to the top of the hill, and back down again. Eventually such activity can become quite demoralising for the proles - as long as one keeps such a tactic strictly within acceptable limits.'

Tristram took notes furiously. *Fascinating.*

'And it saves the local Clientele a days' pay,' added Chuka.

'Precisely,' said Peter. 'Which makes a difference in these ever so... pinched times. But the main thing is morale. You do remember what Napoleon said about the question of morale?'

The boys smiled, nodding in unison.

'If one cannot let out too much pressure through the top for fear of an explosion, one always has the option to cool things internally. That is our main task in Greece at the moment, economically and politically: internal devaluation. Although, as I say, whether matters have not spun beyond our control already is not entirely clear...'

'The referendum is finished, PM,' said Tristram. 'What more can be done?'

'We will see...' said the Lord.

They had passed from economic to political forecasts, and from Greece they moved to news elsewhere. A rash of bad results that the Clientele considered potentially destabilising was discussed. In Spain, the victory of the Podemos and its allies had disturbing echoes of Greece; in Brazil, the discontent and booing among the ranks at the fifth congress of the Workers' Party was a worrying development in a key South American country; in Austria, the Social Democrats in the state of Burgenland had got themselves into a pickle by entering into a coalition with the hard-right FPO. From the outside it appeared most unfortunate, although Peter reminded the boys that the Austrian Social-Democracy was one of the best-priced in Europe. There would be no repeat of what had happened to PASOK. And in Canada, the Social-Democratic NDP had won Alberta for the first time in history, upsetting the oil barons no end. It appeared there was a question mark over whether the Albertan leadership could be trusted to act in the national interest. Nevertheless, the federal NDP leadership was known to be very sensible, thankfully. All signs pointed to a victory in the coming General Election at the end of the year.

Moving on to business, the men assessed their ongoing directives.

They agreed that the leadership nominations had gone smoothly. Chuka reported on the effectiveness of some new Secondary Holdings he had picked up while mobilising support for Corbyn, and they compared notes on the flexibility of various Labour MPs.

The polls were bearing out well. One conducted by *The Independent* was of particular interest. It found that Andy was the clear favourite, with Liz placed not too far behind. Corbyn was safely in last place.

'Ensure that poll is widely circulated,' ordered Peter. 'Nothing breeds success like sucess.'

'However, we have some membership concerns,' Chuka warned. 'Fifty thousand have reportedly joined since the election, a large amount of whom came in after the nominations were confirmed.'

'I thought the three-pound mechanism was designed to keep more members from joining?' said Tristram.

'Hmm... well, we do tend to suffer a little membership surge after a defeat,' said Peter. 'I'm sure it is of no concern.'

They were very happy to hear of another poll which found that Tony Blair was the past leader the public wished Ed Miliband's successor would most resemble. Peter's eyes glassed over, and he was once again moved to remind Tristram and Chuka of the eminent common sense of the British people. Tony would be very pleased indeed.

Only two small reports seemed to run against the grain. The first showed that Corbyn did appear to be gaining the lion's share of the trade union support. Peter thought back to 2010, a chill gripping him for a moment.

However, with the union bloc-vote dissolved, they agreed they need not overly concern themselves. Besides, much of the reported trade union support was rather small-fry: a section of the train drivers, the firefighters, the civil servants – most of whom were not even affiliated to Labour. Among the big unions they remained confident that everything was correctly priced-in.

The second report, however, concerned a party hustings in Birmingham, and it was enough to raise an eyebrow from Peter. More than a thousand members and supporters had attended, and apparently twice could have attended, judging by the ticket demand. What was more, Corbyn had garnered 'genuine and vigorous applause', as one of their Holdings reported, contrasting sharply with the reception given to the other candidates. Corbyn's stance against the Iraq war, the banks, and in support of welfare, appeared very popular.

Peter said nothing, pressing an index finger beneath his nose and gazing out at the heat-blurred Thames. He thought back to their discussion on projections. The business moved on.

Later, as they were standing to leave, Peter interrupted Chuka and Tristram's conversation about the best place in Shoreditch to find Rice Krispies cakes, as if re-finding a trail of thought he had earlier departed from:

'Perhaps it would be prudent,' said Peter, 'if we took measures to ensure that all our Intimates and Holdings are... made completely aware of Mr Corbyn's past?'

The boys raised their eyebrows.

'A little... insurance, on our part? As they say, there's no such thing as bad publicity.'

3

Jeremy and Corbyn were on the train to Durham to address the historic Miners' Gala. Their list of appointments was growing fast. All around the country people were contacting them to ask if they would come to their town and speak. The 'twenty or thirty' meetings John and Jeremy had originally envisioned less than a month ago had become transformed into fifty, possibly sixty, planned campaign rallies.

In the week that had passed since the Greek referendum, Syriza continued to negotiate with the EU, while in Britain the Tory government had announced a new budget. In that time Corbyn's condition had swung between hot, feverish flushes, to cold chills. At one point he seemed to fade away altogether. Then then there were periods when he no longer felt unwell, merely weak, and believed himself to be on the mend. But each recovery proved but an eye in a series of storms that passed over him in early July, after which he soon fell back into a stupor.

But in time Corbyn did recover, slowly but surely, and as the Gala approached the periods of stability became longer, and the fever that has possessed him gave way to mere fatigue. Despite Jeremy's protests he was determined to join the trip. And after promising to merely observe and not over-exert himself, his friend finally agreed.

En route they stopped off at a number of towns to attend the rallies diligently organised by John and his young team. Corbyn managed to play a behind-the-scenes role, reminding Jeremy who the various faces were that approached like distant family relatives, faces he had become acquainted with through his long years of service in the movement. Jeremy confessed that he was impressed. The loyal network of sympathetic ears Corbyn had amassed was considerable and provided comfy beds, excellent cups of tea, and a local base in almost every town they visited.

They were now heading south from Glasgow. After a few false starts the train was hurtling across the Scottish borders toward the north-east of England. In the hours spent between the rallying points Jeremy updated Corbyn on some of the developments that had taken place since he had taken to his bed. The Chancellor had announced a new budget, promising twelve billion pounds of additional austerity cuts.

'More fixing the roof while the sun is shining,' said Corbyn.

'Indeed. And at the same time *The Guardian*,' said Jeremy, 'reports that big business is getting ninety-three billion each year from the government in grants, subsidies, tax breaks and exemptions – companies that pay little or even no corporation tax. Yet the Chancellor has announced he's cutting corporation tax even further.'

'So they do favour a welfare state?' said Corbyn. 'They say charity starts at home.'

Jeremy was encouraged to see his friend in better spirits. 'But the Chancellor buried much of this through his announcement of a new "living wage": Nine pounds an hour by 2020.'

'Well I suppose that's something,' said Corbyn.

'Don't be fooled,' said Jeremy, 'it's all smoke and mirrors. It's only nine quid for the over-twenty-fives, and not for another five years. He's committed himself to virtually nothing until he's booted out of office. According to the Living Wage Foundation the cost of living is seven eighty-five now, while the minimum wage remains at seven-twenty. And in London they say a living wage should be as high as nine pounds fifteen. God knows what it will be in five years' time, once the Chancellor's cuts have been carried out.'

'Benefits for the bosses and cuts for the masses,' said Corbyn. 'Giving with the left and taking with the right.'

'They're taking far more with the right, old boy. But it's not just the state debt that motivates them. It's also the cost of labour.'

'What of it?'

'Apparently it's too cheap.'

'Too cheap?'

'Yes, and it's apparently making wastrels of the bosses - so much so that even the Tories are standing up and paying attention.'

'Why should the Tories care about that? They've always been fond of their masters' vice.'

'Well, it turns out low pay has become more than just a problem for the working class – the problem has trickled up.' Corbyn did not follow.

'Well, for example: Why should the owner of a car wash buy expensive machinery that automatically soaps and sponges your car on a treadmill, when he can employ ten kids with a bucket and sponge to do it on the cheap? The British capitalists have had arms shorter than their pockets for decades. If they could avoid putting their capital into what they regard as the painful process of production, and instead gamble it on the stock market, then all the better for them. That's what Thatcher was all about.'

'But why has it become a problem now all of a sudden?'

'Think of it as a sort of inverted Luddite malaise. It keeps people in bad and cheap jobs like your car-wash shammy or coffee-shop barista, to the detriment of competitive, high-value industrial exports: steel, machine tools, computers, that sort of thing. The mad profits they make from super-flexible, zero-hour workers are just impossible to resist. And the Tories still wouldn't give a hoot about it, but for all the credit agencies getting nervous about Britain's "long-term competitiveness" and the subsequent effect that will have on its ability to pay its debts.'

'Naturally,' said Corbyn.

'If they were to downgrade the credit rating it would "officially" make Britain a riskier economy to invest in. So apart from making us a less tempting place for their rich international friends to park their capital, the Chancellor's immediate problem would be that it would serve to push up interest payments on the debt if the credit rating agencies downgrade us. And we already throw away forty-three billion pounds a year on interest.'

'That's a lot of hospitals. But why does the interest go up?'

'To front-load as much return from what would then be deemed a considerably riskier investment. When it comes down to it, all the Tories are concerned with is that this so-called living wage nudges their business friends into spending in manufacturing, where there are one-off costs for machinery, but relatively few workers, in order to raise productivity.'

'Wouldn't that cause job losses? You think the Tories want that? I think that's a bit far-fetched, even for them.'

'That's what capitalism always does with machinery. Labour-saving devices meaning savings in wages for the bosses, not time for the workers. Yes, the Tories want a living wage, in order to lower the overall cost of the workforce.'

'How long was I out for? Tories raising wages in order to encourage investment!' laughed Corbyn. 'Shows how unreal it has all become. I don't see how we can complain though.'

'Of course you don't,' said Jeremy. 'In other news, a hundred thousand have signed an online petition of no confidence in the health secretary, Jeremy Hunt. That's enough signatures to have it debated in parliament. I think the Tories threatening to make doctors do non-emergency weekend work tipped it over the edge.'

'Tsk – parliamentary petitions aren't meant for things like that. They should debate the policies, not the personalities.'

'And the Tories are carrying out the Queen's promises. They'll lower the benefits cap for families to twenty-three grand a year, and twenty for those outside London. You remember the government's leaked assessment predicting that it would push forty-thousand more children into poverty as a result?'

'I remember. What are the other candidates saying about that?'

'You'll never guess,' said Jeremy. 'They're in favour - all of them – "in principle", whatever that means.'

'If you don't like my principles, I can get new ones,' said Corbyn. 'What a shower.'

'And the government is increasing military spending to two per cent of the budget per year, after the Americans complained,' said

Jeremy. 'But it's just a fiddle. They've added military pensions to bump up the figure!

'Virtuous British enterprise indeed!'

'What else? Oh yes, no housing benefits until you're twenty-one; if you're lucky mum and dad can keep you longer. And student maintenance grants for the poorest students - abolished.'

Jeremy also reported that the mutterings over their candidacy were becoming more frequent among the PLP. One of the kinder remarks held that their nomination proved Labour was resolved to lose the next election. Variations on the theme were making the rounds in the parliamentary tea rooms, mostly gossip of little consequence said Jeremy, but Corbyn insisted on hearing it all the same.

The journalists had not needed to dig very far to unearth their morsels. But however juicy they had first appeared, old girlfriends and the like, they proved slim pickings upon closer inspection. They made more of the fact that Corbyn had invited Sinn Fein to parliament in the 1980s, long before the Good Friday agreement, and that he had taken a similar approach toward Hamas, hoping to assist discussion between the various factions in Palestine.

'I told you not to get mixed up with those people,' said Jeremy. 'They were always just liberals with bombs. If they had real conviction they'd have organised the working class against British rule on both sides of the border - and on the British mainland - through the methods of the class struggle. You can't bomb your way to freedom.'

'But I was proved right, wasn't I?' said Corbyn. 'Only ten years later Blair employed the exact same methods as me. It wasn't troublesome strikes and demonstrations that resolved the situation in Ireland; it was sensible discussion. You have to give Blair that much.'

'You think matters are resolved in Ireland? That's always been your problem,' said Jeremy. 'You imagine anyone can be reasoned with, and for you reason and logic operates like a game of chess. Are the Irish free? Or is Ulster still the most impoverished part of the United Kingdom and Britain's first colony? Sinn Fein and the IRA assisted the British state just as much as the unionists did. They divided Catholic and Protestant when they should have been uniting them as workers against British imperialism. Blair and Adams' reasoned agreement was based on the common disdain they held for British and Irish workers alike.'

They fell into silence. It had always been a sore point between them. That's where rationalism got you, said Jeremy, when it was left to float free of a class point of view. What Corbyn considered irrational was Jeremy's unwillingness to engage with someone without meeting them - to completely write them off. Not to mention how impolite it was. But neither were surprised at the media's response, despite the praise it heaped on Blair for negotiating with Sinn Fein the Good Friday agreement. And who exactly did they think Blair was negotiating with in the Middle East?

Naturally, the media used the case of Sinn Fein to reinforce the idea that they were also sympathetic toward Islamic terrorism. Since the bombings in Tunisia in late June a head of hysteria had built up around the question. Jeremy reported that Harriet had joined in, declaring her inclination toward bombing Syria.

'It's a matter for the UN,' said Corbyn. 'Honestly, after everything we've been through over Iraq. We defeated the government on this question in 2013. You think she'd have more sense.'

'You do realise that the UN sanctions war?' said Jeremy. 'It's no good referring the question to them.'

'But it's an internationalist forum for discussion - a force for good.'

'Yes, and it did the Iraqis a world of good. You know the Romans were quite the "internationalists". So were the Mongols - and the British!'

They spoke no more on the subject. Corbyn was not interested in repeating the same basic argument they had had after the letter to the Prime Minister on the question of Greece's debt.

Happily, Jeremy had in reserve a brighter note they could both move on to. He proudly reported that they had just received backing from Unite, the biggest union in Britain. Corbyn could not believe his ears.

'With Len's blessing?' he asked, quite surprised. 'I thought they were backing Andy?'

'Pressure from below, or so I heard,' said Jeremy, grinning.

'Apparently Andy was still the leadership's man, even after he bit their hand with all his rhetoric about getting away from "union influence". But a tide of demands from the members threatened to overturn the leadership at their conference last week. Len saw which way the wind was blowing and retreated. They're giving Andy a second preference instead. Hedging their grassroots.'

'Pragmatic insurance - I can understand that,' said Corbyn. He turned his gaze out onto the rolling tussled terrain of the Scottish borders with a troubled countenance, as if pondering some difficult mathematical equation.

'Well, quite,' said Jeremy. 'It has all the others in something of a flap, or so John reports: rumours of splits in all three camps; night long re-triangulations; bust-ups over whether to dump the vacuous aspirational rhetoric. Jolly entertaining if you ask me.'

'If we can just do that,' said Corbyn, as the spreading purple heather flew back along the track and into the distance, 'if we can make the winner shift the... narrative, get them to make some honest commitments to hard-working families - things we can hold them to. If we can do that then we'll have accomplished our mission. And then we can all go home.' He looked at Jeremy. A crooked smile broke across his face.

4

As morning became afternoon Corbyn grew tired. He found the brass bands pleasant, but also quite loud, and the cobbled boister of Durham's stone streets made him feel dizzy. The trip had been good for him, on the whole, but he was still far from recovered.

Presently they arrived in the field and took their seats on the raised platform among the various trade union and labour movement figures. They could see none of the other candidates. Liz had been spotted that morning, as had Andy. Perhaps they were still enjoying the march, suggested Corbyn. As for Yvette, no one seemed to know where she was. Time passed and the speeches began. The other candidates did not show.

Maybe they only came for... the brass bands,' said Corbyn, yawning.

'Quite possible,' said Jeremy. 'Blair was a big fan of big band music, as I understand, though I don't know if he ever came to the

Gala.'

'He must have done... his constituency was only ten miles down the road.'

Jeremy listened to the representatives of the labour movement booming across the field. The attendance was reported to be a hundred and fifty thousand, a small fraction of which were gathered around the stage. Beyond, he saw mothers unrolling blankets beneath their family spread, and dads feeding their children to the electric fairground rides huddled on one edge of the green. He looked at his friend sat beside him. He seemed much reduced in comparison to the image he held of him in his mind's eye. *I suppose he's been through a lot these last few weeks.* He had fallen asleep.

Many more lined the streets in the town above, cheering as the last of the brass bands thumped by. They would not leave until they had finished re-cobbling the streets in plastic pint cups, traditionally at some point in the early hours of the next morning. By which time the speeches would be all but finished.

Jeremy was walking through his home, going over one of the points of his speech drawn against the living room wall, when he fancied he heard the ticking of a clock. He felt someone sit down besides him on the stage.

'Jeremy,' cracked a Liverpudlian accent. 'Good to see you up here, comrade.'

'Oh... hello Len,' said Jeremy. The walls of his house trembled. He exited the room and made for the front door. 'It's good to see you too... I hope our message of thanks got to your members for all their support. We were quite surprised when the news came through.'

He considered asking Len what he thought of it, but held back.

'Don't mention it,' said Len, taking a bite out of a pork pie held in a napkin. 'Glad to help in any way we could.' Len looked either side of him, and then elbowed Jeremy in the ribs, baring him a nugget-of-pie-crust grin. 'No sign of the other three, eh? Everyone's backing you, Jeremy. And my people are going to put our offices at your disposal. Because we're very proud to support a man of your... integrity.'

'That really is too kind,' said Jeremy. 'We certainly need all the help we can get.'

'Not at all, comrade. You know, I hear that a few of them Blairites are getting twitchy.' He muffled a laugh as pie crumbs fell into his napkin. 'Anything else we can help you with, you be sure to tell us,' he said, wiping his mouth with his sleeve. Then he stretched out an arm and slapped Jeremy across the back, so hard that it set his glasses crooked.

'Yes,' said Jeremy, straightening in his seat at the sting of Len's palm. 'If they're worried, then I suppose we must be doing something right.' He re-set his glasses and tried changing the topic: 'And how are things in the union at the moment?'

'Oh, you know,' said Len, '*plus ça change*, Jeremy, *plus ça change*... We try to negotiate the best deal for our colleague sisters and brothers, of course, but we need to grow the membership.' He eyed Corbyn, trying to find the answer to the question he would not ask. 'The civil servants are in a bit of a bind. The government's trying to make it more difficult for them to collect their membership fees. I've offered them a comradely merger, but they let the members have the run of that union. But if we're going to grow, we can't stay divided, eh Jeremy? One big union: that must be our aim.'

'Isn't that supposed to be the job of the TUC?' asked Jeremy.

'It should be, Jeremy, but in all honesty, the TUC couldn't catch a cold.' Len's stubbled chin sank into his neck, pulling his face into a purple grimace. 'They fumbled the General Strike. You know Kenny declined to cast the chair's vote to decide that question? Now they've given him a knighthood. That's why they went for us after Falkirk, I reckon... It's why we've got to fight back, eh Jeremy? If we could bring the civil servants into the Labour Party then we'd be able to give you even stronger backing. We've been lending them offices and printing their leaflets. They're indebted to us. Or rather, to the movement, I should say...'

'As long as the members want it,' said Jeremy. 'But can't we find other ways to build the membership? There seems to be so little youth involved these days.'

'Aye,' said McCluskey, looking out onto the field. 'One big union... If we could just be a little stronger, then in one or two years' time, who knows? We could be in a position of real strength. Then we'd be a force to negotiate with.'

'Well, I'm sure that once you show the way, people will join,' said Jeremy, assuming his most diplomatic smile.

'Aye. Once we're bigger, once we're a little stronger,' he repeated, a glazed look momentarily overcoming him. Then he turned to Jeremy and looked him straight in the eye. 'And you realise you're instrumental to it all, don't you? With Labour back in our hands – the hands of working people - we could transform the situation. Imagine a politically united labour movement. Then we can really think about bringing those thieving Tory bastards to account.' He swallowed the last of his pork pie and patted his mouth with his napkin.

'We could bring the government down,' said Jeremy. Len looked at him and laughed.

'That's the spirit, Jezza,' he said, slapping him on the back again. 'You can't even have a joke with the other lot. Even Andy's gone sour, to tell the truth.' His smile petered out and he looked out upon the field once more, the glaze returned and filming his eyes. 'There's just one thing. Naturally, we are going to need our back scratched in return.'

Jeremy looked at Len sharply, disliking the turn of phrase.

'We need to be in the best position possible in order to deal with this government. There's no point stirring things up… Now, I know the firefighters are backing you, but we don't need any of this "worker's MPs on worker's wages" nonsense. It just raises the blood. We need to be turning outwards to more serious issues - not navel gazing. You've seen what this government has in store for ordinary, hard-working people. You see what they're trying to do to us with this trade union bill. I asked them to stop, but they wouldn't reconsider. That's where we should be concentrating our forces. You can see where I'm coming from, can't you?' Jeremy suspected he could.

'Well, it's not something the firefighters have brought up with me, but I've always had the greatest respect for the principle.'

'But it's not even something you practise yourself, Jeremy. You've just had a ten percent pay rise in Westminster while at the same time public sector wages are frozen at one per cent.'

'Yes, you're right, we haven't… but perhaps it's time we started.' He turned and looked at Corbyn, sunk in his snooze.

'We'd be better off discussing raising the wages of working

people, don't you think?' said Len. 'Rather than levelling things off at the bottom?'

'Well, yes, you have a point. It's always the answer I've received when I've raised this question in the past.' Corbyn snorted in his sleep and turned in his chair.

'Aye, that's the other half for you!' Len slapped Jeremy's back again and coughed up a purple cackle.

'Something like that,' muttered Jeremy. 'Anyway, as you say, the main thing is to concentrate on the Tories.' Len could agree to that.

'Another thing,' said Len. 'Will you endorse Andy and Tom? I know they'd do the same for you.'

'Tom would endorse me? Are you quite sure?'

'Well, what about Andy then - as a second preference? I know he's been a bit off-colour lately, but he's a good kid.'

'I don't know about that,' said Jeremy. 'How is he any different from Liz or Yvette? All three of them are dithering over this welfare bill.'

'Aye,' said Len. 'Bloody foolish... don't know they're born. But look, Andy's a good kid really. He's not with that shower that ballsed it up in May. And he's not a Blairite, I think you'll agree.'

Jeremy looked at Len with narrow, sceptical eyes. He could not honestly say what Andy was, thinking about it.

'We're talking to Andy about the welfare bill. He'll come right in the end. If you could see your way to an endorsement, it would mean a lot to... our colleagues.'

'I'll talk to my team,' said Jeremy.

'Cheers Jezza, have a good one - sounds like you're up.'

CHAPTER 9
WELFARE

1

'...but the truth is that within my constituency it's not all fantastic,' said Mhairi, the new member of Parliament for Paisley and Renfrewshire.

'We've watched our town centres deteriorate. We've watched our communities decline. Our unemployment level is higher than that of the UK average. One in five children in my constituency go to bed hungry every night. Paisley Job Centre has the third highest number of sanctions in the whole of Scotland.

'Now, before I was elected, I volunteered for a charitable organisation, and there was a gentleman who I grew very fond of. He was one of these guys who has been battered by life in every way imaginable. You name it, he's been through it. And he used to come in to get food from this charity, and it was the only food that he had access to, and it was the only meal he would get. And I sat with him, and he told me about his fear of going to the Job Centre. He said: "I've heard the stories Mhairi, they try and trick you out, they'll tell you you're a liar. I'm not a liar Mhairi; I'm not."

'And I told him: "It's OK, calm down. Go, be honest, it'll be fine." I then didn't see him for about two or three weeks. I did get very worried, and when he finally did come back in I says to him: "How did you get on?" And without saying a word he burst into tears.

'That grown man, standing in front of a twenty-year-old crying his eyes out because what had happened to him was the money that he would normally use to pay for his travel to come to the charity to get his food; he decided that in order to afford to get to the Job Centre he would save that money. Because of this he didn't eat for five days. He didn't drink. When he was on the bus on the way to the Job Centre he fainted due to exhaustion and dehydration. He was fifteen minutes late for the Job Centre and he was sanctioned for thirteen weeks.

'Now, when the Chancellor spoke in his budget about fixing the roof while the sun is shining, I would have to ask: On who is the sun shining?'

Hear, hear, rose the murmur from the SNP benches.

'When he spoke about benefits not supporting certain kinds of lifestyles, is that the kind of lifestyle that he was talking about?

'If we go back even further, when the Minister for Employment was asked to consider if there was a correlation between the number of sanctions and the rise in food bank use, she stated, and I quote: *"Food banks play an important role in local welfare provision."*

Renfrewshire has the third highest use of food banks, and food bank use is going up and up. Food banks are not part of the welfare state - they are a symbol that the welfare state is failing.'

Hear, hear, rose the murmurs.

'Now, the Government quite rightly pays for me through taxpayers' money to be able to live in London while I serve my constituents. My housing is subsidised by the taxpayer.

'Now, the Chancellor in his Budget said it is not fair that families earning over forty-thousand pounds in London should have their rents paid for by other working people. But it is OK so long as you're an MP?

'In this budget, the Chancellor also abolished any housing benefit for anyone below the age of twenty-one. So we are now in the ridiculous situation whereby, because I am an MP, not only am I the youngest, but I am also the only twenty-year-old in the whole of the UK that the Chancellor is prepared to help with housing.'

The murmurs rose to laughter.

'We now have one of the most uncaring, uncompromising and out of touch governments that the UK has seen since Thatcher.'

Hear, hear, rose the murmurs.

'It is here now that I must turn to those who I share a bench with.

'Now, I have sat in this chamber for ten weeks, and I have very deliberately stayed quiet and have listened intently to everything that has been said. I have heard multiple speeches from Labour benches standing to talk about the worrying rise of nationalism in Scotland, when in actual fact all these speeches have served to do is demonstrate how deep the lack of understanding about Scotland is within the Labour Party.

'I, like so many SNP members, come from a traditional socialist Labour family, and I have never been quiet in my assertion that I feel it is the Labour party that left me, not the other way about.'

Hear, hear, rose the murmurs.

'The SNP did not triumph on a wave of nationalism. In fact, nationalism has nothing to do with what's happened in Scotland. We triumphed on a wave of hope; hope that there was something different, something better to the Thatcherite neo-liberal policies that are produced from this chamber. Hope that representatives genuinely could give a voice to those who don't have one.

'I don't mention this in order to pour salt into wounds which I am sure are very open and very sore for many members on these benches, both politically and personally.

Colleagues, possibly friends, have lost their seats. I mention it in order to hold a mirror to the face of a party that seems to have forgotten the very people they're supposed to represent, the very things they're supposed to fight for.

'After hearing the Labour leader's intentions to support the changes into tax credits that the Chancellor has put forward, I must make this plea to the words of one of your own, and a personal hero of mine.

'Tony Benn once said that in politics there are weathercocks and sign posts. Weathercocks will spin in whatever direction the wind of public opinion may blow them, no matter what principle they have to compromise. And then there are signposts; signposts which stand true, and tall, and principled. And they point in the direction, and they say: This is the way to a better society, and it is my job to convince you why. Tony Benn was right when he said the only people worth remembering in politics were signposts.'

Hear, hear, rose the murmurs.

'Now, yes, we will have political differences. Yes, in other parliaments we may be opposing parties. But within this chamber we are not. No matter how much I may wish it, the SNP is not the sole opposition to this Government. But nor is the Labour party. It is together, with all the parties on these benches that we must form an opposition, and in order to be effective, we must oppose, not abstain.

'So I reach out a genuine hand of friendship which I can only hope will be taken. Let us come together, let us be that opposition, let us be that signpost of a better society. Ultimately, people are needing a voice, people are needing help. Let's give them it.'

The packed SNP benches rose in loud and vigorous cheers. But few other MPs were in the House of Commons to listen. The youngest MP elected to the House of Commons since the Great Reform Act of 1832 took her seat.

2

Amalia 'liked' the video of the young Scottish MP that had been posted by Ross, and shared it on her wall. She had been back in London for over a week now, foregoing her usual family break on the islands in order to complete her studies. Yet, and as before, she found it impossible to concentrate, and was forever finding excuses to leave the library and check her phone for the latest developments back home.

Syriza had increased its popularity following the referendum, and there was much call for a new General Election in order to consolidate the victory they had won in January. An increased majority for Syriza would allow it to govern alone, without the nationalists Anel. But few European leaders seemed to be taking the OXI seriously.

Soon after the vote the European Commission had declared the result 'not legal', and its President, Jean-Claude Juncker, dismissed the decision of the Greek people as an 'irrelevant circus'. The Council of Europe complained that the vote did not meet the standards set by the 'international community'.

Less than a week after the referendum, Amalia was surprised to hear that the Greek government was sending a new proposal to the Troika. It was a promise to implement thirteen billion euros in additional taxes and cuts - fifty per cent more than they had promised in June! However, missing was the corporation tax rise and the one-off tax on business that they had previously demanded. All the old privatisations would continue, and they threw in a few new ones for good measure. Within a week the OXI appeared to have been transformed into a NAI.

Despite all of this, the Germans remained less than impressed. A French newspaper reported that Schauble had asked the Greek negotiating team how much they wanted to leave the Euro, figuring it the cheaper option.

All the Greek political parties backed Syriza's new turn, apart from the Communist Party. In an opinion piece in the mainstream Greek newspaper, *Ekathimerini*, entitled: *"A Short Step from here to Barbarism"*, Amalia read of its lament for the collapse of the traditional Greek system and the *"dangerous behaviour"* of the electorate who were expressing themselves *"...along class lines."* It complained that:

> *"...an atmosphere of intolerance is growing within Greek society, with the 'pro-Europeans' on one side and the 'proud Greeks' on the other. It is but a very short step from here to barbarity."*

A single Syriza minister refused to sign the proposal. The President of the Greek Parliament, Zoe Konstantoupoulo, said she would oppose any new austerity package. Among the leaders of Syriza there appeared real disgust with their government, with one member likening the proposal to the socialists voting for the war credits in 1914, and a betrayal of the popular mandate.

Demonstrations were called. The leaders of one trade union called for a mass mobilisation of the people to defend the OXI. The Communists called a separate demonstration. Amalia could not understand why they did not join hands with the OXI movement.

The government refused to put the proposal to parliament. Instead, Tsipras asked them for a vote of confidence to renew negotiations, re-interpreting the OXI vote as an endorsement of such. They gave him their confidence, but only with the votes of those pro-austerity MPs who had opposed OXI from the beginning.

Much of the online discussion among Amalia's friends revolved around the question of which had primacy: parliament or the referendum? In both Greece and Germany #ThisIsACoup trended in first place, and second internationally - two-hundred thousand times within a matter of hours on Twitter. When Amalia read that the EU was demanding fifty billion euros worth of Greek assets be handed over to them and placed in a Luxemburg-based trust for privatisation, she understood why. And then she read the Troika's demands:

> *"...to fully normalise working methods with the institutions* [The Troika] ... *the government needs to consult and agree with the institutions on all draft legislation in relevant areas with adequate time before submitting it for public consultation or to Parliament."*

From now on Greek law not only had to be approved by the Troika, but the Greek parliament would not even be permitted to propose new laws without its permission. What kind of democracy was this, thought Amalia, when we could do and say what we liked, as long as Brussels and Berlin made all the decisions? Reading her friends debate the issue, Amalia collapsed into a hole. It was true - it was a coup. She had always imagined a coup involved tanks and men in olive fatigues and oil-black sunglasses. What's more, she could see that the Parliament was in reality a living coup, ongoing, behind the backs of the people.

Where did the hinge hang? At what point did the betrayal come upon us? She screwed her eyes and furrowed her brow, but she could not see the perforation marks. She felt for the crease, but could not trace its line. Her mind stumbled, feeling in the dark for points of support. *There must be a fightback. But from whom?* The only organised force remaining was the so-called Communist Party. But they were off in a square somewhere, holding each other's hands.

Her hatred simmered impotently for this man she had worried herself over for so long. Now Tsipras only inspired revulsion. What had he been fighting against, if not austerity? Had he been capitulating all along and she too foolish to notice? She had been made a fool by this jellyfish, this floating invertebrate, pushed hither and thither by the current of the ocean. He was less than a jellyfish. At least they had a sting. He was a sponge, tumbling along on the ocean floor.

She shut down her computer and bowed her head. It was later than she had thought. Simi had invited her to give a report on her experience in Greece at the local Labour women's caucus upon her return to London. She was not particularly interested in attending a women-only meeting, not understanding the point of such an arrangement. But she did have a deep thirst to talk to all and anyone about Greece and the world, and the economy, and the war in Syria and the refugees. She was also hungry to hear what her fellow party members thought of her MP's campaign to become leader. It seemed to her to be gathering momentum. She had volunteered her services at the first opportunity. Jeremy was with the people of Greece - he had said as much to her. If her people saw that the British workers' party was with them, she had no doubt it would give them the necessary morale boost they needed to move once again and take matters into their own hands. And now she knew what the first step would be – to throw out the traitor Tsipras.

As Amalia rose to leave she reflected on how tedious her life in London once was. What was life without coffee and cigarettes and politics? She pulled on her jeans and grabbed her bag and leapt out of her flat into the low evening sun that cut into the second floor corridor, the door slamming behind her as she went.

3

Corbyn had been in relatively good healthy for quite some days now and appeared to have put his bout of summer fever behind him. Laura was not yet home, and so he and Jeremy were surviving on twiglets and salsa as they digested the six o'clock news. Jeremy laid back with his feet on the coffee table and a glass of cold ale to hand. Corbyn sipped his usual green tea.

'I have goals in life like everyone else,' said Reem, the Palestinian teenager, in her best German. *'I want to go to university; that's a goal I want to achieve.'*

Chancellor Merkel hung awkwardly in her green blouse before the group of German school children. A banner hovered above her head:

"Good life in Germany"

'I understand what you are saying...' Frau Merkel struggled to find the right words. *'Nonetheless, politics is hard sometimes. You're right in front of me now, and you're an extremely nice person. But you also know there are thousands more in the Palestinian refugee camps in Lebanon. And if we say: "You can all come here, you can all come from Africa", we just can't manage it.'*

As the Chancellor spoke, Reem smiled and nodded, demonstrating how well she grasped the language of the land that, more than anywhere else in the world, she wanted to call her home. She would not betray the wells that were rising within her, choking her throat sore and paralyzing further speech.

The Chancellor finished and stared at Reem. Unable to hold back any longer, the girl's body shook involuntarily and the tears burst forth.

'Oh come,' said the leader, who had just told a little girl on national television she was being sent back to poverty and war. *'You did it so well.'*

She moved to comfort the girl. The host pressed a finger against his ear.

'I don't think this is about doing it well, Frau Chancellor,' he

said, *'but about this being a very wearing situation for her.'*
The Chancellor turned from Reem, baring her teeth: *'I know that this is a very wearing situation, but I just want to give her a hug now.'* Turning back to Reem, she placed a hand on her shoulder: *'…because we don't want to put you in to such a situation.'*

Reem spluttered, looking up at her unrequited leader. Had she not said the right words? Did she not understand that she wanted very much to be put in such a situation? She wanted to continue in her new school, alongside her new classmates, not go back to the street rubble and night-time fires. Her friend held her, shielding her from the wicked old Chancellor.

'Because this is hard for you and because you have done a very good job of showing to many others how one can get in to such a situation. Ya?'

The sad little scene came to end and the news continued:

'Over five thousand refugees have crossed the Bavarian border this week,' said the reporter, *'and Germany has seen already this year asylum applications reach four-hundred and fifty thousand - more than twice the total for the whole of 2014.'*

Jeremy gestured at the screen. 'Only last year Merkel was celebrating twenty-five years since the fall of the Berlin Wall and how that she, as an East German, understood what it meant to be free. Now look at her: not even a crocodile tear for this poor girl. She'll be traumatised for life!'

'They probably won't deport her now,' said Corbyn. The news cut back to the studio anchor:

'In the Labour leadership contest the New Statesman newspaper has today reported the findings of two privately conducted polls that show that Jeremy Corbyn has developed an astonishing fifteen percent lead over his nearest rival.'

Corbyn spat out his Green tea. 'Did you hear that?' he said, wiping his chin. The anchor continued:

'The polling puts Andy Burnham in second place, despite his recent pledge to vote against the welfare reform bill if the reasoned amendment tabled by Labour is defeated.'

'I thought we were a hundred-to-one shot?' said Corbyn.
'What exactly is a reasoned amendment?' asked Jeremy.

'Basically, it's a way of opposing a bill without opposing it.'

'Oh, well that makes perfect sense.'

'Harriet is basically proposing that the bill not be given a second reading. It stops the process toward voting it into law. So it is an opposition, but the bill is, sort of... disappeared.'

'"Disappeared" - like a parliamentary Mafioso! It sounds more like sticking your fingers in your ears to avoid talking about the subject... It's quite terrifying when one considers the lengths our learned leadership lawyers will go to avoid a political debate.'

'You can understand why they do it,' said Corbyn. 'Better to kick it into the long grass than be exposed in front of the electorate.'

'I suppose they're worried they might upset someone. I think our leaders would be quite happy if Labour became nothing but one long, reasoned amendment. But we'll show them. Isn't that right?'

'Yes,' said Corbyn. 'Good to see Andy is voting against though. That is, if the reasoned amendment doesn't go through - and it almost certainly won't. In that case Harriet is calling for abstention. I'm certain she wants to vote with the Tories. But then again, she says she wants the party to "listen to public opinion". That's a big step forward. Shows we're changing the narrative.'

'Yes,' said Jeremy, sipping his beer, 'the narrative... I think Harriet has always listened to so-called public opinion to be perfectly honest, and that our campaign has very little to do with it. Only, sound public opinion speaks with many wondrous voices, doesn't it? The point is that Harriet and her people have no clue what to listen for; what to value, what to discard. I mean, is public opinion what the *BBC* and *The Guardian* and the *Daily Mail* say it is? Is it the answers to the loaded questions contrived by the polling companies? Or perhaps it's what the focus-groups and think-tanks have to say? Or is it all of these things at once, and a whole host of other self-referential abstractions that have become the shadow cabinet's flavour of the moment? "Public opinion" – these people don't know what day it is!'

The news reported that Prince Phillip enjoyed a delightful joke with a group of East London women, inquiring as to who it was they 'sponged off', as he cut the sponge cake they had prepared for him. Thankfully a Royal aide was on hand to speak to explain the Prince's apparent lack of irony. This was followed by Donald Tusk, the former Polish Prime Minister and head of the European Council, who was reported to have said that he feared a 'pre-revolutionary atmosphere' was developing in Europe after the political fall-out from Greece, warning against:

> '...this radical leftist illusion that you can build some alternative... When impatience becomes not an individual but a social experience of feeling, this is the introduction for revolutions.'

'What time is Benefits Street on?' asked Corbyn.

4

Around the same time that Jeremy and Corbyn were settling down to watch the news, Amalia was climbing the stairs of the Unite building. Eventually she found her way to a bustling office lit by fluorescent tubes. Inside, the place was full of Corbyn supporters, she guessed more than fifty, squashed against each other along the stackable oblong tables.

They were a motley bunch, and at least half of them were as young as her. It was an unfamiliar sight to Amalia. It was not unlike the stuffed seminar rooms of the university, but completely out of context, and with the presence of home she could not say where.

A friendly blonde lady in her thirties led her to a table. She was given a phone and introduced to her neighbours, who were all very excited by the responses they were receiving. That made Amalia a little nervous. But their excitement was infectious and before long they were happily discussing the campaign. They talked of the welfare vote in parliament and the surprise poll that had come out in the *New Statesman* giving Jeremy Corbyn a handsome lead. Some of them even dared to talk openly about what it would be like if he were to win. Everyone was very keen to hear what Amalia had to say about Greece and the OXI referendum, and they were even more impressed when she told them she was actually in Jeremy Corbyn's local party, and that she had met him.

Her audience was a breath of fresh air compared to her previous appointment. The women's caucus had consisted of Amalia, Simi, Geraldine and a little old lady with brightly dyed orange hair who smiled and said nothing, apart from when offering everybody tough, inedible lumps called 'rock cakes'. Amalia had prepared to speak for about twenty minutes, taking care to research the history of the debt and making a list of the myths about Greece that she planned to take apart. The turn-out had been a little disappointing, but she resolved to make the most of it.

Not two minutes into her talk Simi interrupted her with a series of questions about the macho reputation of the Greek male. A minute later she was interrupted again by another question from Simi on the impact on female health since the crisis. Amalia did her best to answer the questions, intersected as they were by clarifications from Geraldine. But then the discussion tailed off into questions about the weather and the local food and the islands, and Simi's reminiscences of her holiday with her boyfriend in Corfu when she was sixteen. Soon a half hour had passed, and Simi suggested moving the meeting over to business. That trundled on for an hour and a half, veering into all manner of obscure tangents, but none of it touching the leadership contest.

At the end of the meeting, under 'Any Other Business', Amalia showed them the advert in the *Revolutionary Newspaper* for the coming rally for Jeremy Corbyn in Camden at the beginning of August. Geraldine caught Simi's eye.

It appeared that Amalia's point was not appropriate, as the caucus was yet to express an opinion concerning the leadership contest. When she proposed they discuss it, it was announced that there was insufficient time.

When Amalia explained to the volunteers at the phone-bank that she had been in the party for more than a year, one or two eyebrows were raised. The only young person known to her neighbours as a member before the General Election was the blonde lady who had shown Amalia to her seat - and she must have been pushing thirty-five. A red-haired student named Ryan said he would leave the party if Corbyn did not win. It was the only reason why he joined in the first place; he would have never considered joining Labour otherwise. Sam, a tall and pale-skinned young English teacher said she had been a member of the Greens before the contest.

During the evening a delivery van arrived and all the volunteers traipsed downstairs to help carry up boxes of new phones. The blonde lady informed them that the campaign had been able to buy them with all the donations that had come in: a thousand pounds a day in small contributions.

As Amalia helped unload the van she was befriended by a shoal of very enthusiastic young students. It soon became clear they had been around the Labour party for a while longer than Ryan and Sam. They were all young men, sweet and good-natured, and uniformly wore tweed beneath long, foppish locks. One tall lad even had a pipe, and she joined him for a smoke on the office balcony when they returned upstairs. The young man told her what a great fan of Tony Benn he was. She said she thought she had heard mention of him in the video of Mhairi Black speaking. When he realised she did not really know who Tony Benn was, she was quite entertained to see his astonishment. He told her how he hoped to be a Unitarian minister one day, how a new call centre for the campaign had just been established in Liverpool, and how Jeremy Corbyn's campaign had attracted almost five thousand volunteers to date. She mostly listened as he talked at length, yet more often she found that her English failed her in the company of these boys with the leather-patched elbows; they spoke an unusual dialect, and far too fast.

At her desk Amalia dialled a few times before anyone picked up, getting through to fewer than ten of the forty numbers she dialled in total. Many were defensive to begin with, until she explained that she was phoning on behalf of Jeremy Corbyn. After that they generally became friendlier and, after a little practice, she found herself chatting away and even enjoying herself. To those on the other end of the line, her English did not fail.

One woman she spoke with, a long-term but inactive party member, was undecided. She worked in the care industry and told Amalia in deepest blue how disgusted she was with the low wages and big profits of the care-home owners. It was not difficult to convince her that Jeremy Corbyn was the best choice to fight poverty wages. One man supported Jeremy Corbyn because he shared the same left-wing views, but he was afraid he was unelectable because he was too 'middle-class'. Amalia had not heard Corbyn described as middle-class before, and would not have guessed it, not having an ear for the peculiar class-based nature of English accents.

At the end of each call she had to ask whether they would like to keep in touch with the campaign after the election, to help carry on building a 'social movement'. Not all said they would vote Corbyn,

5

'I'm making clear I would swim through vomit to vote against this bill,' said John, 'and listening to some of the nauseating speeches tonight I think we might have to.'

Laughter broke inside the house.

'Poverty, poverty in my constituency is not a lifestyle choice'

Hear, hear, rose the murmurs.

'It's imposed upon people. We hear lots about how high the welfare bill is. Let's understand why that's the case.

'The housing benefit bill is so high because for generations we've failed to build council houses, we've failed to control rents. We've done nothing about the three-hundred thousand properties that stand empty in this country.

'The reason tax credits are so high is because pay is so low, and the reason pay is so low is because employers have exploited workers. And we've removed trade union rights that would enable people to be protected at work. We now have less than a third of our workers covered by collective bargaining agreements.

'And the reason unemployment bills are so high is because we've failed to invest in our economy. We've allowed deindustrialisation of the North and Scotland and elsewhere. They're the reasons why the welfare bill is so high, and this welfare reform bill does what all the other welfare reform bills in recent years have done: blame the poor for their own poverty, and not the system.

'On Friday, I brought together in my constituency in a poverty seminar the welfare advice agencies, the local church, and religious groups, to talk about why there are people poor in my constituency.

'The reason they are poor is because rents are so high. People struggle to keep a roof over their heads. What this bill will do, on the cap, is remove sixty-three pounds a week from those families simply trying to keep a decent home over their children's heads.

'The second reason why they're so high is low pay. They depend in my constituency on tax credits to live - parents choosing whether they eat or the children eat that week. This will take sixty pounds a week from every one of those families.

'The other reason why we have got poverty in my constituency is because people have disabilities; they struggle to work and can't do it. This will take thirty pounds a week off people with disabilities who are desperately trying to work, because they're in the work support group trying to get work.

'That's the reasons for the poverty in my constituency. I find it appalling that we sit here in, to be frank, relative wealth ourselves, and we're willing to vote through increased poverty on the people back in our home constituencies themselves.

'And can I say: some of the benefit cuts are going to be absolutely appalling. What is not in this bill, but it is being sneaked through by the government, is the cuts in support allowances for asylum-seeker children - cut by thirty percent - some of the poorest children in our society we're about to ensure that they are pushed into further poverty.

'What we need now is an honest discussion about the reasons for that poverty and how we can invest to ensure we get people out of poverty. And it is some of the things that have been mentioned tonight, it is about lifting wages.

'And to come along and to describe what is a derisory increase in the minimum wage as a living wage when we know a living wage in this country is at least ten pounds and hour - I think it's a disgrace to, well, English rhetoric if nothing else, but also robbing the poor in the face of the poor itself.

'I believe tonight we've seen yet again another way in which we blame the individual for the failings of our society. What we need is a proper debate about how we go forward: in investing in housing, lifting wages, restoring trade union rights, making sure that we actually do ensure that we've got people back to work right the way across the country - that we don't have these high pockets of deprivation in areas around mine, and around the country itself.

'Tonight I think the debate has not served the House of Commons well, to be frank. But I say this to my own side: People down there don't understand reasoned amendments. They want to know: Did you vote for this bill or did you vote against? I say tonight I vote against.'

Hear, hear, rose the murmurs. John sat down.

He spoke well, Corbyn said to Jeremy, but few were present for the debate prior to the vote. They went and sat beside their friend on the green leather benches of the House of Commons.

After dinner that evening, taxi after taxi pulled up outside the Palace of Westminster, and they all piled in.

6

'Orderrr!' growled the speaker of the house. 'Or-dare!'

The Commons was full to overflowing, and fell silent as the tellers came forth.

'The Ayes to the right: three-hundred and eight. The No's to the left: one hundred and twenty-four.'

The murmurs rose and rose, transforming into a pantomime jeer. The Tory benches applauded wholeheartedly the one hundred and eighty-four Labour MPs. With the means in their hands to defeat the bill they had sat tight, watching as the government benches rose to form an orderly queue to vote for a bill that would take billions of pounds out of the hands of working-class people.

'The Ayes have it, the ayes have it,' proclaimed the speaker.

A member of the SNP demanded to speak:

'As mutual arbiter of this house,' he addressed the speaker, 'is there any way you could help me and advise me as to how we could achieve this: Can we rearrange the furniture of this house, so that we become the official opposition?'

The SNP member's voice became drowned under the wild endorsements that rang throughout the Commons:

'The Labour Party can abstain… somewhere in the back benches,' he cried at the top of his voice.

The prostrate Labour MPs slumped in their benches. Some looked to their acting leader, but Harriet only had eyes for the forty-eight MPs who had broken party discipline and defied her. Her scowl fell most of all on the rebel leaders: Jeremy and Corbyn and John.

'Do they really understand what they've done?' said Corbyn, turning away in disgust. 'They've taken billions out of the mouths of the poor.'

'Yes. It's certainly sorted the wheat from the chaff,' said Jeremy. 'I see Ronnie didn't join us. What's his excuse?'

'Neither did Andy. Nor Heidi, Angela, Pat, Owen, Tom… Not even young Hilary,' said Corbyn. 'His father would be spinning in his grave.'

'Harriet just led one hundred and eighty-four of our men into the marsh,' said Jeremy.

'When you add it to the total opposition, we would have beaten the government by twenty. It makes our party culpable,' said Corbyn.

'When you abstain,' said Jeremy, 'you hand your vote to which ever way the wind blows.'

'Yes, to the biggest bully goes the playground.'

'Tony had a pretty accurate measure of his son - he often said as much,' said Jeremy. 'Well, I'm not responsible for the little brat… and you shouldn't wring your hands over him either.' He turned to his friend: 'He's only a Benn in name.'

John came up to them as they filed out of the chamber. 'Looks like our shadow cabinet has selected itself,' said Jeremy, pinching him on the shoulders. John laughed. Sometimes he could not altogether tell whether Jeremy was joking or not.

Corbyn did not see the joke. 'Imagine sifting a shadow cabinet out of this car crash,' he said.

'On their gravestones it will be forever carved: When they came for the workers and the poor, I did nothing,' said Jeremy.

The shrill, public-school whinny of the Tories filled the chamber like a gentleman's bathing house. But as it drained, it was noticeable that there were some from the Tory benches - the less rabid elders-in-waiting - who while voting with their party, nevertheless shook their heads at the nauseating display they had witnessed on the opposition benches.

'At least this Corbyn fellow knows where the stumps are,' said one, passing into the lobby.

'Mules beget no offspring,' another was overheard to remark.

'Good for glue, but I'm afraid not much else,' lamented another.

They pulled on their evening jackets and they made their way back to the gentlemen's club.

***

At the end of July the British Prime Minister warned of the need to protect British borders from the human 'swarm' - seventy-six thousand that month — who had travelled to Europe to escape war and poverty.

CHAPTER 10
JEREMY IN LIVERPOOL

1

In the days that followed the vote on welfare reform angry protests filled social media. Comments registered in the thousands. And those comments were woven into threads. And those threads pulled at the bare gossamer that clothed the emperors of New Labour.

Andy's nest was disturbed more than most. He tried to remind everyone that his opposition to the bill had been through the reasoned amendment, but that he abstained because did not want to plunge the party into 'civil war'.

When Jeremy heard of the responses Andy received to his reasoned argument, he could not help but admire the lyricism of the British public, the spirit of which was all too often passed over by the mainstream rags.

2

Meetings and rallies continued to be added to their schedules, and as July became August the campaign began to take its toll on both Jeremy and Corbyn. Laura's suggested they split their appointments between them, to lighten the burden. Jeremy thought it sensible, and Corbyn agreed immediately, seeing it as a vindication of his previous objections. His expectation had been that Jeremy's ambitious plans would fall foul of the dog days of summer, when Britain was too distracted by the August heat to bother about politics. But in truth, he needed the break.

The Merseyside Association of Trades Councils was hosting a rally. Jeremy volunteered. That suited Corbyn, who had always felt uncomfortable among the Liverpudlians, finding them difficult to follow. Besides, the place reminded him of that awful Kilroy-Silk. On the other hand, Jeremy had always enjoyed his visits to the North-West, and he had had a grand old time of it when visiting Birkenhead the previous month.

After stopping off at Preston for an afternoon rally, Jeremy finally arrived in Liverpool, making his way to the Adelphi hotel. Upon arrival, he was confronted with an enormous queue snaked around the corner, bustling in the final light of the summer's evening. As he approached the entrance they crowded in on him with such force that he initially thought he was being descended upon by an angry mob. But then they spoke:

'Jeremy, you've our traditional values,' said a middle-aged woman. 'Right back to when the party was first set up. It's all about creating a better society isn't it, Jeremy?' Realising he was among friends, and that the press of the crowd was merely the grip of enthusiasm, he relaxed and gladly entered into conversation with the woman as he passed through the hotel entrance. They were squeezing into the lobby when an elderly lady interrupted them:

'I'm with you Jeremy because you've got genuine ideals. You're not one of those careerist politicians like the other three.' Then all three of them began talking, encircled by many fascinated onlookers, about Labour's terrible conduct over the welfare bill. Both women insisted that he sort out the trouble-makers once he was leader. Jeremy was about to reply when a robust, bearded old man with thick glasses burst in from the surrounding crowd:

'You've inspired the working class, Jeremy. You've given us hope because you say what you mean, and you mean what you say! He's galvanizing people!' the old man declared to the two ladies. Then he poked Jeremy in the chest: 'Because you're standing up against austerity and that must be good.'

More approached beneath the Adelphi's chandeliers, and Jeremy spoke with each and every one of them for as long as they wished, and as time went on his assailants began to answer each other, and then it was Jeremy that intervened in their discussions.

And as they spoke, he felt the comradely spirit of *The Internationale* ghost between them, as if being sung by a choir in a far-off room:

> *Arise ye workers from your slumbers,*
> *Arise ye prisoners of want,*
> *For reason in revolt now thunders,*
> *And at last ends the age of cant.*

Finally, he was pulled away by an official, and he bade them farewell. It had set him in a fine mood. By the time he walked into the main hall it was teeming, and he was welcomed with a long applause. He took his seat on stage. When the clapping died down, the chair began:

'When we decided to have the meeting in Liverpool on a Saturday night, some people in the south said: "The Scousers will never turn out, they'll be pissed, they'll be drinking."'

The hall filled with laughter, proud and contrite.

'I said to them: "The thing about Scousers is, they know when to drink, and when not to drink", and I'm really proud - 'cos the television's here... but you're here on a Saturday night - some people from six o'clock.'

The applause was casual, but the gathered mass was of such weight, that it fell upon the platform with a mighty crash.

'I just wanna remind people that Jeremy is one of the only forty-eight Labour MPs that voted against the Tories' bill on welfare.'

The room did not sit back for that, but overflowed with a demanding and superior cheer. Whistles escaped into the air.

'And we only have one other in the whole of Merseyside, and that was Margaret Greenwood. Please write to her and congratulate her for standing up.'

Spontaneous applause echoed in the hall.

'So last week in Manchester,' continued the chair, 'Martin Mayer, the leader of the broad left in Unite, decided to introduce Jeremy as the new leader of the Labour Party and the next Labour socialist Prime Minister!'

The cheers went up and so did the hairs on Jeremy's neck. The chair gave him the floor.

He stood to speak, and a second wave rolled over the first, exploding against the platform's edge. Liverpool rose to its feet with him, and the applause was prolonged, and they honoured him with a mobile phone flash salute. He had not yet uttered a word.

Away with all your superstitions,
Servile masses arise, arise,
We'll change henceforth the old tradition,
And spurn the dust to win the prize.

He looked out upon the Mersey. The chairs stretched back forty rows and were at least as many wide. None went unfilled. Many contained a head greyed by thirty years of waiting, yet a more youthful rim of colour ringed the outer edge, thinner, but with a greater circumference. More youth contorted to peer in from the outside, walling the main doorway closed. Others had to be satisfied with hearing what they could, holding discussions of their own in adjacent rooms.

'A huge thanks to all of you for giving up your Saturday night,' Jeremy began. The cheers went up again. *He speaks!*

'You've come to the Adelphi, and there's not even a dance, so I'm sorry about that.'

They were hardly settled, when outbursts began at the back of the hall. *Have the Blairites sent their thugs?* Then he worried there might be some genuine trouble. Finally, a cry was heard above the others:

'We can't hear you - speak up Jeremy!'

The request was taken up by a hundred polite voices at once. His microphone was too low. He adjusted it and, as he did, they sent him a round of encouragement. Another barrier overcome.

Jeremy began again, making sure to repeat his joke about the dance. He thanked the organisers and praised Liverpool - one of the historic fortresses of socialism – from its struggle against the slave trade, to its proud labour and trade union tradition, to its championing of gay rights. And he made sure to deliver a message from his friend John, a son of the city, who wished he could have been there.

'Now, our campaign is, at one level, an election campaign for the leadership of the Labour Party. *We didn't want that.* We felt that in the aftermath of the defeat in May we should have been doing something different: We should have been examining the policies that led us to that defeat. We should be having that serious policy debate.'

Spontaneous applause echoed in the hall.

'*But the existing leadership did not want that kind of discussion...* and so we entered this leadership campaign. It was extremely difficult because the Parliamentary Labour Party holds the keys to the gate to the election campaign. *The requirement for MP's nominations is an anti-democratic device, one of conservative inertia, designed to keep the rank and file out of the democratic process — something I will change if elected Labour leader.*'

Spontaneous applause echoed in the hall.

'I understand that some of the thirty-six people who signed the nomination papers were apparently very reluctant to do so, and they've made themselves clear since then. Well, I'm sure they'll unclear themselves and clear their minds and be supportive as time goes on. I've no doubt...'

Laughter, and spontaneous applause, echoed in the hall.

'I've no doubt that a sense of clarity will soon prevail.'

More laughter.

'And I want to say a big thank you to those that initially nominated, led by John of course, but also to those also who genuinely thought that there should be an open, democratic debate on the future of our party and our movement.

> *No more deluded by reaction,*
> *On tyrants only we'll make war,*
> *The soldiers too will take strike action,*
> *They'll break ranks and fight no more*

'And I also want to say a big thank you to the thousands and thousands of people all over the country who could observe what was going on, and wanted to make sure that a *working-class, socialist voice* could be heard, and therefore got on to social media, Facebook, Twitter, emails and made sure that that voice was heard there. So…'

Spontaneous applause echoed in the hall.

'…whilst, yes, it is my name on the ballot paper - of course it is, I'm very proud to be that voice – this is a campaign about us, it's a campaign about we, it's a campaign about what we *as the working class* here tonight can achieve: *a socialist society not just in Britain, but worldwide. Therefore, we must be very clear: Our campaign is about how we must take our party back by arming it with a socialist programme.*'

Spontaneous applause echoed in the hall.

'The issues that we are facing are quite simply this: We lost office in 2010 on the back of a *capitalist* crisis *triggered* by the banking collapse in the USA, and the consequent collapse here. *No tinkering with the system could have prevented it, because the crisis was one of overproduction, something we will always have as long as we have capitalism, which is a society based on market-place competition and production for private profit. In all previous societies, crises were caused by underproduction, such as failed crops and bad harvests. But in capitalist society we have the madness of a famine amid plenty, because what is produced cannot be sold profitably by the capitalists. Therefore, you had crazy investments, the sub-prime mortgage crisis, greedy bankers, de-regulation; all symptoms of a system that does not know what to do with itself – it would do anything but put its money into production. Such symptoms were by-products of the contradiction at the heart of the capitalism: the workers are also consumers. If you rob us, you no longer have anyone to sell to. That's what overproduction is – too much produced for the poverty and restricted consumption they have forced upon us. The crisis of 2008 was not a mistake, it was not human error: it was the eruption of something that had been building up in the arteries of their system for decades.* It was not caused by the alleged overpayment of nurses, street cleaners, factory workers or any other worker.'

Spontaneous applause echoed in the hall.

'It was not brought about by the benefits system, or the cost of the National Health Service. And we were told that the only way forward was to set an arbitrary date to move back into budget surplus, an arbitrary date by which we'd pay down the debt. Incidentally, the debt had gone up under George Osborne, not down. And as a result, there would have to be austerity; austerity meaning cuts in public expenditure; loss of several hundred thousand jobs in the civil service; wage freeze for public sector workers; cuts in benefits; cuts in the living standards of the poorest; freeze on council house building virtually through most of the country. And you look at the results. What are the results, really? The richest five families in Britain - the richest five families, the fingers of one hand...' he held up a splayed hand, 'owns the equivalent of the total wealth of twenty percent of the entire population.'

"Shame!" came the declaration from the back of the hall.

'The richest hundred families own the equivalent of thirty percent. We live in a grotesquely unequal society.'

Spontaneous applause echoed in the hall.

'And that inequality is getting worse. My objection to austerity is *not that it coincides with the Tories' most fervent desires; it's a far bigger question than the whim of a single party - even one as nasty as David Cameron's. Plenty of so-called socialist parties in Europe, whose leadership nevertheless accept capitalism, also back austerity. But if you accept capitalism, then you must obey the laws of capitalism - and those laws at present demand brutal attacks on the working class. Just look at what has happened in Greece. Tsipras was not willing to break with capitalism, and so he bent the knee. The great anti-austerity beacon of Europe transformed into a paid servant of the Troika! Let's learn the lessons of Greece. Let's learn the lessons of Syriza: That all attempts to make capitalism humane are as useful as trying to convince a man-eating crocodile to turn vegetarian.'*

Jeremy and Corbyn

> *And if those cannibals keep trying,*
> *To sacrifice us to their pride,*
> *They soon shall hear the bullets flying,*
> *We'll shoot the generals on our own side!*

'My objection goes far beyond the Tories. Saying that austerity is merely an ideological whim is a subjective explanation. It is one that explains precisely nothing! The enormous state debt is an objective reality, and under capitalism someone has to pay. 'I say: Make the bosses pay! Let's take them down, and their system with it!'

Spontaneous applause echoed in the hall.

'But that means taking away their power and resources. After the Second World War, capitalism temporarily flourished. That benefited some of us in the West, but it was an historic aberration. Now the system is reverting to type - it can no longer afford the reforms that the working class conquered in those post-war years. Now it's going back to the 1930s and probably, in George Osborne's mind, more like the 1830s. *They can do nothing else but remake our society after their own ugly image, destroy public services and put the bill onto the working class.* Indeed, David Cameron was thinking aloud a few weeks ago when he said: "How about we get rid of National Insurance and just have individual insurance?"

'Well, that might work very well if you're a wealthy family, to have individual insurance to guarantee yourself against any ill that comes about. The whole point - the whole point - of National Insurance, and the welfare state, is that we all protect each other; we're all protected by each other. *'It is a reform we conquered within their system, and the principle is the basis for socialism. What we know about reforms, however, is that what the masters concede with the left, they will take with the right. 'Therefore, the only real way to defend reforms like National Insurance and the NHS, is not to play the bosses at their own game, but to relieve them of their monopolies, their industry, their wealth — wealth that they have gained on the backs of our class for generations. They have proved time and again that they are too irresponsible to run society. Now comes the time for us to transform it, by taking control and democratically running it ourselves. I think it's called the socialist revolution.'*

Long and spontaneous applause echoed in the hall, and Jeremy felt the stomping of feet move the floor beneath him.

'So, you have to ask yourself a couple of questions. This austerity and inequality – what's it doing? Slicing apart local authority budgets; slicing apart household budgets; closing libraries; closing facilities for the elderly. Closing care centres; closing lots of things; and privatising, privatising, privatising, all along the way. The numbers of families that are hit because of the combination of the change in tax credits and benefit cuts - half of all the families in Liverpool are going to be hit by this budget and this welfare bill that's gone through. That is the strategy they're following. Now, if I asked all of you now to stick your hand up – please don't so as it would be a forest - if you supported the principle of a health service free at the point of use as a human right, you'd all say yes.'

Corbyn had advised Jeremy not to involve the audience too much. He said crowds could be unpredictable, and that it was impolite to put people on the spot. Besides, imagine how embarrassing it would be if no one responded.

"Yes!" they cried as one.

Before Jeremy grew a dark woodland, pushing the Adelphi's crystal chandelier against the ceiling, causing sparkling snowflakes to rain down in the centre of the forest. Looking at the mass of hands reaching for the sky, Jeremy wondered what Corbyn would make of it all. His fears were clearly quite unfounded.

> *No saviour from on high delivers,*
> *No faith have we in prince or peer,*
> *Our own right hand the chains must shiver,*
> *Chains of hatred, greed and fear*

'It was the great achievement of the post-war Labour government; it's the great achievement of Nye Bevan that he managed to push it through. I might add at a time when...'

He was interrupted by spontaneous applause which echoed in the hall.

'Yes, and at a time when the debt ratio was much higher than today. Although we must remember that at that time capitalism, rather than suffering from the plague of overproduction, was actually suffering from underproduction, because of the destruction caused by the Second World War. That allowed capitalism room to expand into, helping it to pay off its debts, which in turn allowed for the establishment of the NHS, through which the Atlee government invested in people, in hope, in the future... Of course, that's not to pretend that that government was perfect - they made mistakes. They made allowances for private beds, an elitist privilege that still haunts the NHS today. And, of course, they invested in nuclear weapons and the war in Korea, and divided the living body of India, causing untold bloodshed - we must never forget that. But with the NHS and the nationalisation of industries they did something good. Today we must go further — we have no choice. We've got to finish the job they started. Because it's not crumbs we want from the tables of the bosses - our mouths won't be silenced with bread. What we demand is nothing less than the entire bakery!'

Jeremy was at one with his audience. He thumped the air, and spontaneous applause echoed in the hall.

'There is something deeply wrong about a system that creates the levels of inequality, desperation, destitution and poverty that exists in modern Britain. The ruling class have no answer to these problems and want to run away from them. 'I'm shocked every time I see somebody living on the streets. I'm shocked when I go to flats and houses around the country where children are growing up in grossly overcrowded conditions. I'm shocked when family's view the onset of the school summer holiday with dread and horror because their children will no longer get a free school meal, and possibly a free school breakfast.' There is something deeply wrong about a *socio-economic system and its ruling class* that is prepared to accept and tolerate the levels of inequality, desperation, destitution, and poverty that exists

in modern Britain *and all around the world. And, to paraphrase something a clever German once said: Here it becomes evident, that the capitalists are no longer fit to be the ruling class in society, and impose upon us their terms of existence as if they were some eternal law. They are unfit to rule because they are incompetent to assure an existence to their workers within their wage-slavery, and because of this they cannot but sink into such a state, that we have to feed them, even though their system prevents us from feeding ourselves. Our class can no longer live under these capitalists, in other words, their existence is no longer compatible with society.* We don't need…'

Spontaneous applause echoed in the hall.

'We don't need to go down the agenda set by 'Benefits Street' and others. *We possess our own working-class, socialist morality.* And that morality simply says this: If society can provide health and education for all, it can also provide housing for all… *There are enough empty houses today to house everybody. Therefore, our principle must be this: A house empty is a house occupied!*

Spontaneous applause echoed in the hall.

'A socialist Labour government's success will not be measured by the normal economic indices, but by the levels of poverty that are reducing; the number of children that are no longer going hungry; the number of people that are no longer sleeping on the streets; the number of people that are able to live and contribute normally within our society… *The need for such measurements in the first years of socialism will be a stark reminder for us of how low humanity sank in the last days of capitalism.'*

Spontaneous applause echoed in the hall.

'Now, that's achieved by two things…' The chair indicated that Jeremy needed to bring his remarks to a close. 'Two areas that I just want to briefly mention, because I think they are very important. The first is education, and the education system as a whole…'

Spontaneous applause echoed in anticipation.

'Every child ought to have a free space in pre-school education. It shouldn't be a lottery, it shouldn't be based

on income, it should be based on the needs of the child; and children's socialisation before they get to school is something that's very important. The children's centres, Sure Start, were a great step forward. It's *criminal* the way they're being destroyed at the moment. *A socialist Labour government will* provide something decent for all our children.'

Spontaneous applause echoed in the hall.

'But the Tories have other ideas, and the other ideas later on in the school age are to turn primary and secondary schools into academies, and any council that wants to open a free school can do so; any council that wants to open a normal, state, community comprehensive - forget it, there's no money available for it. I don't want to close any schools. I want to keep schools open. But I do want to strengthen the whole concept of the local education authority, the family of schools, and bring those academies and free schools back into the normal local authority system. *And by that I mean to say very clearly: We will socialise all vestiges of private education in society.*'

Spontaneous applause echoed in the hall.

'And while we're on with it, I know it sounds very extreme and very far-fetched, but to insist that every teacher in a free school is actually qualified to teach, seems to me quite a good idea.'

Spontaneous applause echoed in the hall.

'But the teachers have been denigrated by this government and sadly, occasionally, even by *those Tories that infest parts of* our own party. In the same way that medical professions are being denigrated now, merely because they've raised concerns about the idea of seven days working without the necessary new staff, recruitment and changes, that can make that a reality. But, there is another issue, and that is the way in which working class youngsters get a chance to go to college, and go to university. The cancellation of the Educational Maintenance Allowance means that many young people simply don't want to stay on at school because they can't afford to, and therefore miss out on A-levels, miss out on the chance of going to university. Those that do go to university, and I was talking to a young man today who just graduated - we were in a rally in Preston - and I congratulated him on his degree and said: "Well done, hope things go well for you", and he was very pleased with the degree he got, and he deserves those congratulations - it's a great achievement. And I said: "What's for you now?" and he said: "Fifty-two thousand pounds worth of debt." Fifty-two thousand pounds worth of debt, because he worked hard, got his A-levels; worked hard, went to university; worked hard, got a degree - and he's now got that level of debt. Well, I voted against the introduction of fees in the first place. I voted it against it...'

Spontaneous applause echoed in the hall.

'...when it was put up to three thousand, I voted against it; when it was put up to nine thousand... and I think we have to look at *the people who run this society* and say: What kind of a society are we in when we penalise someone for being educated? Because if somebody is a good engineer, if somebody is a good lawyer, if somebody is a good doctor, a good surveyor; all the other things that are so important - we all benefit. If there's a good doctor, you benefit - you know the reality.'

Spontaneous applause echoed in the hall.

'Education is not just for the individual. Education is for the society as a whole.'

More spontaneous applause echoed in the hall.

'And when people say we can't afford it - we've done some looking at the figures. We don't know exactly what the situation is going to be like by 2020, *or whenever the next General Election is,* but by the calculations we've been working out – *Corbyn promises me* we've got a good team of people doing it – err... we could raise the corporation tax, instead of cutting it by two percent, raise it by nought-point-eight-five percent, would be enough income to pay for the fees of all students in universities. '*Taxing the rich would be a very good start, but of course that situation would not last long. It would have to be followed up quickly with the expropriation of the big, super-rich companies, before they escaped abroad. And, of course, if they do that, the revolution would go after them to retrieve any stolen wealth and bring it back. Only in that way can we truly, democratically, decide where we want to reinvest the wealth that is produced by all of us, but is currently hoarded by the bosses for themselves.'*

Spontaneous applause echoed in the hall.

'That to me is absolutely a price worth paying. *Such an attitude to education would be an example, inspiring students here and throughout the world, where they're also suffering the same problems. That would help in the spreading of socialism internationally.* But while we're on with it, let's have an attitude to education which is about the value of learning. I'm shocked by the way that adult education is being cut back, opportunities cut back for people with learning difficulties, people with mental health conditions and so many other things. Education isn't just for qualifications for work; it's also for the benefit of society as a whole.'

Spontaneous applause echoed in the hall.

'*The ruling class* don't like us to be too well educated; don't like us to be thinking too much; don't like us to understand our history and where we come from.'

Long and spontaneous applause echoed in the hall. Jeremy felt the stomping of feet again.

> *E'er the thieves will out with their booty,*
> *And give to all a happier lot.*
> *Each at the forge must do their duty,*
> *And we'll strike while the iron is hot.*

'The last point I'll make is this, because it's a hot evening, and I want us to be able to listen to each other and talk to each other a bit as well. It is the issues of the environment and peace and justice around the world. *We cannot go on allowing the corporations, who have invested huge amounts of money into fossil fuels, to keep burning oil, dumping sewage and pollutants into the sea, while holding back the implementation of clean technology. Air pollution, be it nitrous oxide, sulphur dioxide, or anything else, has no respect for national borders. If we pollute anywhere, we pollute everywhere; if we destroy here, we destroy everywhere else.*

'It's not a question of limiting individual consumption — that's just another form of austerity the ruling class try to guilt us into — their wasteful methods create such enormous so-called externalities that the impact of the working class pales into insignificance when you consider the impact of the corporations. No, the fundamental question of the environment means finding, not individual solutions, but carrying out action as a class. That means breaking with the oil cartels and nuclear energy, and putting the value that we produce — the bosses don't produce a penny of it — into clean technology. That poses the question not of a British socialism, not even of a European socialism, but of a socialist world. Only in that way, through overcoming the narrow national interest, can we have a world without borders and treat our environment with respect.'

Spontaneous applause echoed in the hall.

'This city led the way in clean water in the nineteenth century when Liverpool Corporation built Lake Vyrnwy, the pipes and the dam that went with it, and showed what municipal enterprise could achieve... *Socialist municipalities, linked to an overall socialist plan of production, can do the same in every city.*

Spontaneous applause echoed in the hall.

'There is much we have to achieve in those areas; and the inspiration of those people who draw our attention to the destruction of the natural world and the ecosystem - to me they are eco-heroes, and we should respect what they are doing.'

Spontaneous applause echoed in the hall.

'But I also want to conclude with this thought. I voted against the Afghanistan war, the Iraq war, and I was one of the organisers of that million-strong march. And we had massive meetings here in Liverpool against that Iraq war. When wars are over, the victors write the history, the victors decide who's won, and the victors tell the rest of the world who's won.

'What they don't usually tell you is: who's lost? And I'll tell you who's lost: those desperate people in refugee camps in Lebanon; those desperate people in refugee camps in Libya; those desperate people dying in the Mediterranean; and indeed...'

Spontaneous applause echoed in the hall.

'...some of those desperate people in Calais that the Prime Minister describes as a "swarm"... *The imperialist looting of the world for the profit of the giant transnational corporations must stop. In a socialist society we would have no interest in buying oil with the blood of our children throughout the world. The Prime Minister condemns the refugees for pouring into Europe and jumping on the backs of trucks in Calais.* But when somebody is desperate, they do desperate things... *Why would anyone leave their homes and loved ones otherwise? We must rise to our full stature as human beings* and reach out to those humans, and be human, and not *allow the Tories to* condemn them *on our behalf. That is something that we can do, which they cannot. We carry the germ of a humane socialist society within us - no matter how they brutalise us, and sow bitterness, and try to make us think like them. The ruling class, on the other hand, must surround themselves with brutal ideas. They must learn to normalise their brutality. Otherwise, they could not live with themselves. Ours are simple ideas,* based on the aspirations of *human solidarity, social need and justice,* rather than nuclear weapons and the ability to destroy; something that's surely well worth striving for and working for.'

Spontaneous applause echoed in the hall.

'This meeting tonight is about lots of things. At one level it's about an election campaign; at another level, it's about the future of the party; and at another level, it's about the hope that exists within all of us.

Prolonged and persistent spontaneous applause echoed in the hall.

It did not stop as Jeremy continued:

'The hope that we can build a movement, a sustainable movement, that is for social change; that we can stand up to injustice. We can work towards the decent, equal, fair society that those people that founded our unions, and founded this party, and have written, worked so hard, for so long, can be brought about. *We can bring about a society where everyone matters; where people are not pitted the one against the other, but have the free time to relate to one another in a community; a society that has progressed from this archaic class system, based on private profit and the so-called survival of the fittest; and is a* happier, more prosperous, more successful, more peaceful society. *Its name is socialism.*

So comrades, come rally,
And the last fight let us face,
The Internationale unites the human race.

'We have launched a social movement in this, and I'm proud of all the young people that have come forward, and older people that have come out, to help in this campaign. Last night, only five weeks into this campaign, we received our six-thousandth volunteer to sign up to come and help in this campaign.'
Spontaneous applause echoed in the hall.
'Whatever the outcome, please, get organised. Nothing in life worth fighting for is easy. If you haven't done so already, join the Labour Party. If we don't change the party through this leadership contest come September the Twelfth, then I promise you: We're not going anywhere! This is our party, the party of the working class, and we will take what's ours. When a worker has rats in his house, he doesn't walk away; he doesn't look for a new house. He has no other choice but to roll up his sleeves and sweep the house clean, floor by floor, inch by inch, until he is free of the rats, gnawing away at the foundations of his house. We will do this by winning the party back to a socialist programme — a new Clause Four, if you will - that has, as its central demand, the socialist transformation of society through the socialisation of the commanding heights of the economy, under democratic workers' control and management. Only in that way can we win: For ourselves, for our children, and for future generations to come.'
Spontaneous applause echoed in the hall.

'Thank you very much for this meeting this evening!'

The hall exploded, and the guests in the expensive suites on the top floor of the hotel wondered what on earth was going on.

So comrades, come rally,
And the last fight let us face,
The Internationale unites the human race!

Jeremy stayed as long as he could afterwards, drinking heartily in the pub next to Liverpool train station and discussing and joking with old comrades, and teaching the young comrades socialist songs. But before long the last train called and he had to leave. To all he said goodnight, shaking many a hand, and on his way he went.

For most of the return journey he slept, only to wake in a daze as the train pulled into Euston station. Gathering himself together, he walked amid a fog of sleep into the London night.

The night bus was full when it finally arrived. Cold and tired, Jeremy was just about able to squeeze into a corner on the lower deck and passed into a standing sleep as the bus carried him home in the early hours of the morning.

2

The following morning Corbyn was reading a letter at the kitchen table when Jeremy entered in his pyjamas. He was still carrying the night's fog with him as he sat opposite his friend, his grey hair reaching skyward in an alarming tuft.

'I didn't hear you come in last night,' said Corbyn, peering above his glasses. 'You must have been home late... Good meeting in Liverpool?'

'Quite late, the night bus seemed to take an age,' said Jeremy, reaching for Corbyn's toast. 'Very good meeting though - quite incredible, really. There must have been at least a thousand. The comrades thought perhaps even one-and-a-half.'

'Yes, Liverpool has always been keen...,' said Corbyn, returning to his letter. 'The pro-European group have been in touch.'

'Kinnock's group?' said Jeremy, helping himself to Corbyn's coffee. He looked around. 'Where's El Gato?'

'I think he's out seeing one of his queens.'

'It was really something in Liverpool, old boy. I mean the enthusiasm that was there. I put forward the full programme and, I tell you - people responded. There's no need for you to worry about that.'

'Very good…' said Corbyn. 'I don't know whether Kinnock's with them. I'm sure he's knocking about somewhere in the background. They're asking us to state clearly where we stand on the ref…'

He paused and looked up at Jeremy.

'What do you mean: "The full programme"?'

'Do they really need to ask? They should know where we stand on the EU, particularly after what's happened in Greece,' said Jeremy, crunching on Corbyn's toast.

'What do you mean by "The Full Programme"?' said Corbyn more sternly, removing his reading glasses and putting down the letter. 'What exactly did you say last night?'

'Oh, you know; what we stand for, how we're going to get it - that kind of thing. I tell you…' he paused and licked the butter from his fingers, 'you've no need to worry. By their reaction I would judge they're more than on board. I finished by saying that we'll kick the Blairite rats out and bring back Clause Four.'

Corbyn crushed the letter in a clenched fist.

'You said what!?'

'Well, come on old man, we've got to say it straight. We both know that if Labour is ever going to stand up for our class, then it needs to be serious.'

'No one is going to take us seriously if we start harping on about bringing back Clause Four! I hope the press doesn't get hold of this – they'll make a laughing stock out of us.'

'Well, the people of Liverpool seemed to like it – isn't that what counts? It was an interesting little experiment. You're always saying we need to tone down our message, not stir things up. But last night showed that there's quite a number who are receptive. You just have to engage them. And even though you said I shouldn't, I asked people to raise their hand if they supported the NHS, and every hand in the room went up.'

'A thousand hard-lefts in Liverpool would raise their hands. But it's hardly representative of the wider population. People aren't used to these ideas. Half the room probably didn't even understand what had been said, and just stuck their hand up for fear of looking foolish.'

Jeremy furrowed his brow. 'Even if you're right, even if people are unfamiliar with socialist ideas, then isn't our job as socialists to familiarise them with such ideas, rather than assume they can't understand them? Just like on this European question that our friends have written to us about. I'm sure that letter expresses the feelings of a number of people, but we can't just go any way the wind blows. We've got to stick to our principles: there's nothing progressive about the EU - it's just a capitalist club.'

'You might be right. But if we say we're against the EU, then we'll lose the support of a great deal of MPs.'

'Have you forgotten that this contest is one-member-one-vote? There isn't an MP's bloc anymore. They had to give it up to justify getting rid of the trade union bloc.'

'But the MPs still wield influence. What they say can have a decisive impact on what the membership thinks.'

'Maybe so, but our job must be to tell the truth, old boy. What if we were to win this blasted contest? If that were to happen, how could we turn around and say: "Actually, we were against the EU all along?" It'd be dishonest.'

'Look, Jeremy,' said Corbyn, smoothing out the crumpled letter. 'If we don't come out in favour of the European Union, then we place ourselves in the camp of those UKIP bigots. The PLP hates them more than the Tories! And so do young people. The papers are saying that much of our support is coming from the youth, who are very pro-EU. If we oppose it, we'll ruin all the good... narrative, which we've developed on many important issues. After all, you're always saying: *"He who has the youth has the future."*'

'Yes, but not by pandering to them... young people, more than anyone, can tell when you're being disingenuous.'

'Well, then we'll never win. Don't you see that this is politics? If we want to change the EU, if we want to make a difference on any number of things, we've got to win first. We need to be practical. We won't get anything done if we don't win power.'

'If you win the leadership whilst hiding the fact that you're against the EU, then you'll tie your hands going into the referendum.

Besides, I thought this was meant to be about getting the message across? If we're not able to convince everyone, then so be it. Far better to be in a minority and on the right side of history, than support the EU for short-term gain. That would be contradicting your so-called narrative. Need I remind you that the EU is very much in favour of austerity? If we oppose it and lose, at least we lay down a marker for the future.'

'But people don't think of the EU as pro-austerity. They don't think of what is going on in others countries. I mean, how can we align ourselves with the likes of those racists in UKIP? They're against the free movement of labour!'

'UKIP are abhorrent, of course, but are you saying they're any different to the Tories? Are they fundamentally any different to a Prime Minister who says we should stop sea rescues because it only encourages more immigrants to "swarm" their way into Europe? If you're so much in favour of the free movement of people, tell it to the refugees drowning in the Mediterranean… Look, you're right,' Jeremy continued, 'we need to distinguish ourselves from UKIP. They're a bunch of horrible racists. But to do that by saying that the EU is not a racist institution is as deluded as those liberals who think capitalism can have a human face. The EU does not support free movement. In fact, it controls movement, allowing some to move freely within its borders, while letting others drown at sea.'

'But opposing the EU isn't going to solve that problem. If we leave the EU it will mean throwing up even more borders. What about all the legislation protecting workers' rights?'

'Didn't Indian independence from the British empire throw up more borders? Would you have opposed that in the name of 'free movement'? Look, I'm not saying we should just say: *"No to the EU."* We should argue that the EU is a big business club that has no interest in workers' rights. If they quote workers' rights, you quote back what the EU has done to the people of Greece: destruction of the minimum wage; destruction of collective bargaining rights; twenty-five percent unemployed; the Greek parliament controlled from Brussels. We can't talk about the EU protecting British workers while it's happily crushing the Greek workers. We should say: *"No to the EU, Yes to a socialist Europe."*'

'But people would never understand that. If we support leaving

Europe we would lose support not only from liberal-minded people, but we would endanger jobs. Half our exports go to Europe, you know. And you'd endanger EU nationals working in Britain. I'm sorry but this is more of your abstract, pie-in-the-sky talk.'

'Things change, my friend, and so do people. Once upon a time people thought slavery was natural, and that to think otherwise was "pie-in-the-sky". That's why we campaign: to make our point, not paralyze ourselves with fear that it can't be done, or that it won't be popular. Personally, I think you should throw that letter in the bin, and we should both use what little time we have left in this contest to speak out against the EU; speak out against the racists who oppose it, speak out against the racists who support it. Obviously, that will mean supporting a 'Leave' position in the referendum. But we will make the case for it on a socialist basis, distinguishing ourselves from the right wing – just as we should have done in Scotland – by saying we stand for international socialism. Of course, we would have to make a big point about defending all workers, not just EU nationals.'

Corbyn stared at the crumpled piece of paper. Jeremy took his empty plate to the bin and scraped away the crumbs, placing it in the sink, and exiting the kitchen.

'Let's talk about this again later,' called out Corbyn. He folded the crumpled letter and slipped it into his pocket.

CHAPTER 11
INNER PANIC

1

Tristram bounded down the parliamentary corridor after his PM, doing his level best to catch the directives the Lord spilled in his stride. Events seemed to have moved so quickly. He had only been intimate with the Tendency for a matter of months. Now he was about to attend a grand gathering of the Holdings. Even Chuka had only attended such a prestigious event once before. And it was shaping up to be far more of an affair than Tristram could have hoped for. Peter disclosed little about the attendance, but he could hazard many a guess.

There was one attendee, however, Tristram knew would be there for certain: Tony was set to arrive within the next hour, flying in directly from his mission in the Middle East. Tristram could hardly contain himself. Tony may not have been an Intimate of the Tendency, nor even a Holding, but Peter considered his presence vital nonetheless.

'In truth, Tony's necessity is the very reason that he can never become intimate,' said Peter. 'His unique outlook precludes him from being organised along the lines of other men.' For once, Tristram's master appeared nervous. 'The Middle East will still be there when he returns,' said Peter. 'But he also has an interest, naturally. What as dastardly a man as Corbyn could do with this blasted Chilcot Report, one shudders to think.'

The thought had not occurred to Tristram. That was why PM was PM, he supposed. The report was due out next year, and it would just be like those rotten socialists to make use of any little thing they could get their hands on in order to stand in the way of progress. After all, Tony's crusade had been a noble and cost-effective exercise, ridding the world of a tyrant who had no concern for the national interest, and who would almost certainly have destabilised the entire region. At least Gaddafi had been willing to play ball. It was becoming clearer and clearer to Tristram that Corbyn must be stopped at all costs.

'This latest poll is a hell of a thing, don't you think, PM? Points to a fifty-three percent win for Corbyn in the final round. Can you honestly see him as our next leader? Even as our next prime minister?'

'Quite extraordinary, I am sure,' said Peter. He allowed himself a sideways glance at Tristram, running expectantly at his side like a Golden Retriever. 'I do not know what to say, my boy... Only, never ask me to be honest. Among our Holdings such language is deemed... in bad taste. It can cause suspicion. It is probably best if you just listen and learn today; let the grown-ups do the talking.' Tristram's face flushed with a smothering of chastisement. 'The polls let us down at the General Election,' continued Peter. 'Who knows, perhaps they have it wrong again. What I know is that we cannot afford to take any more chances.'

He was not entirely his formidable self, thought Tristram; his Lord's sentences appearing to exhaust themselves before they reached their termination. Nevertheless, Tristram could not but help badger him, so awful and exciting were all the recent going-ons: 'I mean, we knew Corbyn was doing better than expected, but that was all to the good according to the Clientele,' he said, fishing for clues in Peter's face. But his master's face held stiff. 'He's certainly stemmed the bleed in the core base,' continued Tristram, 'split the difference, so to speak. It was only recently reported through one of our Secondaries that the Greens don't know what to do about him, and UKIP isn't best pleased either.' Peter had heard the same. It was certainly news to be welcomed, but at what cost?

'One poll a policy does not make,' said Peter, his voice tightly wound against his apprentice's lappings.

'Quite,' said Tristram, unsure he understood his Lord's meaning. 'Only, it's not the only poll. The *Mirror* has him on forty-two percent, with Yvette second on twenty-three. One has to admit, by all accounts he has a simply monstrous lead.'

Tristram thought back to the nominations, lamenting that he had neglected to put a few quid on Corbyn. He knew that one should always hedge one's funds, but he had been so caught up in the madness of those June days that he had quite neglected to make his way down to the bookies. Peter frowned and said nothing, marching ever on down the long corridor, his finely crafted features simmering below the surface.

'I mean, it's over twenty percent, PM.'

'Under... That is just *Mirror* propaganda – they have always been difficult.' It was clear that Peter was in no mood to discuss the question.

He's probably nervous about Tony's visit. They continued their march in silence, and Tristram carried on his train of thought: *One could retire on those odds... Could one work with Corbyn? They all say how honourable he is... Silly thought - his people would never take me... He seems rather the madman... Besides, the Tendency has my deposit... But he's not like PM, that's for sure... Can I really return to the back benches? What would people think? ...Tory and Labour, Left and right, they're all just different brands at the end of the day... Among honourable chaps and chapettes that means something – one can split the difference... But Corbyn cannot be honourable, not with such 'ideas'... He was only meant to be bait for the core, nothing else... How on earth did we let things slip so?*

They halted at the end of the corridor. Peter took out his phone and unscrolled a message. 'Blast!' he said. 'Tony's plane has arrived early. He will be here any minute.'

'Well, that's good news, isn't it?' said Tristram, the bubbles rising in his throat.

'Yes, yes, of course, my boy. It is Tony's people – they are always the trouble. They want to discuss his fee. Of course, none of them appreciate how much an RAF transport costs these days. Apparently the Whisperjet was without Wi-Fi and he lost a morning's work.' Tristram was captivated, stewing in admiration.

'I shall have to go and get him. You go in and hold the fort - I shall not be long.'

His Lord made his way back down the corridor. Tristram was alone. He looked at the closed door and gently touched the handle. For the briefest of moments he considered that he might slip away and no one might know. He turned and looked back down the long parliamentary corridor, watching Peter diminish in size. They would find him, eventually. His deposit was non-refundable. He pulled himself together and gravely grasped the handle.

As the door opened onto the conference room he was relieved to find some friendly faces among the bustle. It was an oversized room with low ceilings and seemed not to have been decorated in many years, having the feel of a boardroom from the eighties. The attendees were assembled on high-backed leather-set chairs around a long table of sleek polished walnut, placed square in the middle of the wider room. At that moment all eyed were fixed on Alistair, a man Tristram knew to be close to Tony and Peter. He was in the middle of a quarrel with John:

'You did this to yourselves,' fired John, smugness anchoring his accent to the floor. 'I wasn't consulted – nothing to do with me. You're ones who put union's noses out of joint; you're ones who said you didn't need 'em. You've been hoisted on your own petard!'

'You are a moron,' said Alistair. 'And so are those of you who lent him nominations.' Beside him a small, pudgy-faced man with thick glasses nodded vigorously. The MPs on John's side of the table turned simultaneously in their seats. 'Complete fucking morons - totally irresponsible. You know what you've done, don't you? If Corbyn wins, you've voted for your own fucking de-selection! And you know what - I wouldn't blame them.'

Next to John sat Margaret, wringing her hands: 'It was your people who told us to let him in,' she said. 'You said the contest needed credibility. It's not our fault if the other candidates are not viewed with grace and favour.' She laid her hands flat upon the polished walnut and stared at them.

One along from Alistair's pudgy little nodding man sat Chuka. Tristram took a seat between him and an MP named Stephen. Looking around the room, Tristram wondered who was held by whom. Two chairs at the head of the table beside the entrance remained empty. He smiled at Chuka. Everyone else sat silently, watching the spectacle of the two New Labour Bull Seals clashing throats. Peter had said to hold the fort, but Tristram decided on balance that he was better off listening and learning. He turned and greeted Stephen to his right, whose father was something of a hero of his.

'Tristram,' said Stephen aristocratically, not honouring him with eye contact. He may have been the son of a Baron, but so was Tristram - and for longer. A little more respect might have been in order. Stephen may have been heir to a Labour dynasty, but he was still only a first-termer. Tristram, on the other hand, was now serving his third term in the Palace of Westminster.

'PM's just getting Tony,' whispered Tristram.

'Is that right,' said Stephen, unmoved, regarding the unruly exchange taking place at the end of the table contemptuously. 'Complete fucking mess if you ask me. What possessed you to open the party to the circus?'

'Yes, it does seem Labour has taken leave of its senses somewhat,' said Tristram. '"Summer madness"... perhaps it would have been better to have had a brief contest, before everyone became worked up by the heat and taken with this idea of actually joining the party.'

'Militant never went away, you know,' said Stephen, now deigning to turn to face Tristram. 'They've been biding their time, waiting in the wings. I read their websites regularly. Absolute fanatics – haven't let go of the past, you know.'

'It's quite worrying, isn't it?'

'Worrying isn't the word, Tristram. What I'd like to know is: Why is it that people, unknown to us, have it in their heads that they can just waltz in off the streets and receive the same vote as you or I? It's completely undemocratic for those who've worked hard managing this party over the years.'

John brought his fist down on the table with a thud. 'You've egg on your face, Alistair, there's no use whining about it now - clean up your own damn mess!' His amusement was now clear to see. He was having a good old time baiting his opponent across the table. Surely, John was not intimate with the Tendency, thought Tristram. He was far too coarse, far too prone to proletarian outbursts of emotion. Margaret told them to behave themselves - Tony would be here soon.

That was not to Alistair's liking, and he bit back at Margaret, and the whole scene filled once more with bitter words. Then the door swung open. John looked up and fell silent. Alistair backed down. In slid Peter in something of a fluster, fastening the door behind him. He turned to the room, ghosting to one of the empty chairs at the head of the table and composing himself without speaking a word. Tristram noticed that he was quite pink of face, and the hair behind his ears had grown damp.

'Thank you, all, for coming,' said Peter, clearing his throat as he pulled in his seat. 'Tony is close behind. Only,' he stared down the barrel of the walnut table for a moment, as if he had lost his thought. 'Only... there has been something of a wardrobe malfunction. Upon arrival it was discovered that Tony's baggage had been misdirected to The Hague. Most unprofessional, but there we are. Please, let us just act as if everything were normal when he enters - he has not had the best of mornings.'

They waited silently for a long few minutes. No one came. Intermittently Peter looked toward the entrance. Finally, he rose and left the room. A minute later he returned, leaving the door ajar. They remained in silence. Presently, in crept Tony, clad from head to toe in olive and tan fatigues rolled to the elbows, and with tanned leather boots to match. He sat beside Peter and said nothing, not even looking up to acknowledge the room. All watched on in silence. John sucked a curl out of his cheek.

'We all know why we are here,' said Peter, placing his elbows on the table, 'so I will dispose with the formalities. We have a little local difficulty that is presenting us with something of a challenge. No doubt you have seen the latest numbers.' He looked at Tony before turning to the room. Tristram could have sworn that for a split second he saw something like a membrane close over his master's eyes.

'Earlier this morning I met with some important... benefactors. They have also seen the numbers.' Intimates and Holdings nodded gravely. Tony took out a notepad from inside a camouflaged pocket. 'There are grumblings, ladies and gentlemen, deep grumblings. Cash for Questions, MPs expenses, even News of the Word – all storms in teacups by comparison. 'Our task, naturally, is to allay such grumblings, before they career beyond the national interest. I think you have my meaning. So let us come up with a solution. Who would like to begin proceedings?' As he looked around the room he glimpsed Tony out of the corner of his eye. He appeared to be doodling in his notebook.

'We need to go immediately on the offensive,' said Alistair. 'No more dithering - crack everyone into line and start filling the columns. The *Sun*, the *Mail* and most importantly, those sandal-wearers at *The Guardian* – it's time they earned their keep. And who do we have at the *New Statesman*? They've been completely off-message. A full offensive is needed, but we should focus on *The Guardian*... and the *BBC*. We need to work over Corbyn's core support.'

'If Corbyn becomes Prime Minister,' said Frank, who was sat next along to Margaret, 'then Britain will choke in riots and the country will become another basket case. The man's a deficit denier – doesn't believe in the cuts. He'd have us bailed out by the IMF again, like in seventy-six. Why aren't any of the other candidates pointing this out? Margaret was only saying before you came in, Lord Peter,' he bowed his head forward and looked down the table, 'the problem isn't that he's on the ballot. The problem is the other candidates have made such a poor showing of things.'

'Duly noted,' said Peter. 'We certainly could do with stiffening the opposition…'

'He'll hand Scotland to the SNP,' interrupted Frank, his face turning purple with passion, 'he'll put the Royal Family in council housing, raise the Red Flag over Buckingham Palace, and fill it with homeless prostitutes. It'll mean the end of the Labour Party. And it'll mean the end of us!'

'Yes, Frank, that is splendid,' said Peter. He turned to the table. 'Frank says we need to confront Corbyn on policy. Does anyone know what his policies are?'

'"People's Quantitative Easing",' said Morris, a short, bespectacled fellow in a navy blue jumper sat beside Frank.

'And what the devil is that?' asked Peter.

'Well, as we know, Gordon forced the Bank of England to buy hundreds of billions of pounds of debt…'

'So much for the Independence of the Bank of England!' said Caroline, a hard-headed, sedimentary woman with long black hair, sat at the other end of the table.

'That's made borrowing money so cheap,' continued Morris, 'that the Bank of England say interest rates are the now the lowest in five thousand years. How one works that out, I do not know!' Many deflated a titter. 'If you create money, but it signifies no increase in value produced in the economy, it just means there is more money representing the same amount of value. That should make each individual unit of money – a pound sterling – worth less. Now, if your pound is worth less, it's the same as prices going up – all other things being equal.' Tristram turned uneasily in his seat. 'However, even though we've created all this additional money, it hasn't trickled into people's pockets. Therefore, there hasn't been the price inflation you might expect when you magic money out of thin air.'

'So where has money gone?' asked John.

'It's trapped in the atmosphere,' said Morris. 'The banks and companies have it.' John frowned. 'But that's better than inflation, which is what would happen if people started getting hold of that extra cash and spending it,' continued Morris. 'If the business community were to see all that extra demand, they would raise prices. If they didn't, all the extra demand might leave shops empty, or disrupts the supply chain, which could lead to panic buying. Either way, you get inflation, pushing prices further upward in a vortex of cause and effect. Even if things eventually settled down, such instability would be politically... uncosted. Of course, that's a worst-case scenario. But even moderate inflation devalues the currency, making imports more expensive. And we import a lot: electricity, food, gas, cars – the result would mean a further fall in real wages - again, something that could prove to be an irritant.'

Tristram thought it all sounded rather fantastical. He looked to Peter for reassurance. 'But what, pray tell,' said the Lord, 'does this have to do with Corbyn's... what was it?'

'People's Quantitative Easing. If the international community see Corbyn creating more debt,' said Morris, 'they'll worry Britain isn't paying attention to the debts it has already taken on. That could lead to the credit agencies downgrading us as an economy, pushing the interest on the debt up even further.' A murmur spread around the table. 'And of course, if a Corbyn-led Labour government uses this money for creating nationalised industries that are capable of outcompeting the business community, then naturally they will be very upset. They might even refuse to invest.'

'A strike... of capital?' blurted Tristram. All frowns turned on him.

'Good grief,' said Sadiq, sat next to Morris.

'But isn't that what's already happening?' said John.' I mean, capitalists aren't investing with Quantitative Easing we have at moment!'

'What we're basically saying,' said Morris, 'is that Corbyn's version of printing money would be far more dangerous because it would not be seen to be carried out in the national interest. It would upset our debtors, upset the business community, and by stimulating demand and putting money in peoples' pockets it could cause inflation, depending on how it is invested. In any case, it would risk unlocking all the printed money already trapped up there in the clouds, which as it stands could cause quite the deluge.'

'We need to get that message out,' said Alistair, 'in a more comprehendible format. We've still got talented people at the *Mail*, haven't we? Something about the future under Jeremy Corbyn: economic catastrophe leading to strikes, riots, looting, upturned cars – "Britain in flames", that sort of thing.'

'A problem we're coming up against,' chipped in Chuka, 'is that the more we use the moderate press, the more it seems to increase Corbyn's support. We need better product placement. *The Guardian* sows doubts where they can best be reaped, but his supporters don't read the *Daily Mail*. In fact, some of them actually dislike it... Yes, that's right! And the *Sun*, too. They even share their headlines on Twitter and Facebook as some sort of proof that our media is against Corbyn - and that makes them love him even more!'

'But that doesn't make any sense,' said Alistair.

'We can't go by the old methods,' said Chuka. 'What we lack - and this is where we must admit Corbyn has done his homework - is a base in social media. We're not in the 1980s anymore. We can use the *The Guardian*, sure, but every time those *Daily Mail* headlines get online these kids just tear them apart.'

'So how do we go about getting our people inside this "socialist media"?' asked Margaret. 'Who are their writers?' Tristram sighed. She truly was useless.

Jeremy and Corbyn

'We can't get to the writers, Margaret,' said Chuka. 'Corbyn's supporters are the writers.'

'Well, obviously, I didn't mean the Corbyn supporters,' said Margaret, indignant, but somewhat confused. 'But aren't there any sensible journalists in this socialist media? I mean, if it's so important, then there must be, surely?' Chuka's eyebrows became confounded.

'I think we can have the best of both worlds on this one, can't we?' said Tony, all of a sudden. All eyes turned to the man in military fatigues continuing to doodle as he spoke at the head of the table. 'What I mean to say is: It doesn't have to be one or the other, there is always a third way. Peter's man can begin to familiarise himself with the people at this… socialist media,' he said, gesturing to Chuka, 'and Alistair can concentrate on working with our traditional industry friends. I still have Andy and Rebecca's numbers, I think.' No one said a word. Tristram thought the proposal quite reasonable.

Peter studied his old friend for a moment. 'Yes, quite…' he eventually said. 'Alistair - can you do… as Tony said? Start with our friends at the *Mail*, perhaps? And yes, my boy, I will mark you down for that… socialist media task.' Chuka acknowledged, trying his best to unfurrow his brow. 'Well, that is a good start.' Peter scrutinized the room with a pointed grin.

'Corbyn is saying we lost the election because we weren't left-wing enough,' said Simon, a pickled walnut of a man sat beside the sharp and sedimentary Caroline seated at the far end of the table. 'His narrative is gaining a monopoly, and his people repeat it like parrots. And now we've released them into the party. What if they start making trouble?'

'Can't we get rid of them?' said Alan, a grey and oily man sat beside Stephen. 'Or get our people to neutralise them?'

'Do we have - what is the latest figure – forty, fifty thousand little people at our disposal?' said the Lord Peter. 'Of course not - we have always discouraged that sort of thing.'

'They are infiltrators,' declared Stephen. 'How do we know anything about these people? We need to think long and hard about allowing any more to join. You cannot be in the Greens one day and join Labour the next, for heaven's sake!'

'Oh no?' said John, staring hungrily at Stephen. 'Didn't stop this lot welcoming Baron Davies off Tories! You've got to come up with something better than that, lad! What are we saying? To only let people join who've never been in politics before? That's absurd.'

'The point is we knew Davies,' said Stephen. 'We were able to observe his form. With these new elements we don't know where they have been. And it's not just the Greens. As we speak, thousands upon thousands of Trots are licking their lips, watching what Corbyn is doing. I mean, how many did we really expel in the 1980s? One hundred... two hundred members of the Militant? Believe me, there are thousands, if not tens of thousands, of sleeper-cell Trotskyites lying dormant inside our party. They've been there for decades, just waiting for someone to wake them up.'

'Yes,' said John, 'and it was your father who was responsible for all that nonsense.'

'And if you were to ask my father, he would say the same thing to you that he has been saying to me for the past thirty years: "Beware the Trots." He often talks about leaving the job unfinished. I think we ought to be listening to him now.'

His father had to abandon the Miners to deal with the Militant, recalled Tristram. *One has to respect that kind of single-minded willingness to make sacrifices in the national interest.*

'It was Gordon who brought in Baron Davies,' said Tony, 'but I say we should go with young Stephen's proposal. I mean, who is going to bother us with a Tory defection from eight years ago? Where is Gordon by the way? Isn't he coming?'

'No, Gordon will not be joining us,' said Peter. Gordon had not been invited, but Peter knew Tony would not understand that. 'He is in the highlands and cannot be reached. But I think we all know what Gordon would be saying, were he here to speak for himself. He would understand what was at risk. You all remember the midnight visits from his whips when he kept McDonnell off the ballot.' An amused murmur radiated around the table.

Tony interrupted: 'As I was saying, it was Gordon who took in Davies, but what's the problem? We took a man off the Tory benches and increased the number of Labour MPs. Aren't we interested in increasing our presence in parliament? That's just a good chess move – it's not hypocritical.' He had ceased his doodling and was looking past John, toward Stephen on the right of his vision. 'I mean, aren't we interested in recruitment? If a Green MP crossed the floor - fair enough. Defectors often make the most loyal recruits. But the membership is another question. I mean, the Greens? Do we really want environmentalists in our party? That's just fantasy politics. You can't hold back the tide of nature, believe me. And above all, we have to be very honest with people.' The room fell silent. Idly, Tony returned to his doodling. Peter turned a rosy pink once again. Glimpsing Tony's doodle, he saw that it has become quite large and elaborate, sprawling all the way down one side of his notepad.

'Well... I have to say, I think Tony is right,' said Peter. 'To be seen to be... honest, is often the best policy...'

'Yes,' said Tony. Lifting his head again, he scrutinized the room without blinking. He was tail-spinning into the middle distance, raking the embers of his political past. He held out his hands, and his fingers slowly stiffened perpendicular to his thumbs. The room was dry with anticipation. 'That's why... I think what Liz has been doing is absolutely right. Let's... shake up the party; let's be principled; let's... stick to our guns. We need to have an honest conversation – we got it wrong at the last election - we were trying to go two ways at once, abandoning the middle ground. Rent caps; energy caps; immigration caps; did we honestly need to speak so much in caps? Did we honestly need to speak so much... full-stop? I really think our key message about the middle got lost somewhere.'

'I'm sorry Tony,' cried John, fit to burst, 'but you're not here on the ground. Maybe in Syria, or wherever you've been, folk want more of your type of thinking, but people I talk to say Jeremy Corbyn is popular for one thing: they can understand what he's saying! He's a fundamentally kind man, he's got heart – like Old Labour.' A collective gasp let out around the room. 'They're talking about battle for soul of party! And I'm sorry to say it, Tony, but I think they've a point.'

Peter moved quickly. 'What about you, Jonathon?' he asked of the next man along from Sadiq, hoping to push John's discordant remarks to one side. 'We do know how you tried your best to keep poor old Ed on the straight and narrow. What has the fall-out been from all of this? Are Corbyn and his people gaining from this so-called anti-austerity politics?'

'Not according to my findings, sir,' said Jonathon. He was a shy, working-class man, always deferential to his betters, and who rarely spoke unless spoken to. 'Fifty-eight percent of our focus agrees with the statement: *"We must live within our means, so cutting the deficit is the top priority."* People understand the need for austerity. They voted for it, and figures don't lie... That's why the Tories won. If Labour wants to win, we need to acknowledge that. We need to look at what UKIP did: *"Family, Faith and Flag"* - that's the sort of message the public want. We failed to deliver, although I tried and tried with that boy until I was blue in the face.' Many on Jonathon's right nodded in agreement.

'If I may,' oozed Alan, 'all this left-wing drivel that Corbyn's spouting about why we lost the election emanates from the hard-left loonies around him. Completely intolerant, violent ideas. They have a sexual fixation with Lenin, I'm telling you - they're the ones organising this. Now, we've been very kind to Corbyn and the unions over the years. We've tolerated their finger-jabbing nonsense, allowing them to remain on their soggy side of the party. Why they should betray us now, by linking up with these anti-Labour lunatics, I do not know. It's most disappointing. But that's what happened, and we've got to be firm with these people – they are a virus, plain and simple. We have to deliver the antidote. I agree with Stephen. We need to check them. We need to veto them. We need to build a wall around the Labour Party to keep them out.'

'Sir, if I may, sir?' said Jonathon. 'Thank you. The problem is Corbyn has this sort of anti-politics personality. It's hip right now. But it's confined to a small Haringey elite. It's really more of a lifestyle choice. And you can't make policy out of a lifestyle.'

'What people want is to return to the 1930s,' said Morris, picking up Jonathon's point. 'That is a time they remember fondly: when people pulled together; when communities organised hikes across the local countryside; a kinder time, when people came together and did not trespass against each other; when they organised with working-class pride around issues such as the campaign for parliamentary democracy in Spain. That's why we should learn the lessons of UKIP and the English Defence League. They are what I describe as "purposeful social movements". Labour also needs to be a purposeful social movement.'

'We have to have policies for the country, not the party,' said Alistair impatiently. 'The Labour Party isn't the electorate. I've said it before: It was utterly moronic for you to let him on the ballot sheet in the first place. I hope you've learned a lesson from all of this.' He turned to Tony as he finished, and the pudgy little man beside Alistair nodded vigorously once more. The row opposite rearranged themselves. John was about to bark back, but Tony began to speak, and so he held his tongue.

'You know, under my reign,' his notepaper now full with doodles, 'we modernised the NHS, and now we have choice. We introduced a minimum wage and we all became richer. We put education first, and now every child goes to university so that afterwards they'll be able to get a good job. And our tuition fees provide the young generation with the opportunity to take on responsibility at an early age, like we had to. Cherie and I were very young when we took out our first mortgage... We didn't need to dismantle Mrs Thatcher's property-owning democracy; instead we built an education-owning democracy on its very solid foundations. Education, education, education - like I always said.' Tony saw the heads of his disciples rolling around the room in approval. The younger ones felt themselves in the presence of genuine historical privilege. 'We toppled dictators and brought democracy to far-off lands, making the world a better place to live. I mean - come on!' His eyes grew wildly. 'I never understood the unions, you know? They always had a complaint. Never a "Well done, Tony" or a "Thanks, Tony" or a "Keep up the good work, Tony". They always wanted more... one way or another, Alan,' he said, looking across at the ever-slickening grey man. 'They never approached us as friends. It was always clear they had an ulterior motive. I mean, why should we have repealed the anti-trade union laws? The Tories weren't in power! You know I made this point to them on numerous occasions, but they never listened. I told them that all they had to do was get out the vote, keep Labour in power, and there would never be a need to repeal the anti-trade union laws. No government ever abolished the spinning wheel or the bronze axe, did they? No. They just fell into disuse. And I'm sorry, we can't do everything... Alan, you need to tell the TUC firmly to get their troops in order. How can we do that if individual unions are making all this fuss about Corbyn? All I achieved... our legacy, it's at risk.' Alan smeared out his deference and said he would see what could be done. 'I think it's important what was said by Peter,' continued Tony, 'about the conversation he had with his people: the Business Peoples. They're really quite remarkable people, don't you know? They know how to talk to the market. They can track money for days, and can smell out sentiment from great distances. Only last week I met this fellow who told me he had spent whole weeks at a time in his office - they don't do a regular ten to three, Monday to Wednesday, like you or I. And that man could name over two-thousand financial products, just from memory alone. They're brought up to be completely at one with their environment, don't you know? I mean, isn't that simply exceptional? Such knowledge can't be learned by anyone... It's a unique culture that we need to protect. Peter has touched base with some of their leaders, and they've been clear about the whole thing: The market rejects Corbyn. Some of the little people might not like that, but don't we have a share in the democratic process, too?'

'Yes Tony, but ...,' said John. But Tony cut back in.

'And one more thing, John, one more thing... To all those who would complain that Labour hasn't a heart, I say this: 'I'm a Labour leader... but it's not about me. In the end, it's not even about our members. It's about the country, and what it needs.... I think we need to stress that. It's not that Corbyn couldn't become Prime Minister, although personally I think it unlikely. But even if he did, it wouldn't be right... because it wouldn't take the country forward. It would take us backwards.' Heads nodded urgently; throats thrummed with approval. 'So that's why it's not the right thing to do.' Tony turned his eyes to the ceiling, as if to channel a higher level of profundity. All hung by his lips. 'That's why, when people say: "Well, you know my heart says I should really be with that politics..." Well, get a transplant - because that's just daft!'

Their applause was solemn at first, but soon broke into joyous hand-smacking. Some held back, such as Peter, who considered naked displays of emotion a tad vulgar. But when he looked into the eyes of his Messiah, he could not help but feel the love steam across his ectothermic heart. Yes, even the Lord Peter could feel love. It was a love that longed for Tony to return to him and take back the reins. A second coming would spin awfully well. But he knew his longing to be indulgent. His friend had moved on to bigger and brighter things. Peter looked long upon his old leader, until he realised he had forgotten where he was. The clapping had stopped and the room was silent once more. Then John spoke up. *Oaf!*

'Calm down Tony,' said John. He also had not joined in the applause. 'That kind of language is just abuse, like Alistair calling this poor... like calling Margaret, and Frank and Sadiq here, "morons". I won't stand for it, and neither should you, Margaret.' She offered John a beaten smile. 'You're not going to win by hurling slander at them, nor by expelling them, neither. I say: take them on! Take them on, and take their supporters' money in the process.'

'These so-called supporters,' said Simon, wrinkling into a pickle, 'have been allowed to choose our leader for the price of a Tesco meal-deal. How can we allow that?'

'You've made your bed with contest,' said John, firing back. 'Now you have to lie in it. 'And you may think some of the unions are ungrateful, Tony, but your lot have forgotten how to talk with them. I mean, look at this meeting here - where are sandwiches? Where are pork pies? Aren't I right, Alan?' Alan averted his slippery, embarrassed eyes.

'Corbyn's been endorsed by the RMT and the firefighters,' said Simon. 'Those are non-Labour unions. Surely we can have him suspended for that?'

'Kenny has kept a lid on his people,' continued John. 'Now we need to look to our people. What about Tom - he's a sensible lad, and looks like he might get Deputy. That man is key for you now, Peter. If Corbyn wins by the margins they're saying, then he'll have hell of a mandate. Tom needs bringing properly into fold.'

'I don't think we want to involve Tom', said Tony, becoming alert. 'That man is disloyal, discourteous and just plain wrong. Do you remember when he led the cabinet resignations against my leadership? What kind of man plays dirty tricks like that? Not to mention the upset he caused Rupert.'

'Many of the men I still keep in touch with are pretty discontent,' said Alan. 'Although most are dirtied dishrags by now, not fit for polishing boots. But if they say is anything to go by, then we've got something to work with. The last thing they want is someone like Corbyn showing them up.'

'These lads may make a fuss from time to time,' said John, 'but better to have them inside tent pissing out, than outside tent pissing in. That's what I always say. And it's what you never understood, Tony. Stephen's father — at least he relied on other union leaders to stop miners getting out of hand; he relied on them to stop Liverpool and Lambeth getting out of hand; and it was them who helped expel leaders of Militant. And while you and Alistair have been away it's been likes of Unite and GMB who have held line. We could have had five winters of discontent and five miners' strikes, way Tories have behaved. But our union friends stuck with us despite you lot. Of course, they have to make some grumbling; that's par for the course.'

'Personally, I think we should look at getting the whole thing called off,' said Stephen.

'Agreed,' said Alan. Frank and Simon backed him. They all looked to the head of the table.

'That... does seem a sensible proposal, I must say,' said Peter.

'There appears to be clear evidence of party infiltration,' said Tony, coming alive once again. 'The question is: How can we have a fair and democratic contest until these Greens and UKIPers and Trotskyites are removed?'

'Yes. It does appear that they have taken advantage of the letter of our new rules, rather than being guided by their spirit,' said Peter. He turned to Chuka. 'I believe you have sounded out Harriet on this question, my boy, have you not?'

'Yes, but it's not got wings,' said Chuka. '"Deadline-focused credibility", she says. They assure us they have some little people working on the new members, a real around-the-clock operation apparently, but actual contest suspension - cuts no ice. They've so few little people to pick from that they've had to outsource to employment agencies, and Harriet says that so many have swarmed in that she's finding it hard to hold back the tide. She said it could take until next summer to pick away at the new members. We can't be leaderless for a whole year.'

'You know, there is a chance he won't get it,' said Margery, an elderly MP who sat at the far end between Jonathon and Simon. 'None of the polls report Corbyn having more than half of first preferences. Apart from the fanatics that follow him, everyone else will put him down as fourth preference — if they preference him at all.'

'Margery has a valid point,' said Frank, 'the only trouble is our candidates are drowning out each other's message. Can't we agree on a single candidate to oppose him?'

'Tristram, my boy,' said Peter. 'I think you have something to say on this?'

'Yes, I've been in touch with our candidates, and they agree. All their private polling indicates it would be better if everyone else stood down.'

'Well, I think we should choose Liz,' said Simon, and Margery loaned him a *'hear, hear.'*

'Mmm, yes,' said Peter. 'Unfortunately this Corbyn… over-correction, shall we say, presents us with a difficult choice. It appears that Liz does not have the numbers.'

'I'm sorry,' said John, 'but I think we've got to back Andy.'

'Well, I think Andy should step down for a female candidate,' said Margery.

'Margery raises an important point,' said Peter. 'We should not discount the feminist angle. It has always served us well when we need to deal with irritants, especially when they are of the straight white male variety. We used it well in ninety-seven, as I recall.' He turned to Tony and smiled.

'"Blair's babes",' murmured a grinning Tony, not taking his eyes from his note-pad.

'The only problem,' said Jonathon 'is that the polls show that sixty-one percent of women voters back Corbyn.'

'You want the unions on side?' said John. 'Then you've got to give them their man. They don't want Yvette –too close to Red Ed. And they aren't going for Liz because she's the so-called Blairite candidate.' Tony looked up at John, but said nothing.

'John has a point,' said Alan. 'But I think you'll find Lord Peter's had the superior argument. We should field a woman - either of them will do. Then, even if Corbyn was to win, we will be well-positioned to continue a feminist narrative against him. And Corbyn's supporters in the PLP are so few that they would have trouble filling a shadow cabinet without taking on a few women under our… influence.'

'Look, we need to do a number of things,' said Alistair. 'Peter is right - we need to look into getting the whole thing called off. Get the lawyers to look at it. We can make something up: it's the first time; it was a dry run; we've identified flaws in the system; that sort of thing. And Stephen's entyrist angle is important. We were able to terrify the little people with the Militant in the 1980s. We need to ramp up the rhetoric regarding illegal alien elements entering: Tory infiltrators, spongers who don't have the interests of the party at heart, who don't speak our language. And we should unify opposition in one candidate. It's A.B.C stuff. Quite frankly, it doesn't matter who we choose.'

'The question of infiltration is more important than the candidate,' said Stephen. 'Even if we somehow manage to rid ourselves of Corbyn, we now have to process thousands of little Corbyns. Harriet should be told to use all the new money gained from these infiltrators' membership fees against them – to employ more agency staff to weed them out. Beef up the Compliance Unit. We could even establish a shadow compliance unit to assist her.'

'Why not tell them we're full up?' said Frank. 'At least from now on. Worked on the Mersey for years in the old days.'

'I could run it by Harriet,' said Chuka. 'But Corbyn has a hundred and fifty local parties supporting him. All the others combined have only one-hundred and eighty or so. It shows what Stephen said: It's not just the new members that support Corbyn, there appears a D.U.D. layer embedded in the party. That's going to be a lot tougher to shift.'

'Who would have known it?' said Tristram in such despair that he spoke his thoughts out loud. But there was no response. Then he added: 'I've certainly never heard of such elements in my local party.'

'It was the same with the Militant,' said Stephen, becoming more agitated. 'We never knew until it was almost too late. That's how they worked: on the fringes of the party, quietly putting people in place like Corbyn. And then, when the time is right: Bam!' he punched a fist into the palm of his hand, 'the party is overrun with marauding Trots selling "newspapers" and demanding "political discussion", all the while concealing their bloodthirsty politics with a comradely manner and an insistence on "democratic procedure".'

'Yes, thank you, Stephen,' said Peter. 'We are all aware of your family's intimate knowledge of the problems of entrism. But we need to think soberly about this. There is no evidence to say that the local parties are overrun. We still have our little people on the ground -

they are our listening posts - and if there had been infiltration I think we would have had some indication. Nevertheless, we should inform our people and instruct them to be vigilant.'

'The problem is that ordinary members don't think like us,' said Alan. 'Many will naively welcome these new members. Therefore, what we need to do in the event of a Corbyn victory is to fall back and lay siege through the local parties.'

'And the parliamentary party,' said Simon.

'Judging by the polls,' said Jonathon, 'Corbyn could get a quarter of a million votes. How could we lay siege to that?'

Lord Peter steepled his fingers. 'Napoleon once said that a thousand French soldiers would invariably defeat one-and-a-half thousand Mamelukes,' said the Lord, 'even though the Egyptian Knights were far superior warriors, taken individually. There are many examples in history where a smaller, better organised army, has defeated a larger force. We are organised. We must ensure Corbyn's people are not. We must brief our little people to disorganise and demoralise his ranks.'

'To be fair,' said Alan, 'if these young people come in and see the state of the local parties discussing dog shit and double-yellow lines, then they'll bounce right out again. That's our best defence. And it's one that's worked for many years.'

'And let's make it clear to the PLP,' said Tony, 'how serious it all is: their careers are in danger. Imagine what Corbyn will do to all those MPs who stood up for the people of the Middle East?

'How many MPs put loyalty to the government first back then?' said Margery. 'Not Corbyn. And he doesn't deserve our loyalty now.'

'I think what Alan and Margery are saying is right. We should start laying plans for defeat,' said Alistair. 'Guerrilla warfare.'

'Yes, I have been informed that the man rebelled against Tony over five hundred times,' said Peter. 'I think if it comes to it we are going to have to explain to our colleagues that "what is good for the goose is good for the gander". If he can afford to have principles, then so can we... I think we need to get to work. Everyone talk to their contacts in the press, start writing columns and discussing with the other candidates and the whole parliamentary party – anyone who has the wherewithal to understand.'

Peter brought the meeting to a close. As they stood, he beckoned his young apprentices to one side. 'We are going to have to start expanding operations. We need to bring in more people and increase our Holdings. We will meet on Monday to discuss our new directives.' The brothers nodded and went on their way.

As Tristram neared the exit he could not help but approach Tony, who had remained seated: 'It's a pleasure to meet you, sir. And may I just compliment you on your smashing fatigues.'

Tony looked up with a bewildered smile and offered Tristram his hand. Seeing what was taking place, Peter intervened and swept his earnest apprentice along. The room emptied. Tony and Peter remained. 'It seems it is just us again,' said Peter. 'Like old times.'

'Peter, has anyone mentioned my fee?'

CHAPTER 12
CORBYN IN CAMDEN

1

Amalia turned the corner into Bidborough Street and was amazed at what she saw. Initially deciding against making the trip upon realising she would arrive too late to help sell the *Revolutionary Newspaper*, and with no ticket for the rally, she figured there was little point in loitering outside a closed door all evening. But Bob had called her and insisted she come down, late or not, and 'witness history in the making'. After the disappointment of Greece, Amalia had salted her expectations, yet the tide on which her MP was riding caused her to think again - she could see he was gathering momentum. In the end she took little convincing and a bus to Camden.

Finding herself blocked by a mass of people, she wondered how she would find the rally. Then she saw high above the rows of heads at the other end of the street a little man leaning against a railing that had been fastened to the top of a red fire engine. Pushing past the clammy shoulders in the close summer's evening, she kept her eye on that little man, until she eventually arrived at the front.

Corbyn felt insecure against the railing. It was draped in a large white banner emblazoned with the slogan of the movement in bold red letters:

'Straight talking, honest politics'

Each time he saw that slogan he heard Jeremy asking whether it was meant ironically, and each time he felt in the pit of his stomach the acidic truth underpinning his friend's cruel question. He never expected to get to this stage; never expected to see his throw-away remark flapping in front of thousands in the August breeze. Now, as he looked upon his overflowing following, there seemed something sinister about the whole thing.

The fireman indicated to Corbyn that they were ready. Beneath the platform he felt bolts unscrewing. The top of a spreading chestnut tree swayed above him in the evening breeze, its trunk held rooted below, unmoved. Sweat lined his face and the wind chilled against it, causing him to shiver. Nothing seemed steady. Perhaps it was only the earth that swayed. He saw the many faces fixing their expectations upon his shrunken outline. To the left of his field of vision *The Dolphin* was doing a roaring trade along the sweaty membrane pushed up against its doors. Many in his congregation held pint glasses, and he suspected some had just wandered out from the bar to see what all the fuss was about. How else could one explain such numbers? That was the problem with open meetings: anyone could turn up. He doubted his audience, unsure where to pitch his remarks. Approaching the microphone, he asked if they could hear him. They said they could, and added that they were only too proud to listen. They bade him begin:

> 'We've had a bit of overflow of numbers tonight so we've got, erm…, we've got two overflow meetings in the Camden Centre and in the town hall, and we've now got this one out on the street. Can I say thank you for all coming along and I hope it stays dry for the rest of the evening, and I hope *The Dolphin* does well out of our attendance here this evening.'

They laughed at his joke, hoping to will him on. They told him to relax and to speak as he saw fit, and that he should not be nervous:

> 'This is a campaign, at one level, about the Labour Party leadership; but on another level it is about a lot of other things. We entered the campaign…'

Corbyn tried turning to the right, but met resistance. His microphone was caught. Distracted, he turned and saw a fireman at his feet, struggling with a knotted cable. Soon it came loose and the fireman winked him some encouragement. He managed to fumble out some words:

'...and I hope we keep the wires on the microphone... with succeeding there.'

He turned back toward the crowd and, as he did, the Fire Brigade Union's flag slapped him in the face. He flinched and was unsteadied, and as he grasped the railing he thought he felt the stage slip forward. His heart jumped. He looked out at the expectant faces as they bent their hope around the benefit of his doubt. He looked beyond them, to his home in Islington, and the approaching safety of his front gate:

'I want to say first of all - big thank you to the FBU for giving us this facility this evening; for the work that all firefighters do, all the time.'

He had gone no further when they spontaneously exclaimed their approval, saying that they knew he was genuine, and that if any of the other candidates had said the same thing they would have considered it merely a calculated remark to curry favour.

'They keep us all safe,' he continued '...and for the best slogan ever: "We rescue people, not banks." Thank you, FBU, for what you do.'

They called out their approval. They said the others would never have acknowledged such a slogan. That gave his words weight.

'This campaign is about the leadership of the Labour Party. But it's also about an alternative. When we lost the election in May all of us were pretty devastated by that defeat, obviously. We were devastated of what the possibilities were for the future - and there was some good stuff in that Labour manifesto. But I believe the fundamental problem was that the banking crisis of 2008-9 was not caused by firefighters, street cleaners, nurses, teachers, or anybody else in our valuable public services. It was caused by deregulation; it was caused by speculation; it was caused by sheer levels of greed. And whilst taking the banks into public ownership was absolutely the right thing to do, the problem was: they weren't kept in public ownership, the banks weren't forced to work for the rest of us and the rest of the economy; they were allowed to carry on in their own sweet way. So when we got to the

2010 election we were offering more austerity, more cuts, more punishment on the poorest in this country. David Cameron claimed we were all in it together - I don't think so David Cameron, I don't think we're all in this together at all. I think you think everybody else is in it together, except you and your party and the people around you. So we then have had five years of opposition, we've seen what the coalition government has done. The levels of jobs that have been lost in the public sector; the wage freeze; the lower wages for those in the private sector; the zero-hour contracts; the brutality of much of the benefit system and what it is doing to the poorest and most vulnerable within our society. So when we came to the 2015 election, surely we should have been able to offer something other than austerity, and say that we believe the function of government is to deal with the poorest in our society, and ensure that poverty is eliminated and promote an economy that is expanding with jobs, opportunities and work for all, and not apply the process of austerity.'

He paused as they shouted their wholehearted agreement with his assessment. Not because they thought the previous leader was capable of offering anything other than austerity, but because they believed that Labour deserved a leader that should have.

'And so we entered this leadership contest in order that there could be that debate and that alternative. And the response has been truly amazing. The thousands of people that have come out to take part in this discussion, saying the things about the kind of society they want to live in.'

Following his trip to Liverpool, Jeremy had encouraged Corbyn to engage with the audience more. It was not as if he did not understand the importance of such gestures. At the June 20th demonstration he had asked for anyone that had caused the banking crisis to raise their hands. All had kept their hands down, aside from one or two jokers. But casting his eyes over the faces stood below him in Camden he felt the burdensome weight of their expectation. As the sunglasses and football shirts and plastic pint glasses spilled out of *The Dolphin* he realised he could not bring himself to do it, He fell into the safety-net of supposition:

> 'If... I asked you all to raise your hands if you supported healthcare as a human right, free at the point of use, every hand would go up...'

Drips of embarrassment echoed along the sound system as his eyes hunted desperately for a raised hand. After an eternity, which was less than a second, the hands went up. Every hand went up. *What about those people in the... oh no, they've raised their hands too.*

> 'Yes... every single hand is going up. Even though more than three rows into the back were slightly slower in raising their hands, it's okay.'

They sang out to him that they approved of this consultation. They knew he asked because he understood they were worthy of consultation. They said he should feel free to ask again. Forgiving him any hesitancy, they suggested he continue with his remarks:

> 'Yes, we would all support that,' he said as the waves churned beneath him, 'and we recognise what an incredible achievement it was for the labour movement when we got the NHS in 1948 - before I was born. We also, in the same year, got the welfare state. But somewhere along the line, we lost our way; somewhere along the line, we gave in to Benefits Street; we gave into abuse of people who are justly, legally and correctly claiming that to which they are entitled. Somewhere along the line we have allowed the cheapness of the media to take over and abuse people on disability benefits, abuse people...'

He was interrupted by their cries for him to please stop. They understood what he was saying, but would he not say 'we' so much? It was most inappropriate. They did not wish to be associated with the sins he listed, and were at a loss to understand why he should include himself in such unnecessary self-flagellation. But he did not hear them:

> '...abuse people in very difficult situations... and declared fit for work when clearly they are not. People have committed suicide as a result of that. Can we be bold enough and strong enough and clear enough as a party and as a labour movement to say we want to live in a society where we don't pass by, on the other side, when

somebody is going through a crisis? We don't pass by, on the other side, when a family is forced to live on the street because they can no longer afford the flat or house that they are living in? We don't pass by, on the other side, and leave the poorest to fend for themselves whilst the richest keep on getting richer and richer at our expense, with their investments in property which they use as a cash cow for the future? Can we be proud of wanting to live in a civilised society where everybody cares for everybody else, and everybody cares for each another? Surely that is something worth aspiring to?'

'*Yes!*' came their answer – '*generally, and to all your questions*'. But they also made sure to add that they would much rather live in a society where personal crises were not dealt with by them, but by well-trained professionals working for a socially owned and controlled health service. And they said that they would much prefer to live in a society where people could not be evicted. A society where evictions had been deemed a crime, and landlordism outlawed. They said that they would much prefer to live in a society where the poor no longer existed, not because they had been socially cleansed from the earth, but because the rich no longer existed, and instead it was only society that was rich. And they clamoured to mention that they never felt good about 'walking by', as he so put it, but sometimes they had not the time, nor the energy, nor the money to stop and talk with the homeless. It was truly a terrible state of affairs they had to admit, but with what little they could achieve as individuals, they were concerned that such brief contributions would merely be patronising and fruitless.

Should that helpless individual guilt be turned inwards, against them? If he had been addressing one of those humans who enjoyed joint ownership of the whole misery-creating system, then he might have had a point, they submitted. But they were not, and they would not accept any burden of responsibility. They all wanted a kinder, fairer politics. But at the same time they had not turned up to join the bloody Samaritans…

'I am accused of being out of date and that this is desperately old-fashioned, desperately outdated, 1980s stuff. No, it's not. It's a 21st-century world, where a lot of people have had enough of free-market economies. They've had enough of being told that "trickle-down" works. They've had enough of being told that austerity works, knowing full well that it does not. So let's be practical about the things we want to do. The things we want to do are to create an economy where we invest in high-skilled manufacturing industry; where we invest in sustainable development; where we invest in green-energy jobs and green-energy resources; where we invest in rail infrastructure; where we invest in council housing; where we invest in giving people a decent place to live; where we don't have a housing policy that deliberately drives people out of central London as a whole process of social cleansing as a combination of higher rents and insufficiency of benefits. This can be done.'

They held their peace for the moment. They understood the importance of being practical, and agreed that whether something was old or not was quite meaningless. But they weren't going to make a song-and-dance about that. 'High-skilled manufacturing', 'sustainable development', 'green energy', 'rail and housing': they all sounded perfectly reasonable, particularly when the proposed solutions were decent homes, cheaper rents and greater benefits. They could do without rents and benefits altogether if they were honest about it, but in the name of Corbyn's plea for 'practicality', they allowed him the benefit of the doubt. And this word that he kept repeating: 'invest' - sounded a lot like casting their nets on the other side. And sort of slow. Those among them who had saving accounts and endowment mortgages were unaccustomed to anything but measly returns on their investments in the best of times.

'Our students are leaving university with massive debts: fifty-thousand, sixty-thousand, seventy-thousand, worth of debts. What kind of reward or start in life is that for young people who studied hard, worked hard and achieved a great deal at university? We've worked out that it is possible, actually, to fund university education. My generation had free education. I personally didn't take it up; I am not claiming any hardship - that was my choice. But I had that opportunity. It is not mine to take away from the next or subsequent generations.'

They re-registered their approval. All remembered the heroic struggle of the students. They said that the comparison he made with his generation raised an important point. Surely the imposition of student debt was an unmistakable sign that society was being taken backwards?

Below the stage, penned in among the forest of shoulders, Amalia wondered whether her MP proposed to include her debt in his railing against the current state of affairs. He had not explicitly stated he would annul all student debt, but surely he could mean nothing less? She paid her fees in London, but her debt existed in Greece. She knew he stood with the Greek people, so surely he would refund all ill-gotten debt if he became the Prime Minister? Her parents were already considering whether they could pay for little her sisters' education - and they were not poor.

As she listened, someone tapped her on the shoulder. She turned to see Bob glowing in his yellow hi-vis tunic. He had a big smile beneath his sunglasses and wisp of white hair.

'You should have seen it earlier, girl,' he said. 'Astonishing - they were queuing round the corner. I tell you, in all my fifty years in the Labour Party, never seen nothing like it.' Above them Corbyn continued to explain his ideas for students:

'And so, by increasing corporation tax by nought-point-five percent, we could achieve free university education for all. A price worth paying, I believe.'

'Not a bad start', said Bob, raising his shades above his kindly wrinkled eyes with mischievous sympathy. 'Let's hope those corporations don't have passports.' Amalia smiled. 'Here look, I've sold sixty papers - you want to help me at the back for when people start walking away? They've been lapping it up.' She consented, and as they made their way toward the thinning outer edges, she continued listening.

'I am going to conclude before I have to disappear,' said Corbyn, 'because I received the magic one-minute sign before I have got to go somewhere else. I would just say this: This campaign, at one level, is about a position in the Labour Party. I have been in the Labour Party all my life. I opposed the Iraq war, I oppose nuclear weapons.'

Yes! And good on you for sticking with it, they cried.

'I stand by a tradition that's something very different. And I am inspired by all those people who have come together; who are put off by personality politics; by the politics of personal abuse; by the politics of celebrity; and want something stronger. So, I am not indulging in personal abuse of anybody. I don't do it - never have, never will. There isn't time; it is a waste of energy; it puts people off. I want on September 12th, whatever the result, for us to be together, to stay together, to keep on being together, in order to develop the policies that will bring real social justice; that will bring policies that will help bring peace, therefore, to the world; that will help bring a just and environmentally sustainable world.'

Sensing the conclusion, they opened their applause ahead of time and reached out and placed their hands beneath his feet. A crack of energy from below whipped Corbyn above the rising tide:

'We can together do it! Let's be strong! Thank you very much for coming out tonight!'

The waves rushed against the fire engine steps as he descended, and he found himself waist-high and wading in the ocean current. His eyes rocked with the tide and the wind hurled itself upon him. He became unsteady and frightened. A coordinator in a hi-vis jacket shielded him with her clipboard.

"Jez we can!" they submitted.

"Jez we can!" they declared.

"Jez we can" they concurred and, understanding that their man was needed elsewhere, let him pass. Then among themselves they gathered and discussed, resolving to help spread the word to the best of their abilities.

2

Amalia looked back at the gap in nature that had opened up, revealing the ocean floor. It sucked against the fire engine as seagulls hung above, suspended in mid-air. Then the wave let out a gasp and broke, falling back and flooding past her in countless drunken discussions. She held the paper around her chest. The headline strap read:

*"From Greece to Britain: Vote Corbyn,
Fight for International Socialism!"*

It was a good message, and she felt proud to support Corbyn as a Greek, straddling the two pillars of the summer. The *Revolutionary Newspaper* was only a monthly, and because of that the headline could miss the mark. The July edition had carried something typically forgettable like: *'We must struggle'* or *'Begin the fightback!'*

Many greeted Amalia and the paper's sentiments, and did not just stop to transact, but talked with her at length and with rare English enthusiasm. It occurred to her that, gathered and cheered as they all were, it was the physical exchange of the newspaper that allowed the Corbyn supporters to bridge beyond their own friendship groups, and only then with trepidation. Yet, despite their traditionally stiff upper lips, they overflowed. It was something she had not experienced in this country. And while she spoke with one group, five more washed by to whom she could just as easily have sold. All this she considered later. In the moment she had no time to stand outside herself.

Toward the end of her bundle, ears soaked in spittle and hands smeared in newspaper ink, a young lady approached her. It was Sam from the phone bank, and with her, Ryan. She had not noticed it before, but they appeared to be a couple. They bought Amalia's last two papers and were as friendly as ever. Ryan made fun of the black inky smudge that marked the freckles beneath her right eye. They talked for some time, and she felt a genuine warmth of friendship often so difficult to detect in England, this land of polite and tiresome subtleties.

Bob eventually came over them and introduced himself with a sovereign-splashed handshake, and momentarily Amalia became bitten beneath her ear with anxiety as her funny-looking friend associated himself with her. But before long he had worked his silly charm and had them laughing. Then she twisted her hair beneath her ears in shame. Bob invited them to the pub for a pint.

'Actually, we were thinking of seeing if we could sneak in,' said Sam. 'Want to try?' Amalia agreed immediately, jumping at the chance to know them better, but Bob made his excuses. As he left she embraced him tightly, and off he went on his bike, ex-blonde wisps flapping in the dusk.

Jeremy and Corbyn

At the entrance they were frustrated by Corbyn's army of stewards. They were a motivated bunch, and Amalia regretted not having asked to borrow Bob's hi-vis jacket. They walked around the building for a while, and were about to give up, when Sam spied an open window above a stack of metal railings which had earlier been used to channel the rising tide. From inside a voice boomed out, followed by intervals of applause.

The window was at least eight foot high, but with a leap Ryan gripped the granite ledge and hauled himself up, finding his feet on a small ridge. He peeked through the window and then turned to Sam and offered her his hand. She was tall and made the leap easily enough. Amalia, being neither tall nor athletic, eventually scrambled up with help from both of them. They all tiptoed on the ledge, four feet above the pavement, and peered inside. The hall was full and alive in anticipation. A microphone went *thud-thud*:

'Hullo,' said the man.

The crowd whistled and rewarded him with a round of applause.

'Can I, erm... first of all say: My name is Mark Serwotka. I'm the general secretary of the PCS trade union, and I...' they applauded that, too. 'Oh right, I'll have to come again!' he said in his happy Welsh accent. 'I'm going to be chairing tonight's meeting. I'm just going to make a few introductory remarks. Can I thank you for your patience. I know it's very, very warm... like a typical South Wales day, and we've had some problems getting everybody in - you'll have seen from the crowds, there's massive crowds. There are three meetings going on simultaneously - and some of our speakers will be leaving here to go and address the other two meetings, so anyone who speaks and leaves the stage, they're not being rude, they're actually going to talk to colleagues outside in the other meetings themselves. I was delighted to be asked to chair this meeting because we are all here, I think, because we want to see a better Britain, a better world, and we want some hope and inspiration in our politics, and if you think that Jeremy is offering that ...'

They stopped him and, to his delight, decided he had earned another applause.

'Fantastic. Now, Jeremy's schedule is absolutely incredible. He's running around the country doing massive meetings. Since he's been told by MumsNet he is the sexiest man in Britain... err, he's err...'

They broke into laughter.

'We are all growing beards now by the way!' More laughter. '...he's had a real packed schedule. But this meeting had a particular theme to it, and what this meeting represents is the type of social movements that Jeremy has spent a lifetime backing; being at the meeting and speaking to you tonight. It's to make the case that we all want Jeremy to be Labour leader. We want Jeremy to be Prime Minister.'

They could agree to that, throwing out another long applause.

'But Jeremy, more than anybody, knows that you don't change things just through Parliament - you change it with what's going on outside of Parliament. So what you're going to find tonight is speakers from a load of movements that Jeremy supports, all coming to show their support for Jeremy. And he'll be joining us towards the end of the rally, obviously, to give the keynote address... Can I just put a shout out? There's a lot of campaigning organisations here: disabled people against the cuts; we have housing campaigns; anti-racist campaigns; and Jeremy wants to thank everybody for their support. And I want to publicly say this: that in PCS we've had more strikes in Britain than most other unions. And one thing's been common to every one of those strikes is Jeremy Corbyn always supports us, and he's always on the picket line.'

They knew and understood, applauding with polite vigour, those who had always known it, and those who had come to understand it of late.

'And that's why we want Jeremy to win this election - because he supports workers in struggle. And if you don't know it, in a week or so's time, our members at the National Gallery are starting an all-out indefinite strike after fifty-two days of action trying to stop privatisation.'

That they applauded with grave respect. Some of the workers in that dispute were present, and whom joined in the applause for their fellow workers who had been unable to attend.

'So, like Jeremy, I hope you all get down to the picket line. The last thing I want to say is this: I always grew up being told the left is childish; they threw insults around; they weren't grown-up. Isn't it appalling to see the spectacle of all these Blairites trying to trash Jeremy in TV studios up and down the country?'

They agreed it was, and said so loudly.

'And this morning we had Chris Leslie, the shadow chancellor, telling everybody that Jeremy's not electable and he doesn't have a credible economic policy. What I think we all agree: that it is his economic policy that is not credible. Jeremy's is what we need to give people hope in this country.'

A point well-made, they said.

'So, maybe Chris Leslie shouldn't be so presumptuous and say he won't serve in a shadow cabinet - he hasn't even been bloody asked yet!'

Yes, they laughed, *it is rather presumptuous when one thinks about it!* They sincerely hoped Jeremy would not be asking Mr Leslie to join him.

'Now, my mother always told me it was presumptuous to assume something before you are asked, so maybe he wants to calm down a little bit.'

Their laughter was extended as they imagined their mothers raining a little common sense upon the shadow chancellor's pink cheeks.

'And my last remark is to Tony Blair. Now, Tony Blair made one of the most crass and insensitive remarks when he said that anybody who wanted Jeremy to win in the labour movement should get a heart transplant.'

They grumbled *shame!* beneath their collective breath.

'Now, let me tell you this: I am unfortunate enough to be one of two-hundred and eighty-four people in Britain who is currently waiting for a heart transplant. This device I have around my neck keeps my artificial heart going until I can get a heart transplant. And I just want to say this: If I get called in tonight for my transplant, I will go into hospital hoping Jeremy wins, and I will wake up with a new heart still wanting Jeremy to win the Labour leadership campaign!'

They burst into applause. Not standing or animated applause, for it was a hot night and they were Londoners. But it was applause full of empathy because it came from a man waiting for a heart. They too had been waiting for a heart. Tony Blair had taken theirs and in its place become the black pit of despair where their heart once beat. Now they thumped hard into that vacuum of expectation that had been carved open, delivering oxygen to tissue long considered dead.

'So... that's erm, that's enough from me for the opening remarks,' he said, as they continued to whack the hot night air. 'I said we've got a fantastic array of speakers. No one better than to kick off tonight than the former Mayor of London, lifelong socialist, campaigner for Jeremy, and the supporter of so many just causes over the years. I give you Ken Livingston.'

The weighty name was greeted with cheers carried over from enjoyment generated by the chair's opening remarks.

Amalia and her friends leapt off the ledge as the nasal wheeze of the former mayor fogged the hall. It seemed Jeremy Corbyn would not speak for a while, and in truth there was little point waiting on a precipice so long for a speech they had already heard. But they had broken in upon a little window of history and become its witness. They decided they fancied that pint after all.

3

'How the situation has arisen no longer matters,' said Tom, mashing his pad.

Chuka leaned into Tom as he turned a corner, tapping 'X' repeatedly. 'That's the way Peter sees it,' said Chuka. 'And we all agree that we need a man like you, Tom, to help broker the peace.'

Tristram perched on the arm of the little sofa in silent green envy, his face flashing blue and yellow as polygons collided across the screen.

'We all think you played a great role in bringing us all together for the New Year's celebrations. Well... all except the Scots, of course.'

'Their days were numbered anyway,' said Tom, 'once Gordon decided to step down.' Chuka looked over at Tristram with dead eyes. 'Aha!' shouted Tom, his thick-rimmed glasses momentarily bathed in a deep yellow flash that screened his eyes. 'Got you – you missed the level-up!'

'You win again, Tom,' said Chuka.

'Is it my turn to play now?' asked Tristram.

'Yes, in a minute...' said Chuka, irritated. 'You're right, Tom: The Scots let us all down. But for the moment we've bigger fish to fry.'

'I can see what you guys were thinking,' said Tom, planting a mine in Chuka's path. 'It was a good plan – didn't occur to me at the time. To be honest, I stopped playing the trade union game after Falkirk. Len handled that all very poorly. And by the time the Collins Review came out, I was too busy with the new GTA.'

'That's something we wanted to ask,' said Chuka. 'How are your contacts in the unions these days?'

'They're still a good summon. Obviously nerfed a bit since they started backing Corbyn - bit of an Easter egg, that.'

'Quite,' said Chuka, re-spawning after being eaten by a sewer crocodile. 'But it goes to show how much we really have in common.'

'Yes, I've always said the same to our people. It's the bug our platform always had. It's like when Street Fighter II came out - everyone wanted to be Dhalsim because he had the "Yoga Inferno". But that soon wears thin when he's the only character anyone plays.'

'I remember,' said Tristram nostalgically. 'My favourite was Ryu... Hadouken!' he shouted, crossing his wrists. Tom turned from the screen for a second and stared at Tristram, his mouth agape. Then he turned back and just managed to dodge Chuka's rocket launcher.

'But this is an open-ended game,' continued Tom, 'and we share the same ultimate mission-quest. That was the problem with Tony. He wanted to keep on playing and wasn't prepared to pass the controller.'

'Steady on,' said Tristram. 'The man defeated the Tories three times. Gordon couldn't even win the leadership contest - let alone the General Election!'

Chuka flashed him an angry stare, and Tristram felt foolish for letting his temper get the better of him.

'Well, anyway, that game is third-generation,' said Tom. 'You can't take it back to the shop and sell it second-hand to recoup your losses.'

'And the trade unions?' asked Chuka.

'I think once the deputy leadership contest finishes they'll have served their purpose. They were only ever a useful piece on the board when playing against you guys. To tell the truth, they have so many complex side-missions and obligatory tasks, their game becomes a bit dull in the end.'

'I can imagine,' said Chuka. 'I think our game will be much more to your liking.'

'If you want my opinion,' said Tom, 'you need to stop concentrating on the contest. That mission is lost. You need to start thinking long-term.'

'Yes, the point has been made,' said Chuka, slashing at Tom with a rusty chain-saw.

'We all know that when an individual member of the PLP becomes an irritant,' continued Tom, 'they're not difficult to dispose of. Groups of irritants, harder - you have to slice them up like salami and consume them one by one. Large groups are much more of a problem. Tony learned that, eventually.'

Tristram trembled on the arm of the sofa with indignation at the disrespect displayed by this common little man. But Chuka stretched out his arm and held him back.

'If Corbyn gets past level one, we'll have to teach him that the shadow cabinet is a spider's web in which small men get caught. There are plenty of moves I can show you boys. You're aware of the feminist cheat?'

'Of course,' said Chuka.

'And you know about the worm-holes?'

'We've only recently discovered them. But it seems we have much to discuss.'

'Plenty.'

'So, we have an accord,' said Chuka, smiling. He stretched out his hand to Tom.

'Pleasure doing business with you,' said Tom, not taking his yellow-tinted eyes from the screen as he shook Chuka's hand. 'By the way, have I ever told you boys about some very interesting investment opportunities I could involve you in?'

CHAPTER 13
AMALIA'S EXPULSION

1

The warmth and the light of August made Amalia feel at home in London, and regular visits to Victoria Park supplemented the sun she carried back from her Greek July. It was not exactly the Aegean, but then what could possibly compare with the islands and their summer winds?

Her flatmates were away until next month and the house was hers. She sat at the counter eating a late lunch. It was the cleanest the flat had been all year, so much so that for once she felt comfortable enough to walk barefoot. Now the lino only stuck on account of the heat. Her feet dangled off the stool as she picked over her tomato and feta, staring once again at the letter that had come through her door that morning:

It has been brought to our attention, with supporting evidence, that as well as being a member of the Labour Party, you are also a member of Syriza.

What did that matter? It was the politics of her country. It wasn't as if the British Labour Party existed in Greece.

Chapter 2.1.3 C of Labour's rules requires that Labour Party members ...are not members of political parties or organisations ancillary or subsidiary thereto declared by party conference or by the NEC in pursuance of party conference decisions to be ineligible for affiliation to the party.

Many of the words were arranged beyond her grasp, and in such a way so as to express apparent upset about the fact that Syriza could not, or would not, affiliate to the Labour Party. It was a strange thing to be upset about, she thought. Her phone vibrated on the counter. She let it ring.

It has also been brought to our attention, with supporting evidence, that you have publicly demonstrated support for the Scottish National Party and Revolutionary Newspaper. This has included posting a video of an SNP MP on 17 July, and selling the Revolutionary Newspaper at a Labour Party event.

Were they snooping on her Facebook? For a moment she wondered if she was the victim of a practical joke. She remembered the video of Mhairi Black, but to the best of her recollection the young MP's remarks had been in support of Labour. Amalia recalled she had even quoted Tony Benn. If she was expected to share only Labour videos on her wall, and only support Labour politicians, then did she have to support all of them, even the ones she did not like? Even the ones that contradicted the others? What about the MPs who supported Tory cuts? Did that constitute 'support for another party'? And what was wrong with supporting the *Revolutionary Newspaper*? They were Labour members, like Bob, who supported Jeremy Corbyn. Then she wondered if Bob had received the same letter.

Chapter 2.1.4B of Labour's rules states:

A member of the party who joins and / or supports a political organisation other than an official Labour group or other unit of the party, or supports any candidate who stands against an official Labour candidate, or publicly declares their intent to stand against a Labour candidate, shall automatically be ineligible to be or remain a party member, subject to the provisions of Chapter 6.I.2 below of the disciplinary rules. You are therefore ineligible to remain a member of the Labour Party.

If in the future you are in a position to comply with Labour's rules, under Chapter 6.1.2 of the Rules, you may apply for re-admission, but this must be made directly to the National Executive Committee for their consideration. Chapter 6.1.2 states: When a person applies for re-admission to the party following an expulsion by the NCC on whatever basis or by automatic exclusion under 2.14 of the membership rules, the application shall be submitted to the NEC for consideration and decision. Such applications shall not normally be considered by the NEC until a minimum of five years has elapsed. The decision of the NEC shall be binding on the individual concerned and on the CLP relevant to the application.

The National Executive will only relax the 'five year' exclusion period in what it deems to be exceptional circumstances. Any re-application should be sent directly to the Labour Party's Compliance Unit at the Newcastle address given above."

Many words served to hedge the simple fact that she had been expelled for five years. It seemed a lifetime. Her phone vibrated, again she let it ring. Her trial and sentence had apparently not only been *in absentia*, but also *sine scientia*. She had a vague recollection of receiving a rule book when she joined the party, but surely no one seriously expected her to have read it? Why had they not phoned her to talk if they were upset? No matter from what angle she approached it, she could not find reason in the letter. It spoke of Amalia, recognised her by name, but the person they described was a stranger. That person was wrong, they said, and such wrongness only deserved rejection. She felt dirty like shame. Had she actually deceived them through negligence? The seeming triviality of her crimes made her feel all the more irresponsible. Simi and Geraldine, and Bob, and Jeremy Corbyn, would think her foolish.

Eventually the buzzer rang. It was Bob. Tonight her branch met, and as usual he had called for her on his route. Earlier she had phoned him and explained the letter, and that therefore she would not be able to attend as usual.

'Alright,' said Bob as she opened the door. He was holding the August edition of the *Revolutionary Newspaper*, her name scribbled in pencil above the banner. Having sold out at the Camden rally, she had forgotten to take a copy for herself. As always he wore his dark shades and high-vis jacket. He had carried up his bicycle, attached to which was an orange side-bag full of personal effects and a bicycle pump and a further bundle of *Revolutionary Newspapers*. Resting his bike in the hallway, he went through with Amalia to the kitchen and took a seat at the counter. She made him a cup of tea and resumed picking at her salad. 'So... how are you feeling?'

'Pretty upset at first, I guess, but now - I don't know. You didn't sound surprised on the phone.'

'That's 'cos you're not the only one, Amalia - they're doing it everywhere.' He explained the rash of expulsions being reported throughout the country. For some reason it gave her comfort. 'Let's have a look at it then,' he said, putting on his reading glasses. The sight of his magnified old eyes caused her to giggle. He muttered the boring bits beneath his breath. '"...member of Syriza." Who told them that?'

'Well, I am... I don't know - they probably saw it on Facebook.'

'Facebook?' he said, looking up from his glasses. 'What... and they keep the membership lists on there?'

'No, it's just a group... Like, to speak to people - you don't actually have to be a member of Syriza.'

Unimpressed, he read on: 'Chapter two-point-one-three – C! - of Labour's rules requires... blah, blah, blah.' He blew a raspberry. 'What a load of old cobblers. There's no way in hell that conference or the NEC has taken the time to declare membership of Syriza "incompatible with Labour membership."'

'It's not like I hardly go or anything,' said Amalia. 'I can't stand those Syriza kids.' As he read the letter to the end, Amalia's mobile vibrated once more. Again she let it ring.

'Rubbish - that's all I'll say about that.' She appreciated Bob's display of solidarity. 'I mean, what are you saying?' he said, holding his glasses and arguing directly with the piece of paper. 'If you're a member of "Amnesty" or "Save the Whale" you're gonna boot her out too? Don't make me laugh!' Amalia smiled at her indignant old friend. 'What about the Right, eh? What about "Progress" and "Blue Labour" and all that? You telling me they're gonna expel Blair for supporting "Progress"? Not an affiliated section of the Labour Party!' He removed his glasses. 'I'm very sorry Amalia, but I think you'll find this is what Karl Marx technically referred to in *Capital* volume three, part two, chapter four as... bullshit.' Amalia laughed. '"Suh-Reet-Sar" – you're having a laugh! As for the newspaper - it's a newspaper, for crying out loud! Aint *The Guardian* newspaper organised? Don't they meet up and talk about what they're gonna write? Or do all their articles just materialise out of thin air? They gonna start expelling *Guardian* journalists next? Give me a break! Look girl, the most important thing is: Do not let these bastards grind you down. They're arguing on this or that technicality. It's so flimsy - they must know it isn't going to stick! That's not what they're after. What they want most of all is to demoralise you, and demoralise Jeremy Corbyn's supporters, especially the young, energetic ones like yourself. They're terrified of you far more than him. And they're hoping you'll lose heart and go away – so don't.'

'Yeah... I guess you're right,' said Amalia, rattling her fork along the bottom of her salad bowl.

'You know I'm right. Why do you think they've done nothing about an old fart like me? I've been selling the paper for donkey's years. They don't care because they think I'm a harmless old eccentric who's good for nothing but stuffing letterboxes and buying a fiver's worth of raffle tickets at the CLP. You've been in the party more than a year and you're expelled just as it's dawning on the Right that they're gonna lose they party? Don't make me laugh! You know what it shows, don't you? That they're weak. And they're terrified of losing control of the party. Gets them worried over losing all their perks and privileges, you see.'

'Do you think I should clean up my Facebook wall?' asked Amalia.

'Don't know... why should you? You haven't got nothing to hide.'

'Well, I suppose I did share a video of Mhairi Black for the SNP - but she was talking about Tony Benn.'

'Pfft... Look, it's not about that. One way or another they'll go for you, whether you're on Facebook or not.'

'You're on there too, Bob, selling the paper.'

'Am I?' She showed him the pictures of them and other supporters of the *Revolutionary Newspaper* selling outside the underground. 'Oh yes... very good,' he said, unimpressed. 'Don't understand it, don't want to understand it. Sounds like a whole lot of grief...' Amalia minimized the window. 'Here, can you look up an old girlfriend of mine on that?'

'Do you think I should come to the branch? I emailed a few of the guys about the letter. They told me to speak to Simi, but she emailed me an hour ago asking me to send her the details of the letter to be read out, and that I shouldn't come.'

'Not come? She can't do that.'

'The letter says I'm not a member anymore. Look,' she said, opening her inbox, 'she said she didn't even know I was expelled until I told her about it.'

'Is that right?' said Bob.

'I know... I feel stupid for telling her now; I thought she would already know. Now she says I mustn't come under any circumstances. Look, she's even underlined it and put it in capitals:

<u>YOU CANNOT COME TO THE MEETING, YOU ARE NOT ALLOWED – SEND AN EMAIL TO BE READ OUT IN THE MEETING BUT DO NOT COME!</u>

'If you only got this an hour ago, say you didn't read it.'

'She'll know – she's already been phoning me and I haven't picked up. I can't believe she's being like this. What does it matter if I go along, at least to tell the comrades and explain to them? Geraldine said I might be able to come as a guest to ask the branch for their support.'

'Look, the branch has a right to know what's going on. It's not like you've just arrived – you've been involved since you got here, haven't you?'

'Pretty much.'

'The comrades know you; you've gone out campaigning with them. Whilst you was away some of them was talking about making you a delegate to the CLP as far as I'd heard. They're going to want to know why you're expelled all of a sudden.'

'I guess.'

'I know... Come on, you'll come tonight - we'll go along and see what's what. I'll back you up.'

2

They walked the busy lane to the community hall where the branch met, *Revolutionary Newspapers* under their arms. Amalia was nervous. What would people think of her being expelled, no longer one of them? Bob did his best to reassure her and distract her with silly jokes. She had not before noticed the Union Jack bunting that lined the hall's guttering, left over from some past celebration. The setting sun bathed everything in an alien light.

Occasionally some of the elderly members had been hard to fathom. Sometimes they had asked her to repeat what she was saying. But they had always made her feel welcome. Now she was uneasy, as if she were attending a meeting for the first time; as if she were an intruder, an impediment to their comradely discussion. Bob suggested they go early. That way, if the comrades really were determined to keep her from attending the meeting, then at least she could speak to them before it began. As they turned into the little cul-de-sac where the entrance to the hall was, they saw Simi's car parked outside. Simi and Geraldine were sat in the front.

'Uh-oh,' said Bob without moving his lips 'looks like we're caught! Keep... walking,' he said conspiratorially, trying to distract Amalia with his silliness from her anxiety. But Simi stepped out of the car.

'Am-Ah-Lee-Ah! Can I talk to you, please?'

Bob saw Jack and Neville, a couple of old party hands, at the entrance. 'I'll go on in,' said Bob. 'Try and work on them. See you inside.'

Before she knew it Amalia was abandoned on the concrete cul-de-sac. Simi marched forth, her assassin's baby-face coldly set. Beyond her, she saw Geraldine step out of the other side of Simi's car.

'Am-Ah-Lee-Ah!' she cried, as if the maid had spilt her coffee. 'I thought I told you to stay away? Didn't you read my email?'

'I'm sorry,' said Amalia, seeing that her presence was clearly no small thing. 'I just wanted... to come down, and explain. Can't I speak to the comrades?' Simi pulled close to Amalia's face, causing her to grasp the *Revolutionary Newspapers* tightly.

'I've been trying to phone you all afternoon. Why didn't you pick up? I've already said to you Am-Ah-Lee-Ah: you can't come in. Are you trying to undermine my authority?'

'What? No... I just... didn't think it would be a big deal if I could at least talk to people? Geraldine said maybe I could attend as a guest.'

Geraldine was walking over and as she passed Amalia, placed a hand on her shoulder and squeezed it sympathetically with a mole-ish squint – it was a piteous offering to the leper, poorly masking the revulsion. To Amalia's eyes it was the kiss in the garden. Until that moment she had held out hope that Geraldine might understand, not just walk on by, on the other side. Then Amalia became paranoid. What had they been discussing in the car? Had Simi been instructing her? Disciplining her? Was Geraldine just Simi's lackey?

'Yes,' said Simi. 'We had been talking about you attending as a guest. But now I'm not so sure, the way you're behaving.' Amalia had never been comfortable with Simi's playful overtures, feeling more like she was being prodded than befriended. But she had not suspected the inner spite the woman held, now visible at close quarters coursing through her veins. Amalia generally considered herself tough, especially when compared to the anxious English, but now she felt small and wanted to cry.

Inside the hall, Bob had begun to work on the two old-timers. Jack, who had a long and wispy beard, was a little younger than Bob. He was a known member of the 'Campaign for Labour Party Democracy.' Amalia had already emailed him about her expulsion.

'What do you make of it then?' probed Bob.

'Yes,' said Jack, wandering through the stackable chairs with his hands folded as if paying his respects. 'It's quite a predicament.' Bob was not surprised.

'What is it, Militant Tendency?' asked Neville, the oldest of the three, taking a seat near the entrance.

'Something like that, I s'pose,' said Bob. 'Depends on your meaning. You know that girl's done nothing wrong. Expelled for selling the *Revolutionary Newspaper*? I've been selling it here for years!'

'Yes, but you know as well as I do… what you've got to understand, you see, is that all these new 'uns have got involved in the party and the 'igh-ups don't like it… It aint right, but it's the way it always is.'

'How can they expel her for selling a paper,' said Bob, slapping his own bundle down onto the little coffee table in the middle of the room, 'when I sell it all the time - long before she came around. It's… arbitrary.' Bob felt he was failing to inspire the support he needed from these desiccated coconuts.

Geraldine walked in, and Bob popped his head outside to see if anyone else was coming who he could petition. He saw Simi approaching. Beyond her, he could see Amalia, stood where he had left her, chin buried in her shoulder. He walked out of the room to attend to his friend, passing Simi without saying a word.

'What a fucking bitch,' said Amalia, blowing cigarette smoke.

'Here, you know those things will kill you…' he said, waving the smoke out of his face. 'What she tell you?'

'Nothing. I just can't believe she's being so hostile. She said I was "undermining her authority", and that she had been going to let me attend and explain things, but now she can't make any promises.'

They stood in silence while Amalia composed herself and recalled her encounter. The two friends had been intent on kicking up a fuss, but now it felt as if the wind had deserted their sails. Other members arrived in due course. They were the same old faces. By the time the meeting was due to begin eight were present - a surprisingly large meeting for that time of year. But both Bob and Amalia had lost confidence in their petition, sensing it would fall upon deaf ears.

'What do you want to do then? It's up to you,' said Bob.

Amalia took a long draw on her cigarette and through it on the road. 'Shall we go in?'

'Yeah, if you want to girl…' said Bob. 'Look, it's not quite seven o'clock; the meeting hasn't even begun yet. Let's just go in and ask to say a few words before they start. They can't object to that, can they?' Amalia agreed it was reasonable, though she dreaded it.

Creaking open the door, they saw the branch assembled in a circle of unfolded chairs, and all turned toward Amalia and Bob, littering the room with unfinished sentences. Simi, Geraldine, Jack and Neville had been joined by George, a trade unionist in his early fifties, Mel, and the couple Tania and Gareth, the latter three all of the generation of Geraldine's thinned ring. Geraldine herself stared at Amalia, startled eyes widening, as if Amalia were about to do something obscene.

'I'm sorry Amalia,' said Simi, letting go a puerile howl. 'I thought I made it clear - you can't come in!'

'Yes, I know, Simi,' said Amalia, screwing her courage to the fact of the matter, 'but I just wanted to say…'

'Amalia, will you please go!' shouted Simi from the edge of her chair.

'Look… the meeting doesn't start till seven,' said Bob, pointing to the classroom clock on the wall.

'At the moment we're just… a friendly gathering of people, not a Labour Party branch.'

'We're in a room booked by the Labour Party,' replied Gareth, who was a local councillor.

'Not yet,' said Bob.

'Amalia,' said Geraldine, in her sternest Librarian timbre. 'I think it is best that you go.'

Feeling reinforced, Simi all of a sudden became angry with Bob: 'Oh, don't you come here with your dirty left-wing tactics!' she cried, bile overflowing from a deeper place than anyone could imagine.

'What's that supposed to mean?' asked Bob, in all sincerity.

'Get out Amalia!' cried Simi very loudly, rising out of her chair and losing all decorum. Then she quickly sat back down and her voice deadened:

'You're going to have to leave,' she said, folding her hands on her knees. 'We'll discuss whether you can attend the meeting once you allow us to begin.' So Amalia left, and an awkward silence descended on the branch.

What a miserable shower his comrades were, thought Bob. The only ones who had spoken up were those who for years had succeeded in making everyone else feel as if they were merely tenants in the local party, working somebody else's land. And now they had just moved on an apparently dangerous field-hand. Despite Jack and Neville knowing the injustice of it all, they had remained silent. It was as if thirty years had never passed. Bob looked at the clock. A minute remained until the meeting was due to begin, so he went to check on his friend.

Up the cul-de-sac to the lane he walked, but he could not see Amalia. He hoped she was not too upset. Then he worried that when they called her in, if she were not there, they would use it against her. He went back into the meeting.

Simi had opened proceedings without him. The printed agenda was circulating and Jack was asking a question about the summer barbeque. They agreed to discuss it before the planned political discussion on the leadership contest. Bob looked at the agenda, annoyed. There appeared to be no point on the agenda for a discussion on Amalia's situation. He wanted to complain for the way his friend had been treated.

Minutes
Apologies
Councillors reports
Correspondence
BBQ
Political Discussion on Labour leadership contest
AOB

That they were due to have a political discussion at all was a small miracle. He worried about Amalia. She would not have wanted to miss such a discussion. 'So at what point are we going to discuss Amalia's situation?' he asked.

Simi stared at Bob like stone, as if his enquiry was utterly disrespectful. 'Bob… it will be discussed under correspondence.' For one so young to talk to him as she did would have caused offence in your typical veteran comrade. Neville was offended for him, though he kept quiet about it. But in this instance Bob's strength was his weakness. He did not consider himself old.

The meeting recalled in him something he had last felt a long time ago, when half this lot were in swaddling. That was after he had met *Militant*, who had introduced him to the Labour Party. He had joined with cheer and made the struggle his life's work. Then they expelled him, and those who called themselves 'Left' collapsed like marrow jelly. He remembered the disappointment, which was worse than pain, which is at least sharp and short-lived. But that disappointment gnawed at him for years from the inside. He had not been naïve. He had had the measure of his comrades then, as he did now. He knew what their words were worth. But it was their personal showing that was so bitterly disappointing; the itchy palms of those he had joked and broken beer with for years; their sudden preoccupation with their shoelaces, unable to form a sentence without consulting the party rulebook. Then he was out, and the phone stopped ringing. For them he stopped existing. For him the party became a phantom limb, amputated, but still grasping.

They sat in silence, pretending to read the Councillors' reports, not voiced by their authors, but distributed in dumb printed matter, and artful in their dullness. No discussion of the councillors' well-intentioned cuts took place.

'Now,' said Simi, moving matters on. 'I received from Amalia an email yesterday where she told me she had been expelled from the party. I did write back today to tell her not to attend, but she chose not to reply and instead came to the meeting anyway, despite what I said.' Bob shook his head. 'So I think it's important that - people can get very emotional about these types of things, understandably - but I think it's important that we keep calm,' she said, swiping a furtive glance in Bob's direction, 'and discuss things through first as a group...'

'And also decide,' said Neville, leaning back in his chair and pressing his thumbs under his arms, 'if we want to let her back into the room.'

'Yes, and decide if we want to let her into the room... So, who would like to begin?'

'Yes, well, I did speak to Amalia the other day,' Jack wheezed through his nasal passage, 'when she raised this with me over the phone. I said to her that first of all, of course, she should raise it with Simi. But what she appears to be accused of is being a member of Syriza, the Greek party in government, when the party rules state that you can only be part of another Labour Party 'unit' or 'group', officially sanctioned by the party.' Gareth and Tania nodded solemnly at the utterance of the rules. 'They also say she is a member of the "*Revolutionary Newspaper*". Now, we all know that Bob has been selling the paper for years. And if you look it up online, you can see it is quite clearly a grouping of Labour Party supporters.' Bob nodded, although he had never seen the website. 'Finally, she's accused of supporting a party other than Labour by sharing a speech on Facebook of an SNP MP.' Gasps were drawn at that tantalising revelation. Neville spoke next:

'Well, I remember this kinda thing hapnin' in the eighties,' he said, coughing out an East London accent and decades of tar. 'Whenever they're afraid they pull this kinda thing. But the last few months - I don't think I've ever seen what I seen recently... Now, it don't matta what you think of Jeremy Corbyn - tens of thousands have joined the party! What was you saying before we started, Geraldine? That this branch alone has doubled in members in the last three months? S'gonna be a job to get 'em in, but last thing we want is to start playing silly buggers. Now, the girl... Am-lee-ah - been round a while, and she's a good girl, puts the work in. I don't know about this SNP business, but it don't do any harm - same with the newspaper, if you ask me.' Simi brought in Bob:

'First of all, I'd just like to say I agree with what Simi said. It's important not to get heated in situations like these, but to remain calm and respectful. Now, Amalia is a dear friend of mine, and so even from that point of view, let alone because comrades should always be civil to one another, I'm duty bound to protest the way she has just been treated. Attacking people for supposed 'left-wing tactics,' whatever that means...'

'Umm,' interrupted Simi, 'I was saying that at you Bob, not Amalia.'

'Well, whatever – don't make it any better. And please, don't interrupt me; you're supposed to be chairing this meeting.' He continued: 'Where was I... yes, to then be making accusations about her purposefully ignoring emails, phone calls, making insinuations about...' This time it was Geraldine who interrupted:

'Bob, you're not helping!'

'And why are you being so hostile all of a sudden?' he snapped, immediately regretting it. From time to time Geraldine seemed to show something of a decent party spirit about her, unlike Simi, but after Amalia told him of Geraldine's poor showing at the entrance earlier, his suspicion had been growing fast.

'Excuse me, Bob,' shouted Simi, 'but I think we could do without that kind of aggressive behaviour - especially towards female colleagues! And, for your information, Amalia just admitted to me outside that she purposefully didn't reply to me.'

'You're making accusations of her while she's not here,' he said, hoping Amalia had not been so foolish as to admit such a thing, 'when she don't have the opportunity to reply herself.'

'That's what she said,' repeated Simi.

'Well, I think you are misinterpreting her words quite frankly, and anyway, I'm just saying - I protest how she's been treated.' He finished abruptly, annoyed by the interruptions which he knew were designed to make him lose his train of thought.

'Well,' said George, the trade unionist. 'I think we had better have Amalia in to speak.'

Simi said nothing for a second. Then: 'So... what do people think about that?'

'I'd like to hear what she has to say,' said Mel, a friend of Geraldine's.

'The thing is,' continued George, 'because they've actually formally expelled Amalia, rather than suspended her from meetings, she is - formally speaking, you see - no longer a Labour Party member, and therefore not under our control, per se. So we could invite her in, to attend as a guest.' A muttering of approval broke out. *Trust the union man to come up with that one.*

'OK,' said Simi, 'let's give her five minutes, and then we can ask her to leave again and continue to discuss what to do next.' She left the room to find Amalia. All sat in silence, looking at their feet and trying to fathom which way the wind was blowing.

'Bob! I can't find her, Bob!' cried Simi, marching back into the room. 'Can you see where she's got to?'

He was relieved to find her at the top of the cul-de-sac, perched on a railing beneath the ragged bunting, a cigarette pinched between her folded arms. Red eyes showed she had been crying.

'I can't believe she made me cry, I'm so embarrassed,' said Amalia, the tears loosened in her old friend's presence. 'What the fuck am I doing this for?' She sucked in the smoke hard, exhaling it in his direction, but he forgave her this time.

'Hey, don't let Simi get the better of you - you're better than that. She's a twat, Amalia - plain and simple... and she's threatened by you, don't you see? You see, you're younger than her, you're better looking... although you won't be for long if you don't cut those fags out!' he smiled to see her choke a laugh through the tears. 'Look, Simi's just another talentless careerist who is probably thinking that all that time she spent licking the party's arse could be all for nought if Jeremy Corbyn and his barbarians take over. Her life begins and ends in this CLP.'

'I can't believe how disgusting they've made me feel,' said Amalia, wiping her eyes. 'I thought they were pretty sad, but I thought they were... you know, at least nice people.'

'Hey, don't you know the song, girl?' He rocked his head as he sang to her:

> *'Never smile at a crocodile,*
> *'No, you can't get friendly with a crocodile,*
> *'Don't be taken in by his welcome grin,*
> *'He's imagining how well you'd fit within his skin.'*

They both laughed. 'I used to sing that to my kids.'

'Thanks Bob,' she said.

'Look, if you don't want to go in, don't... but I think you might regret it. You should go in there and tell them to go fuck themselves - I'll back you.' She laughed again. She was no longer crying.

3

'I wanted to attend the branch tonight,' said Amalia, the red marks merged with the freckles beneath her eyes, 'so I could explain for myself what has happened and show I have nothing to hide about my conduct or my politics.

'I think the branch should know what's happened to me, that I have been expelled, not only because the branch has the right to know, but because you are the people in the party that know me best. If anyone decides I should no longer be a member, it shouldn't be some unelected "Compliance Unit" but you, who know how I have been involved in the Labour Party since I came to this country. I've knocked on doors campaigning for the party in the General Election; I've attended the branch meetings and CLP meetings and women's meetings,' said Amalia. 'The branch officers even talked about me becoming a delegate to the General Committee.' She stole a glance at Simi, who kept her eyes firmly on the floor. 'I proposed doing stalls because I thought we could go into the street and attract young people to the party.' Her comrades had nodded and politely ignored that suggestion, but she thought it worth saying anyway.

'I ask the branch to please discuss whether you would be happy to vote for my expulsion. Here is the letter.' She held it up for all to see and summarised the crimes it listed. 'Simi said I should email her the details, but I didn't want to send sensitive information out that way and not know where it might end up. But here it is.' She passed her expulsion letter round the group. Simi eyed it greedily. 'Please, I'm happy for you all to read it. Pass it round and decide for yourself whether you think I should be expelled.'

From the beginning I have never hidden my politics. I've always said that I am a socialist, and I helped Bob sell the *Revolutionary Newspaper* – I've done that since I joined. It is not against party policy to sell a paper, and the *Revolutionary Newspaper* is not a banned publication. In fact, I find it quite worrying to think that any socialist ideas should be "banned". If we disagree as a party, then we should discuss our differences, not start expelling each other! I joined Labour when I arrived in this country because it was the party of the working class in Britain, the same as Syriza has become the party of the working class in Greece. As for Scotland, I think we should discuss what has happened to the Labour Party there. To me it seems similar to what has happened to PASOK in my country. But what won't resolve anything, is people paid by the Labour Party to snoop on my social media accounts to check on what I've been doing because I might have a different point of view. Those are the actions of a party that is afraid. That's why I support Jeremy Corbyn, because he is the socialist candidate and he's not afraid to say it. He is standing up for lots of people and by doing so he is making them less afraid, too. I think he has the potential to attract a lot of individuals to the party who can help fight for socialism. So, the more I think about it, the more I think it is not an accident that I've been expelled.' She looked at Bob and he nodded, the only one who would meet her eye.

'The expulsion is political. It's happened here because I support Jeremy Corbyn, just like others are being expelled around the country. You can talk about newspapers. You can talk about Syriza and Scotland. But the only real reason

I'm expelled is that those who oppose Jeremy Corbyn cannot beat him in a real debate, so they resort to all sorts of dishonest manoeuvres to defeat him. But that won't solve their problems, not in the long run. So that's why I think I've been expelled. In one way it is disappointing to me, but in another way I should not be surprised. I've seen in my home country this summer how people who stand up against the establishment are treated. They disregard us. They try to sweep us under the carpet and write off as an anomaly. The question I ask is this: When does the anomaly become so frequent that it stops being dismissed as an anomaly, and become recognised as the new rule?

'I've always voted Labour since I came to this country, I intend to continue to vote Labour whether I am expelled or not. Because it is the party of the working class, and I think that the working class are the only ones that can make socialism happen. I ask for the support of the branch. If you think it unfair that I have been expelled, then please let me continue to attend meetings until I am reinstated.'

They thanked her and she left.

Simi opened the discussion about what the branch should do. John proposed a letter in support of Amalia be sent from the branch to the Compliance Unit. Mel said that she thought Amalia was terrific, and that we should back her because she did not just show up to vote, she got stuck in with the branch and had helped during the General Election and everything else besides. Old Neville nodded in agreement and repeated what he said before about the ''igh-ups. Geraldine said nothing supportive of Amalia personally, but agreed they should send the letter.

Bob said that neither Syriza nor the *Revolutionary Newspaper* could be considered banned by the party, nor in opposition to the party. Gareth, the councillor, responded by saying that being a member of Syriza was in opposition to PASOK, the Labour Party's sister-party in Greece, and as Amalia was Greek she could not vote in the General Election, meaning she was not on the electoral register, and therefore ineligible for party membership.

She was an EU citizen said Bob, and therefore was on the electoral register, and he added that arguing working-class immigrants shouldn't be members of the Labour Party just because they haven't got a vote in the General Election was a scandalous thing to say. Every worker had something to offer the party. At the end of the day it's the Labour Party that should be offering something to them, he said, not the other way round. Neville liked that.

'You know what Amalia's crime is? It's not being Greek or videoing some SNP thing on the internet, and it certainly aint for selling the *Revolutionary Newspaper*. I've been selling it here for years and none of you have said a thing.'

'Well, Bob, people have asked questions about it actually,' interrupted Geraldine.

'Well, if anyone has any questions, they should be asking me. I certainly haven't heard anything,' he said, staring Geraldine straight in the eye until she looked away and slunk into her seat. 'If you lot let them expel this comrade, it'll be a crime against the party. What's more, they'll come for the rest of you next - just like in the eighties. I mean, what's next? Expelled for buying the WI calendar? They're testing the waters with the likes of Amalia to see what they can get away with.' No one disagreed openly. They agreed to write the letter, and most wanted the business to move on. Then Bob repeated the proposal that Amalia had made: that she be allowed to attend as a guest until the matter was resolved.

They turned in their seats uncomfortably and grumblings were made that the meeting had run on far too late already, and that there was still the political discussion to be had. Some were very insistent that such a proposal should not be discussed, but Bob pressed them, and got Neville to second his proposal.

They raised their hands. The vote was tied four-to-four, and so the proposal fell. Then they decided not to have the political discussion as time had run on.

Toward the end Patrick arrived, a man in his fifties, and slight of character. They updated him on the events of the meeting. Having only joined the party himself because of Jeremy Corbyn, he was privately intrigued to hear that a real-life expulsion was being discussed in his local party. But all he asked, rather meekly, was whether she had broken any rules. The discussion had caused them to grow sick of the sight of each other. The newcomer's question received abrupt and conditional answers, and the meeting was declared closed. Thank god for that, thought Bob.

***

In August more than one-hundred and thirty thousand refugees crossed into Europe.

CHAPTER 14
VICTORY

1

"Jez he did! Jez he did!" shouted a small and vocal band of supporters.

'I'd like to begin by thanking all the participants in this leadership contest. Given our party's recent past, you provided the necessary opposition. As we know, history progresses not without a little pain. Thank you, all of you, for providing that.'

Jeremy looked at the rows of heads before him. The response was underwhelming. Undeterred, he continued:

'For example, Harriet - I thank you. Where would we have all been if you hadn't the honesty to stand up for what you absolutely believe in by leading the abstention on the Tories' hated welfare bill? By doing so, you exposed the rotten sympathy swathes of our MPs have for the Tory cuts. You could have swept that under the carpet. But you didn't. You made it known, and in the process provided the necessary gag reflex that is now vomiting your people out all over the Queen Elizabeth Centre's lovely floor. And for that, Harriet, and all the other candidates: Andy, Yvette, Liz - I thank you.'

Harriet turned in her seat and forced into position the grooved muscles of her profession as the cameras flashed, as did Yvette and Liz in turn. Andy just looked glum.

'Nevertheless, despite the best efforts of said rotten swathe, our campaign attracted the support of sixteen thousand volunteers all over the country; organisers in each part of the country who organised all the events and meetings that we have held, and in total, we have done ninety-nine of those events - today is the century!'

"Jez he did! Jez he did!"

'This contest proved a huge democratic exercise of more than half a million people all across the country. During these amazing three months our party has changed. We've grown enormously. We've grown enormously because of the hopes of so many ordinary people for a different Britain, a better Britain, a more equal Britain, a more decent Britain. It's no secret, of course, that Corbyn and I have had our differences. And I realise that has resulted in policies that are not always completely consistent. But, let me tell you, he's coming round!

'And what this contest has shown him, shown both of us, is that the working class is waking from its slumber. That has not necessarily happened because people are completely clear about what they want. But they know what they don't want! They don't want privatisation, they don't want cuts, they don't want war. All these issues brought people in, in a spirit of hope and optimism, as well as in an understanding of the need to completely annihilate the clique of self-serving careerists who have dwelt within out party for far too long. So I say to the new members of the party, or those who have joined as registered supporters or affiliated supporters: Welcome! Welcome to our party, welcome to our movement. And I say to those returning to the party who were in it before, and felt disillusioned and went away: Welcome back. Welcome back to your party, welcome back to your home.

'The media, and our former party leaders, simply did not understand the views of many young people in our society.

They had been written off as a non-political generation who were simply not interested, hence the relatively low turn-out and low level of registration of young people in the last General Election. They weren't. They are a very political generation that were turned off by the way in which politics was being conducted, and not attracted and not interested in it. We have to and must change that.

'I want to say a big thank you, they all know who they are, to my many personal friends, many people, everyone in Islington North Labour Party, for electing me to Parliament eight times up until May this year. Their fantastic comradeship, friendship and support; it's been quite amazing, and I absolutely value their advice. Sometimes it's advice you don't really want to receive, but that's the best advice you get. And I say thank you to all of them in Islington North. And I also say a huge thank you to all of my widest family. All of them. Because they have been through the most appalling levels of abuse from some of our media over the past three months. It's been intrusive, it's been abusive, it's been simply wrong. And I say to journalists: Attack public political figures, make criticisms of them, that's okay, that's what politics is about. But please, don't attack people who didn't ask to be put in the limelight, who merely want to get on with their lives. Leave them alone. Leave them alone in all circumstances.

'I'd like to congratulate Tom Watson on his winning the deputy leadership. The role he played in bringing down the *News of the World* in 2011 of course brought him to all our attention. It also brought the standing of the Murdoch's dirty media empire and the ruling-class press to an all-time low. In that way Tom helped pave the way for our victory. We don't need them, eh Tom?' Tom sat in his seat as solemn as Buddha.

'If you want a born... organiser, Tom's your man. Some people are already calling us "Tom and Jeremy"! Well, I'm sure that with the party voting in a socialist leadership, combined with Tom's intimate knowledge of the party machine, the only cartoon violence we'll be witnessing is a mobilised and organised working class dropping an anvil on the Tories!'

"Jez he did! Jez he did!"

'I'd like to thank our former leader, Ed Miliband, for the role that he has played. Over the years he has had to stand up to a torrent of racist abuse from the bosses' press about his Jewish roots and his father's contribution to socialism. It's another symptom of the degeneration of the establishment. Added to that, since this contest began, he has had to face additional attacks from even those in his own party who blame him for our victory. Is there any way to interpret this behaviour other than as a complete contempt for party democracy?

'I spoke with Ed the other day and he suggested I reach out to these elements; that Labour is a broad church and that I should make efforts to bring them into the new leadership. Well, we'll have to see. Corbyn likes the idea, but I'm unconvinced. I told Ed: "My mandate comes from the party as a whole, not the PLP, and I intend to represent the majority view. After all, is that not the meaning of democracy?" He said democracy means taking into account the different talents of the MPs. Well, all I can say to that is: fat lot of good it did him.

'No, we're going to start a new kind of politics. And if this contest has taught me anything, it is that our new democratic system for choosing a leader is at odds with the rest of our internal structures. So we're going to restore annual party conference to its rightful place as the supreme decision-making body, which will decide policy in full view of the membership, not in shady back alley forums controlled by cliques in the PLP. We're going to employ digital referenda to consult the members. We're going to bring back mandatory re-selection of MPs, councillors, and all our elected public positions by the local parties. And we'll end the superficial system of so-called positive discrimination to all positions within the party that do not warrant it. From now on we'll elect our representatives for the ideas they stand for, and not the appearances through which capitalism seeks to divide us.

'Of course, to achieve all this, we need the new members to flood the party demanding change. Don't let the buggers intimidate you. It's your party - take it! Because I am just one man. It is you who must become the real leadership. The fight for the soul of our party has just begun. And with that, we will change the situation in Britain. I think we are already having an effect.

'Look at the refugee crisis. All along we have been speaking out about it. And I don't mean the crocodile tears that have been shed by the Prime Minister in the last two weeks because the mainstream media, desperate to use the tragic picture of little Alan Kurdi washed up on a beach to sell their newspapers, inadvertently forced the Tories to change their policy toward this humanitarian crisis. Rather, I mean our long-term opposition to Blair's oil wars, and the imperialist looting of the world in general, which is the cause of the refugee crisis. Once Labour is back in government I pledge to have our special forces bring Tony Blair back to this country to stand trial, not for war crimes – all capitalist war is a crime against the working class – but for his role in the betrayal of the labour movement, which ultimately culminated in untold destruction, and the death of hundreds of thousands in the Middle East.

"Jez he did! Jez he did!"

'Exactly. And we'll take that two-hundred million pound fortune he has made on the blood and bones of this party and the Arab peoples, and put it into a special fund to provide housing and jobs for those refugees currently in tired and hungry despair filing along the many border fences of Fortress Europe.

One of my first acts as the leader of the party will be to go to the demonstration this afternoon to show support for the way refugees must be treated, and should be treated, in this country. Andy, Yvette, Liz, Harriet, all of you here today, I invite you to join me.' Confused exchanges travelled along the front rows.

'Marvin and Sadiq, our Mayoral Candidates in Bristol and London, we're going to be seeing a lot more of each other!' Dawning realisation fell across the faces of the two men. 'That's right - we're going to be campaigning together! Particularly on the crucial issue of housing. I am fed up with the social cleansing by this Tory Government. We need Mayors who put an end to sky-high rents; put an end to the insecurity of those living in the private rented sector. And that's just to begin with. We must learn from our Welsh comrades who have put an end to the market in the health service in Wales, something we need to do in the rest of Britain. We must learn the lessons of our disastrous alliance with the Tories in the so-called "Better Together" campaign and the subsequent rise of the SNP, by granting Scotland full economic autonomy. Beyond that, the only way to cut across national divisions is by the conscious combination of Scots, Welsh, Irish, English – all the peoples of Britain - into a single class, consciously organised and mobilised against capitalism. This nightmare capitalism, which has sent more than two thousand people with disabilities in Britain to an early grave in these past three years. We will unite against it at home and abroad and break free from NATO and the EU and the UN - all tools of imperialism - and instead reach out and build an international socialist organisation which will be our tool for the building of a world without borders.

'I'd also like to thank the MPs who nominated me,' he said, watching with a twinkle in his eye the Labour dignitaries and donors in the front seats, 'even those who did so reluctantly - it has been reported.'

"Jez he did! Jez he did!"

'And I thank the unions that nominated me: Unite, Unison, the TSSA, ASLEF, the Communication Workers Union, the Prison Officers Association, the Bakers' Union, the Socialist Education Association, the Socialist Health Association, and also thank you for the support received from the RMT union and the FBU. And thank you to all the other unions that took part in this campaign.

'To those last two mentioned unions I would say this: I understand why you left, or put yourself in a position to be expelled. There have been a lot of expulsions recently, something that must come to an end. And to others who may be outside looking in: Now is the time to come back, now is the time to join and help us make our party clean once again. I fully understand the importance of unions at the workplace defending people's rights, standing up for their members, and that's why our party will oppose this Government's attempts to shackle the unions into this Trade Union Bill they are bringing forward on Monday. I encourage you all, in the words of Shelly:

> *'Rise, like lions after slumber*
> *In unvanquishable number!*
> *Shake your chains to earth like dew,*
> *Which in sleep had fallen on you,*
> *Ye are many — they are few!*

'I will conclude by this: The Tories did not use the economic crisis of 2008 to impose a terrible burden on the poorest people of this country. It was the crisis that used them. And the same applies whether you are Tory, Labour, Green or even Syriza: If you accept the capitalism system, you must accept its laws, and that means imposing a terrible burden on those who cannot afford to even sustain themselves properly, those who now rely on food banks to get by. It's not right, it's not necessary, and it's got to change. That is why we must stand for the socialist transformation of society — a socialist revolution — not just here, but everywhere. Ultimately, only such a transformation can improve people's lives, expand our economy, and reach out to care for everybody. It is something you cannot do while the economy remains in private hands. We need to develop a socialist programme so that our party is about justice, is about democracy. It is about the great traditions we walk upon. We're going to show the working class of Britain that our socialism is intact. That is what brought us all into this wonderful party and this wonderful movement in the first place - isn't it?'

He heard once again from a distant corner of the hall:

"Jez he did! Jez he did!"

'We can all live well, we can all live fairly, prosperity is possible, things can, and they will, change!'

2

Jeremy rolled from side to side and woke with a snort. He was in bed, and he was alone. The radio alarm read eight as it mumbled the morning news, reporting that today was the penultimate day of the Labour leadership contest. Tomorrow the winner would be announced.

He rolled onto the other side of the bed where Laura's warmth had lingered. Out the window it looked set to be a beautiful day, although if the usual drift of thieving clouds were to put in an appearance, it would not be until mid-morning. For the moment the sunlight gave him energy. Sitting up in bed, he reached for Corbyn's "*Controls on Immigration*" mug and took a sip of water.

There was still no sign of Corbyn, who had not come home the evening before last. Jeremy had lied to Laura to reassure her by saying he had gone to visit his brother - stress of the contest and all that. It was not a complete lie. Corbyn had become quite stressed, even jittery, in recent weeks. He began complaining about aches and pains and the September heat, which was admittedly close even for the time of year. Finding it difficult to sleep, Corbyn had developed the habit of taking long midnight walks by himself. Jeremy had given it little thought, supposing that in his condition it was not the worst of ideas. And then, two days ago, he had not come back. No one seemed to know where he had gone. There was no note. John had not seen him, nor had his sons, and Jeremy knew he was not with his brother, Piers. He even tried phoning Diane, but she was none the wiser. He tried talking it over with El Gato, but being a cat, El Gato failed to see what the fuss was about. Sometimes he did not come home for a whole week, he said, and he told Jeremy he should let the man alone. But nevertheless, he did make one worthwhile suggestion: The allotment.

Jeremy judged it worth trying. He cooked some bacon, eggs, sausages, hash browns, fried mushrooms and baked beans, and sat down to breakfast with the morning paper, reading an article about the recent revelations that thousands of people had died in the past few years within six weeks of being forced by the government to find work. He washed it all down with a mug of black coffee, finished, and left the house.

Exiting through the front door, he received a slap from the rose bush that framed the entrance, grazing his cheek. The point was well made. It had been neglected and had started to grow somewhat wild. Jeremy had been ducking beneath it for some time now. He normally left the gardening to Corbyn, who had been meaning to tie it back, but the contest had of late distracted him from his gardening. Jeremy bade farewell to El Gato, closing the door behind him. On the street he spied a few lurking photographers, but managed to pass on by them unseen.

When he arrived at the allotment he was somewhat surprised to find that his friend's strip of green was in rather a sorry state. A cloud of flies could be heard whirring over the compost heap, which had turned decidedly ripe, and around the tree a skirt of the apples had fallen and turned rotten. The grass path was dishevelled and sun-bleached, overrun by collapsed rhubarb that crawled with weevils. The potato plants had died away, and the tubers that had floated to the surface had shrivelled and turned green and were swamped with aphids. The speckled sweet corn had fared slightly better, though it had been pecked by crows. Only the red currants seemed to have held their own, their berries bunching brightly in the morning light.

The garden shed was ajar, but Corbyn was not inside. Removing a deck chair, Jeremy sat and looked upon the wreckage, recounting the period leading up to his friend's disappearance. The heavy flow of attacks against his friend as a racist; as an anti-Semite; as a terrorist sympathiser; as a homophobe and sexist; all had undoubtedly taken their toll on his friend. The press had not become bored, but had grown ever more rabid. They had even put it around that he was a Bin-Laden supporter because he once said he would prefer the man be subjected to trial and due process, rather than trial by assassination. Jeremy thought Corbyn would have become accustomed to their abuse by now; after all, he was far more used to the limelight than he. But it seemed he had underestimated how much his friend had been hurt. It was all frightfully unfair.

He had tried to persuade his friend how it showed how desperate they had all become, but each time he said it (and he had said it many times over the summer) Corbyn appeared less and less convinced. One day, as they were travelling by train back from a hustings, in an attempt to lift his spirits, Jeremy reported on the hashtag that was currently trending: #suggestcorbynsmear.

The outrageous behaviour of the press had not gone unnoticed by those who loved him. In fact, it had developed to such intensity that it had turned into its opposite. Thousands were parodying the tabloid absurdities, and some were rather good. Jeremy showed Corbyn some of his favourites:

Jeremy Corbyn...

"...won't give his neighbour's ball back."

"...did nothing to prevent dinosaurs becoming extinct. Probably happy about it."

"...says that there are plenty of businesses like show business, and that we should invest in them."

"...refuses to say Starbursts, says Opal Fruits instead."

"...puts unexpected items in the bagging area."

"...can't see both sides on welfare cuts, chooses one side over another."

"...is really Keyser Söze."

"...regularly tells you how many days there are until Christmas."

"...made me doubt The Guardian."

Corbyn was highly amused, and wondered how they knew about the Opal Fruits. Jeremy said it was an internet phenomenon, and that thousands were contributing. That cheered Corbyn somewhat. Jeremy added that if Tories like Louise Mensch were tweeting them abuse (he tried to explain to Corbyn how her attempt had backfired, but he did not really understand) and the Tory grandee Ken Clarke was warning his party against hubris because Jeremy Corbyn could become Prime Minister, it showed how much the entire establishment was panicked - not just the Blairites. But, rather than being cheered, that seemed to push him back into his seat.

Jeremy tried to reflate him, but Corbyn only stared out the

window as the countryside rolled by, mumbling to himself about how he had to prove them wrong; that he was not as they portrayed him. Then he turned to Jeremy and said that Labour was a big train and they should make a point of making special allowances for women and minorities if they won the contest. *Cover all the bases...*

Sat in the allotment recollecting all this, Jeremy's attention became drawn to something moving in the corner of his eye, down beside the greenhouse on the bank of the stream. A bundle of clothes appeared to be flapping in the breeze.

Rising from his deck chair, he walked a few paces down the untidy strip of lawn, careful not to trip on the drunken rhubarb. As he approached, he saw that the bundle was not a bundle at all, but a man, squatting on the flats of his heels. His arms flayed frantically from side to side as he rocked back and forth. Jeremy halted at the greenhouse. The tomatoes were melted on their stalks, attracting yet more flies. The bundled man by the stream shivered in the breeze.

'Corbyn... Is that you, old friend?' The man sent a stone soaring - *plunk!* - into the water. Then he turned to Jeremy, slowly unfolding:

'Hello, Jeremy...,' whispered Corbyn.

'Hadn't we better be getting you home, old boy? Laura will be worrying if she doesn't see you at the embassy.' They were due to attend a commemoration of the 1971 coup in Chile that evening at Bolivar Hall.

'Jeremy... do you remember that time we ran away?'

'When we were little boys? Yes, of course... although I seem to recall we didn't get very far. Didn't you pretend to twist your ankle not half a mile from home?

'It was the only way I could get you to turn back,' said Corbyn. 'No one ever knew we were gone.'

'Yes, and it can be the same for you now if we leave soon. Look, what's this all about?'

'I don't know if I want to. There's too much... it's the expectation. I've been thinking: it's not too late to pull out of the contest. We've done a really splendid job gathering so much support. We could say we've made our point: The party needs to change. With all these new members and supporters, I'm sure it will...' He looked up at Corbyn with a sort of bleak hope written upon his face.

'I think it's a bit too late for that, old boy. The party is already changed. But if you don't go through with this, then it'll be all for nought. Those new members joined because of you. Half of them will tear their party cards up on the spot if you stand down.'

'But that's why it's all so unhealthy; to join a party over one fellow. It's not right, Jeremy.'

'I'm afraid that's the way it has worked out.'

'Well... perhaps they haven't joined because of me... It's like we always say: people are fed up with austerity - they'd vote for anyone who said the same.'

'I think it's more than an economic question, old boy. It's a question of principles, a question of hope and optimism.'

'Well, what about doing it without me? After all, it was your idea. I certainly never wanted this. And most of the policies are yours, anyway. Perhaps I could pop in and see you from time to time, see how you're getting on...'

'You know the ideas are both of ours,' said Jeremy, hoping to console him. 'What about this latest one? About taxpayers opting out of contributions to the armed forces – definitely wasn't one of mine!'

'I said that fifteen years ago! Now the *Telegraph* has dug it up and is calling it bonkers. Even the generals are calling it bonkers!'

'Hey, come on, don't listen to what those Generals have to say - they're bound to say that kind of thing.'

'You think it's bonkers,' said Corbyn, sorely wedging his chin between his knees.

'Well, you know, it's not what I would have said. It's, well... pacifist,' he said, struggling to find the right diplomatic words. 'But I suppose it makes a useful point about where our taxes go.' Corbyn turned his eyes up at him like a puppy hoping for redemption.

'I mean... we need to get that kind of thing right, old boy. I've always been surprised by the weight you give to consumer boycotts. They're so individualistic, hardly your cup of tea. They accept the idea that markets decide. So-called voting for goods and services just means the rich get more votes.'

'Well, I'm not advocating that now,' protested Corbyn. 'They clearly don't like it...'

'Clearly,' said Jeremy.

'It's just that there's so much expectation... The whole thing is like one cruel joke, and tomorrow I'll be fed to the crocodiles. I mean, what are we going to do? We can't hope to fight the PLP - we're completely outnumbered! Even the thirty-six who nominated us aren't all completely with us...'

'Well, come on, we all know that old boy.'

'Yes, but you would have thought they would be more reasonable. I can already hear them plotting. They'll lay siege to us, Jeremy. They'll outnumber us. They'll ridicule me and when it's all done we'll be worse off than when we started. It'll be Michael Foot all over again.'

'Foot lost because he didn't have the balls to carry out his programme. He bottled it and allowed himself to get distracted by the witch-hunt, cared too much about what people thought of him. And there was the small matter of the SDP split.'

'And the Falklands,' said Corbyn, rubbing beneath his eyes. He looked as if he had not slept for a week.

'Yes, and the Falklands, that probably had an effect too. A little bit of war hysteria... But then look at Ed. He lost because he had the brass balls to have no programme at all!'

'That's unfair.'

'But we needn't make that mistake,' said Jeremy. 'It's like you're always saying - we need to learn the lessons of the past.'

'He who does not learn from history will be forever doomed to repeat it.'

'Yes, exactly - Santayana. Chilean, wasn't he?'

'I could use it... in the meeting, tonight?'

'I dare say you could. Why don't we get up off this bank?'

He took Corbyn by the arm and lifted him up. Standing side-by-side, Corbyn seemed somewhat shrivelled, appearing to stand shorter. Perhaps it was the slope of the bank. They made their way out of the shade of the greenhouse and the apple tree.

'This garden has gone to waste,' said Jeremy.

'Yes, I think that's what set me off. I came here to get away from it all. You know, clear my head? But when I saw what a mess the place had become...'

Jeremy helped his friend into the deck chair and sat down on the ground beside him. They both stared at the chaotic allotment.

'I think what you have to realise,' said Jeremy, adopting his most sympathetic voice, 'is that this is about more than just you. Millions of people have been under so much pressure for so long; sooner or later that dam was sure to burst. You just happened to be where it went off... the "hole in the dyke", so to speak.'

'Can't we just put a finger in it? It's bound to burst somewhere else, sooner or later. I just don't see why it has to be me.' He extended a gaunt forearm. 'Look, my hands are literally shaking.'

'Isn't it natural to be nervous when embarking upon a great project?'

'But, it's as if... it's as if we haven't even laid the foundations of the house yet, and now we're raising the roof.'

'Come on,' said Jeremy, 'these foundations were laid long ago. They were laid by the sixty-one million jobs destroyed since the crisis and the - what is it - eighty-five billionaires who now own half the world's wealth? They were laid by the five million homeless in a Europe of eleven million empty homes. They were laid by the measly three percent of full-time jobs created in Britain since the crisis, and the two million now using food banks. They were laid by Eddy promising to match Tory spending. They were laid by the earthquake in Scotland.'

'Yes, yes, I know all that,' said Corbyn. 'What I mean is we don't have an organisation. How on earth are you and I, and a few other decent chaps like John, going to hold the line against the massed forces of Blairism? It's a suicide mission. It would be magnificent, of course, but it would not be war.'

'But we do have an organisation. It exists in the supporters and the new members. It exists in the one-hundred and fifty-two local parties that voted for you. And if you become leader tomorrow, you'll have the majority.'

'Yes, but we're not organised. They'll cut through us like hot steel through butter.'

'But we have the wind behind us and they're on the retreat.'

'They'll be back, and they'll be seriously organised next time. Besides, do you think all these supporters who've been whipped up in the summer breeze will last the winter? They'll drop like flies. They'll get bogged down in the snow. And I have to say – don't tell anyone - but when I think about it, that might be for the best...'

Jeremy frowned. 'What on earth are you talking about?'

'Can you imagine the mess they would make? No experience, no finesse, no understanding of the rules of engagement. They'll be like bulls in a china shop!' Jeremy was growing annoyed. 'That is if they stick around. I expect they'll go to ground and leave it to muggins here to clean up, as they have done for the past thirty years. I really wouldn't be surprised if...'

'Look,' said Jeremy, fed up, 'if you truly are determined not to press ahead, then alright, I'll go it alone. But be sure this is what you want.' He turned and looked at Corbyn square in the eye. 'You are right,' said Jeremy, 'there's going to be a hell of a lot of pressure, and if you have made up your mind then I suppose there's not much I can do to talk you out of it.' He stared at the red berries twinkling on the vine, hoping his friend did not think him abrupt.

In truth, Corbyn had not expected Jeremy to agree. Whatever relief it brought him became immediately mixed with new and opposite misgivings. He pulled on his watch strap.

'I'm going to have to select a shadow cabinet,' said Jeremy. 'That's not going to be fun. I mean, who is there? I suppose at least the campaign group youngsters will bolster us. Then I'm going to have to get the trade union leaders around the table at the TUC, and Labour Party conference - I'll have to speak there, too. I expect they'll be demanding I hob-nob with everyone... but I'll wriggle out of it, somehow.'

'Well, I'm not sure that's a good idea', said Jeremy. 'You'll need allies if you're going to take this on. And you have to meet with the union leaders; they have a lot of influence in the party - even among the Blairites.'

'If you say so, old boy... but the main thing is to push the message to the union ranks. That'll get them twitching!' he chuckled, a toothy grin spreading across his face.

'Well, I don't think that's a very good idea. And you'll want to speak at the conference, the leader always does that. You can't be an absentee leader.'

'Yes, yes – you're right, I know I should go. The trick will be how to appeal over the heads of the conference to the wider party.'

'That doesn't seem very democratic. I thought you were all in favour of making conference the supreme body?'

'With this year's delegates? They were nominated six months ago! This conference will represent the old party. It'll be as out-of-date as the Constituent Assembly. But you're right, I should speak. I'm sure we can rely on the media to relay the message: "We stand for the socialisation of the banks and giant corporations under workers' democratic control." At least it'll be entertaining watching their jaws drop.'

'What?! Jeremy, I think that's far too extreme,' he did privately agree that their faces would likely paint a rather amusing picture, but he kept that to himself.

'Imagine all the people you'll upset. Imagine the reaction of the PLP? Imagine the press! You'll embarrass yourself…'

'Excuse me, but you're not the one who's going to have to put up with this, thank you very much! I'm well aware they'll be coming for me, and from all angles. With sword and steel and the Queen wielding the kitchen sink, I'm sure. But how else can I approach them other with a sense of humour and with the knowledge that all I can rely on is the membership?'

Corbyn had never met the Queen. Jeremy wouldn't know how to speak to her. He was beginning to pity his friend. *A lamb to the slaughter.*

They were quiet for some time; Jeremy lost in thought, hatching little plans and amusing himself with the imagined horror of the Blairites. All the while Corbyn looked at him and thought conflicted thoughts. After a while, he sloped forward in his deck chair:

'You know, perhaps I won't throw the towel in after all.'

'You won't?' said Jeremy. His face broke between relief and despair, so that Corbyn was not sure what to read in it.

'No, I won't. I can't leave you to fight them alone - I can see you need me. We're a team, you and I. We come as a package, or not at all.'

'I say, that's right old chap – just like old times?'

'Just like old times,' said Corbyn. *I can't just let him go off on his own. It wouldn't be… proper.*

'So, shall we be getting back then?' said Jeremy. 'Laura will have dinner ready soon.' They brushed off the allotment, and Corbyn put the deck chair back and closed the shed door. Jeremy felt happy to have his friend back.

'I think you're right,' said Jeremy as they walked toward the main gate. 'What you raised - about the foundations? About being better organised. They'll come for us, that's for sure. And, as you say, the only way to fight them is by being prepared on the ground.' Corbyn was not convinced he did say that, but he let Jeremy continue: 'So I think we need to get organised, as you say. The fight doesn't stop tomorrow. We've a tremendous momentum behind us, but we need to start bringing it together, concentrating it. Otherwise it won't count for much when the cannons sound.'

'Let's talk about that later,' said Corbyn, putting an arm around Jeremy.

'Sure... so, Allende tonight is it? Now there's a lesson from history.'

'Indeed. Incidentally, you did stay on the couch while I was gone, didn't you?'

'Let's talk about that later,' said Jeremy, putting his arm around Corbyn.

3

The next day a hundred-thousand-strong swarm descended upon London to declare that refugees were welcome and that the government should open its borders. It was part of an international day of action, with similar protests taking place in other cities in Britain and across Europe.

Seventy-six thousand refugees and migrants crossed into Europe in July through Italy, Spain and, most of all, Greece. They joined the chains of gangs already shackled to the winged chariots of free trade, stumbling across the Balkans and Hungary and Austria, where seventy-one Syrians were found suffocated in a truck, and as far as Sweden, harried at every step by riot police and barbed wire and detention and deportation. Those were the fortunate ones, who had escaped death by ISIS: the latest strain of a plague the market had sown in the desert of the twentieth century. They had survived the desert. They had survived the black market currents – two-and-a-half thousand had not. And they arrived not only from Syria, but from Afghanistan and Pakistan, Eritrea and Somalia, Libya, Nigeria, and beyond. They arrived from the many lands laid waste by Capital, far beyond the blue waters and emerald cities that lay behind the walls of the National Interest. There were sixty million in all: the most displaced movement of human beings the world had ever seen. If the escaped inmates of the crisis could survive all that, then surely they deserved to be put to work in the fenced-off fields of Europe.

Outside the underground station, Amalia had a number of missions to fulfil. First, she would tell to those who would listen of her mother's free clinics that had come to the assistance of the refugees, and of the holiday makers and Greek islanders who had hauled them onto the land; of the people of Belgrade who had embraced them as they and other Yugoslavians had needed embracing not so long before; of the people of Budapest, who had assisted them at the train station, and who marched against the particular brutality with which their government treated the refugees; of the thirty thousand who marched in Vienna and who organised cars and coaches for them; of the local government of Ada Colau in Barcelona - the Mayor on a workers' wage - which was overwhelmed by the volunteers who came forward after announcing its plans to receive the refugees.

Second, she would ask people to help sign the petition, already signed by four hundred thousand, demanding the British government take in more refugees. Third, she would help Bob sell the *Revolutionary Newspaper* — something she did now as an act of defiance against her expulsion as much as anything else. Finally, she would celebrate for Jeremy Corbyn. Passionate as she was about the refugees, regrettably their struggle would still be their tomorrow. But what dominated her thoughts was the leadership contest's grand finale. All she could think about as she swayed on the London underground was what a big thing it would be if he won. Surely he would. Her expulsion was a fact that was not yet real. She was still carried in the moment of the summer, still feeling herself to be part of Jeremy Corbyn's party.

She was a late Greek, and Bob showed her his watch. He was never harsh, but he always made you know that you were selling a *Revolutionary Newspaper* because you were a revolutionary, and that was a serious business. She understood and readily joined the sale outside the Marble Arch as thousands vaulted forth from the subterranean darkness.

It was not a difficult sale. People streamed toward her eagerly to exchange opinion. There was one brief moment when she encountered an aggressive and well-to-do Syrian lady, who demanded to know why Amalia did not support bombing Syria – was she not against Assad? But for the most part the morning was lively and in good spirits, and the sun shone, and more often than not people stopped to talk about Jeremy Corbyn.

Then the news filtered through. Jeremy Corbyn had won with fifty-nine-point-five percent of the vote on the first round. It meant that a quarter of a million people had decided there was no need for second preferences. Then she knew it was always going to happen. But to have hold of it in the shell of her ears was something new and wonderful. Without hesitation she dropped her clipboard and grabbed a bundle of *Revolutionary Newspaper*s and marched toward the station entrance. Like a town-crier she began proudly pronouncing their victory with the paper's pro-Corbyn headline to those emerging with blinking eyes from beneath the earth. Then the *Revolutionary Newspaper* became cold water on a hot day, quenching the migrating thirst.

Amalia was close to running out of papers when a hand grabbed her shoulder. She twisted on her heels mid-cry and saw Sam and Ryan. They stopped and talked and each bought a paper, and as more emerged from beneath the earth they soon found themselves being washed downstream. By the time they realised, they were almost at Hyde Park corner. Amalia turned around and could no longer see Bob or his stall. The lights changed, and they were carried across the road, Sam holding onto Ryan's hand tightly.

Once inside, the tide fanned out into the park. She figured she could continue with them a little while longer - Bob had most likely become driftwood himself. They discussed the homemade placards and the special, dedicated attendees of all London protests whom they spotted, and who have become minor demonstrations in their own right. They spoke about the victory of Jeremy Corbyn, and Amalia's expulsion, and her experience at her local party meeting. They talked about their work and their studies, and then her new friends asked her what she was doing this year. Amalia said she would be in London for another year at least, doing her postgraduate degree. Sam asked her if she had a place to stay, and she told them her tenancy had another month to run before its renewal.

As they walked deeper into the park they saw Corbyn supporters in red T-shirts jumping up and down in a circle. Amalia recognised some of them as the leather-elbow-patched boys in tweed from the phone bank. They chanted:

"Jez we can! Jez we can!"

The park was no crucible as in Ermou Street, yet she saw that the same faces were present, and the same hairs pricked the back of her neck. The circle was swelling with onlookers. They decided to walk over to take a better look.

4

'Tragically, wars don't end when the last bullet is fired, or the last bomb is dropped. The mourning and the loss of soldiers of all uniforms goes on. The mourning and the loss of families who lost loved ones because of bombardment and fighting - that goes on. The refugees move on and on. And there are whole generations of refugees around the world that are victims of various wars. Those desperate people in camps in Lebanon, in Jordan, in Libya and so many other places; desperate people trying to cross into Turkey and other places. They are all, in a sense, victims of wars.'

Jeremy stopped speaking. He looked out onto the sea of his apprehension. The moment was overwhelming him, and he stepped back. Corbyn took the microphone:

'So surely, surely, surely, our objectives ought to be: to find peaceful solutions to the problems of this world!'

The horizon rocked back and forth as they cheered him. Jeremy moved to one side and watched on.

Upon the stage they could see a strange new hope placed among them. Always suspecting he was of their number, the little grey man had proved his worth by bringing them the head of the Labour Party. In doing so, the chronic weariness vanished as he spoke words they had never heard before, and which they later learned were what confidence sounds like.

The faces arrayed before Corbyn were all the colours of the former empire, and the many shades of the fracturing new. Whether they had lived in London all their lives, or had just hitched over from Calais, all were victims of war.

Not a war of bullets. Nor a war of bombs. But a war nonetheless, ongoing, since people first had the tools to write about it, and the great mother of all violence.

Wars inevitably recruit.

For years the dying waves had retreated beyond the horizon, binding them to the tide-pools and the lichen. Year piled upon year, defeat piled upon defeat, and layer crumbled into sedimentary layer. And all that could be seen was dead fish upon the sand.

Jeremy looked up and saw seagulls hovering overhead. They were crying out to those below, sounding the coming tide. He turned to Corbyn.

'Together in peace! Together in justice! Together in humanity! That, surely, must be our way forward! Thank you!'

Corbyn stepped step back and heard a rumbling in the distance. It grew into a roar. Then he saw it, and Jeremy saw it too. The tide was turning, countless waves crashing one upon the other, rising seven, eight, nine feet high. Faster and faster it came, far faster than he expected, too late to get out of the way. Jeremy saw the terrible white water crash around Corbyn's eyes.

And then it was in his eyes, too.

***

One-hundred and seventy-three thousand in September.
Two-hundred and twenty-one thousand in October.
One-hundred and fifty-five thousand in November.
One-hundred and nineteen thousand in December.

Printed in Great Britain
by Amazon